LONGSWORD'S LADY

COUNTESS ELA OF SALISBURY

BY

J.P. REEDMAN

Copyright 2020 J.P. REEDMAN/HERNE'S CAVE

Cover-Pixabay/J.P. Reedman

Note: The castle and cathedral foundations we call 'Old Sarum' today are referred to as Salisbury Castle and Salisbury Cathedral throughout this novel until 'New Salisbury' is founded....

Written about Ela of Salisbury in her own time:

'...*a woman indeed worthy of praise*...' The Register of St Osmund

CHAPTER ONE

The Avon twisted through the heart of Amesbury, gliding around the feet of the hill that separated the town from the Great Plain beyond. A black dragon, crouched, the trees on its summit thrust like pointed spines against the sky, while its shadows hung long over the moving water. My nurses eyed it with superstitious dread. One, Hella, who had a mark on her cheek that people called an elf-kiss, muttered that it was a 'haunted place' and crossed herself whenever she was forced to glance in that direction.

But I, Ela, daughter of the mighty Earl William Fitzpatrick, was unconcerned by either haunts or dragons. The field by the river was sunlight-drenched, filled by daisies and by swans that floated in flood-pools left by harsh rains. A little further away, the new priory of St Mary, founded by old King Henry to atone for the death of Thomas a Becket, crouched amidst a stand of pale birches swinging their slender boughs like arms. Nuns of the Fontevraultine order dwelt within, pious sisters I knew by name, for Amesbury manor house was my birthplace and my mother, Eleanore de Vitre, visited the priory when time permitted.

I stood on the riverbank, the cold, clear water licking my toes through the tips of my pattens; I glanced surreptitiously at my nurses—it would not please them to see the despoilment of the expensive shoes hidden by their mundane outer coverings, but they were arguing over some triviality—Was it true Queen Guinevere died in Amesbury or did Lancelot carry her away?—and not paying much attention to my actions. Ahead of me, the river rippled, the faint sunlight gilding the surface of the water. A fish leapt, scales glistening silver; stepping from a clump of river bushes, a huge, stalk-legged heron snapped at it with a long beak—missing its prey by inches.

Reaching down, I grasped a pebble and flung it, watching it skip on the river surface—alarmed, the heron unfurled its wings and flapped away. Immediately, guilt consumed me. It was not in my nature to affright or maltreat animals but today my mood was dark, my thoughts anxious, and I was not my usual self. Nurses, beasts, birds…I wanted all to leave me be.

My father was ill, lying abed at Salisbury Castle with physicians gathered around him, trying out potions and possets to make him well again. Mama had dragged me to Amesbury for fear I would contract whatever had felled him.

Worry knotting my insides, I recalled how thin and jaundiced he looked when I had said my farewells from the doorway—I was not even permitted to kiss his brow in parting. He appeared shrunken, aged, not the powerful Earl of Salisbury, former Sheriff of Dorset and Somerset, who had carried King Richard's sceptre at his first Coronation and bore the Canopy of State at his second after Richard had returned from his captivity in Durnstein Castle. Father now resembled a discarded doll, limbs loose, head lolling on his neck.

I was my parents' only child hence the extreme caution taken with my own health. My birth had wounded my mother so that she could never bear another child—hence I was my sire's heir. One day I would bear the title of Countess of Salisbury in my own right, not through a husband. My future inheritance also made me a grand marriage prize for some nobleman; from the young and ambitious, to the old and avaricious, both seeking an Earl's title. The thought of men with no real care for me squabbling for my hand horrified me, making me shiver despite the brightness of the day. *Papa will recover*…I thought fiercely, hurling another stone into the water. *He will. He is strong, he fought with the King. He will recover…*

I heard a voice calling me. I turned, the waters chill around my ankles. My hair, the hue of an autumn leaf mixed with rich honey, blew out in a stiff gust of cold wind that skirled down from the Plain. A cloud scudded over the sun.

A young messenger-boy had run into the meadow on foot and was talking animatedly to my nurses and the solitary guard my mother had sent with me, a tall, lean swordsman called Hal. Amesbury was a small, quiet place compared to many other towns, but Mama was well aware of my value and would not risk an abduction. It was Hella who was frantically calling; her face was white, her blue eyes strangely staring in her thin visage. "Lady Ela, child, come quickly; do not delay."

Lifting up my skirts, I rushed to her side, almost slipping on the dewy grass. "What is it, Hella?" Fear kindled in me, a small flame that swiftly grew into a conflagration. Cold sweat slid down the nape of my neck beneath my horse's mane of hair.

"Ela, you must go to the manor house at once. Lady Eleonore needs to see you! It is urgent!"

I dared not asked more of Hella; the faces of my companions looked grim, as did that of the messenger boy. I saw his feet were caked with mud and bleeding. Head bowed to hide my terror, I let the two nurses take either arm, keeping me close, and Hal, his calloused hand on his sword hilt, escort me back to my home.

The manor house had never seemed so gloomy as when I entered its main door that day. My mother, Eleonore, stood alone, wrapped in her red cloak; in her hands, she clutched her rosary, its black jet beads glistening in the dull candlelight. Her lips were moving in silent prayer.

I had never seen her so pale, so intense. A native of Brittany in France, daughter of the Baron of Vitre, she was usually ebullient and laughing, her green eyes mirthful, the freckles on her nose fine as gold dust—beneath her wimple, her hair was fiery to go with those freckles. Today, however, the little dots stood out like blemishes on the drained mask of her face

"Ela...daughter..." she rasped as she glanced up.

"What is happening, Mama?" My voice wavered, sounding thin and plaintive.

"You—go! This is between me and my daughter" Mother beckoned to my nurses and Hal. Hastily they fled the solar without even the customary bow or curtsey.

It was now just Mama and me, the smell of candle wax, and the faint scratch-scratch of a mouse scampering somewhere in the walls.

Mama's mouth moved; it was as if she had difficulty forming the words she wanted to speak. Finally, they tumbled out in a floundering rush. "Ela, my dearest child, I have received grievous news. News from Salisbury. Your father…"

"He has got worse?" I cried. "The medicines have not worked?"

She breathed deeply, painfully, as if each breath hurt. "Child, I can find no easy way to say it—at around *Terce* today, your sire departed to the arms of God." She crossed herself and her tears began to flow.

A child statue, I stood frozen. I felt as if God had stricken me too, freezing my limbs, stilling the beating of my heart. Tears would not come; my eyes were dry as a dusty tomb. Yet a yawning chasm gaped inside, filling me with agony as if an unseen hand tore at the very fabric of my being.

At last I found my voice, weak and wobbling. "God assoil dear Father. Still, we must go to him, Mama, to see him washed and wrapped in white linen…to see him laid to eternal rest."

Mother took another deep breath, her hands knotted in her rosary beads until I thought the string might break and send them whirling in a black cascade upon the floor. "Yes, I must go anon to my poor husband's deathbed and see that all is done as it should be. I fear the wolves will soon be out to try and wrench away what is his…and yours, my little Ela…You must be kept safe…"

"Mama?" Renewed fear struck me like a blow. She was saying, in not so many words, that she would not let me see my father one last time. And there was something else she clearly did not want to tell me…

I caught her hanging sleeve; good cloth, the edges patterned with silver thread in flowery curlicues. "Why do you not want me to go with you? Surely, it is my right. I am not afraid, Mama. After all, I am my father's heir."

Her tears flowed harder, forming a glittering row on her small, pointed chin, like hanging diamonds. "Your inheritance is the problem, Ela."

I shook my head. "What problem can there be? I am his legitimate daughter."

"We have spoken of this matter before. You are not a naive girl despite your youth. You may inherit but every manner of man both good and wicked will want to wed you. Many have wished to already, attracted by the sweetness of your birthright, but now they will swarm like bees—and bees may sting. You are in danger, child; I fear such men would not stop at an abduction, and subject you to a forced marriage even at your tender age." Her fingers stroked my face, fingers trembling. "You are so young. What they would do would be a crime against God."

Letting her hand fall, she began to pace the chamber, her long skirts swishing through the rushes strewn across the flagstones. "I—I must think on what should be done. The King must be informed; due to your vast inheritance, he will doubtless want you as his ward."

"His ward! But that means I shall have to go away, will it not? Leave Amesbury and Salisbury."

She bowed her head, nodding. "Yes, for a while, at least, Ela."

I felt my face grow red and furious. My manner was disrespectful of Mama's grief, but what she proposed filled me with abject terror. "Do you think that becoming King Richard's ward would save me from wicked men seeking my fortune? He would marry me to one of his horrid old favourites in a heartbeat." The tears that would not come earlier began to threaten. My eyes blurred; Mama's slender shape wavered in the candlelight.

"Yes," she said, "you are not wrong, Ela, and that truth is something you must have the courage to face. But a marriage proposed by Richard is by far the best marriage you will make, and would put paid to those who might behave less honourably towards you. The youngest you might join your husband's household would be no less than thirteen, I deem, and maybe later if you and I speak the King fair—or his mother, the Dowager Queen Eleanor. Anything he suggests would be preferable to a rogue baron laying hold of you and carrying you off…"

At that moment, hoofbeats sounded in the courtyard, clattering on the cobbles. Mother gasped, her hand flying up to her mouth. "Who could it be? Surely not so soon. Ela…come with me."

A loud knocking sounded on the front door; someone was pummelling the old, worn oak with a curled fist. One of the servants scurried into view and rushed towards the insistent sound. "Halt, halt!" cried Mama. "I bid you do not…"

The man's hand was on the bar, half-lifting it. Hearing Mama's frightened cry, he paused in confusion. Another crash sounded, louder than the first; now it was if someone put his shoulder full-force to the door. The servant yelped in fear and tumbled backwards onto the flagstones as the door burst inwards and men poured into the hallway.

Mama grabbed me, pushing me behind her. "If I tell you to run," she said, "go out through the kitchen and into the fields. Keep on running and do not turn back. Do not go on the road. Hide on Wall Hill if you have to…"

"But Hella says it's haunted!" I gasped.

"You are wiser than that! It is not ghosts you need fear!" She shook me fiercely. "When night has fallen, climb the priory wall. Go to the nuns; they will help you."

The men who had invaded our home were approaching, stomping into the neat little hall with its musty age-blackened beams. Hooded and cloaked, swords girt at their sides, they looked like wraiths out of some terrible ancient legend. Their leader stalked towards Mama, then abruptly halted and flung back his hood.

My fear vanished in a trice. It was only Philip, Father's younger brother. He was not there to harm us. I did not know him well, but still, he was family…" Uncle Philip!" I cried, rushing in his direction

Mama lunged, grabbing me about the waist and dragging me back against her. "No, Ela!" she snapped. "Stay still."

"But it's only Uncle Philip…" Confused, I wriggled in her grip.

"Yes, listen to the girl, Eleonore," said Philip. Some years younger than father, Philip would have been attractive save that his gaunt cheeks gave him a slightly vulpine appearance. A small jagged scar marred his cheek, glowing white against his tanned complexion. "Only Uncle Philip."

"Philip, I do not know why you are here but I am not happy with this intrusion, especially in this unseemly manner. I will have much to deal with over the next few days." Mama's face was white as curds. Her hands upon my waist were cold as ice and trembling.

"I am here to offer my condolences over William's death," he said, "and to see to little Ela's safety."

"What do you mean by that?" She eyed him suspiciously. "The King will have her as his ward. That is safe enough for me. You know well what often happens to heiresses without strong male protection, and she is of such tender years."

"Ah, but she *has* male protection." He jerked his thumb towards himself in a cocky motion. "It is my intention to take Ela away—for safety—out of England and into Normandy."

"No!" Mama looked horrified. "You are mad, Philip! You will anger the King if you remove her from England. Besides, where would she be safer from predatory men than in the King's household? As a ward, she might even be placed with his mother, the great Queen Eleanor."

"Ah, Eleonore, how naive you are." Philip shook his head in mock sadness. "Richard will have no care for her youth; he will have her betrothed in a week to benefit his finances—and you know what that also means? For you, and for the remaining sons of Earl Patrick? It means we have lost control of the entire Salisbury fortune. Forever." A feverish flush mounted his cheeks. "It is not right that some other man should hold that which belonged to my father!"

"It was God's will that no son was born to William and me," said Mama weakly. "Ela alone is heir to the Salisbury earldom; you must accept that truth, Philip."

"Oh, I accept it—but not that all its accumulated wealth and prestige will drift away from our family and their affinity." He peered at me, his eyes hard and dark, observant. "She will be pretty one day. Ela, come with me…."

I glanced up at Mother. "No," she said weakly, "it is too dangerous."

"Eleonore, once the King has Ela in his grasp and has wedded her off to one of his cronies, you will find yourself going without—and begging to be married off to whatever lord will have you. Why do you suspect *me* of some sort of wickedness? Give me the girl before the King's officials—or worse miscreants—arrive in Amesbury. Who knows what ruffians gallop over the Plain even as we stand here arguing? News travels fast, the death of an Earl with no son is a grave matter, and when men smell money…"

"I swear if you harm her...or give her in marriage to one of *your* cronies, I will kill you!" hissed Mama, and I had never heard such venom in her voice. "Remember, my father's lands border Normandy—he would surely find you if I asked."

"I am a knight and honourable," snorted Philip.

"Honourable knights." Mama's tone was mocking. "One thing I have learnt in this life is that honour is swiftly forgotten when wealth and advancement lie within one's grasp."

"So...I must go with Uncle Philip?" Confused, I gazed at Mama. "I am not being sent to the King after all?"

She pressed a limp hand to her brow, nigh close to fainting. "Perhaps Philip is right—perhaps it is for the best. Until things have settled, till the will is proved. The King is not even in England at present; he's off fighting for the right to build a new castle in Normandy. Left alone in one of his palaces, without him to keep order...anything could happen to you."

"He would not care. As long as he got a hearty amount of payment for her marriage. Every penny of her fortune would end up in Richard's coffers or her new husband's," said Philip, pressing home his advantage as he saw Mama waver. "Come now, let me take the girl—time is pressing." Philip was tapping the toe of his boot on the flagstones, an incessant, irritating noise.

Mama called for Hella to bring my warmest cloak. With shaking fingers, the girl draped it around my shoulders. Philip stepped over and yanked up my hood. "You must not be seen, do you understand, Ela? We have a long journey ahead of us and we may be stopped if it is suspected what we are about."

I was afraid, deathly afraid, and also wracked with grief for poor Father, lying cold and white in Salisbury Castle upon its windy hill while the chapel's passing bell tolled. My vision blurred with another torrent of stinging tears.

But he would not want me to cry. He would wish me to show courage. He never had a son but I would be as fearless as any son— and trust his brother Philip with my wellbeing.

I put out my hand and Philip took it, surprisingly gentle. Then I was whisked away into the growing dusk. Rain had arrived, dappling the puddles on the rutted track, and a blue twilight pall clung over

Amesbury, eerie and wavering. Philip's men were waiting with horses and a small carriage. I climbed inside and the door was slammed firmly shut. Through a crack in the drape that shrouded the narrow window, I saw Mama standing in the manor house door, clutching the carved stonework for support.

Shakily, I waved. Then, as Uncle Philip dug his spurs into his courser's flanks and headed for the main road to Salisbury, I passed out of my life in Amesbury and away into a gathering storm.

Uncle Philip's manor in Normandy was small and remote, ideal for our situation. He insisted neither King nor unwelcome suitors would ever find me. Oh, soon though there were suitors enough; local barons, even distant kinsmen, who came to look me over as if I were a prize cow. Disdainfully, I glared down my small nose at them, but below the brave veneer, I was deeply frightened. Philip had sworn to Mother to keep me safe, but as the days flew by, my mistrust of his motives grew. It was clear he wanted the wealth of the Earldom of Salisbury to remain in the family and not pass to a husband outside of it, and there was only one way to make sure of that. To marry me off to a distant family member or to some minion Philip had firmly under his thumb, obedient and compliant.

I decided, with a child's flawed logic, to misbehave whenever the chance arose. Maybe I would be so much trouble he would send me back home. I do believe he was having a few second thoughts even before I started my little game, as it dawned on him that perhaps carrying off the King's would-be ward might bring trouble in the future. One did not want to make the Lionheart roar by stepping on the royal prerogative! But motivated by greed, Philip had acted in haste and now he could only step forward, not back.

My first act of disobedience came in needlework lessons. I refused to sew or stitch with the women he had employed to cater to my needs, and when they tried to force the needle into my grip, I stabbed one woman in the hand instead, making her scream and run about the hall, bleeding. On Philip's orders, I was duly punished, but a few nights eating gruel in seclusion was no great hardship and quelled my rebellion not at all. When my next needlework session rolled around, I showed how diligent I was now by sewing the other ladies' skirts together so that they tripped and fell when they stood up.

It wasn't just my attendants who suffered my mischief. Whenever Philip brought in the local barons and knights, the distant cousins, to gawp at me, I chose my ugliest dress and put on a show of frowning, sulking and acting if a sensible thought had never passed through my head. Before their horrified gaze, I would eat like an uncouth farm boy, smearing my mouth with gravy, while my hair hung down in tangles, half-hiding my bored, disinterested face.

Finally, Philip approached me, red-faced and fit to explode, after I knocked a cup of wine into the lap of one of the local lordlings whilst at meat. In the panicked aftermath of splashed wine, ruined tunic and apologies, I had escaped to the vineyards, where I was eating the fat purple grapes, dangling them inelegantly over my open mouth. He snatched them away and threw them in the dirt. I glared at him evilly.

"What is this all about, Ela?" he raged. "You are much changed since coming to Normandy. Where have your manners gone? You are rude to my friends and insolent to me. Your nurses and women are scared of you—one said she feared you might bite her if you did not have your way. What has possessed you?"

"I miss my mother and my home," I said simply and truthfully. "I want to go back."

"Eleonore agreed that you should come here." He waggled an accusing ring-spangled finger beneath my nose. "You know that is so—you were there when she gave her consent."

"Consent under duress hardly counts, does it, Uncle? Mama hardly knew up from down on that unhappy day."

Brows bristling, he stared hard at me. "Surprising words from a little maid not yet ten summers, and proof that you are not the scatterbrain you pretend to be in front of visitors. Well, I shall not accept more of this charade. You will behave as a child of your station, not the village idiot."

"Or what, Uncle? Will you beat me? I shall contact Mama."

"Shall you now? What will you do—send a crow to tell her, like some witch in a story? I would not put it past you. Listen to me, girl, I have had enough of your insolence. You have no idea what I've saved you from."

"Oh, I know. Wardship. Marriage. A loss of the Salisbury inheritance to my new husband. Hm, I take it you are enjoying the benefits of some of that inheritance at present?"

"It was my father's!" he roared suddenly, eyes flashing

Steeliness filled me, despite my age and sex. "It was *my* father's after him," I said coolly. "And he left it, in the rightness of law, to *ME*."

Philip began to sputter. "Be silent, you little harpy! From now on, I am confining you to the tower in the east wing of the manor. Tutors will visit every day and report on your progress—you will co-operate and not behave like a simpleton or buffoon. You will show me your needlework daily, and if it is of insufficient quality, I will make you unpick it and start again, even if you must stay up all night. I desire to hear of your proficiency in Latin and religious education— you are so eager to be a Countess, but you are not fit to be one. As of now, you are only an impertinent chit with no respect for her elders."

"I do not want to live here anymore!" I shouted, stamping my foot, as sudden tears sprang to my eyes. "I would rather be with the King than you! At least I'd know my fate with him! I…I truly do not know what you intend for me, only that it is clear you desire my fortune. Would you make of me a nun?"

His face bleached of colour and his mouth moved soundlessly. I knew then that the thought of a convent was foremost in his mind, not a marriage alliance with one of our many distant relatives after all. If I took the veil, retreated from the world, that way he could hang on to the Salisbury inheritance. He would tell King Richard that I had become possessed of the Holy Spirit and begged for a cloistered life. I would name the loving uncle who had guided me to God as my heir…

"It's true, isn't it?" I cried shrilly, hands knotting into impotent fists at my sides. "You want to force me into orders!"

"You are too forward for your age," he snapped, his eyes wild, dangerous. "Get you from my sight."

Sobbing, I fled the vineyard.

The east wing of the manor house, with its great round tower capped by a conical red roof, was an older part of the building and less used than the rest. Ivy grew up the tower's flank, infiltrating chinks in the stonework, making small cracks through which the wind whistled. The room at the top where Philip installed me had recently been plastered and paintings of the Virgin decorated the wall, but despite that nod to comfort and homeliness, the place still seemed isolated and unfriendly. Warped floorboards creaked at night, and I slept badly, dreaming of ghosts that walked in the halls, of men who came to force me to the altar or the cloister.

True to his word, Philip sent scores of stern-faced tutors to the tower to procure an education. I dared show no more defiance, for I realised I was powerless, despite my strong words. The fire in me had died after my last blaze of insolence; I just prayed that my knowledge and dismissal of Philip's plans to see me veiled would shame him into abandoning them.

Attentively I settled down to my Latin and other studies and despite my unhappiness, excelled in all—I was an 'exceptional girl' my tutor said, which gave me some pleasure in my confinement. I even embroidered Uncle's Coat of Arms to please him, noting that one of the animals on it was a bull. Aye, he was bull-headed—but so was I.

Philip must have been pleased by my apparent submission, for although he did not release me from my solitary tower, he sent me a stack of books. It was lovely to pore over the trials of the tragic Tristan and Iseult and, even better, *Yvain ou le Chevalier au Lion*, in which the hero Yvain rescues a lion from a dragon and the beast becomes his stalwart companion, defending him against giants, evil knights and even hellish demons. In the end, Yvain is safely reunited with his wife, Laudine.

As summer progressed, my captivity began to rankle once again. Hot weather descended over Normandy, but I could only look from the narrow-arched window at the rolling green landscape across the moat, or the tempting dark forest where Uncle Philip and his men hunted wild boar and dappled deer. The sun beat with fierceness on the roof of the tower, adding to my misery. My nurses were florid and sweating, the tutors equally damp—and pungent.

One evening, after reading a romance that contained a particularly thrilling chase, I decided I had more than enough of stuffy confinement. I was going to escape—for a night anyway. I had to return, for I had no way of finding my way about Normandy, but at least I could breathe the cool night air and feel the summer dew on my skin.

Creeping from my bed, I opened the bedchamber door a crack. My nurses and tiring women lay on the landing outside, snoring and rolling over like great sea-beasts in their sleep. I was glad then that the tower room was puny; normally, they would have slept within, waiting for orders. I grinned like an imp and quietly closed the door again.

Approaching my bed, I ripped off the linen sheets and knotted them together. I pulled on the ends with all my strength to see if they would part. They held firm, and I beamed with inner pride. I was a good knot-binder. When in England, I had learnt to tie knots by emulating Father's squires—perhaps to show my parents that it was not so terrible that I was a girl and not their longed-for son. That I could do more than sew and dance…

Biting my tongue in concentration, I tied the end of the sheet to one of the wooden posts supporting the canopy of my bed. I prayed the wood would not buckle; it was a fine bed, as befitting my status, but not terribly sturdy compared to the one I'd slept in back in Salisbury Castle. If the post should give, the whole bed would collapse, the carven headboard depicting the Annunciation falling inwards, while the canopy that kept spiders and woodlice off would descend like a deflating blancmange pudding. And I would end up falling to the ground outside….

I swallowed, now a little nervous about my audacious plan. Clutching my makeshift rope, I straddled the window and gazed down. Below was a stretch of grass; the eastern wing faced out over the spacious gardens. And the tower itself was not so high, not compared to the towers at Salisbury, which was a royal castle. This was only a fortified house; the tower was mere artifice, giving the place the illusion of strong defence. There was a moat, firmly locked in the shadows, but neither water nor wall would keep a foe out for long.

I was going to do it. Worst that could happen, I told myself, would be a bruised bottom if I fell partway down. Carefully, I swung one leg over the window ledge and eased myself forward, clutching my knotted sheets. I stared upwards at the misty globe of the moon, burnt deep gold by the hot summer and round as a coin, and uttered a quick little prayer to Mother Mary. Then I began my brave (or foolhardy) descent from my prison.

My rope held. I was glad I was a thin, light-boned girl of little weight. Within a few minutes, my feet touched the grass and I was running barefoot and wild beneath the moon.

It seemed a magical night in that burst of newfound freedom. My head was spinning with fantasies engendered by my fevered romantic reading and I imagined a great knight like Sir Lancelot riding out of the gloom to whisk me away.

Hair flying, I ran through the empty gardens, taking in great gulps of the clean air. Roses hung on trellises, fragrance filling the night, their petals faded by the moon and dripping with dew.

I stopped, glanced around and then lapped up one speck of dew with my tongue like a cat. Local villagers claimed summer dew was the tears of faeries and would make a girl breathtakingly beautiful...

I careered onwards, skipping and jumping over the herb-beds. Rosemary, mint, thyme was crushed beneath my toes, which I curled in the rich, cool soil. Lavender sprays thrust out fragrant purple arms; I tumbled into their embrace, trying to control my laughter.

I must not be foolish and give myself away!

And then I heard it, over by the wall where it dropped down to the moat. A man was quietly singing a plaintive ballad. My heart pounded and once again I envisioned Sir Lancelot and heart-sick Tristan. Keeping close to the shadows, I skirted the wall to observe the singer if I could.

Soon I spied him, in the copse across the moat, ringed in a pallid circle of moonlight. He was a little disappointing—not like I imagined Lancelot or Tristan at all—with a snub-nosed face, full cheeks and a weak chin. He wore no shining armour, just simple homespun and a battered cap upon his dusky blonde curls. Half-hidden by a bristly shrub, he was singing in a low voice,

"To wake sweet delight once more,
That has lain too long asleep,
And worth that be exiled deep
Close to gather and restore:
These thoughts I long have laboured for!"

Excitement gripped my young heart; that song was familiar! "You…you over the moat!" I hissed, trying not to raise my voice too much. "I can hear you. Are you Giraut de Bornell, the troubadour of the Viscount of Limoges? That is his song!"

Immediately the singer sputtered into silence and ducked behind the night-furled shrub, although I could still see the pointed peak of his cap bobbing over the top of the foliage.

"I know you are there," I said somewhat crossly, folding my arms. "If you have no business with the lord of this manor, you are liable to find yourself struck by an arrow. The bush you are sitting in does not hide you at all."

Branches rustled. Slowly the man arose like some woodwose climbing from its leafy lair. "Forgive me, but you startled me. Who are you?"

"It is more important to know who *you* are, wandering about the woods in the dark. I take it, you are not Bornell."

"No, I am not, nor am I a real troubadour…just a traveller who enjoys a song. I was advised in the village down the road that this is the home of Philip Fitzpatrick, son of Patrick of Salisbury."

"Yes, that is my uncle and this is his manor…but he is not at home," I blurted and instantly regretted my loose tongue. Why was this man *really* skulking in the woods? He seemed harmless enough, even a bit foolish, but looks could be deceptive. I glanced up at the roofline. The manor was so remote that Uncle kept only a small contingent of men on hand—and most of them had departed with him on his overnight hunting trip. The remainder were stationed by the entry bridge over the moat, since no one ever imagined a determined little girl would climb down from the east tower into the secluded garden.

The man in the hat was peering at me through the murk, full of curiosity. "Do not fear, I have no wish to see Lord Philip…"

I breathed a little sigh of relief.

"I am seeking his niece, the Countess of Salisbury. His Grace King Richard desires her presence as his ward. He has long missed her."

My breath of relief became a startled gasp.

"I ask you, Lady—you call Fitzpatrick 'uncle.' Are you the Countess Ela, daughter of William Fitzpatrick and Eleonore de Vitre?"

I said nothing, standing glumly, guiltily, in my nightgown. The magic of the night, the excitement of my escape from the tower vanished. I felt exposed, vulnerable.

"You *are* her, aren't you?" the man said, visage lighting up with excitement. He stepped from the bush, striding down to the water's edge as if he wanted to cast himself into the moat and swim across.

Again, I held my tongue.

"You need not fear me, my Lady," he said. "I am a knight, Sir William Talbot, and I mean you no harm."

"If you mean me no harm, you will go away," I blurted, then hated myself, for if my sullen silence had not told him all he wanted to know, my own treacherous, over-swift tongue had.

"Go away I shall," replied Sir William, "but let it be known that I am sworn to serve King Richard and will deliver the findings of my journey to him."

"Where is the King now?" I asked boldly.

"In his fortress of Chateau Gaillard, where he is overseeing the building."

"Chateau Gaillard? That is many miles hence, I believe. By the time you fare back to him, my uncle and I might have fled miles hence. You'd never catch us."

William Talbot smiled; under the moonlight; I did not like the look of that smile. "The King is a generous and forgiving man," he said softly, "but not *too* forgiving. As things stand, he is *grateful* that the Lord Philip kept the King's ward in safety while he was busy. He is willing to forget that she was taken from England without his permission. He is wise enough to know men act out of character in the throes of grief, and Lord Philip had lost his beloved brother, Earl William. But now…the King wants the Countess of Salisbury under his protection. If she is denied him, I think his patience will wear rather thin, and an offer of pardon be withdrawn…"

So…a threat. I chewed on my lip. Although not pleased that Uncle Philip had torn me from Mama, considered forcing me into a nunnery, and banished me to the dilapidated east wing, I wished him no real ill. He was my father's brother and Father had loved him for all his faults. I did not want Philip harmed or imprisoned.

"Do what you must do, Sir William Talbot," I murmured.

"My Lady, I see that you are a child of intelligence as well as beauty and grace. I will go to King Richard." He bowed, then turned on his heel and vanished like some woodland spirit into the depths of the trees.

Rubbing my now-freezing arms, dotted with sudden goose pimples, I stood staring after Talbot. The delicious coolness of the night after the day's stifling heat was replaced by a distinct chill. In the heart of the woods, an owl hooted—remote, lonely, eerie. A cloud slipped across the face of the moon and suddenly I wanted nothing more than to return to the safety of my tower room.

I raced back through the gardens, slipping on the dewy grass. The roses and other flowers wept, their petals rimed with dangling beads of moisture. Grasping my makeshift rope, still dangling down like a white serpent, I dragged myself up toward the window inch by inch. It was far harder going up than down; my arms ached and trembled with the strain. Gritting my teeth, I clung on tenaciously, fearful that I would get halfway up then plunge back to the ground. The night-chill, first lovely then uncomfortable, vanished again as I began to sweat with my efforts. My face burned and my body was bruised through my thin shift by the hard stonework of the tower.

At last, I managed to grasp the window ledge and pull myself in. Panting like a dog, I dragged my 'rope' in behind me and untied the knots with trembling fingers. Then I threw the dirtied sheets in a bundle on my bed and hurled myself after them, and slept an uneasy sleep till the red rays of the boiling sun found their way into the chamber the next morning and the tiring women burst in, bustling about and reminding me that it was time for Mass.

"Your shift!" one of them exclaimed, glancing suspiciously at the greenish stains down the front. "Whatever have you been doing, my Lady?"

I shrugged. Let them guess. Soon it would not matter.

William Talbot, King's man, knew I was here. Richard the Lionheart, King of England, Duke of Aquitaine, would soon send for me and I would never endure those tutting nursemaids again....

Uncle Philip returned from his hunt beaming with pleasure and in a jolly mood. He and his companions had not only brought down several fine stags but a ferocious, if not exactly huge, wild boar.

Sitting at the high table in the hall, he feasted on his catch, and he even summoned me to partake of the many courses. I could not meet his eyes throughout the banquet and picked listlessly at my food; Philip thought this both hilarious and, at the same time, a good sign—a token of improved manners and maidenliness.

"My niece Ela's wilfulness pride has been broken," he roared to his companions, as he gulped down goblet after goblet of wine. "She will make a fine—and wealthy—wife for someone, now that I have tamed her. Why, I'd be tempted to wed her myself if she wasn't my niece..."

"But you're already married!" some knight shouted from further down the hall.

Philip flushed. "It was just a jest...a *jest*." He and his wife were estranged; she lived in England and I'd never met her. "And truth be told, she'd make a better nun, that wife. The girl can read Latin, you know. Nose in her books rather than her sewing."

I wished I could fall under the trestle table as my merits as either potential wife or cloistered nun were discussed. I wondered if I should pretend to faint but decided against it—I had not the skills of a player and would not be at all convincing.

Uncle, I thought. *I dare not tell you the truth of what is coming. But soon you shall know..."*

A knot of genuine sickness bloomed in my belly at the thought. Head whirling, I rose from my bench.

"Ela?" Philip frowned at me over the rim of his cup. "Whatever is the matter? You are as white as curdled milk!"

"My Lord Uncle, may I be excused?" I asked, clutching my belly.

One of the nurses swept in from the shadows at the end of the hall to support me. "She has the megrims, poor child," she told Philip. "She hasn't been herself for days. It must be the unseasonable heat…."

"Yes, the heat…" I groaned. I was sweating now, sickly pains needling my stomach.

"Go…*go*!" Philip waved his hand. "Nursemaid, report to me on my niece's wellbeing later when my feast is over."

With my nurse, heavy-set, titanic Ortense puffing and panting behind me, I bolted for the privy and was sick.

"I am going to put you to bed, my Lady," said Ortense. "Too much heat, too much rich food—both can upset the wellbeing of a young girl."

I was glad to be tucked into bed and left alone. Here, in my isolated chamber, I would not have to carry on my deception, pretending that I had submitted to Philip's will. Pretending that I would not soon become a ward of the Crown.

Falling into a restless slumber, I dreamed a strange and ominous dream. I was in a field full of white daisies and white lilies, emblem of the Virgin. A company of knights on horseback drew near, their mail shining in the sunlight. Above them flew the greatest banner of all, red and gold, a lion roaring upon it.

Suddenly the banner fell. In horror, I tried to grab it but miraculously the lion upon it tore free of the crumpled cloth—becoming a real lion, not just an image. He set huge paws upon my shoulders, pushing me to the ground, crushing daisies. Terrified, I beat at him with my hands.

I am Lionheart, Ela…and you are mine to do with as I will.

I wept, choking on thick, tawny fur, believing he intended to devour me.

But he merely showed his great, white, spiky teeth. *If you obey my commands, I will not bite. It is your destiny to dwell with the Devil's Brood....*

Devils! Abruptly I awoke, heart hammering, breath railing in my lungs. Outside there was a flash of lightning; a storm was coming in to break the oppressive heat. Moments later, torrential rain began to beat on the conical roof of the tower, a fierce *ratatatat* that obliterated even the distant rumbles of thunder.

The storm was coming—and so was Richard Lionheart.

CHAPTER TWO

It was not the King himself who arrived at Uncle Philip's abode but one of his emissaries—one that was much feared, the ruthless Provencal mercenary, Mercadier.

Dark and sullen, clad all in black with a silver badge bearing three Lions Passant on his shoulder, he arrived at the manor house followed by a stone-faced array of fighting men. Without waiting for an invitation, he pushed past the bridge guards, waving a writ from Richard, and strode straight into the hall, where I was breaking my morning fast with Uncle Philip and other members of the household.

Philip blanched when he saw the dark, saturnine figure and his dish of sops fell from his fingers with a clang, sending a spray of red wine over the rushes.

"How…how dare you barge in here like this?" he managed to splutter, but there was true terror in his eyes despite his angry words.

"I believe you know me," said the mercenary. "I am Mercadier, right-hand man of his Grace, Richard Coeur de Leon. I come to you on King's business…important business."

I sat still as a stone on my bench. Under the table, my nurse Ortense squeezed my fingers so hard I thought they might snap. Even a maid as young as I knew of the exploits of Mercadier, Richard's brutal right-hand man. With a band of Brabancon mercenaries, he had burned the lands of Aimar of Limoges, driving fleeing peasants before his fury; he had taken thirteen castles from the Count of Toulouse with fire and sword. He had served Richard in the Holy Land upon the Third Crusade, fighting manfully at the King's side and buying glory with the shedding of blood. Richard adored Mercadier and spoke highly of his deeds; other men, even Richard's closest colleagues, feared and loathed the mercenary.

Philip rose from his seat, wiping droplets of red wine from his tunic. "Of course I know you," he said, somewhat sharply. "Who doesn't? That still does not excuse your…your gross imposition."

"Does it not?" Thick black brows lifted under a cascade of greasy raven hair. "The King would beg to differ. I think you have something of his, Philip. Something he wants very badly. You were most...*audacious*...to take it from him."

"The girl..." Philip's face had become mottled with purple as if he might have a fit of apoplexy.

"The Countess of Salisbury." Mercadier's voice was the lash of a whip. His gaze lifted from Uncle Philip, running down the trestle table until it landed on me. His eyes were black and piercing. Even though I was in no wise guilty of any wrong-doing, a sensation of queasiness and fear gripped me. But when Mercadier approached, it was with all courtesy, bowing and even offering what seemed to be a smile, although it came off more as a wolfish grin.

"Lady Ela, I presume?" he asked, his voice oddly light and cheerful, without the sarcasm he had used on Uncle Philip.

Disentangling my fingers from Ortense, who looked as if she might faint dead away, I stood up. "I am Ela of Salisbury." I tried to keep my voice steady.

"His Grace the King sends you a message, my Lady." Mercadier cleared his throat. "He has missed the presence of his ward and commiserates with her over the death of her esteemed father, William Earl of Salisbury. He summons you to his side at once, to take up the position worthy of your rank."

Uncle Philip's face was now truly empurpled. "He just wants her as a reward for one of his cronies! The whole earldom of Salisbury will be given to some toadying sellsword, no doubt!"

Mercadier held up a black-gloved hand; gold studs pierced the leather, pointed enough to rip a man's cheek or eye. I wondered if he would strike Uncle Philip.

"Silence, sir; speak not another word least the King decides he is no longer grateful to you."

"Grateful?" Uncle Philip's eyes bulged in confusion.

"Grateful," smirked Mercadier, stroking one of his lethal-looking gloves as if he stroked a black cat. "Naturally, he is grateful that his dear ward was so well cared-for during her absence. *Grateful...*" His hand uncurled, and he held it out meaningfully.

Uncle Philip uttered a strangled, choking noise.

"You wouldn't want to see his *gratitude* fade, would you? To make his Grace reconsider his benevolence and perhaps declare you a traitor, the kidnapper of a royal ward?" The swarthy face was fierce as a Saracen's now, the jaw thrust forward with its small black beard bristling. "Pay up, Philip, and all will be forgotten. Otherwise…" He glanced over his shoulder. "Out beyond the walls, I have far more men than those I came in with. Brabancon mercenaries. They would leave this place in smoking ruins if I told them to."

Philip's anger had retreated to fear; he was white again, his eyes darting around in their sockets. "This…this is *outrageous*!"

Mercadier swept towards him, his ebon cloak swirling. I cringed, fearing he'd either smite him with that studded fist or pull out one of the daggers ranged about his thick leather belt. "No, what *you* did is outrageous. Pay what you owe. I grow tired of waiting."

Weakly Philip stood back, his shoulders slumped in defeat and beckoned for his steward. "Go to my counting house, Walter, and fill a casket for the King."

Mercadier beckoned to one of his Brabancons, a burly fellow with a bald head and a lip that had been split by the blow of a weapon at some point. It had healed but flapped outwards like a gummy flag. "Raoul, go with Sir Philip and make sure that the King is well recompensed."

Philip and the steward marched out of the chamber, Raoul hovering behind them like a huge, ominous shadow, his sheathed sword jingling against his leg.

Mercadier turned back to me. "I know it is early, my Lady, but I would not linger, and his Grace is eager to have you safely at his side."

"I…I will have to pack my things," I informed him, hating the way my voice sounded childish and whining in my own ears. "My hair…I'll need to change my gown."

The hint of a sneer curled his lip. 'It will not be necessary. The King will replace any lost goods—with better ones."

His tone told me that argument was useless, and also that his temper was growing short. And that despite my noble blood, I had no say over his actions, nor would I receive any special treatment. I was the King's possession and Mercadier had come to collect me and take me to his Grace in the same manner as a prized broodmare or herd of cows.

"Very well," I squeaked. "But surely...surely, you must see it is not fitting for a maid of my tender years to travel alone with so many men."

The sneer again, only now holding a trace of mockery. "Do not fear, Lady Ela. No man of my company would dare lay a hand on such as you, any more than they would plunder King Richard's coffers or break the walls of his castle. If they did, I would cut off that offending hand myself. Nonetheless, to prevent evil rumours, yes, bring an attendant..." He gestured to Ortense, who had clutched my hand so tightly under the table. "Take that one—she's ugly enough not to cause distraction!"

"Ooh!" cried Ortense, her round face turning scarlet. "I cannot go just like that! I have a husband in the village..."

Mercadier ignored her and gestured to me. "My Lady, outside if you would, without delay. We have brought a chariot for your use."

Ortense was still wittering about her man. Selfish in my own uncertainty, I grasped her arm and patted it. "Do not be afraid. Once the King decides where he wants me to stay, I will ask him to send you straight home."

"But my Pierre—he'll think I've been kidnapped!" she bawled, tears springing from her eyes. "Kidnapped and had my virtue compromised!"

"I will have a message sent..."

"He can't *read*, milady!" she wept. "Oh, wicked day, wicked, wicked day..."

Mercadier's expression was growing stony. "Outside, my Lady, *now*," he snapped, "and that great cow with you, or do I need to get a cattle-prod to her backside."

That silenced Ortense's wails. Clutching her hand, I led her from the hall into the courtyard. Mercadier's Brabancon mercenaries were everywhere, heavily-armed, sinister, reeking of subdued violence. I tried to avoid their hot, interested and amused gazes as I walked over the horse-befouled flagstones to the carriage waiting near the gate. Ortense lolloped along beside me, mouth opening and shutting soundlessly like that of a hooked fish. I feared she might collapse, and thought it odd that I, the child, her noble charge, should end up taking care of her.

Gently I pushed her massive backside into the chariot and she collapsed on the seat, puffing as she wiped at her wet face with her apron. Unassisted, I climbed in and sat beside her. Mercadier was a few paces behind; mercifully, he did not enter the chariot, but his lean, sharp face hung framed by the window slit. "You are well, my Lady?"

I wanted to say 'no', that I had expected my 'rescue' from Uncle Philip would not leave me feeling even more like a prisoner, but I held my peace and nodded. There was a full wineskin in the carriage, and a parcel of fruit and cheese, and a pisspot should we need one. What else could we ask for?

"Good," declared Mercadier, "we make for Chateau Gaillard." He grasped the rich red curtain that was tied back from the window and let it fall. Ortense and I were plunged into shadow. The nursemaid started to moan as the horses drawing the chariot began to move, their hooves clopping on the stones of the courtyard.

I sat motionless, hands curled in my lap, and thought of the future. Soon I would reach King Richard's castle. Soon I would stand in the presence of the great Lionheart, bravest and most honourable of monarchs.

And what would happen to me then?

CHAPTER THREE

Chateau Gaillard was the King's newest castle, still only half-complete. As our company began the ascent of the eminence on which it stood, I peeled away the concealing curtain and gazed out, uncaring that Mercadier's Brabancons might leer in at me and Ortense.

At the top of the rise stretched a vast plateau dense with earthworks. On a jutting tongue of land stood the donjon, round rather than rectangular, faced with interlocking white and grey stones that shone as the strong sunlight beamed down upon them. Ladders and scaffolding clung to stonework; masons and apprentices swarmed over surrounding walls like ants spilling from an unseen anthill. The sound of stone-cutters striking blocks with hammers and carpenters hewing timbers reached my ears above the buzz of daily activity in the inhabited baileys above.

Mercadier noticed my inquisitive face peering out and let his horse drop back a few paces to trot alongside the carriage. I thought he might chide me for exposing myself to all men's eyes, but instead, he said, "A fair fortress, is it not? Chateau Gaillard—the Saucy Castle. His Grace, King Richard, was saucy indeed to build it here. Philip Augustus of France is furious."

"Why so?" I asked. "Were they not once friends?"

He raised a bushy black brow that made him look like the villain in an old tale, the black knight who would die on the sword of Arthur or Lancelot. "You know an awful lot for a little girl."

"I am not just any little girl, as you know," I said haughtily. "And no matter my age, I am still 'my Lady' to you, Mercadier. I am the Countess of Salisbury."

"So you are...*my Lady*," drawled Mercadier, "and I do believe it is not just his Grace's wondrous castle that is 'saucy.'"

He spurred on before I could think of a rebuke, which I would have given him. Now that I was safely in Richard's domain, my earlier fears of the mercenaries had lifted. Even Ortense had ceased her wailing; before this day, she had travelled no more than ten miles from her birthplace, and this journey was new and exciting, even if somewhat terrifying.

I had no more time to think on Mercadier's impertinence, however, for we had now topped the height and clattered over a wooden bridge into the outer bailey, encircled by five huge towers gleaming pale against the sky. Here stood workshops and stables; horses trotted by, led by their grooms, while a smith hammered away inside a forge that belched black smoke and a stone-cutter bashed a mallet against a huge slab of limestone. An apprentice mason sat cross-legged on the parched ground, tongue thrust between lips in concentration as he carved a wimpled woman's head, no doubt meant as a decoration for the King's Great Hall. I wondered if it was meant to be the King's mother, Queen Eleanor.

The outer bailey soon ended and our party rode over another bridge stretching into the middle bailey. If the outer defences fell, that bridge would go up in flames or be cast down into the deep dry moat, but I doubted anyone would dare attack such a massive fortress with its glaring rings of towers. More towers poked up in the middle bailey too—great stark cylinders with birds floating around their turrets. Another cluster of workshops was set up within the shadow of the walls; to our left, a huge slab of stone was being gradually hoisted to the top of the wall, which was dotted with strange stone projections. At first, I had thought them gargoyles or other water-spouts for the rainy season, but on closer inspection, they were clearly something else.

Mercadier dropped back to the carriage window again. "You are impressed, my Lady?"

Grudgingly I nodded. "But Salisbury is a fine castle too. Very strong…"

"Yes, King Richard's dear mother, the Dowager Queen, often testifies to its stoutness."

I flushed, remembering that Father had been her gaoler there, after her estrangement from King Henry.

"Don't worry, I do not think she will hold her imprisonment against you," laughed Mercadier.

"I was just a baby; I do not remember anything of her at all!" I insisted.

The little entourage rolled on, approaching the inner bailey and the great donjon. Entering the gatehouse, I glanced up to see more stone projections from the turret above, pierced with holes...and finally I guessed their purpose. "They are for dropping missiles!" I cried, to myself more than anyone else, but the ever-alert Mercadier heard me and grinned.

"Ah, so you've spotted the 'murder holes', Lady. They are used to drop boiling oil and pitch onto an enemy's head. The King took the idea from the fortresses he visited in the Holy Land. But look, even finer at keeping the foe outside the castle—the wall of the inner ward."

I eyed the great pale wall rising ahead, a ring enclosing the keep. Slashed only by arrow-slits, it had no towers or other visible features.

"No siege engine can destroy it," Mercadier explained proudly. "The wall is even, with little for a foe to aim at and nothing a grappling hook might catch upon. There are no towers to undermine. By building Chateau Gaillard, King Richard has shown he is a great master-builder as well as a warrior!"

At last, we were past that great slab of impregnable stone, and servants swarmed out to meet the incoming party. Mercadier walked off without a backwards glance, evidently pleased that his work was done, and I was now in the hands of a gaggle of bowing, scraping servants. A steward handed me down from the chariot with care. He let Ortense stumble out on her own; her ankles had grown puffy in the heat and she nearly fell into the dust. I thought she might cry; she seemed horribly out of place, staring up at the frowning keep as if she gazed into the hell-mouth itself.

The steward led us up the broad sweep of the keep's stairs; I grew aware of eyes following my every step. Holding my head high, I attempted to move with a Countess' grace.

"Poor little mite," I heard one woman say, down below in the bailey.

Her words rang like an ominous bell in my head, but I pretended that I had heard nothing. Inside the keep, I was escorted to a private chamber with walls decorated by red silks from afar. Lions were sewn upon these hangings, while strange mats lay across the floor, green as grass...but curious, not woven from reeds or rushes, but cloth. Towering candelabrum with reaching arms cast shadows and the air was scented with unfamiliar fragrances, sweet and luxurious, redolent of Outremer and other eastern lands.

My nerves were jangled, for I expected to see the King in this lavish chamber. Instead, three women entered the room, the sweep of their gorgeous robes disturbing the green woven rug, making it buckle and toss like a sea of grass. All three glimmered like jewels, one in sapphire-blue like the Virgin's blessed robe; another in vivid yellow, a sunburst in the gloom; the third in silver-grey, mist and moonlight.

The grey-clad lady cleared her throat, recognising that, unaware of their identities, I did not know how to approach them with courtesy. "Greetings, Ela Countess of Salisbury," she smiled. "Berengaria, Queen of England, gives greeting to the King's ward." She gestured with a graceful hand to the woman who stood in the middle of the three, the one robed in blue like the Virgin.

Queen Berengaria! My face burned with shame for not realising she might be at Chateau Gaillard! Many back home shamefully forgot they had a Queen—for Berengaria had never once set foot upon England's shores. Nor had she produced an heir, and cruel gossips whispered she never would. The King had been temporarily estranged from her, his reason unknown to all save his Confessor, but Pope Celestine had ordered a reconciliation, and after suffering a grave illness, Richard's heart had softened and he promised to show the Queen fidelity and accompany her to church each Sunday.

Richard was a man of his word, or so I'd heard, and so Berengaria was at the Chateau, perhaps, hoping to produce an heir. My knowledge of how the latter might occur was sparse, only that men and women should ideally dwell in blessed matrimony for that happy event to follow...

"Your Grace." I made a deep curtsey, well aware of my travel-rumpled and sweaty gown and the tangles in my hair. Behind me, Ortense uttered a strange sound and fell to her knees with a crash.

"Arise, child." Berengaria's voice was deep, rich, and gentle.

Getting up, I looked at the Queen. Men said she was more wise than fair, and I agreed she was not perhaps so beautiful. Her face was thin without the lily-white complexion so favoured, and her brows were thick and black. Yet her eyes, a deep, rich brown, were captivating, and above all, they were kind. A cross set with rubies burned bright against her sapphire dress, and her headdress was bound by a modest gold circlet patterned with leaves. Not, as Queens and nobles went, an ostentatious lady…

"Welcome to Chateau Gaillard. My Lord Richard will see you later; at present he is busy with his masons. As you can see, this castle is in a perennial uproar; Richard wants it finished soon. It will be a marvel, a triumph to all who worked upon it—a castle of huge size and incredible strength raised in but two years!"

"It is very impressive, your Grace," I said. "I look forward to my time here."

"I do not believe the King will keep you at Gaillard overlong," she said. "It is too busy for a young girl, and you need a ladies' education. However, an important aspect of your future must be dealt with before you fare elsewhere." Suddenly pensive, she sighed deeply. "My ladies-in-waiting, Ada and Giraude, will look after you in the meantime."

"Ooh, your Grace…that feller, Master Mercadier, told me I was to look after Countess Ela." Ortense was breathing down my neck, nervous and puffing.

The Queen gazed solemnly at the servant. "Who is this woman, Countess Ela?"

"She is Ortense, a kindly soul; one of the nurses in my uncle's house. I beg you treat her well, for she is far from home and did not foresee a long journey."

"Mercadier forced her to come with you."

I nodded. "I needed a female escort for propriety."

Berengaria sighed. "True enough, but Richard should have arranged such niceties before his captain set forth. Sometimes my husband acts in haste without much thought. Unless it is war. He is good at war, but not so diligent in other things." She laughed, but her laugh was a little strained, and Ada and Giraude joined in, their laughter equally false.

The Queen then gestured to her women. "My ladies will attend you from now onwards; they are more fitting for a Countess than an uneducated nursemaid from some provincial village."

Ortense turned puce and began to shake. It was obvious she thought the Queen would order her dismissed, leaving her wandering in strange country miles from home, but she dared not voice her fears in such high company. She began to wring her hands, the big fingers twisting like sausages about to burst.

"Your Grace, you won't send my servant away right now, will you?" I blurted "She cannot find her way home on her own; nor can she walk the path alone."

Queen Berengaria looked surprised by my forthrightness but smiled as if my concern pleased her. "I had no intention of doing so, Countess. She will accompany you to your chambers for the night, and when I can arrange it, I will have her sent back to your uncle's house."

Ortense let out a relieved sigh then, realising how loud she had been, pressed a hand to her mouth.

"Come this way, Lady Ela," said the lady called Geraude. She was the one in yellow, her thick, tawny hair bound in two braids speckled with minute, dark-purple jewels. "We will show you the way, have a bath drawn, and see that fitting clothes are brought."

Giraude and Ada led us from the donjon, back into the middle bailey where the hall-block and chapel stood. Ortense and I were taken to a chamber at the back of the apartments, leaning out over the curtain wall. The room was compact but well-fitted out for visitors. A bed stood in one corner, covered by a canopy, and paillasses for the ladies were arranged on the floor. Three walls were brightened by white-wash, while the fourth, above the bed, bore a skilful painting of the Annunciation. An unfashionably large window with two thick wooden shutters gave a view beyond the castle to the village of Andelys, lying below with the deep blue serpent of the Seine twisting before its tall stone houses.

Ortense huffed down in a corner while Giraude circled me, measuring me with her eyes. "As you might imagine, Lady Ela, the castle is not full of young girls and it would take time to summon a tailor. You are quite tall for your age, though—I am certain one of my gowns can be altered to fit. You will then be ready for your audience with the King. I will also dress your hair when the time comes. The Queen says I have skill with hair and allows me to dress her own."

"I have no such skill," laughed Ada, a slender, fawn-like girl with waist-length dark braids visible beneath her veil, "but I will get the servants to bring the tub for you to bathe in. I am also sure you must be famished."

"Well, if Ela isn't, I am!" blurted Ortense. The Queen's women looked at her. She blushed, quivering in embarrassment.

"Yes, it has been a long journey," I interjected, hoping to spare my servant's blushes. "Ortense and I had little food with us, and the heat of the day turned it rancid."

Ada inclined her head and she inched towards the door. "I will send to the kitchen."

The bathing tub soon arrived, carried on the back of muscled servant-boys with sweating brows and cheeky smiles. They glanced sideways at me; clearly wondering who I might be. Assuming my most maidenly airs, I turned from them and observed the painting of Our Lady confronted by handsome Angel Gabriel with outspread wings painted in gold. Beneath his bare feet were written the words of Luke—*He will reign over the house of Jacob forever, and of His kingdom there will be no end.*

The servants were shooed out by Berengaria's women, and another group arrived hauling boiled water in huge ewers to pour into the tub. A third wave of servants brought the food on silver trays. Steam fanned throughout the room. The scent of roses and herbs rose deliciously into the air.

Then I was left to the ministration of Ada and Giraude, who disrobed me with deft fingers and helped me up the steps into the tub. I sank into the sweet-smelling waters up to my neck, as Ada rubbed my back with a large chunk of soap. It smelt fairer than any soap I had used in the past; back at Salisbury, soap was made from mutton fat, potash and soda, and was functional but not pleasant to the nostrils.

"What is that soap made from?" I asked Ada. "It smells like…like heaven!"

"It is an old recipe; one devised by the Moslems!" Ada said. "It is popular in Spain. It contains olive oil to smooth the complexion, a pinch of lime to brighten the skin…but not too much, else it might burn! And herbs. Sprigs of rosemary are in this bar!"

"It…is it a heathen soap then?" I queried, feeling as if I might have sinned by enjoying such decadent luxury.

"I doubt God will be angered." Ada pursed her lips, eyes twinkling. "After all, is it not said cleanliness is near to Godliness?"

I was determined to say an extra prayer later on, just in case Ada was wrong…but now my belly was growling as I examined the array of treats set out on the wooden board laid across the tub. Mince tarts beckoned, roasted nuts, fritters, cuts of cheese and custards. There were also candied oranges and strange green and black vegetables that resembled large beads. They had a startling, pungent taste upon consumption; I could not decide whether I liked them or not.

"What are these?" I held one up, half-eaten.

"Have you never had one before, Lady Ela?" asked Giraude. "Well, I suppose you wouldn't have in England. The climate is too cold there. They are called 'olives.'"

Bath time soon ended. The two ladies wrapped me in a bleached sheet and rubbed me dry. Ortense came to help, eating the olives and the remains of anything I had left as she did so.

Before long I was dry, smelling of roses and herbs, with my hair tangling to my waist and a white nightdress frothing to my ankles. Ada was lighting the tall candles spaced around the room. Shadows capered across the walls, seeming to make the Angel Gabriel smile.

"We will let you rest now, Lady Ela," said Giraude. "Ada and I shall lie outside the door if you need us."

The two ladies exited, taking their paillasses with them, and I was left with Ortense, who was finishing the last crumbs of my meal. I headed to the window, loose nightgown trailing. Putting my elbows on the stone sill, I peered out. The streets of Andelys were filled by torchlight; a lone star twinkled over the tip of the church spire. The Seine was dark as wine, rushing along its course. Within the castle, a few workmen still hammered and chiselled, some whistling as they worked, others singing merrily, while night-birds swooped between the great towers on shimmering, night-dimmed wings.

"Isn't it *wonderful*, Ortense?" I breathed as the nurse waddled up behind me, smelling of olives and cheese.

"I don't know, milady," she muttered. "Too high up, it's making my head spin. Oh, I wonder what Pierre is doing tonight? I hope he's not drunk…and that he's fed the chickens…and that he's missing me…"

"It is my fault you're away from home, and I'm sorry." I retreated from the window and let her pull the shutters closed. "I won't let them forget to send you home."

"You're a good girl, Ela," said Ortense, "to think of a humble soul like me. I'm grateful but I must admit, leaving you here worries me a little. Such a huge castle, such high and mighty lords and ladies…and such a little maid, even if a bright one." Tears moistened her eyes. "Yet, I do miss Pierre already and my cottage, humble as it is."

"You must go—in fact, I bid you go," I said. "*This*…castles and great nobles…this is my destiny, Ortense. I am where I should be, as decreed by God. I am the King's ward; no harm will come to me."

Her face screwed up and I thought, with alarm, she might really bawl, but she held herself in check. "You are a dear girl," she managed at length, "and so, so innocent. Long may it be so, Lady Ela."

The next day, a carriage was readied to take Ortense home. I insisted on accompanying her into the bailey and asked Ada to make sure she had refreshments and a comfortable pillow for the journey. Ada and Giraude seemed amused that I should be so bothered about a servant, but I was insistent. As the chariot rolled out of the bailey, I waved, but Ortense, hidden within, could not see my frantic efforts.

I stood staring after the carriage, and a new sense of loss struck me despite my earlier brave words. I was alone in a foreign country with no kin to speak for me. And I had yet to meet the mighty Lionheart, King of England.

It was not long before that time would come, though. "Hasten now, Ela," prompted Ada. "We must not stand out in the bailey for too long—the workers are gawping at us and it is not seemly."

Giraude giggled and pressed a languid hand to her mouth; the masons and apprentices, carpenters and stone-cutters were indeed glancing over, no doubt wondering why the Queen's ladies were wandering about away from their mistress accompanied by a well-dressed child.

Resigned, I sighed. "Let us go then if you think that to look is evil."

Giraude and Ada eyed each other and burst out laughing.

"We must make ready for your presentation to his Grace anyway," soothed Giraude, noting my cross expression. "King Richard is going to give you a private audience in the throne room. You are very fortunate. You are just like one of the royal family."

"What do you mean?" I asked. "The King's great friend, the Marshal, is my distant kin, but I am not royal-blooded myself."

Ada gave her companion a slightly disapproving glance, although it was tinged with mirth by the faint upward curve of her lip. "Giraude sometimes talks too much, Lady Ela; the Queen often reprimands her for her loose tongue. Let us get you prepared, and then you will learn what his Grace plans for his dearest ward."

The ladies ushered me back to my chamber where I was primped and pampered, bathed and perfumed like a great lady. Giraude's dress, tailored to fit my child-like form, was a lush leaf-green, embossed with pinecones in golden thread. The sleeves hung down almost to the floor, lined with pale, imported silks of a colour tender as the blush of dawn. As Ada tied the laces at the back, Giraude toyed artfully with my hair, braiding thick strands with blue ribbons after rubbing in mystical oils from the east to make the hair shine. A simple polished circlet was set on my brow when she was satisfied.

"Shall we put some dried safflower cream to add redness to her cheeks? Or what about lily-root powder to whiten her complexion?" asked Ada thoughtfully. "Or would that look too *advanced* for a girl her age?"

"I think the Countess is fine as she is," smiled Giraude. "I am sure his Grace will agree."

Time passed. A light meal was brought for the three of us—frumenty, fish jellies and boiled millet. As the light outside died away and servants wandered around lighting fire braziers and torches, my companions grew more serious in mood, even nervous.

Without success, I tried to quell my own nerves. I knew every second brought me closer to meeting the most famous King in Christendom—my own sovereign lord, who held my future within his hands.

Finally, Giraude rose, dabbed at her pretty mouth and said, "Did you not hear the bell? It is time. His Grace will have dined and is waiting for the Countess Ela."

Ada cast me a reassuring smile. "Are you ready, my Lady? The King likes punctuality. As you can imagine, he is a very busy man."

I nodded, but my stomach was doing somersaults. What if he did not like me when we met? What if he thought I should be immured in a convent or given to some beastly old man? I began to wish I had begged Ada and Geraude for their lily-root and safflower powders to make me prettier!

In silence, I followed the ladies through the corridors, the mingled castle scents of cooking, burning torches, tallow and the distant privy making my nervous tummy churn.

I inside the keep, I was deposited at the door to the King's Audience Chamber—Richard's throne room. "Here we must leave you," Ada whispered in my ear, giving my upper arm a reassuring squeeze. "It is not meant for the likes of us unless invited. Good luck, little bird."

At the door, a man stood wearing a bright tunic emblazoned with the King's *Leopards Passant*—that some called Lions. In his hand, he held a brazen trumpet. Giraude walked over to him, speaking in low tones. Moments later, he raised the trumpet to his lips and blue a blast. "The Lady Ela, Countess of Salisbury!" he then cried in a ringing voice, announcing my presence to all within the audience chamber.

Giraude whirled to face me, giving my cheek an affectionate pinch. "Go now, little Countess. Be brave. Look him in the eye; he likes courage!"

As if in a dream, I floated past the trumpeter and into King Richard's throne room. The walls were very pale, unpainted and smooth, glowing gold in the light of dozens of bracketed torches. The roof was vaulted and without decoration, beautiful in its graceful starkness. A niche at the far end held Richard's throne, raised upon three marble steps. Its back was gilded, and a Cross rose upon the top, while the base was inlaid by blue and green gems. Candelabras stood on either side, each holding seven long white candles.

However, the King was not sitting on the throne. I was gazing awe-struck at an empty seat...

Disconcerted, I glanced around. Courtiers were gathered on the edges of the room clad in expensive raiment—samite tunics, silks, brocades, hats with dyed feathers, particoloured trousers, gilt belts, fine boots with silver buckles. They stared past me as if I did not exist. They had likely been told *not* to stare, but it made me feel as if I had become invisible. I worried that somehow I had offended Richard, who would leave me standing alone, hapless and helpless, as if I were a mummer who had forgotten his lines.

But then a plush purple curtain twitched aside near the throne and the arched doorway to a private ante-chamber was revealed. Two men walked out, and it was as if the clouds parted to reveal the shining sun.

Although I had never seen him before, I knew the King at once, lion by name and leonine in appearance. He stood a good head taller than most men; dusky-gold hair curled on his shoulders and his reddish beard was neatly trimmed. Lance-keen blue eyes peered from under darker brows; little lines from squinting into a harsh foreign sun sprayed out around them. Massively muscled shoulders moved beneath a vair-lined mantle of scarlet cloth.

The other man's identity was a mystery; I presumed he was one of the King's advisers. He was as tall as Richard but much leaner, and his hair and beard were darkish brown, though also holding hints of both gold and red. He wore a sea-green *bliaut* with wide, hanging sleeves over a striped blue shirt and forest-green hose. He was younger than Richard; I guessed in his mid-twenties at the latest.

The King sat upon his throne as I dropped into the deepest curtsey possible—so deep I feared I might fall over. When I finally rose, the Lionheart's lance-sharp eyes were upon me, scrutinising. A hot blush coloured my cheeks—I was now glad I had not used Giraude's creams, for I should have looked sunburnt as a peasant toiling in the fields.

"So, my Lady Countess…" The King's voice rolled out, not the roar of a Lion, although I could well imagine him roaring in battle, as he led his soldiers on to victory. "We meet at last, my ward. I have long searched for you."

"Yes, your Grace," I said. "My Uncle Philip Fitzpatrick thought my family should care for me instead."

"Did he now?" Richard laughed gruffly into his beard. The man at his shoulder gave a faint smile. "Did he indeed? He thought it proper to take you away from your King and your guardian?"

"My Lord King, have mercy on him," I said. "I will say it—he is nought like my father, Earl William. Uncle Philip is a very stupid and grasping man. When Mercadier and his men ransacked his treasury, I imagine he was punished enough."

The court burst into laughter. Tears rolled down the cheeks of some of the men gathered before Richard's throne. I did not know, at that moment, if I did good or ill speaking with such frankness about Uncle Philip.

Lionheart was mopping at his eyes. Mirthful tears ran from them, wetting his cheeks. "Ah, you speak boldly, little Countess. Does she not, Will? He glanced at the younger man near his shoulder.

"She does, indeed," replied the man. "That is not such a bad thing—in this matter, at any rate. As long as she does not become a tongue-lashing shrew!"

I flushed with fury at this oaf's mocking words. Who was he to assume anything about my future character?

"You malign me, sir!" My voice held frost; my eyes narrowed.

The court descended into laughter again. The King's friend, Will, grinned at me, bold as brass.

Confusion and anger made my head spin. All I wanted now was the King to tell me his plans, then send me forth. At best, I might end up in Queen Berengaria's household, I supposed; at worst sent to be educated at some gloomy backwater of a convent with an abbess known for harsh discipline.

King Richard seemed to be growing weary of his fellows' laughter, for which I was thankful. He held up his hand and silence fell.

"As you know, your wardship entails not only your education but the matter of your marriage. While my man Talbot sought you out, I dwelt long and hard on these matters …" He glanced at the man by the throne again.

"Seeing you, I have decided. You are to marry my half-brother William Longespee—Longsword. Marriage to a Countess who holds an earldom in her own right is precisely what he needs to take his proper place in the world…"

Longespee! I had heard his name whispered amongst Mother's maids, who were wont to gossip. Longsword, the *bastard* brother to the King, son from one of old King Henry's many liaisons. Some folk whispered that his mother was the beautiful Rosamund Clifford, whom it was rumoured Queen Eleanor had poisoned, but Mama had sniffed at such an idea. "Foolishness! Eleanor was locked up in our own castle when Rosamund died, so unless she truly was a shapeshifting witch and could fly on a besom to Godstow Priory, she never touched the girl. As for William Longsword's mother, anyone with any knowledge is aware that it is Ida de Tosny, who was a relative of Rosamund and resembled her. Ida did well out of the union and ended up as wife to Hugh Bigod, Earl of Norfolk."

I fought to keep my face steady. A King's brother was a fine match, but not so much when he was tainted by *bastardy*. My inheritance was to go to shore up a man who could inherit nothing due to his birth…My lower lip trembled a little, but I told myself to find courage. Women had to be brave in these matters. At least I would live in Salisbury Castle and not go to some draughty heap in some horrid place like the Fenlands, where strange, sinister men roamed about with webbed hands and feet. Or so I'd been told.

"Well, Ela, what do you think?" asked the King. "You will be part of my family with all that position entails."

"Your Grace is too kind," I said, my lack of enthusiasm clear.

"Come now, he is not as bad as all that, child!" laughed the King.

"I would not know, your Grace. I have never seen this William Longespee."

"Oh, but you have, Lady Ela. He stands at my side, my loyal brother, even if born on the wrong side of the blanket."

I gave a loud gasp and my horrified gaze flicked over to the man in the sea-green bliaut whose resemblance to Richard was now obvious. The man who had thought I might grow up to speak shrewish scold!

He gave me a wry grin and said, "It has been a pleasure meeting you for the first time…*wife*."

"But…but we are not wed yet!" I cried.

"Obviously not," said the King. "You are past the age of reason but not yet of the age of consent. However, as of this day, you shall be betrothed, and barring any mishaps, when you are above the age of twelve, you shall be truly wed to dear William. Come, take my brother's hand…"

"What about my dowry?" I gibbered.

"You need not worry—it is all dealt with," said Richard.

I felt quite ill. I wondered what part, if any, my mother had played in these negotiations. I wished she was here now, and childishly hoped she would step from the shadows, an angel come to save me.

Instead, William, my future husband, stepped in my direction, tall and lean, the torches making a golden nimbus around his shoulder-length brown hair. Up close, I supposed he was not so bad—at least ten years my senior, but not old, and he had all his teeth and no disfigurements.

But he thought I was shrewish…!

"Lady Ela?" he said quietly but firmly. He extended his hand and with reluctance I took it. His palm was warm, rough, sword calloused. My own hand drowned in clammy sweat.

"I will take you as my wife," said William, looking not towards me but to the King and the rest of the assembled witnesses.

I knew the words—what girl did not?—but for a second my tongue faltered. Then my voice emerged, a whispery, shivering sigh. "I-I take you, William Longespee, as my husband."

Silence fell. Then Richard descended from his throne, bluff and magnificent, the Lion of England. He clapped William on the shoulder. "There…it is done. After long bachelorhood, my brother William has taken a fitting wife. He will be the Earl of Salisbury."

"Hail to the Earl of Salisbury!" someone shouted, and the cry was taken up.

Tears stung at my eyes. My *father* was the Earl of Salisbury.

But he was dead, and I was his only heir, and now I had a husband who would have my inheritance as his own for good or for ill…

"We must feast!" roared Richard. "We must make merry and celebrate. To the hall, my friends, my stalwart fellows!"

William released my hand and without a single backwards glance, strolled over to the King and together they vanished into Richard's private ante-chamber. The courtiers in the throne room hastily dispersed.

Feeling adrift, I turned to follow them out, but suddenly Giraude appeared, taking my arm. "You did well, little Countess,"

"Am I suitably dressed for the banquet?" I asked. The back of my dress was damp with sweat.

"The banquet?"

"Yes, the King said he was to feast with William…my …my husband." I swallowed.

"Oh, no; the feast is for Richard and his friends only, not little girls. I must get you prepared."

"Prepared for what?" *What now?*

"Did his Grace not tell you? How remiss. On the morrow, you are to be sent away for a proper lady's education. You are going to the Abbey of Fontevrault…"

I knew it, some bad-tempered, crow-like Abbess!

"…to learn not only from the holy sisters but to dwell under the protection of the King's mother, the Dowager Queen, Eleanor of Aquitaine."

CHAPTER FOUR

Bells boomed, waking me from a troubled sleep. Springing upright with a gasp, I clutched the sides of my seat as it rocked back and forth. For a moment I had dreamt I was back at Salisbury castle …but no, I was in a chariot on my way to the Abbey of Fontevrault, where the Dowager Queen spent much time, although she was not a nun and had not fully retired from the world either.

Ada sat across from me, sewing quietly. As she saw me wake, she nodded in my direction. "We are here at last, little Countess."

Wiping the sleep from my eyes, I peered through the filmy curtains that veiled the chariot windows from curious gazes.

The Abbey was huge, almost a monastic town. The church of the *Grand Moutier*, the Great Mother, towered above the rest, its pinnacles and arches wrought from white limestone, smooth and severe. A lesser church, St Benoit's, huddled in its shadow like a timid child, smaller but no less stark and serene, while beyond stood other chapels, their roof tiles shining in the sun and their bells ringing. Monks and nuns flocked everywhere as far as the eye could see, the men toiling at daily duties while the women processed through the complex, singing hymns and holding their hands to heaven. Poor folk from the local town flooded in to be fed; the crippled and sick were carried past on stretchers, hymn-singing nuns accompanying them.

"I have never seen such a grand foundation!" I said excitedly. The priory at Amesbury was a daughter-house of Fontevrault, founded by King Henry as penance for Becket's murder, but unlike its Mother House, it was small and compact, although the lands it owned stretched down to the river and up to the haunted heathen stones on the Plain. It held only nuns, but here there were monks too and sisters in different garb from the Benedictines I was used to.

"It is certainly a busy house," said Ada. "Five communities dwell here as set out by the founder, Robert d'Arbrissel, who was a preacher from Brittany. There are men from all walks of life and women too—queens and nobles like her Grace, but also widows and poor women without dowries. Some are virgins who dedicated their lives to Christ from the earliest age, some merely wish to escape the evils of the world, some reside in St Benoit's for healing of the flesh, and some are...*fallen women* who have repented of their immoral ways. The brothers and sisters also run a Lazar hospital..."

"*Lepers*!" I squealed. I was afraid of lepers with their eaten pus-stained rags, and ringing bells. Mother had told me to avert my eyes if I saw one, and never to let one touch me in case I was afflicted by their malady.

"Do not fear those sorry creatures," reassured Ada. "They are nowhere near where you will be staying." She pushed the curtain open a little more. "See—that small chapel is for the monks, St. Jean de l'Habit—the Evangelist. Further out—you can see it against the compound wall—is La Madeleine, the chapel of the Magdalen, where sinful women repent. The Lazar House is also sheltered by the wall and has its own enclosure to separate the sick from the well; it is the smallest of the chapels and, of necessity, the most private."

The chariot slowed then ground to a juddering halt. Monks and nuns were surreptitiously glancing in our direction. The townsfolk were openly pointing and gawking; they had spotted King Richard's lions painted on the canvas stretched over the chariot.

"It is time," said Ada, when I did not move. "We are here."

The door-hatch was opened by one of our attendants, and I stepped blinking in the sunlight into the courtyard of the abbey. At once I was approached by a diminutive, wizened nun. "I am Sister Sybille. I will take you to the Abbess Mathilde, Countess Ela. Mademoiselle Ada, I leave you to the hosteller to find lodgings for the night."

So I was on my own. Ada disappeared into the guest house and I was led into the cloister by Sister Sybille, who moved terribly fast for one so aged and spindly. She guided me past rows of candles, over smooth, polished floor-slabs until we reached the offices of the Abbess Mathilde.

The Abbess sat before a wooden desk massed with scrolls. Candelabrums gave light, as did a slit window filled with expensive greenish glass, a novelty that was becoming fashionable in France and England. Paintings of the Virgin adorned one wall while St James and his scallop shells graced the other.

The Abbess was reading from a ledger as I entered with Sister Sybille. As I was announced, she put the book down with a quiet shuffle of page. "So—the young Countess of Salisbury is here."

She looked me up and down. Mathilde was a woman of middle years with a plump and unlined visage that shone like a moon in the candlelight, exuding peace and serenity.

"My Lady Abbess."

Mathilde cleared her throat. "You are welcome to God's House of Fontevrault. Before I take you to Queen Eleanor, your guardian during your stay, you must know that this is a house of learning and that maidens who do not have a calling are few. You shall be expected to live as the novices do, under the same rules and laws. Can you read?"

"Yes, my Lady Abbess. Quite well. My father thought it important since he had no sons."

Abbess Mathilde nodded, clearly pleased. "And can you sing?"

"I—I think so." I did not know if my voice sounded sweet but hoped it was.

"Well, yes or no, Ela?"

"Y-Yes!" I stammered.

"Good." She returned to her ledgers. "Sister Sybille will find you the garments of an oblate, and take you to Queen Eleanor."

Soon I was clothed in a hot, itchy, woollen robe that the nun Sybille had procured. My head was decently covered but not by a professed nun's wimple, rather a simple white veil. I was glad I was not required to cut my hair like the sisters.

Sybille picked up a candle, for impending dusk was turning the cloister violet-blue and the saints' statues and painted walls were sinking into a heavy gloom. It was almost like going on an adventure, navigating the long passageways that bored through the heart of the immense abbey.

The Dowager Queen had quarters separate from the actual nuns. I suspected she paid Abbess Mathilde handsomely for them in tributes of wood, lands and coin. I was excited to meet this famous, even infamous lady, but apprehensive too, for she was known for being forthright, even blunt. My sire had once been her reluctant gaoler—and had told many tales of their conversations.

Sybille beckoned me up a staircase that twisted in a spiral. Then we were standing outside a broad door with a torch bracketed over it. "Her Grace awaits," said the whiskery-chinned old nun, and she drifted away into the body of the abbey like a passing wraith.

Taking a deep breath, I tapped on the door with my knuckles. An imperious voice called, "Enter!"

With trembling fingers, I grasped the door-ring, and stepped over the threshold into Eleanor of Aquitaine's living quarters.

The Queen was sitting on a stool padded with cushions. She had a book open on her lap. I assumed it was a religious text, but as she closed it, I glimpsed illustrations of knights and giants—and to my astonishment, a picture of the mighty heathen stones that stood on the Plain above Amesbury.

Eleanor noticed my startled look. "I am reading Wace," she explained. "Henry and I had this book commissioned. It contains tales of King Arthur and other histories." Her lip quirked. "Henry was always trying to legitimise his reign. He wanted to be seen as a true descendant of Arthur."

I blushed that her keen gaze had noticed my inquisitive one. "Your Grace, glad am I to come here."

She shrugged. "Where else could you go? You are Richard's ward, but he has little use for young maidens. Castle building and warfare cover the bulk of Richard's interest. Berengaria…a sweet enough girl, but she needs to turn her attentions to my son and getting an heir—you, I fear, would be too much of a distraction in the household. Come over, let me look at you."

I walked toward the old Queen, trying to appear confident but not *too* confident, in case she thought me gauche and arrogant. I was curious to behold her, this infamous woman, Queen to two Kings, and instigator of the troubles between her sons and their father. Her battles with Henry are what caused her to end up locked in Salisbury Castle

She was, I thought, still of considerable beauty despite her great age, her jaw quite firm beneath the band of her barbette, her deep green-brown eyes wide-set, bright and full of lively interest. She did not have rosy cheeks or fashionable lily-white skin, but a honey-like complexion remarkably fresh for a woman so ancient—I guessed she must be around seventy summers. I was sure I had never met anyone so old before.

Eleanor appraised me, head to toe. "A well-grown girl. I knew your sire, you know…"

"Yes, your Grace. He spoke fondly of you…" In fact, he had not; he pitied her imprisonment, but I heard him tell Mother the old Queen was something of a termagant…

"Did he now? I doubt that." Eleanor gave a most unqueenly guffaw. Her teeth were still good, strong and white. It was easy to see where King Richard got his looks, although his colouring was pure Plantagenet. "Still, he treated me as well as possible under the circumstances. He only obeyed orders and we were certainly not enemies—I thought greatly of his father, your grandsire Patrick. Did you know what he did for me?"

I had heard the tale many times from parents and nursemaids but dared not say so. The Queen clearly wanted to tell the tale. "No, your Grace."

She gave a deep sigh, eyes misting at the memory. "I was riding to my capital at Poitiers while Henry dealt with rebellion—the obnoxious Lusignans were at their usual trouble-making alongside the Count of Angouleme—another devious snake—and the Count of La Marche. Henry had captured the Lusignans' fortress, but for whatever foolish reason decided to leave me there while he carried on fighting elsewhere. As a protection, he left me with Earl Patrick, whose reputation as a knight was excellent. Soon that reputation was put to the test…one day, as we rode through the woods, the Lusignans attacked like so many ravening wolves! With no regard for his own safety, Patrick fought his way through the mob and bore me to safety at the castle. But when he mounted a return attack on Guy de Lusignan's men, Guy himself sprang from a tree and stabbed him in the back—a coward's blow and one that shall ever live in infamy! Young William Marshal then attacked, a lion in his ferocity, but he was captured and dragged away. I ransomed him, you know; gave him his start in life…How he has risen, my dear Marshal…" She smiled to herself, caught in a reverie of olden times.

"You were very generous, your Grace. William Marshal is kin to me; his mother, Sybil, was my grandsire's sister."

Queen Eleanor sat up, focussing on me once more. "You are part of my family now—the royal family of England. William is close to both my sons, even if he is only a bastard. I pray he will always lend them the strength of his arm."

I flushed.

"His mother was Ida, the least vapid of Henry's mistresses. She was his ward; I suspect she felt she could not say no. I preferred her to that frowzy little redhead Rosamund Clifford—and see, I was right! Ida made a good marriage with Hugh Bigod and has given him children, without a whiff of further scandal, while Rosamund just turned up her toes and died…" She let out a sharp laugh; I was not certain whether her words were humorous or not, considering the rumours…

Abruptly, she changed the subject. "You can read and write, I trust."

"And sing," I responded. "Abbess Mathilde already asked."

"Your education will continue with me. I will make certain you receive full religious education here…Other duties required of young ladies will be taught in my castle of Poitiers."

I almost clapped my hands in joy. Although the Abbey was overwhelmingly grand, I was well aware of its many strictures. "Is—is that permitted? Will the Abbess let me go?"

"She can hardly hold you. While she would not be the first abbess to try and coerce a young noblewoman into taking vows, Mathilde is not that sort. I am not a nun here, you understand, Ela. I may one day take vows or I may not. A convent is an ideal place for an old woman to retire to commune with God and atone for her sins. My bones are beginning to ache—but I am not ready to withdraw entirely from the world. Not yet. Grown men though they are, my sons still need me. Richard is too reckless by far, and John…well…Johnny…" She shook her head. "He is incorrigible. Henry's favourite, but of all my brood, he's the one who broke his father's heart. I worry how it should be…if Richard should die without heirs."

Outside the narrow window, a wandering owl hooted, voice echoing eerily amidst the pinnacles on church and chapels. I shuddered; I fancied so did the Dowager Queen. Then she leaned back and sighed. "And here I am, rambling on at a travel-weary child like an old crone in her dotage. None of my worries is of any concern to you—although they may well be, one day, now that you have joined the family. Come now, we will eat..." She gestured to a table where cheeses, bread and fruits lay on a plain pewter dish. "It is simple fare, as you might expect in a House of Benedictines, but it is wholesome. Oh, and I have a small gift for you, on the occasion of your betrothal." Stiffly climbing to her feet, she opened a cedarwood chest and drew out a book wrapped in a silk scarf. "I am sure this will help you get through the more arduous times in the abbey."

"Is it a prayerbook?" I asked, unwilling to tear off the wrapping like a greedy babe. "Thank you, your Grace."

"Prayerbook," Eleanor of Aquitaine snorted derisively, folding her arms. "Certainly not. Abbess Mathilde can supply you with such. It is *The Knight of the Cart* by Chretien de Troyes, in which Arthur's right-hand man, Lancelot, first meets Queen Guinevere."

I spent the next months as Queen Eleanor's shadow. I sang in the choir and dispensed bread to the poor at the gates. I received religious instruction from the Abbess herself and from the Obedientaries, the senior nuns. I was permitted to do some copying in the Scriptorium—Sister Agnes said my hand was clear and my eyes keen for the close-up work—and I embroidered robes for use in church services. I was not so good at that, but Sister Gisela guided me and soon I found my stitchery much improved. I had been unsure of residing with the nuns, but they were good and kind—and when days grew dull and I had spent a hot hour in prayers while the summer sun blazed onto the church roof, I could always retire to the quarters I shared with the Queen, lie upon my straw-stuffed paillasse, draw out my handsome gift and read the tale of the noble Lancelot...

But then one day the following Spring, after a visit to the Scriptorium, I noticed Eleanor frowning and pacing the chamber floor. I dared not ask what the matter was. I noticed she held a parchment, half-rolled, in her hand.

I stood in silence for a while, afraid to approach lest my presence be unwelcome. At length, the Dowager Queen acknowledged me with a motion of her hand. Her mouth was tight; it made her look older—and her eyes were weary. "Well, Ela, it looks as though you will see my capital at Poitiers soon."

"Your Grace?"

She licked her lips, fiddled with the letter then slowly tore it to pieces. "There may be trouble. I have received unwelcome tidings. When one lives as long as I have, Ela, one gets a sense when something is amiss. A feeling of unease, a feeling that I may soon be needed. Pack your things. I have spoken to Mathilde already. A chariot will arrive at dawn. We leave for Poitiers on the morrow."

I spent the night tossing and turning, wondering what had happened to unnerve the Queen, but secretly pleased she was taking me with her and not leaving me with the nuns. As the light of the rising sun turned the abbey towers to columns of blood, I clambered up, bleary-eyed from lack of proper sleep, and was bundled into the waiting carriage.

"Make haste!" Eleanor called out to the grooms leading the horses. "We must not dally. It is important I arrive at my palace as soon as possible."

On the way to Poitiers, the Queen finally told me what she had learnt. "A Queen, even a Dowager one, must keep her spies," she said briskly. "Richard would tell me nothing otherwise—he thinks I should retire, as a good woman should. Well, I'm not a good woman, as I am sure you have heard before."

I spluttered on the small beer we'd brought from the abbey. Eleanor continued, "As it happens, I have heard that the Count of Limoges has risen in revolt against the King. Richard rides out to meet him with fire and sword."

"The King is a very brave and a great warrior. I do not think you need fear, Madam."

"But a mother always does, Ela—hopefully you will learn that yourself one day if God gives you many children. Anyway, it is not Richard's prowess in warfare that makes me fearful—it is his rashness, his foolhardiness. He is bored since returning from Crusade; I fear he will think he is invincible."

"He is the Lion of England."

"He is just a man," Eleanor said sharply. "One who I saw come wailing from my womb. He has his faults and none know them better than I. Oh, Richard, Richard, you gave me so much pride—why could you not have given me a grandson too, to make the inheritance secure?"

She glanced away and began to toy with her rosary beads which were made of a clear blue glass frosted with pure gold. Outside, rain began to fall, thrumming on the canopy roof. Several drops leached through the heavy, waxed cloth, dripping into my lap. I brushed them away distractedly, thinking of Eleanor's clear distress.

The rain still fell in sheets when we reached Poitiers. I was wet through but the Dowager Queen, although drenched herself, had regained some cheerfulness. As the carriage rattled through the gateway and the townsfolk came out the cheer and hurl bouquets, a wan smile touched her lips.

"This is my family's stronghold," she told me. "It has one of the oldest churches in the whole of Europe, the Baptistry. I placed my own mark on the town, too—Henry and I built the cathedral, and immortalised ourselves and our four sons in coloured glass." She shook her head, a shadow passing over her features. "Alas, I had four sons when the window was wrought—now I have but two."

Slowly the chariot progressed down the main street, barely able to make headway due to mobs of well-wishers. It was obvious that Eleanor was well-loved in the town. Up ahead, a large palace came into view, heavily fortified with an imposing donjon facing the townward side. The great tower's shadow fell black over the cobbled street; from the pinnacle of the red-tiled turret flapped a banner bearing the Arms of Aquitaine, a single, blue-clawed lion on a crimson background.

"It's an impressive Tower, is it not?" said Eleanor. "And rather daunting to the eye, I dare say. It is called the Maubergeonne. My grandfather, William, built it to house my grandmother, Dangereuse de l'Isle Bouchard."

"Dangerous!" I cried, surprised. I had never heard of man or woman called 'Dangerous' before.

Eleanor gave a little laugh. "Her true name was Amauberge, but dangerous she was and the name stuck; she cared not for the laws of men and scorned them. She was my grandfather's mistress, not his wife. Now many men have mistresses, but there was more to it than that. Her daughter was my mother, Aenor, so Dangereuse was bedding her own daughter's husband."

"Oh!" I blushed, thinking I had never heard anything quite so scandalous.

"My family has never been quite like others—so many lusts and entanglements! But it is not quite as bad as it sounds; my mother had already died when grandmother became grandfather's leman. He did have another wife, though—Philippa—and she was most distressed to find Dangereuse in her home and herself banished to Toulouse! She retired to Fontevrault in high dudgeon and there conspired against Dangereuse with grandfather William's *first* wife, Ermengarde, whom he had put aside due to her insufferable moods…Ah, child, I am sure you do not want to hear such wicked, wicked tales."

I murmured that I was happy to hear whatever the Dowager Queen said, even if I did not understand it all. "You will one day, I am sure," she said, with one of her enigmatic wry smiles. "Now—here we are."

We entered the palace as servants dropped curtseys and bows. Eleanor went to the Great Hall for a while and sat on the dais as people from the town came bearing gifts—and sometimes bringing their grievances too. Their lady had been long away. The hall was huge, larger than the Great Hall of Salisbury, and much more modern—Eleanor and Henry had remodelled it in the Angevin style. Great wooden beams carved with angels and grotesques spanned the ceiling, while the walls were a series of graceful arches, unpainted, almost stark, gleaming white-gold in the light of candles and cressets.

I was allowed to watch the procession of newcomers and Eleanor's response to them; she told me it was my duty to learn, for I would need such knowledge as William's wife. "You are a clever girl," she said. "I saw that from the first. You won't be merely a vessel, bearing children to William Longespee—although, God willing, you will also do that, as it is your duty. I foresee you working in tandem with your husband, Countess not just in name but a figure of hope and respect to the folk of Wiltshire. After all, had you not been born a woman, your title would have been Earl—and those people are yours and will look to you, female or no."

Much pleased by her kindly assessment, I waited with patience and heeded every word as she dealt with troubles brought before her—disputes over land, tales of outlaws in the nearby woods, a bridge that needed rebuilding, a church with a leaking roof.

Once she was done, she retired, and I was taken by her favourite lady, Amaria, who had shared her imprisonment in Salisbury, to my own tiny chamber. I was to dwell with one other lady-in-waiting, Lucienne, who was young, lively and pretty. She would sleep on a pallet while I had a small, compact bed.

For a week or more, I saw little of the Dowager Queen, who was closeted away with advisers and stewards, treasurers and chamberlains, mayors and aldermen. With Lucienne and other ladies, I journeyed into town to see the famous sights of Poitiers. We walked alongside the swelling River Clain and visited the cathedral where the rare painted glass glowed jewel-rich, depicting not only the Queen and her sons, but also Biblical scenes—the Women at the Empty Tomb, the Dead Arising, a blind-folded St Paul awaiting martyrdom, St Peter on an upside-down Crucifix being tormented by the Roman Emperor Nero. A smirking blue devil was hissing encouragement in Nero's ear.

The devil's malicious cobalt grin unnerved me, and since I did not like to dwell on ugly things, I turned my mind to bygone times, when the beautiful, vivacious Eleanor had married young King Henry on that very spot.

Later, my little gaggle of women travelled on through the market, where we bought gewgaws and fresh pastries before stopping at the ancient Baptistery with its great fonts and colourful frescos that showed, among the expected religious images, strutting peacocks with dazzling green and blue plumage and a contingent of horsemen in flowing cloaks.

"That one is a Roman emperor!" Lucienne gestured to a particularly martial-looking rider. "Have you heard of Constantine, Lady Ela?"

"Of course!" I replied, smugly. "He was proclaimed Emperor in Britain and his mother was a British princess called Helena! Henry of Huntingdon wrote about it—the Queen let me read her copy." The ladies all glanced to each other and smiled indulgently; I was just glad Eleanor allowed me access to her many books, even if some tales in them were partly a writer's invention.

My smugness vanished when I arrived back at the Palace. No sooner had I changed garments and washed the dust from my face in a basin of rosewater, Lucienne raced through the door in a flap, her face pallid beneath her headdress. "Countess, the Dowager Queen sends orders that you must come at once."

Straightening my rumpled skirts, I quickly followed her to Eleanor's apartments. The Queen was pacing the tiles, a trapped lioness. She was dressed in a plain white robe and her hair hung free, a waist-length cascade of dark slate grey. Amaria stood beside her, trying to put a blue cloak around her shoulders. She ignored the maid's efforts, continued to pace.

"What is it, your Grace?" I asked. "You seem…distressed."

Eleanor turned to me, and it seemed as if all the long years of her life had crashed down upon her in one fell swoop. "News has come from Chalus-Chabrol." Her voice was a harsh croak, torn from trembling lips. "Terrible news. That fool of a son of mine, Richard, believed the castellan was hiding Roman treasure after hearing a story that a peasant had dug some up; he was desperate for money, as ever. He besieged the castle, as small and unimportant as it was…The fool…the fool…"

She slumped over as if about to faint; Amaria clasped her around the waist, ever a tower of strength. The Queen seemed to recover, grasping the edge of the nearby table for support. "Richard went to view the siege engines without wearing his mail. He got too close to the defenders. One of them fired a crossbow bolt and it struck him here…" She touched her left shoulder.

I gasped and put my hand to my throat in shock. "Your Grace, surely the King…the King is not…"

"No, not yet." Her eyes were stormy, dark, rain-filled. "But the wound has gone bad. Nought can be done. Richard's life is now in God's hands." She stalked to the window, throwing open the shutters; the sun had just set and the horizon beyond blazed blood-red, the clouds limned by streaks of fire. "I must go to him...my son, my precious son. If he must die, I would be at his side. I ride out for Chalus tonight."

"Tonight?" cried Lucienne who stood behind me. "But madam, dusk has fallen. Wicked men ride upon the roads..."

"This is my ancestral land," snarled Eleanor. "I fear no one who walks upon it, do you hear me? I will ride through hell if need be to reach my son. Summon the steward. Have him call for the horse-master and grooms. Have my carriage readied for immediate departure."

"Your Grace, I sorrow to hear this grievous news." I thought of golden Lionheart...merrily handing me over to his brother, William Longespee in Château Gaillard. "I wish I could offer my help but..."

"You are a child, I know." Eleanor motioned for Amaria to get her travelling garments from their cedarwood chest. "You must stay here at Poitiers; Lucienne will look after you. Be sure you practice your embroidery and dancing..."

"Madam!" Words burst from my mouth, unexpected. "Let me go with you. I am the King's ward, but also family, wed to the King's half-brother. I would stand by you, support you in need even though I am only a child."

Eleanor paused. "What an odd girl you are. It is often said only children mature long before those who come from a large brood. Maybe it is true—but no, a castle under siege and a dying King is not a fitting place for a maid of tender years."

"I beg you, your Grace," I implored. "I feel it is my...my duty. My father, God assoil him, always impressed upon me from my earliest days that it was my duty to serve. My grandsire Patrick also believed this—and so he gave his life to defend you when you were attacked by the Lusignans. If you have respect for my forebear and his deed, let me go with you."

"Patrick..." Eleanor whispered and she shook her head. "They say there is no fool like an old fool...and I guess I am that fool. You may accompany me as my lady-in-waiting in training. Amaria shall travel with us too. You must agree to obey her in all things as I may not be free to guide you."

"I swear it!" I said. My belly was doing nervous flipflops. Why I so desperately wanted to join Eleanor on such a dreadful journey, I scarcely knew despite my avowal of 'duty'. I did believe in my father's words, but there was more to it. Deep inside, I wanted to *be* Eleanor, not some pampered lady confined to my bower with my stitchery throughout the long years of my marriage. I would bow to my husband's wishes since God had ordained it so, but I would play the part of a mindless ninny for no one. I was the Countess of Salisbury, and it was more than a mere title...

Bundled in heavy, hooded travelling cloaks, we left within the hour. The sky had become hard jet, the palace lit by a thousand fire braziers circling the towers. The great gates, studded with burnished bronze, clanged aside and the Queen's carriage rattled out into the night, surrounded by her boldest knights on strong destriers, mailed and helmed. A standard-bearer carried her banner, flapping noisily in the night-wind.

Huddled in my mantle, I sat next to the silent Eleanor. I was going on a great, terrible, frightening adventure, and as in the final tales of the glorious King Arthur, no happy ending was in sight...

The sun had set.

The Lion of England had fallen.

CHAPTER FIVE

The castle of Chalus Chabrol was a cheerless place, guarding the passage to Limoges on one side and the road to Spain on the other. The oldest part, a solitary round tower, stretched high into the sky like a warning finger, dwarfing the other buildings massed on the bleak hilltop. The roof of a sullen, unlovely hall rose a few feet above the thick blackish walls, as did a spire on the castle chapel. No defenders were visible, save for a lone guard above the gate, half-hidden by a stone projection, but greasy smoke curled from within, perhaps where a building had caught alight in a storm of fire-arrows.

King Richard's siege engines sat around the edge of the castle ditch, unmanned. Soldiers walked about as if in a daze, armed but not in battle array. The pavilions of the captains, set back on the hillside, were unusually quiet, with no one coming in or out. The King's pavilion, largest of all, painted with Biblical phrases and capped with gold, stood silent, its flaps pulled closed.

Queen Eleanor climbed from the chariot without waiting for any assistance. Amaria scrambled after her and I followed, desperate to keep up.

Unbelievably spry for one so old, Eleanor pushed aside her own soldiers and strode purposefully towards Richard's tent, her face stony as granite and nearly as grey. The ground beneath her calfskin travelling boots was trampled and churned; mud squelched up, sucking at her ankles. I slipped and nearly fell; Amaria dragged me up, more interested in keeping pace with her mistress than saving my dignity.

As we neared the King's pavilion, a lanky man in black emerged from the surrounding tents and swiftly approached us, bowing low before the Dowager Queen. I was surprised to see Mercadier, leaner and spindlier than I remembered, his hair an oily tangle around his bony moustached face.

"Your Grace," he said, "I greet you with great sorrow…Would that we met in happier times."

"Well, God has willed it otherwise, Mercadier," said Eleanor gruffly. "How fares my son?"

"Not well. The physics attend but the wound has gone rotten."

"Could not the arm be taken?"

Mercadier shook his head. "The King would not hear of it, Madam. And then…it was too late. Indeed, I bid you not dally, for the world slips away from him. A priest already attends, to give Extreme Unction…"

Eleanor took a steadying breath, a flicker of grief rushing over her features. "I will go to him then. Are there lodgings ready for me, my maid and the girl?"

Mercadier nodded. "I ordered a tent set up for you next to the King's pavilion; food, such as we have, and warm spiced wine await you."

"Go, Amaria, and take the child," said Eleanor. "I must be with Richard."

"Lady…" began Amaria. "I would be with you."

"A-and I!" I stammered, although the thought of seeing the brave, bright King, the golden lion, on his death-bed was terrifying.

"Go!" ordered Eleanor, waving her hand in our direction. "Do not argue with me, either of you! Do not waste my last moments with my boy!"

The Dowager Queen hoisted up her muddied skirts and ploughed determinedly over the sodden hilltop toward Richard's tent.

Mercadier turned towards Amaria and me. "Ladies, follow me. I will take you to your pavilion, where you may rest. Pages wait to serve you." Suddenly he halted in his tracks, staring down into my updrawn hood. "I remember you! Ela, niece of Philip Fitzpatrick, and Countess of Salisbury, is it not? You have grown. What are you doing here?"

"I am indeed Ela," I retorted, "and I am now also wed to the King's half-brother, William. Therefore, I am family as well as part of Queen Eleanor's household. And so I have come."

"You are brave, faring to a rough camp where a King is about to meet his maker."

"I *am* brave, and why should I fear? All is in God's hands." The wind was blowing cold over the hilltop, whining between tents, driving smoke from watchfires into my eyes. "Only King Richard matters...and the welfare of the Dowager. She has been kind to me."

Amaria and I went to our tent and sat inside, drinking spiced wine to warm our chilled bones. The wind grew stronger, and the canvas above rippled and swelled. A page with bobbed golden hair served us pasties and tarts on a tray. He was about my age and looked miserable, his eyes red-rimmed as if he had spent the last day weeping.

Amaria noticed him too. "You are Thomas, one of Richard's own pages."

"Yes, Lady," he said in a tremulous voice. "For nigh on two years. They will not let me see his Grace now."

"His bedside is not the place for a young boy—even a loyal page," said Amaria kindly, placing her hand on his shoulder. "Not now."

The lad flushed, fighting to keep his emotions in check. He did not weep, but words burst forth instead of tears. "I would have given my own life for his, I swear it. He was inspecting the engines...when a bolt came from the blue and struck his shoulder. He fell back, but even as he lay on the ground in pain, he said he forgave the one who shot him and ordered that when the castle fell, he was not to be harmed."

I was surprised. "Why did he do that?"

"Because it was a boy who shot him...just a boy. They say his name is Bertran. The King vowed he would not take revenge on a child who thought he was defending his home from an enemy. Many do not believe his Grace to be overly merciful—but he is honest and he is fair."

Outside the wind gave a shriek like a soul in torment; the tent poles clattered and the flaps billowed. I shivered as cold draughts rushed over me; so did Thomas.

"Hostilities have ceased," he continued, "at least for now. Even the lord of Chalus did not want the King hurt. He only wanted him to take his army elsewhere. He swears there is no treasure."

"Stay here with us, boy," said Amaria as the storm-wind gusted again, shuddering the tent. "The night is dark and unhappiness reigns. If the King should...Well, I think it best if you remain with Countess Ela and me."

Thomas looked glad of the companionship. "I will guard the door," he said, although there were already two soldiers outside, leaning on their pikes and peering through the downpour toward the sullen walls of Chalus.

"What a chivalrous young man you are!" exclaimed Amaria. "But it seems to me that you are already weary from great deeds in the service of your sovereign. Here...take my extra coverlet and lie before the brazier."

Thomas took the cover and squatted before the flames. Amaria handed him a sweetmeat she had saved. "I truly shouldn't," he murmured, but he did.

And then he was sound asleep.

I gazed longingly toward my own couch. I felt weary, dirty and upset. "Go get some sleep, Lady Ela," said Amaria. "But keep your raiment on, even your shoes. One never knows if one must flee in the night. That's what Queen Eleanor always said to me."

Unfastening my cloak, I curled up under the embroidered cover, drawing both the cloak and a sheepskin over me for further warmth. Overhead, rain rattled on the canvas, like nervous fingers drumming. I tried not to think of bony hands reaching in the dark or strange voices howling in the wind...or, more mundanely, of what would happen if someone inadvertently touched the canvas and started a leak.

An uncomfortable, unrefreshing sleep consumed me. Some hours later, I was woken by a shriek, a desolate sound that filled the night. I sat bolt upright. Amaria was still asleep, snoring, a rug up round her ears to filter out the noise of the weather.

My heart banged against my ribs as the cry came again then tailed off. Could it have been a fox? They were given to unearthly shrieks in the night. But would any fox skulk around a busy army camp?

I glanced at Thomas. He was awake too, eyes bright and fearful, their surfaces shining in the dim light. "Did you hear that? What do you think it was?"

Dazedly, he shook his head. "Go back to sleep, milady. I'll protect you."

"Protect me—your eyes are like moons! You're shivering too, even though you are right by the brazier."

He opened his mouth, no doubt to once again inform me that, although barely my size, he would look after me—but out in the night a bell began tolling in the castle chapel, low, stony, dismal. We could hear shuffling and clanking and horses neighing as men moved around the tent.

Racing to the doorway, I untied the flap and flung it back, receiving a face full of rain. Thomas was right at my heels. Our guards had vanished. The camp was full of torchlight and moving figures of men; huge knights bowed their heads and wept, tears mingling with the heavy rain.

At my back, I heard Amaria shift, mumble sleepily. I did not want to wake her for fear she would hold me back. I wanted to find the Queen…

The bells tolled on. "They are opening the castle gate," murmured Thomas. "Have they surrendered?"

"We'll find out." I darted out into the night, Thomas running after me.

"We mustn't!" he said.

"We must. I am the King's ward."

We rounded several captains' pavilions; men were inside, on their knees, praying on their *prie-dieus* before portable altars. A priest ran by, head bowed; camp followers were fleeing, their faces taut with sorrow and fear. I saw Mercadier, followed by a wedge of huge, brutal Brabancons, striding toward the gatehouse of Chalus, his black moustache bristling, a murderous appearance making him seem half a demon. He was a fierce man who never baulked at shedding blood, but only tonight of all nights did his strained, staring countenance truly frighten me.

The King's tent loomed. Great warriors and mighty barons streamed out into the deluge. I heard the sounds of praying and sobbing. Men sobbing. I had not heard such raw grief before, and knew in my heart that the Lionheart, greatest warrior of his age, was gone, felled by a crossbow bolt shot by an angry boy.

No one paid much attention to me or Thomas, who had started to snivel. I grasped his hand to give him strength and comfort—and in a small way to give myself some too. It was not good to be alone. At the threshold of the pavilion, we paused, staring in.

The Dowager Queen knelt on the floor beside a rich couch, holding the body of Richard, King of England, in her arms. His head was thrown back, his features already greyed by death. His outspread golden-red hair washed over her arm like a sea of sun-touched wheat. His shoulder, visible beneath the sheet lying over him, was a mangled black mess of putrefied flesh and splintered bone. A priest stood over the couch; behind him, pots of incense helped diffuse the smell of sickness, of decay and death.

Thomas made a thin wailing noise, feeble as a kitten's cry. I made to pull him away but Eleanor glanced up, saw us both. For a moment her eyes were flinty and my heart missed a beat, then she gestured us to enter. "He was your King, after all," she said, in a pain-dulled voice.

I entered the pavilion, aware that some of those gathered in the gloom were shocked, even angered by my presence. Thomas slunk after, clearly afraid he would receive a beating for trespassing into a place meant only for adults.

Queen Eleanor rocked back on her heels and laid the King's head down onto a cushion. "And so you see the end of life, the end of greatness, Ela. He was your brother by marriage. Do not forget that, and honour his memory by honouring his kinsman, William Longsword."

"I shall," I said reverently.

"Kiss him farewell, Ela. It is the last time you shall see him thus. The embalmers come. His bowels shall be removed and buried in the Chalus' chapel, signifying to all the treachery of the filth who felled my son. His heart will then be sent to Rouen, a city he loved, his brain to Charroux abbey, and his body to Fontevrault, to lie forever at his father's feet."

Hesitantly I knelt, laid my lips lightly to the King's cold cheek. A waft of putrefaction from his wound reached into my nostrils, turning my belly. "I swear I will ever give honour to your family," I murmured, "for my children will have the royal blood in their veins."

I wondered if William was near at hand, or if he was in England. If he was at Chalus, he made no move to see me, his betrothed wife.

Stiffly Eleanor rose; a servant rushed over with a bowl of rosewater and a towel. The Queen laved her hands; blood stained the water. I glanced away.

Eleanor placed a hand on my shoulder, leaning on me as if I were a sturdy pilgrim's staff. "I must retire. I did all I could for Richard. It was not enough, of course, but even a Queen cannot counter the will of God Almighty." She paused, staring out the tent toward the grim, rain-beaten hump of Chalus. "You must not stay outside much longer, Ela. Things are going to turn ugly at the castle. You must not watch. It is unfit for a woman's eyes."

"I thought the garrison might have surrendered," I said.

"It has. Their lord is as horrified by Richard's death as any by all accounts. But my son's men, his sellswords, Mercadier...they will want their revenge. Richard forgave Bertran, who shot the fatal bolt. Mercadier will not."

The Dowager Queen shepherded Thomas and me through the storm back to our tent. Amaria stood silhouetted in the doorway, hair bedraggled, a skin slung around her shoulders. "Lady Ela!" she cried. "I was about to begin a search. Whatever possessed you of such folly?" And then she saw Eleanor and the Queen's bereft expression, and she fell to the ground in a frenzy of weeping.

"Amaria, get hold of yourself," said Eleanor, but although her words were harsh, her tone was not unkind. "Grieve we all shall, but as ever we must look forward to tomorrow." She pushed into the pavilion, Thomas and I trailing at her skirts. Heeding her mistress, Amaria clambered to her feet, grabbed a linen cloth and began wiping rain from her mistress's visage and raiment.

"Boy..." Eleanor craned her head around to gaze at Thomas, "can you run fast? The *trouvere* Blondel is in the camp, as you must know. Find him and bring him at once."

"Yes, your Grace." Thomas bowed until the ends of his hair swept the floor and then he was off, bounding like a frightened hare into the stormy darkness.

"The *trouvere*, madame?" Amaria gave Eleanor a quizzical glance.

"Yes." Eleanor sat on a stool and ripped off her headdress. Her thick greying hair tumbled loose, shining in the dying embers in the brazier. "Definitely. We need some music, some distraction…"

"From our grief."

"No, not from that. Only time can mend a heart…not music. There is another reason." She cast her maid a meaningful look. "With the children here."

"Aah," breathed Amaria, and I swore her cheeks whitened.

The tent flaps were pushed aside, allowing in more rain, and the wet shapes of Thomas and a tall lean man bearing a lute beneath his arm. Fair locks flowed in sodden coils about his blue-clad shoulders. "Your Highness." He fell to one knee before Eleanor and wept like a babe.

The Queen put her hand on the golden head. "Blondel…Jean. You served my son Richard well in the past, finding him within his prison by singing your songs. Sing again, this night of all nights, as loudly and as merrily as you can."

"Whatever my Queen demands," said the *trouvere*, who was none other than the famed Jean de Nesle, commonly known as Blondel, who had sought for the King when Richard was imprisoned in the castle of Durnstein. He began to adjust his lute.

Outside the rain was beginning to lessen. I noted that the bell in the castle had ceased to toll. There were a few thuds and thumps and the shouts of men. And then there was a scream, a high almost inhuman cry that went on and on and on…

"Sing!" commanded Eleanor. "I do not care if your lute is out of tune. Just sing!"

Blondel nodded and his sweet, sad voice rang out, filling our surroundings, "*Merry it be while summer lasts,*
   Sweet with the song of birds…"

Another scream rang out in the distance, more tortured than the last.

"*Louder,*" snapped Eleanor, expression rigid. She poured herself a goblet of wine, drank it swiftly. I huddled on my paillasse, with Thomas crouched near me like a dog.

"*And now comes the harsh weather,*
and the winter wind's cruel blast…"

Another blood-curdling screech came from the direction of the castle. The wind shrieked along with it. Thomas put his hands over his ears.

"Alas, Alas! How long this night is!
While I, most unjustly, sorrow, mourn and fast...."

The screaming ceased. We all sat in silence. Around us, we could hear the jingle of mail, the neighing of horses, the tramp of feet.

"What—what was that cry?" I finally asked between tight lips.

Eleanor stared off into the dark. "Mercadier has taken revenge for his lord."

The next morning, I found out exactly what had happened in the castle of Chalus. Mercadier had stormed in and demanded to be given Bertran, the lad who had shot the King. The lad Richard had forgiven on his deathbed. Who Richard had wanted to spare.

Fearful for the entire garrison, the castellan had handed him over to the mercenary leader. Mercadier had flayed the boy alive, then hanged him from gallows set up high on the castle wall for all the world to see.

I beheld Bertran's slight body, neck crooked at an odd angle, twirling like a leaf in the high winds. Hastily I averted my eyes. "Why did he do it?" I murmured to myself, but Thomas the page, still trailing me and the Dowager Queen, thought I had spoken to him.

"He killed the greatest King of all time!" said Thomas, as if daring me to argue. "He deserved death!"

"But Richard had forgiven him and asked that he be spared. It just seems *dishonourable*…"

Eleanor, who had been arranging transport for the King's body, walked up behind us, clad in gold and in dark blue, the colour of mourning. "You will find, my dear child, that in the heat of battle, or of love, honour flies away like the birds in winter."

"Justice was served," said Thomas stoutly, sounding like a man twice his age.

I hung my head. I grieved for the King, of course, as was expected—but I also thought of that small figure dangling in the wind from the dour walls of Chalus. Justice must be served—but what of mercy?

The embalmers arrived and did their work on the King. His heart, brain and entrails were removed and the inside of his body washed with wine and vinegar. Ablutions completed, his insides were stuffed full of grass, straw and reams of cloth, and then by huge quantities of herbs and spices to keep the stench down on his final journey to Fontevrault. A linen shroud was wrapped around him, followed by an outer layer of waxy cerecloth, before he was placed in a lead coffin hastily made to hold the royal corpse.

A delegation of monks from a nearby monastery took the royal entrails in a simple pine box up to Chalus, where they were interred to remind the castle's lord of the infamy committed by one of his own men. Richard's heart was placed into a finer oak chest and given into Eleanor's keeping. A funeral hearse was constructed, covered in cloth of gold and hundreds of banners. Images of Christ on a rainbow decorated it, and a wood-carver even made a crude effigy of the King to ride above the coffined body.

"It is time to go," Eleanor told me. "Our own chariot awaits, ready to follow the hearse of the King." She was holding the heart-box in her hands. "We must journey to Rouen, to the Cathedral of Notre Dame, before going on to Fontevrault."

I glanced around hastily. Where was Thomas? I wished to say farewell. I caught sight of him helping other pages and squires to dismantle a tent. "Thomas," I called. "It is I, Ela."

The other boys glanced quizzically at young Thomas, who went red to the tips of his ears.

"Who's your wench?" asked one of the eldest, a lad perhaps fifteen summers old with a freckled face and pointy nose.

Thomas went even redder. "She's no wench; have some respect. That's the Countess of Salisbury and she's wed to the King's brother."

The boys froze and then fell to bowing, embarrassed and even a little fearful. "Ah, Thomas, you are my gallant," I said. "What will you do now that the King is dead?"

"Return to my father's household," he replied. "I expect he'll try to find another placement for me. It will never be as good as it was in Richard's court, though. I wonder what his brother, John, is like?"

"I do not think you'd like John," I said. I had never met him but had heard many tales, none flattering. He had once risen against Richard while he was imprisoned, hoping to usurp his throne. "I wish you well in all that you do."

"Maybe we will meet again?"

I laughed, shaking my head. "I doubt it. In a few years I will go to England to be with my husband, William Longespee."

"Then it is farewell." Bending, he plucked a solitary yellow trefoil, trampled and bruised by the frantic activity going on around it. With a bow and flourish, he handed it to me.

He was only a little boy, maybe a year younger than me, but I blushed as I thrust the flower into the lacing on my bodice. The squires cheered and threw their caps in the air, a little bit of levity in the dark days following the Lionheart's demise.

The smell of the Rouen's market place reached into my nostrils, a mixture of dung and cooking. Piemen barked from street corners, merchants in bright hats wandered by, children and dogs cavorted in the gutter, while beggars and cripples jostled with all manner of nuns and monks in robes of black, grey, white and brown.

As the funeral cortege approached, an unearthly silence descended on the square. Even the dogs ceased to bark and the pieman stopped yelling. Men and women fell to their knees, weeping as if they had known the King personally. They rushed towards the hearse with its rattling wooden effigy of Richard, but the guards kept them away with the points of their spears.

Inside the cathedral, the nave and aisles were heavily fragrant with incense. Candles burnt bright in welcome as Eleanor, still wearing her mourning blue, carried the heart-box of the King through the ambulatory and choir up to the High Altar, where she was greeted by the Archbishop, Walter de Coutances, who had invested Richard as Duke of Normandy and journeyed with him as far as Sicily at the beginning of the Third Crusade.

I glanced around; tombs packed the nave and chantry chapels. Empress Maude lay here, grandmother to Richard, the woman who had torn England apart to press her claim to the throne over that of the usurper Stephen. William Fitz Empress, one of her three sons, rested near her grave—they say he died of a broken heart when he was refused marriage to Isabelle de Warenne. Most poignant for the Dowager Queen was the tomb of her son William, known as the Young King. He was Richard's older brother, a great tournament-goer, who died of dysentery shortly after pillaging an abbey to pay his sellswords for an unjust battle against his father and Richard. Nonetheless, he repented of his wickedness at life's end, crawling naked before a crucifix and clutching his sire's ring in his hand.

His tomb lay opposite from where the Archbishop planned to bury Richard's heart. Ringed by lines of candles, I could see the effigy, cowled, a sceptre clasped in the hands, the carved face clean-shaven with hair to the shoulders. The Young King and Richard had fought in life, but now the brothers would both lie silent in death.

It was a sobering thought.

The Requiem was sung, the voices of the clergy and the choir ringing through the high arches:

"Libera me, Domine, de morte aeterna
in die illa tremenda
quando coeli movendi sunt et terra,
dum veneris judicare saeculum per ignem.
Tremens factus sum ego et timeo,
dum discussion venerit atque venture ira:
quando coeli movendi sunt et terra."

I am seized with fear and trembling...there, in that House of God, I was thus seized, for my world was changing and nought I could do would control it. Lionheart was gone. I had been his ward; another waited for the crown—what was I now?

The journey back to Fontevrault with the rest of Richard's remains seemed an eternity. The skies wept for him, throwing down sheets of dark rain that made footing treacherous. The hearse and the pall got wet, the body reeked despite the embalming, and the whole party began to suffer gripings of the gut. And from across the rain-drenched countryside came hundreds of peasants, wandering towards us in a green and brown cloud—some genuine mourners, some just curious to see a King taken to his final rest.

My weariness struck to the bone, and I was glad when finally the gleaming walls of the abbey complex rose up before our company. Climbing down from the carriage, I slipped and fell awkwardly in the mud of the courtyard. Then I began to weep for all that had taken place—for the uncertainty of my future.

"Whatever was her Grace thinking, allowing you on such a journey at such a time. I knew it was wrong!" Amaria's breath tickled my ear and her strong, capable hands slid under my arms, pulling me back to my feet, muddy but unharmed. "Come, I must put you to bed before you sicken!"

Sicken I did and ended up with a burning fever that laid me low for nigh on a week, so I did not see the King's body lowered into the tomb at his father's feet in the abbey church. Nor did I see the Dowager Queen wipe away her final tears for her favourite son and, filled with her usual determination, call for a scribe. She would write to the new King, the man the childless Richard had named heir despite his past behaviour.

In the dead of night, Queen Eleanor sent a letter to England, fastened by her own seal that read *Eleanor, by the Grace of God, Queen of the English, Duchess of the Normans.*

She was writing to the Count of Mortain—her youngest child, once called Lackland as an insult, who was now, by his brother's dying wish, King John.

CHAPTER SIX

"I must go on a long progress across Aquitaine, child." The Dowager Queen turned, the morning sun stroking her face, picking out lines that had not been there before, tracing a blue vein along her temple. "John will need my assistance to get his affairs in order. Many voices still clamour for my grandson, Arthur of Brittany, to be King of England, not least of all his mother, that hard-headed Constance—I must silence them."

"And me, madam?" I asked in a small voice.

"I fear our time together must end. You were Richard's ward; now Richard is dead. I think it is time you returned to England."

"To the new King's court?"

"Jesu, no. I would not have a girl like you in John's court. Even at your age…too much temptation, and I do not know anyone I could trust there."

"My mother, then?" I was a little unsure of that. Word had reached me that she had married again, for the fourth time, to a knight called Gilbert de Malesmains.

"No, Ela, I have written to your husband's mother, Ida, Countess of Norfolk. She and her husband, Ralph Bigod, will keep you safe until you are old enough to live in your own household in Salisbury."

I hung my head; it would be strange not to live in Eleanor's worldly-wise company.

"Oh, do not look so glum, Ela." She placed one hand on my shoulder, chucking me beneath the chin with the other so that I glanced up and met her steady gaze. "I am sure you will not face hardship under Ida's watch. You are now going on thirteen. Your stay there will only be for a few years. I believe William visits his mother often; perhaps you will come to know him, and a bond grow between you both that will engender a harmonious marriage."

I remembered the grinning lordling in Richard's throne room and doubted it somehow, but I dared not voice my concerns to Eleanor. It would make no difference anyway. My fate was set, as it was for all noblewomen. My husband was chosen and that was that.

"When must I leave Fontevrault, your Grace?" I asked.

"As soon as possible," replied Eleanor. "Trouble brews in Brittany. Constance rides at the head of an army, trying to capture John so that her son may rule."

"King John is here in France?"

"Yes, of course. He took sail as soon as news reached him of Richard's death. He has taken possession of the royal treasury at Chinon but was then forced to flee to Normandy. I am not greatly worried, however; the Marshal has stepped in, ensuring that the Norman barons will mount defences against the Bretons even when John must return to England. I have already sent Mercadier and his Brabancons into Anjou; they will make men kneel to John with fire and sword if need be."

A sudden hardness turned her once-lovely countenance to stone, and I felt an unexpected surge of anxiety. The Eleanor of the Courts of Love, the book-loving Queen who favoured troubadours and chivalry seemed to have vanished. Now there was only the tigress Eleanor, who had thrown off an unsuitable saintly King to marry a fiery younger one; who had abandoned her daughters and conspired with her sons against her own husband. Her sole ambition now was to ensure that her youngest boy sat securely on the English throne. Her grandson Arthur meant nothing; and, hard as it was to accept, neither did I.

Without a word, I curtseyed to the stern-visaged Dowager Queen and crept back to my chamber, where I began to pack my belongings for the long journey to come.

It was Summer and I was in England, walking in the orchard at Framlingham Castle. Countess Ida was sitting in an arbour with her ladies, while I poked around the edges of a little fishpond. The pond was a riot of dragonflies with green and blue wings as iridescent as peacock feathers, and spindly-legged water-spiders that skimmed the surface. Deeper below, bream, perch and tench flashed by, shadows in the greenish gloom, their tails waving like weeds and their gills pumping. The eel…the solitary eel that Earl Bigod had earmarked for the Christmas feast, I spied him too, flitting through the murk, his pointed head with its nasty row of teeth jutting into the darkness. Secretly I called him 'John' after the King.

I did not like the King.

When I first arrived in England, the country was prepared for John's Coronation at Westminster, a most solemn and splendid event. The Earl and Countess of Norfolk left Framlingham and went to London for the event. They had returned quite shocked. I overheard them speaking in the hall, unguarded in their speech. I could not resist peeping around the corner of the door from my hiding-spot in the corridor.

"I could not believe what I was seeing," growled Earl Ralph, a dark-eyed man with thinning close-cropped hair and a neat beard. "The King behaved with levity rather than solemnity, as if he was at a revel, not as his own Coronation. I swear I heard him giggle like a foolish maid as the Archbishop rubbed on the Holy Chrism!"

"Yes," agreed Countess Ida, hand to her breast as if the memory of the goings-on in London had taken her breath away, "and he did not take the Sacrament! And where was his wife, Hadwisa of Gloucester? Why was she not crowned at his side?"

The Earl made an angry sound. "You *know* why, Ida. He's looking elsewhere. He was never satisfied with Hadwisa from the start; she's too plain for one, and she's borne no children after ten years of marriage. He only ever wanted her for her lands because he was Lackland back then. And now…" He shrugged. "He is King."

Ida looked scandalised. "Do you truly think he will put her aside, Roger? For what reason would he…*discard* her?"

"The usual way, Ida—consanguinity. Both descend from Henry I. John made noises about getting a dispensation when they first wed, but it appears it was never granted."

"Oh." Ida bowed her head. She was beautiful; I could understand why old King Henry wanted her as his leman. She had flawless ivory skin, green cat's eyes, and her waving hair was a deep, tawny reddish colour. Men whispered that she had the look of her kinswoman, Rosamund Clifford, who Henry had loved to distraction—and who Queen Eleanor had loathed most of all his mistresses.

"And, wife…" Roger Bigod walked around the smouldering fire-pit, exuding agitation, "John is free and easy where women other than his wife are concerned. This is why we must impress upon your son William not to speak of his little Ela when around the King. She must remain safely in Norfolk until they are formally bedded."

"Roger, surely you do not think…"

"My dearest, you of all people know how a King cannot be dissuaded when he has his heart set on such a goal." Ida blushed to the roots of her hair. "I do not say that with condemnation, Ida, you know that. John is a lecher; he has many bastards already. One of them was even begotten on his cousin, the daughter of Hamelin the Earl of Surrey, who was half-brother to King Henry. It was a disgrace…"

Ida cringed. "All such behaviour is a disgrace and I have atoned for my great sin…"

"Your sins are all in the past," Roger reassured her. "But John's may lie in the future. He will want another Queen…"

"You do not think he would gaze at his own kinsman's wife…"

"She is pleasing of aspect and, best of all, she is the Countess of Salisbury, so she is far from penniless, although Salisbury is not such a rich earldom as some. I cannot say for certain such wickedness would ever happen in truth, but John is an envious man and covets what others own—and if his behaviour is challenged, he claims it is all in jest."

"We will keep Ela safe then," said Ida. "It shall not be long before she and William can be married in more than name. Let no man tear asunder…"

I shuddered as I remembered Ida's words all those months ago, and glanced over to the arbour in the castle gardens. The ladies were sewing, as they always did. Ida's small daughters were there, Margery, Mary and Alice. Margery, the eldest, was learning to sew, while Mary sniffed at a flower and Alice was dandled on a nurse's knee. They all seemed happy and content; I was not. I had not seen my husband since arriving in England, not that I had expected to. He was too busy cosying up to his brother, the King. From what I understood, he was close to John. It made me tearful at times, thinking he might be of similar temperament to his half-brother.

Something splashed in the fishpond and I jumped, thinking of the evil old eel leaping up behind me with his spiky jaws agape. Instead, I turned to see Hugh, the Earl and Ida's eldest son, who was a few years older than me, almost seventeen. He had been visiting Settrington in Yorkshire, newly granted to him by his father, but had returned for a visit to his parents and siblings. "Oh, Hugh, I nearly leapt out of my skin!" I chided.

"Did you think it was my older brother, William?" he teased. "Did your heart beat faster, little Ela?"

Had he been reading my thoughts? My cheeks burned. "You're awful, Hugh!" I knelt down and splashed him with pond water.

He yelped as it struck his saffron tunic, pretending to be offended, but by the grin on his face, his indignation was clearly false. His sisters were too young to tease, so he had me instead, a sister by marriage.

"I'll bet you won't do that to William when he arrives," he said, wiping at a damp spot on his sleeve.

"What do you mean 'when he arrives'?"

His brows shot up into his unruly brown hair. "No one has told you? Jesu! He is returning from court for a time; that is also why I returned to Framlingham. And to be honest..." he gazed out at the stark profile of the castle walls, rebuilt after being razed to the ground in the time of Earl Roger's father, "it's a little more comfortable here than in my cold, northern manor of Settrington."

My heart was racing. "When is he coming?" I gasped.

Bemused, he glanced over at me. "Why? Are you planning to run away?"

"Of course not, but...but...Oh, I do not know why I am so affrighted!" Tears pricked my eyelids and I stared down at my toes. "I am afraid he won't like me. Or that I won't like him. I only met him once; he made fun of me and treated me like a baby, and I have heard nought since."

"Did you expect to?"

"Well, no..." My chin jutted out, defiance replacing my momentary loss of confidence. "But it would have been nice if he did!"

"Knights aren't 'nice'!" Hugh laughed, but before I could admonish him, he was pounced upon by two of his younger brothers, Ralph and Roger, who had spent the afternoon clattering around the bailey with wooden swords.

I retreated into the garden, fearful of being struck by the swords the lads were still waving. Going to the bedchamber I shared with Ida's ladies, I lifted up a glass mirror, imported from the Moorish regions of Spain, which was a gift from my mother last Christmas. I peered at myself—growing wildly like a weed, my hair longer, darkened with adolescence until it was brownish honey. A big spot bulged to the right of my nose.

"I look like a witch!"

I wanted to weep but would not allow myself. Why was I upset anyway? He had already implied I was shrewish. What made me think wives and husbands had to like each other anyway?

William Longsword was here. Ida was making a great fuss of her eldest child. The Earl had retreated to his apartments, allowing mother and son to converse alone. He seemed at times a stern, almost emotionless man, but it seemed he treated his wife's son as a true part of the family, with no rancour for the accident of his birth.

I sat waiting in my chamber, as Ida had told me to. I wore a sky-blue kirtle fringed with embroidered gold pine-cones. My sleeves were gauzy green with fur trim and dangled to the floor. A circlet held my tightly bound braids from my face and a filmy twilight-lavender veil was wound round them. Muriel, a maid assigned me by Ida, had lanced the nasty boil on my face and covered it by white paste, which she also blended into my cheeks. She examined her handiwork with satisfaction, and said I looked 'as fair as a flower', although I still feared I appeared like some terrible pallid revenant risen from the grave…

A knock sounded on the door and I called out a shaky welcome. Countess Ida swept into the chamber, followed by my husband, William Longespee. Muriel dropped into a curtsey and was given a hasty dismissal with a hand gesture from Ida.

William had not changed much since Chateau Gaillard. A little broader, his hair a little longer, he stepped forward to politely kiss my hand. But as he glanced up, I was startled. His eyes, an intense dark green-blue, were looking straight into mine as if he had never seen me before. They were intense and bright—and made me blush beneath my white paste.

"Lady Ela," he said, "I would scarcely have recognised you. How you have matured…"

"She is coming up fourteen now," Ida reminded. "Girls change greatly after eleven or twelve."

"I can see that," murmured William. "Lady, I have a gift for you." Reaching beneath his cloak, he brought out a box and opened it. Inside lay a golden cloak clasp, studded with pearls and the rare pale red rubies known as *balas*.

"Thank you, my lord husband," I gasped. It must have cost him a fortune to source those pale red stones.

"Look at the reverse, my dear," prompted Ida.

I turned it over, read the words graven there. *Pour amor, say douc.* "For love, so sweet," I said softly. Below the thick fall of my braids, the tips of my ears burned like fire.

"Yes…" Now it was William's turn, although a grown man, to sound nervous. "I pray it will be so. Mother, what do you think…?" He faced Ida, looking almost like a little lad seeking his mother's assurance.

"I think one more year and it will be enough," she smiled.

"A year…" He seemed crestfallen.

"A year. It is for the best. As a woman, let me tell you this." She put a hand on his arm. "You do not want to risk losing your wife soon after the bedding, do you understand? A woman's lot is a perilous one if there is a child—especially if she is *too young*…."

It was William's turn to blush a rosy shade. "I-I understand what you say, Mother. I want no harm to come to my wife. I will heed your wise words. A year it is."

So a date for the final 'perfection' of our marriage was set by Countess Ida. I hardly knew whether to be joyous or afraid. But as I observed my husband as he conversed with Earl Roger in the Great Hall, I grew more interested in him. Not enamoured—I was not like those flighty maids who swooned and sighed over every knight or troubadour they laid their insipid eyes upon—but intrigued, desirous of knowledge. He seemed loyal to his royal brother and fearless in regards to battle, speaking with enthusiasm of upcoming diplomatic forays into hostile territories. He was no sluggard, it seemed, and was ambitious yet not overtly grasping.

Ida contrived for me to meet her son again in the castle gardens. "Ask him about his life; he will like that," she told me, pushing me out of the narrow door that led to the orchard.

Muriel and Ida's own ladies had dressed me again, giggling and enjoying every moment of primping and poking. I wore a long, scarlet bliaut with golden side-lacing made as tight as possible to accentuate my burgeoning figure, and the sleeves were knotted to keep them from sweeping the ground. My hair was tucked under a crisp white barbette and my lips daubed by a strawberry concoction brewed up by Muriel. At least it tasted nice. I wore a tight silver belt around my waist, clasped by my husband's gift.

Together, William and I walked through the trees, Longsword every inch the courtly knight without a flaw. I marvelled at how tall he was when we stood side by side; I was a big girl for my age, taller than many grown women by several fingers, but he towered over me, imposing, god-like. I had not noticed it so much in Chateau Gaillard where the golden, forceful Richard Coeur de Lion had dominated the meeting.

"What, er, do you enjoy, Lady Ela?" he asked, somewhat awkwardly. "Dancing…sewing?"

"Not particularly," I answered with honesty. "I enjoy reading books when I can lay my hands on them. Religious texts, romances, lays…all are good."

"Oh, yes," he said, still unsure, "you abided with the old Queen, did you not? She has a sharp mind…and a sharp tongue."

"As do I," I teased, "you said it yourself upon our first meeting."

"Did I truly?" William looked flustered. "If I did, that was churlish of me. I beg your forgiveness, Lady."

"Forgiveness was given long ago," I lied. "But come, tell me about yourself, about your time at court. It is lovely here at

Framlingham but Suffolk is, well, rather far away from any bustle and excitement. It is even quieter than Salisbury."

William stared at his feet then up at the sky. I wondered if he would change the subject, but then he said in a conspiratorial whisper, "You have heard that my brother John had his marriage to Hadwisa of Gloucester annulled?"

I nodded. "Yes, such an event could not stay hidden, even in far-flung Suffolk. Your father had guessed it long before."

"Well, it is more exciting than that! John already has a new bride picked out."

"Who?" I goggled, curious.

He leaned in, still whispering, "Isabella de Angouleme, daughter of Count Aymer."

The name meant nought to me. I shook my head. "Is this Isabella a great heiress?"

"A marriage with her is strategically sound," said William, "but she is younger than you, my dear wife—only twelve summers. John plans to wed her in Angouleme this August. She is said to have great beauty and that John is enamoured of her beyond reason—God's Blood, my brother is susceptible to a pretty face!"

"I pray they will find much happiness together," I said dutifully, although I had heard that John was the runt of the Plantagenet litter in looks, and the foulest in manner. But he was King; that would count for much.

"I pray so too but I advised him against the match."

"That was bold."

"He is my King but also my brother; I often tell him when I deem him foolish, even if he does not listen. This marriage is causing great scandal and unrest—Isabella was already betrothed to Hugh le Brun, Count of Lusignan. John stole her beneath Hugh's very nose…with the connivance of Aymer of course, who wanted that pretty crown for his daughter's fair head."

"Will this mean war?" The afternoon seemed to darken.

"Most likely. Philip of France is threatening to confiscate all French lands owned by John. Hugh is gathering men."

"Could he not have found a better bride?" I wrinkled my nose.

William laughed. "No doubt, but John is John; he oftimes acts impetuously and likes to play the wayward imp. He is truly enamoured of this maid, however, and will not be dissuaded."

"What will happen to his first wife now—Hadwisa?"

William chewed on his lip, once again appearing a little flustered. "Well, she is back in wardship…"

"But she is old!" I blurted with all a child's tactlessness.

"Ah, but John does not wish for the Gloucester inheritance to get away…besides, he has a task for her; he wants Hadwisa to care for the new Queen while she is still of tender years."

I folded my arms across my chest, indignant for this spurned woman I had never met. "I find that rather cruel, William. Having the marriage annulled…then using his cast-off as a nursemaid!"

"I will tell the King," he said with sarcasm. "I am sure he will value your opinion…"

I was abashed. I was speaking out of turn and behaving like a shrew—and at Chateau Gaillard he had implied her already thought me shrewish! "Oh…please do not tell him!" I begged. "I did not mean it. It is not my place to judge. I should not have spoken so freely; please do not look upon me as a nag!"

"A nag!" He laughed out loud, and then he bent and took my chin between his fingers, tilting my head up towards him. "I have no fear of that, little Ela, for you are too wise to become so. And never fear to speak out; I would not have it otherwise. Some men may want timid dormice for wives; I want a helpmeet whose head contains more than embroidery patterns."

Shyly, I looked up at him and smiled. Maybe this marriage would work. Arranged for us by Richard, but approved by both parties in the end. Such things happened sometimes, like magic.

To my deep pleasure, William Longespee, tall, stately and handsome as Lancelot, smiled back.

CHAPTER SEVEN

I was fifteen, a true wife, and I was going home to Salisbury. Excitement welled up in my heart as I peered out of my litter at the old familiar roads, hills, and villages of Wiltshire. Three months ago, William and I had finally commenced our married life together at Framlingham, and it was more glorious than I had dreamed possible. He had recently returned from the King's business, where he had tracked down the infamous outlaw, Fulke Fitzwarin, besieging him in Stanley Abbey and accepting his surrender. The whole Bigod family had clustered round to hear his tale, treating William as if he were a figure from knightly legend. I, wimpled like a modest wife, decked in the new jewels he had bought me, basked in reflected glory.

However, as is found so often in life, heaven has its shadow, and our time together was cut short—John recalled William to London on urgent business. I asked if I might come, but he touched my face and shook his head. "No, it is no place for you, sweetling. Besides, I believe the King is sending me overseas to make a treaty with Sancho of Navarre."

So William had ridden to the King to receive his next mission and I had been left with Countess Ida. "A husband's absence is something noblewomen must accept," she told me. "It is not always a bad thing to spend time apart—it does a woman no good to bear a child year after year; your teeth will fall out and your hair will thin."

I made a face, touching my long, thick braid. Ida was not finished, however. "William has given instructions that you should return to your castle of Salisbury, where you shall set up your life together upon his return. The people there already know you, and it is time you were re-acquainted, so that castle and town will dwell side by side in harmony with William as their new lord."

With that, she had called the servants to start packing. Before sunrise two days hence, I had left Framlingham, its line of towers strung out along the horizon. Stalwartly, I turned my face towards the west and my old much-loved home.

As my litter was borne down the Roman road known as the Portway, I stared out the draperies to the dark, oddly-formed hill growing ever larger on the horizon. Salisbury Hill was ancient, far older than the castle on its summit—my nurses used to clutch crucifixes when they walked across the bailey at night after telling tales of dead Roman soldiers and wild men decked in lurid paint. There was a massive earthen bank around the exterior, with huge ditches that descended to a great depth. Beasts and even children sometimes tumbled down them to their doom. The town clustered in the first set of earthworks and ranged over the ward behind; a cluster of cobb and thatch, rubble and timber. Beyond was another ditch, more recently dug and just as deep, but filled with rows of sharpened wooden stakes—the moat, crossed by a long wooden bridge, that protected the heart of Salisbury, its royal castle.

It was a cold and windy place, the fortress perched atop the hill's cone like the centrepiece on a vast subtlety at a banquet, but of late its stark grandeur had haunted my dreams. It was home, *my* home. I was its Lady, and I meant to do well by the people who lived within those high earth banks and stern stone walls.

The entourage was approaching the main eastern entrance through a gap hewn in the bank. Tears flowed as the townsfolk dropped the tools of their trade and came running to wave and shout greetings. The bells in the little chapel of St James began to jangle merrily, and up in the castle itself the bells of Holy Cross over Eastgate boomed out, followed by peels from St Nicholas. From around the side of the outer ward, deeper bells tolled from the bell-tower of the cathedral built by Saint Osmund.

Passing into the inner ward, more crowds were waiting, alerted by the sound of the bells. I waved frantically at the baker in his apron, the black-bearded smith with tongs in hand, the barber before his shop with its striped pole. I remembered dozens of faces from my childhood, albeit they now seemed old…and it appeared they remembered me in kind. "God bless the Lady Ela, daughter of good William Fitz Patrick, Earl of Salisbury!" cried a sot stumbling from a nearby tavern called The Hog, and others began to chant the same. Pipers began to play and a bagpipe wheezed; men whisked women away from washing-tubs and looms, and the townsfolk began to dance as if it was a festival day.

Then the great motte reared up, a slumbering giant. The sun swung behind its shoulder, putting its pudding-shape into stark silhouette. I heard the lead rider of the company cry out to draw rein; we slowed to a snail's pace. Hooves clopped hollowly on the wood of the lowered drawbridge; the litter swayed and its canvas flapped as the wind that blew day and night on that height caught hold of it. Ahead, the gatehouse turrets soared, with the chapel of St Cross perched above, its roofline grotesques leering down. The walls bristled with archers wearing William's colours; mailed sentries with blue cloaks stepped aside to let the entourage access the inner bailey.

It was much as I remembered. Sorrow filled me, remembering the last time I set foot within these walls. My father had lain abed, dying—and I had not realised the seriousness of his condition. An innocent child, I had gone merrily with Mama to Amesbury manor to keep out of the way...

I drank in the old familiar sights—the bakehouse where I had stolen slabs of butter-drenched bread, the tidy courtyard with the hall running alongside and the Great Chamber overlooking it. The neat little servants' chapel of St Margaret, huddled near the hall, while St Nicholas, which was for the family and visiting dignitaries, straddled St Margaret's back. The lower chapel was accessed from the courtyard, while the other was through the upper floor of the Great Chamber.

The entourage ground to a halt, and I clambered from my litter, brushing down my skirts. A man in a scarlet robe emerged from the Great Tower, a strong rectangular stone block built by old King Henry. This was where he had imprisoned Eleanor for many years, Amaria her only loyal companion, away from the Courts of Love, away from all but the constant sighing of the wind.

"My Lady Ela?" The man drew near. He wore a chain of office and his robes were fur-lined but I did not recognise him from my father's household.

"Yes...and you are?"

"I am Earl William's steward, Hobart de Lynom.

"Earl William? I do not remember you..."

His balding head grew flame-red with embarrassment. "The *new* Earl William, not the old, milady."

"Ah," I gasped, feeling foolish. He referred to my husband, Earl through right of our marriage, not my father.

"I welcome you to Salisbury Castle, Countess. I hope you find it pleasing."

"I am pleased, more pleased than you can imagine. It is where I grew up."

He and escorted me through the courtyard. "Mama!" To my surprise, my mother was standing by the steps into the apartments. She hurried towards me, and I admit I wept and so did she as we embraced.

"You have grown so—you are a woman now."

"And William Longespee's true wife. All that intrigue and fleeing England after Father died, and yet I ended up as the King's ward nonetheless and married to his brother."

Mother coloured slightly as if my flight with Uncle Philip was something she did not wish to discuss. "No matter, all has turned out well by the will of God. You know, I expect, that I have remarried—to Gilbert de Malesmains?"

I nodded. "Word reached me, Mama. I pray you are content."

"You—you are not cross?" she said cautiously. "My remarriage was very soon after your father's demise. I cared deeply for William, you know, but a woman needs a man to protect her interests in these uneasy times. Gilbert and I thought to marry in haste, lest one of the King's knights put in a monetary bid for my hand that we could not outdo. John makes much money out of widows…Oh, I suppose I should not speak so, now that you are wed to his brother."

"William is close to John; I would say nothing against him in his presence. I have not met his Grace, not yet, and truth be told, I have no great desire to, from what I've heard. Now, let us go refresh ourselves, and see what delicacies the kitchens can concoct for our pleasure."

Just before sunset, Mother and I took a leisurely stroll atop the castle walls. The sky was red and clear, with frothy clouds mounded on the horizons. The banks below were mist-shrouded, the fog pierced by tiny lights from cottages and the flambeaux held by the patrolling night sentries. St Osmund's cathedral squatted amidst the huddle of houses, its walls of intermixed green and white stone now bathed in a hazy deep pink. Lanterns bucked in the attached cloister as the clergy went about their nightly business. As usual, the wind was shrieking over the ramparts and the crenels.

"They want to move it, you know…" said Mother, holding a kerchief to her eyes as the wind made them tear. Or *was* it the wind?

"Move what?" I stared down at the swirling lights, ethereal as the candles of will o' the wisps.

"The cathedral," she said. "I suppose you would not have heard."

"I have been long away…Too long, it seems. What evil news, mother—*evil*!" My heart felt leaden; it was as if my joyous homecoming had been ruined. The cathedral had always stood there, a gleaming symbol on the hillside. Its bells had greeted my mornings, noons and bedtimes, and many a time had I visited the tomb of the saintly Bishop Osmund, lighting a candle before his sarcophagus of black Tournai stone. Osmond was a candidate for sainthood; moon-mad men claimed he had restored their wits, while others said he caused cripples to walk. He even helped the pain of toothache.

"I know it seems sad and strange." Mother patted my shoulder comfortingly. "But Bishop Herbert Poore and his brother Richard insist it would be best to move the cathedral down toward the Avon, near the flood lands."

"But *why* should they move it?" I asked in high dudgeon, anger replacing my shock. The wind ripped at my veil, made it lash at my face. "It took tremendous effort to build. Five days after its consecration, a great storm felled part of the nave…"

"Perhaps that is why," said Mother dryly, dabbing at her eyes again. "The wind never stops up here. It is bad enough in the castle but the curtain wall shields us, save at the top of the Great Tower. The cathedral is not so fortunate—you will have surely noticed how the wind drowns out the choir and shakes the expensive glass panes in the windows. I would much rather say my devotions in St Nicholas'; at least I have no fear that masonry might drop on my head."

I stamped my foot huffily, unconvinced. "Surely this mad plan needs the assent of the King!"

"It was given while Richard lived. The lack of water and the roaring wind were the reasons given. Peter of Blois wrote harsh words on the state of the cathedral; he called it '*a captive on the hill where it was built, like the ark of God shut up in the profane house of Baal.*'"

"Harsh words indeed—and untrue!"

"If it ever happens, it will not be for a long time yet," soothed Mother. "Such great efforts take time, and the present King may not take much interest in the project; he may even scupper it. He is not over-fond of churches, and trouble stirs in Normandy again. Serious trouble."

I froze. William had left for Westminster in a hurry. "What trouble?"

"Let us go down from these walls." Mama hurried along the breastwork toward the staircase near the Postern Tower.

"You have not answered me!" The relentless wind whipped the words from my lips, carrying them to her ears.

"It is best if your husband, Earl William, tells you," she said, vanishing down the stairs. Sleeves and cloak flapping, she strode across the night-touched bailey.

"But he's not here!" I cried out, attempting to run after her. The wind struck against me, pummelling me with invisible fists, pushing me against a jagged crenelation. Mama was at the hall's door, not even glancing back; I would never catch her now.

Heart heavy, I trudged down the staircase, ignoring the servants who bowed as I passed. More than anything, I wished that William *was* here.

I was a child no longer. My responsibilities were legion. I needed to know the affairs of the land so that I could, if need be, defend my people, the folk of Salisbury town. Feeling defeated, I sought my apartments in the upper floor of the Great Chamber—and saw to my surprise, a messenger waiting in the vestibule, escorted by two knights.

I tore the parchment he bore from his hand; William's seal gleamed upon it in blood-hued wax. Hurriedly I ripped it open and read, my heart thudding against my ribs: *I will be home by the sabbath but can stay only a day or two. Then I must take ship for Normandy. I pray this news will not bring you distress…*

Distress? I was both troubled and perturbed. I sent for a sleeping draught from the herbalist who lived without the gate, but the liquid burnt my tongue and gave no relief. I tossed and turned upon my bed, while my tiring woman Muriel, sent from Framlingham by Countess Ida, snored on her paillasse in the corner, mercifully unaware of my discomfiture. At length I fell into a light, uncomfortable sleep, the coverlet twined around my legs, and my head, pounding with fevered thoughts, resting on my arm.

An indeterminate time later, I awoke. The room was full of deep blue shadows. Grey light crept through holes around the edges of the shutters that covered the window-slits. The wind was even higher, rattling and whistling over the castle. Drawing a thick fur around my shoulders, I sat upright.

The fire brazier was full of ash and the room smelt cold. Glancing at the paillasse, I noticed that Muriel was missing. I frowned. Mayhap she had run to the nearest privy, although we had earthenware pots for our nightly needs.

A shadow moved just out of eye-range, partly hidden by the voluminous bed-curtains. Someone was in the room with me—a floorboard creaked beneath a furtive bootheel.

My spine prickled. I did not think it was Muriel creeping about the chamber. Why would she? If she was up, she would be stoking the fire or collecting sops from the kitchen for me to break my fast.

Breathing heavily, I slid from the bed and took up a great basin of rosewater that stood on a chest. If there was an unwelcome intruder, he would get a face full of freezing water. I did not know who would dare accost me in my own castle, but stranger things had happened, and now that John was on the throne, my husband was an important man, a powerful adviser and an Earl. He would have enemies who might benefit from a hostage…Aiming for furtiveness, I inched forward, the bowl clutched in my hands.

"You're not going to throw that over me, are you?" a man's voice asked. "I have only just dried out from the rain on the road last night!"

"William!" I cried and lost hold of the basin.

My husband sprang into action and caught the bowl deftly as it fell, thrusting it back onto the chest without spilling a drop. I noticed he was still dressed in travelling gear—muddy boots, a dark green cloak with the hood raised.

"How long have you been there?" I asked, hastily pulling on a robe.

"I arrived in Salisbury sooner than I expected. Hobart said you had retired; I did not want to wake you. I sent Muriel about her morning tasks and said I would keep guard over you."

He pushed back his hood; his face was drawn, tired, stubble blue above the line of his neat beard. I went to him and he brightened a little, kissing me gently and then with greater ardour.

But then he pulled away, sighed, and sat on one of my stools, stretching out his long legs as if they ached. "Would that I could stay longer. There is nothing I would like more than to spend a peaceful week in the arms of my sweet bride."

My cheeks reddened. I was aware we were alone—at least until Emma returned. However, William released me and stood back, hands resting on my shoulders. "I came to Salisbury as quick as I might, but I have to leave again soon. By the end of the day, alas."

"The end of the day!" I cried in dismay.

"Yes, I must go back to Normandy with the King. Disturbances have broken out, ones that need a firm hand lest they spiral beyond control."

"Is it over the treaty with Sancho?"

"No, that was finalised to the satisfaction of all."

"Then *what*? I thought the problems there were done and over! That John had placated the Lusignans over his stolen Queen. You've already been back and forth from Normandy…"

Grimly he shook his head. "It is Arthur…Arthur of Brittany. He has risen in rebellion. This is far more serious than indignant Lusignans. Philip of France is meddling, as he always does. Not that Johnny has helped himself—he can be stubborn. Philip has declared him a 'contumacious vassal' after he refused to give up two castles as surety."

William slammed his fist on the sideboard, making me jump. "John's lands have been declared forfeit. Philip has moved his armies into Normandy and razed John fortress, Boutavant, to the ground. He now eyes other castles—and John wants me to join him in defence of his strongholds."

"And what of Arthur—what part has he played in this matter? He's only a boy, scarcely older than me!"

William's eyes grew troubled. "It has come to light that last year Philip betrothed his infant daughter, Marie, to Arthur, and granted him Maine, Anjou, Touraine, even Aquitaine."

"But how? Surely they are John's?"

"In Philip's eyes, John forfeited them all. Not long ago, he did homage to Philip for them and the French King now believes he has broken his vows. But Philip has not just given Arthur John's lands, he has given him two hundred knights and linked him up with the Lusignans, who are eager to punish John over the theft of Isabella. It is war, Ela—and Arthur is desirous of John's crown. And so I must go, taking the fastest ship from Southampton. My levies are already at the port, waiting."

"But still you came to see me."

"I am here, am I not?"

I flung myself into his arms. "It is too short a time! Ah, this meeting pains me beyond words—yet it would have been worse if you had departed with no meeting at all."

"That would never happen, my little dove." He ran a hand along my cheek, wiping away a stray tear. "I swear I will always put your wellbeing foremost when I can. But you must swear to me…"

"Whatever it is, I shall swear it!"

"Swear that you will be strong, come what may. In my absence, run Salisbury as your sire did, with both honour and justice. Your mother Eleonore has agreed to remain here to guide you, and my chamberlain Ralph and steward Hobart are honest and skilled men."

"I swear I will do my best, but William…" I bit my lip.

"What, my love?"

"What about the cathedral?"

"What about it?"

Surely, he must know. "Mother said there is talk of …of moving it! It seems preposterous!"

"I have heard. It does not please me as having a cathedral has brought prestige to Salisbury, but the decision is not for me to make—or you. But I would not fear, little one. As things stand, it will take years for such a move to be made if it ever happens."

I breathed a sigh of relief. Who knows what the future might hold?

I stood up on my tiptoes, looping my arms about my husband's neck, and then thought no more of the cathedral, or the war breaking out in Normandy and Aquitaine, but only of William and me.

CHAPTER EIGHT

My days were spent learning the duties of a chatelaine. I had already received some training from the Dowager Queen, but now, under the hand of Mother, I could put it into practice. Mama's new husband, Gilbert de Malesmains, came to abide with her at Salisbury; he was a short man with a ruddy face, a rounded belly and a loud laugh that set my teeth on edge—but he seemed kindly enough, and appeared to make her happy, despite his lack of great means. It seemed a comedown for Mama, after being an Earl's wife, but perhaps it was a relief to choose her own husband after having the other three chosen for her by powerful men.

I did not realise, as we ordered and organised and oversaw repairs around the castle that I would not see William again for a year and I would learn that patience was a woman's lot…

Finally, however, the happy day came—William returned to Salisbury. I awaited his arrival in the solar, heart drumming in anticipation, wearing a silver bliaut with marten trim and silvered embroidery. The chamber had been scrubbed floor to ceiling, the rush mats changed, the soot marks removed from the murals on the wall.

When William's footsteps sounded in the corridor, I rose from my stool to greet him. I bit back a cry as he entered. As if a wizard's hand had swept over him, he had changed. He looked older, grimmer. Although an experienced warrior in Richard's service even before we wed, lines of care were now etched on his face and a haunted quality lurked in his eyes. He did not smile as he approached me in his blue tabard with the lions leaping golden upon it, based on the arms of his forebear Geoffrey Plantagenet, Count of Anjou.

"Ela…" he said, his voice a hoarse whisper, and then his arms were around me, strong iron bands, and his face buried in my hair. "There were times when I was away that I thought I would never see your sweet, pure face again."

"Was it very dangerous? Here in England, we heard of nought but victory after victory for the King. Was not the rebel Arthur captured at Mirabeau, along with his sister? Poor Queen Eleanor, my dearest teacher and mentor. I cannot imagine her holed up in Mirabeau, with Arthur laying siege to his own grandmother's castle!"

"Arthur…" murmured William uncomfortably. "Ela, call for meat and drink to be brought and I will tell you of my journeys. I will only tell the tale once, and afterwards, you must never speak of it to anyone."

"Why?" I asked shakily, wondering at his strange dark mood.

"Danger. To you…even to me. Do you understand?"

I nodded. "Yes, I would never deceive you and go forth with flapping tongue. You know what is best."

I called for food and wine, and this was duly brought from the kitchens: venison pasties and capon in saffron, with honeyed pears and wine from Bordeaux. Despite asking for food, William picked at the fare with listless motions, which troubled me. He was changed.

At length, I dismissed all the servants, barred the door and refilled his wine goblet. I noticed how his fingers trembled as he took it. Whatever haunted him must be evil indeed.

He released a deep sigh and suddenly slouched forward. I went to my knees next to him, hand on his knee. "William, you are frightening me! Are you ill? Do you need the physician?"

He shook his head. "No. I am sick at heart, that is all. Listen, and I shall tell you why."

I settled down at his feet. His two hounds, Fortuna and Parsefal, crowded in next to me, comforting me with their warm, furry flanks and inquisitive black noses. So loyal…

As was my husband. To John. And in my heart, before William even said a single word, I knew John Lackland would play a part in his sorry tale…

"When John heard his mother was imperilled, his wrath knew no bounds, Ela. He gathered his forces and we rode from Le Mans— nearly a hundred miles!—reaching Mirabeau in a mere two days!"

I gasped. "You flew like the wind!"

"When we arrived, the town was in Arthur's control and Queen Eleanor inside the keep. It was early morning and our enemies were breaking their fast. We managed to burst through one gate they had foolishly forgotten to barricade. Many a helm was staved in, and

Geoffrey de Lusignan was taken prisoner in his tent while dining on pigeons! Arthur was captured too, while his men fled or were taken prisoner. Arthur's sister, Eleanor of Brittany, was watching from a nearby rise and she was seized also. John wrote a letter back to his officials in England saying, *God be praised for our Happy Success.*"

"That poor girl, Eleanor of Brittany," I murmured, thinking of Arthur's sister, who so strikingly beautiful she was known as 'the Fair Maid' or 'the Pearl.' What will happen to her now? I suppose John will marry her off to one of his barons."

William shook his head. "No…he is going to imprison her, Ela. For life. She is royal; as Geoffrey's daughter, she has a strong claim to the throne. She will always be a danger to John."

"But she has done no wrong! To imprison her is unjust!"

"Her blood is her crime," said William wearily, passing a hand across his forehead as if to wipe away evil memories.

I heartily wanted to rail against John, but dared not speak. I pressed my face against Fortuna's warm brown fur and she gave a sympathetic whine.

"There is more, though." William's voice sounded even more tired, shaky—almost as if he might weep. It was a strange sound to hear from a born warrior.

"Dare I ask what it is?" I whispered. I glanced up from Fortuna's fur; the firelight was shining golden on my husband's glassy, wet eyes.

"Arthur…" he croaked. "My nephew. John's nephew…"

My head started to thud. I dreaded what might come next. "Arthur…"

"Once he was in chains, John rode victoriously for Falaise and imprisoned him in the donjon of the castle. He also sent prisoners of war all over the land, and to England as well. He mistreated those men, and only William des Roches protested and fought for Arthur's dignity."

Sickness gripped me, but I champed down on my tongue. *Why did you not stand for these unfortunates, my husband! Loyalty to family is one thing…but this…*

"Arthur was shackled with three pairs of manacles. Des Roches tried to convince John that the boy was merely a pawn in the hands of King Philip and others, but John would not listen, so des Roches departed in anger to his own lands."

I thought of that young boy, near in age to me, sitting in a chamber within a high tower, his limbs laden with chains. A piteous fate for a royal prince, even a rebellious one.

William poured himself another goblet of wine. I feared he might get drunk, but if the drink gave him some relief from his burden, then that was maybe not such a bad thing.

"John then descended on Brittany and sacked many towns; he forged on to fire Le Mans, Tours and Angers. However, des Roches retaliated, having joined the rebels. John was furious—he flung himself on the rushes and gnawed them with his teeth."

I grimaced, my expression hidden in Fortuna's fur. Gnawing rushes? He seemed more a mad dog than a ruler

"It went on and on, John storming towns and cities, and the Bretons and their allies retaliating. 'Free Arthur!' they cried. "He is more noble than you! He should be King in your stead!' John could not bear that, so he…came to a decision."

William bowed over, unexpectedly hiding his face in his hands. "Some of his advisers counselled that he deal with Arthur *harshly*… finish the boy's chance at kingship."

"What do you mean 'harshly'? My voice was a croak.

William sat upright again, hands falling limp into his lap. "The advisers, not me I hope you realise, said he should be blinded and castrated to make him unfit to rule. John agreed."

In horror, I cried out and pulled away from him. The dogs scattered. Shaking, I leaned against the tapestry on the wall, a white unicorn, symbol of purity and innocence. I felt my innocence was being washed away by William's words, destroyed by my new life of Kings, crowns and cruelty…

Blearily, he gazed at me. "It was not done. John sent three assassins to Falaise, but two of them vanished, not wishing to commit such a crime, even for much gold. Only one turned up at the castle and when he went for Arthur with his dagger, the boy struck out and knocked him to the floor. Hubert de Burgh, the Chamberlain, was watching through a doorway and was filled with pity for Arthur, and he called his own guards and had the assassin thrown from the castle. He then put out a rumour that the mutilation had occurred and Arthur had died from his injuries."

My heart brightened. "So Hubert de Burgh fooled the King. Arthur was alive and unharmed all along! It is like a tale told round the fire, where the young hero escapes. Not that Arthur is a hero; he has been a fool."

Shadows darkened William's face. "Unlike such tales, there is no happy ending here. De Burgh fooled John only for a short while. Soon the Bretons heard of Arthur's supposed demise and their destruction of John's castles increased tenfold. De Burgh became so afraid he admitted that Arthur was still alive."

"Was the King furious? Did he kill de Burgh for his lie?"

"Kill him? He wanted to kiss him!" A laugh that was half a strangled sob tore from William's throat. "The best way to appease the Bretons, John now thought, was to produce the living, unmutilated Arthur...and he did so. He even went so far as to meet with the boy and speak kind words, offering him not only freedom but many rewards of lands and honours if he should bend his knee and renounce his claim to the throne. But Arthur, damn him, played the part of the proud Plantagenet—he told John, to his face, that he alone was rightful heir to the entire Angevin Empire. He would never bow to John's wishes and would cause him grief for the rest of his days."

"What a stupid, prideful boy!" I cried, putting my own hands to my face in shock. "He should never have spoken so."

"Because of his rashness, good men died," William said. "John wrote the orders to all castellans who held prisoners from Brittany and Anjou. The captives were all sent to Corfe."

I nodded; Corfe was a huge and powerful fortress, not so far away in Dorset. "I heard that the prisoners taken abroad were being gathered there."

"Beloved, I hate to speak of dire events to a female of tender years and gentle birth, but as I will often be away, I deem you must know the wickedness of the world, so you will never trust too much. Ela...John ordered the men moved—and then starved to death in Corfe's oubliette. They are all dead. Not one escaped."

Bile stung my mouth; I felt my knees grow weak. I wanted to scream at my husband to rise in rebellion against his brother, that this was unnatural, that no King in recent times had behaved with such malicious cruelty. But I dared not. I knew my place; knew that not only would William not listen to my protestations; any interference might destroy the fledgeling bonds of love and trust in our marriage.

"As for Arthur," William continued, "John called a council. I was there, along with Reginald de Cornhill, William de Braose, Peter de Maulay, and Geoffrey Fitz Peter."

"Fitz Peter is the justiciar of England," I said. "He holds the regency in John's absence. Whatever the King wanted must have been very important…"

"Very…" murmured William "A decision was made, and…and…" he began to stammer and take great gasping breaths, "on the Thursday before Easter, John drank himself into a frenzy. He…he acted as if possessed by the Devil. He ordered the rest of us to prepare a boat for him at the castle sallyport, and then to bring Arthur down to him. We got the boy…Ela, he thought he was about to be set free. Christ, Christ…I cannot bear it. How can I tell you what happened next?"

"Because you must!" I said in a tiny whisper. My hands curled, the palms sweating. "You are burdened by whatever happened. Speak to me, if you cannot speak to a confessor!"

"Arthur got into the boat—and a look of pure terror crossed his face as John climbed in after him. He started to struggle but de Maulay was in the boat too, grabbing his arms from behind. The boat drifted down the Seine, and then John and de Mauley both drew daggers and stabbed Arthur to death. They tied a weight to his body, and hurled it into the Seine…"

Leaping from his chair, William began to pace the room. "I—I am to blame as much as any. I agreed that the boy needed to be dealt with, yet somehow, I-I did not think… I must shoulder the blame."

I ran forward, clutching his tunic. "No, no, you are *not* to blame. It was John's will, his hand that wielded the blade…"

William pressed his hand over my mouth suddenly, heavily. My eyes widened with blossoming terror; I could not breathe. "Keep your voice down! You must never speak of this matter, never tell anyone what you know. This is not to protect John, but you, me, and all we hold dear."

His hand fell away, and I collapsed into his arms, gasping for air, fear causing me to tremble head to toe. All my short life, I had seen my family as mighty and untouchable—now I had learned it was not so. No different from any peasant, if I said the wrong thing, revealed dark secrets in an unguarded moment, I could end up entering the gloom of Corfe's oubliette—the place of Forgetfulness, whence none returned alive.

William pulled me closer to his chest; he had begun to weep in earnest, unashamed. It was a terrible, heart-wrenching sound, and I wanted to put my hands over my ears but dared not move. His chin rested atop the crown of my head; I felt the parting in my hair grow wet. "I do not expect you to understand, Ela," he said. "For all that he has done evil…John is still my brother. *My brother…*"

CHAPTER NINE

The King had returned to England, and William departed in haste for Worcester, where the Welsh Prince Llewellyn was meeting John to negotiate marriage with John's bastard daughter, Joanna. I was left to my own devices, with only my mother and my newly-chosen tiring women, Mabella and Felyse, for company—Muriel had returned to Countess Ida's service—and my troubled thoughts. Word had come that Normandy was fully under Philip of France's control—Chateau Gaillard, that seemingly impregnable fortress, had fallen. John, paying no heed to his military advisers, had built an extra level to the chapel and inserted large windows to beautify it; the besiegers had managed to gain entrance after smashing through the shutters. After that, Caen quickly capitulated to the French king, followed by Falaise; Barfleur and Cherbourg were captured like so many chess pieces.

Amidst all this bad news, I continued my work around the Castle under Mother's watchful eye. A woman's work is never done, they say, and that is even true of a high-born lady married to a King's brother. Servants I had plenty but I still had much to do, young and inexperienced though I was. At dawn, I attended Mass in St Nicolas' chapel, my eyes often still bleary with sleep—mindful that my suffering would be good for my soul! Then, as Mabella and Felyse dressed my hair, I broke my fast, sometimes having sops—bread dipped in rich wine—but at other times a little salt fish or demain bread, which made me feel most decadent. After eating, my attention was given to the ledgers—checking that they balanced and that the suppliers of various goods had not taken advantage and given us too little or unsuitable stock. Following that, I would ride into town with the steward to collect the Lady Day rents from the folk who dwelt beyond the gate. Salisbury was prosperous but sometimes a family could not pay full rent because the father was ill or had died or suffered some other misfortune. I attempted to be fair in those circumstances and would bring a priest in to witness arrangements for payments in arrears. Some others might have driven a lax tenant forth, threatened prison or imposed punitive fines, but I refused to do so unless the tenant tried to cheat me. I had known these folk from the time I was a little girl and had sworn to help, not harm.

Later in the day, I'd tour the kitchen and supervise the meals after checking the stores in buttery and pantry. That out of the way, I settled to embroidery or dance practice with my ladies and Mama, until it was time for our prayers—and then dinner. With William away, we ate frugally: dumplings, fritters or pasties mostly, or smoke herring or mackerels, followed by cheese and wafers, or fruit dipped in a paste of rose and violet.

Finally, when the day was done, I would retire to my chamber, and Mabella or Felyse would shoo out the great ginger mouser, a cat called Tibelda, who liked to curl up by the brazier. Angry, she would lash her tail before stalking from the room, slanted eyes glowing green evil, and go to find renewed warmth, and maybe a mouse, in the kitchens. Felyse would remove my wimple and comb my hair, while Mabella untied my garments and slipped a white linen robe over my head before ushering me to bed.

Despite the constant busy-ness of Salisbury, I grew a little tired of each day's similarity and craved some amusement, so I hired a Fool to entertain in the evenings. His name was Proudfoot, and like many Fools, he was a dwarf, never growing beyond a child's height. He rollicked when he walked and had an oversized head of wild blond curls. He would follow me about the castle along with William's hounds; I caught him riding on one once and told him off sternly.

April arrived in a rush of sunshine, and although news coming out of Normandy was still dire, the warmer breezes soothed my troubled thoughts, and the banks below the curtain walls were teeming with wildflowers, their scents vibrant and renewing. On the outskirts of the town and in the fields beyond, the ploughmen were out and peas, beans, barley and oats were sewn. Life was returning to the world, and soon, I hoped, William would return from his business with the King.

I wanted him here. I wanted him at my side.

I wanted to give him an heir, although Mother flung up her hands in frustration at my complaints, and chided, "Ela, do not fret about such matters so soon. It is safer to bear a babe when you are a few years older."

Right she may have been but the worry of barrenness nagged at my soul; Mama had only borne one child to my father, not the hoped-for son…but me. She had one other daughter by her second husband, Gilbert de Tillières, a girl in France whom I'd never met, but that was all. Four husbands and only two girls to show for it.

Morose, I wandered the wall-walk after completing my daily tasks. Mabella was suffering a cold and Felyse was tending to her with apothecary's potions, so I allowed them some free time till later that evening. Instead of the ladies, Proudfoot came hopping after me—he had a limp through a deformity of the hips that made his gait uneven—shrieking and gibbering as the winds whipped over the crenels and nearly blew him into the bailey. "I am not a tumbler but I shall tumble, I fear, before long, Lady!" he cried.

"Perhaps you should not have come up here," I said over my shoulder. "Little legs make little speed! And you are so small, you might blow away like a dandelion's head!"

"I prayed a gracious lady might carry me in her arms as tenderly as any babe!"

"You would make a rather ugly babe, Proudfoot!"

He placed a hand over his heart. "You wound me, sweet Lady, but then, that is the lot of a Fool. To be wounded. No Lady ever gives me her eye, or her hand…or anything else!"

His talk was risqué but I ignored it, rolling my eyes. "Proudfoot, Proudfoot, *I* am no Fool. I know you've half a dozen mistresses in the town, and one or two baseborn children as well!"

He leapt in the air, clicking his heels and arms windmilling. "My secret is out!" A gust of wind nearly carried him off for real this time; I snatched his collar and yanked him back from the edge of the wall.

"Proudfoot!"

Panting, he squatted on the ground. "My thanks, Lady. Your arms are as strong as they are fair. To think—if you hadn't caught me, all my lovely lemans in Salisbury would have been weeping tonight. *Boohoohooo.*" He made an obnoxious bawling noise and pretended to rub tearful eyes with his strange little knuckles.

I rolled my eyes again. "We had best go down; the wind's grown even stronger and it's nearly time for Mass..."

Suddenly, from down below, on the far side of the wall, there was a *boom*. One of the deep bells of the cathedral. Leaving Proudfoot sitting in a heap, I peered over the edge toward the town. Another bell peeled, its sound deep and thunderous. "Why...why are they ringing the bells?"

"If I could grow wings, I'd sail over to find out for you, milady." Proudfoot waddled up to me and peered over the edge as best he could.

"This bodes ill," I said. "There is no reason to sound the bells, save fire, flood, invasion...or death."

"Shall we go find out?" The dwarf gestured to the stone staircase.

I picked up my skirts and fled towards the stairs, descending to the bailey with my little companion keeping good pace despite his afflictions.

A courier had arrived and was speaking to Hobart de Lynom. I noticed the Lions of England upon the stranger's tabard. "Oh no, no," I whispered, imagining the worst. My knees felt weak. "I cannot face it. It must be William..." I thought of terrible things, from accidents, to duels, to murder. Maybe John had found out he'd spoken of Arthur; maybe he'd been thrown into the oubliette at Corfe like the French and Breton knights.

"Lady, if you cannot—I will go forth as your champion." Proudfoot gave a bow; his eyes were kind, sympathetic, and in that moment, I guessed the poor creature was more than a little in love with me. I reached out to hold him back, but the fabric of his jerkin slipped through my trembling fingers, and he was loping across the courtyard, his blond mop waving like a wheatfield in a gale.

I saw the messenger and de Lynom stop conversing and turn to stare; then their gazes fell upon me, standing there like a terrified ninny, my skirts blowing in disarray and my veil almost strangling me.

They started in my direction but were blocked by Proudfoot, who made wild gesticulations with his large, mobile hands, all the while shaking his head. De Lynom halted, put a hand up to tell the courier not to approach, and my Fool rollicked back towards me, puffing and blowing.

"There is good news and bad," said Proudfoot. "Earl William is well and hale and still wiping John-boy's arse."

Tears of relief burnt my eyes. "Oh, Proudfoot, you Fool, you shouldn't speak like that of John…even if you are a Fool!"

He shrugged. "A Fool's duty is to mock the great and good and not so good! But now, I beg you, listen to the sorrowful news. I fear it will make you weep, although all knew this day would come soon, for our lives rarely exceed three score and ten, the span allotted man by God most high."

"Speak," I said. "I must know." In the distance, the cathedral bells continued their funereal clangour.

"On the first day of April, a light went out," sighed Proudfoot. "A bright and beautiful light, once the most beautiful in Europe, or so men tell. *If the world were all mine from the sea up to the Rhine, this I would willingly forego to have the queen of England lie in my arms"*

I knew then who had died, and yes, the tears flowed, even though some years had passed since we had parted. Queen Eleanor, wonderful, learned, talented Eleanor of Aquitaine, the wonder of her age, scandalous and shocking, yet full of wisdom and grace.

"I cannot bear to see you weep," said Proudfoot. "How can I make My Lady smile?"

"At the moment, you cannot," I said. "Another day, Proudfoot. For now, I must be alone."

He bounced around me like a frolicking puppy, bowing and kissing the hem of my dress, then hastened away towards the servants' quarters.

Composing myself, I approached the messenger, a man of middling height, neither old nor young but with kind, tired eyes. "Sir, this is grievous news you bring. Who sent you? I see you bear the King's insignia."

The man bowed his head. "I serve his Grace, the King, but have come to Salisbury on behalf of his lordship the Earl, Countess Ela. He said you must be told of the Dowager Queen's death, for at one time you were close to her."

"If only he were here to comfort me!" I said piteously, hating myself for my weakness. "Such a dreadful message is hard to bear when one must grieve alone."

The messenger stared uncomfortably at the toes of his boots. "The Earl gives advice—and solace—to the King after the death of his esteemed mother."

I said nothing, unwilling to believe that John cared about anyone but himself, even though he *had* sped to Eleanor's defence at Mirabeau. And even if he did, did he need his half-brother's solace as much as his wife did?

"You may go," I informed the courier, then, turning to Hubert de Lynom, "See this man is given small beer, meat and bread and receives some coin for his efforts before he heads back to court. See that I am not disturbed for the rest of the day. I intend to spend the next hours in prayer for the soul of the late Queen Eleanor."

With Mabella, Felyse and several stout armed fellows, I left the castle and descended over the wooden bridge and walked to the cathedral. Its green and white walls glimmered in the weak sunlight; the garishly painted saints on the west front raised tormented eyes to heaven. Inside, monks and nuns scuffled from chapel to chapel, robes making a sound like the scamper of mice-feet. Beeswax candles shuddered in great chandeliers as the wind struck the building with relentless, unseen fists. Frankincense and myrrh—the rich scents coiled into my nostrils as I passed the Rood Screen to kneel before the high altar.

I thought of Eleanor, her brilliant life ended, although in truth that brilliance had waned in her last years; her wits had wandered in her dotage. She was a sinner and freely admitted so, but I was sure God would be merciful and admit such a bright star to heaven. And if He did not, I wagered she would merely smile and say that then it must be her duty to brighten the long hours men spent in Hell...

Tears slid down my cheeks, hot, endless. What must her last years have been like? Her lands in turmoil, besieged in her own castle, John losing most of the familial territories. She must have also known about Arthur, and even though he had treated her abominably, I doubted she would have wished him dead... No wonder her mind had faltered at the end.

As I moved away from the altar, I caught sight of Bishop Herbert Poore striding through the aisles in a billow of robes. I mused about whether to pretend I had not seen him; I had little enough to do with the cathedral in my daily life and was less inclined to after learning about Poore's plans to move it to Merryfields, the lands near the river owned by his brother. However, it was too late to avoid detection—his head swung in my direction and a moment later he glided over to my side.

"Countess Ela, it has been long since last you graced the cathedral with your presence."

"Yes, my lord Bishop; it is not common for a woman whose husband is away to wander far from her castle. But today I have suffered great sadness. Queen Eleanor was kind to me in my youth."

"And so the bells ring out for her," said Poore. "She will not be forgotten. I remember her well from when I handled the finances for the vacant See of Sarum." His lips pursed and his eyes narrowed; he had only become a bishop after great hardship. He had been nominated for a position in Lincoln, but the King had refused consent, preferring another. He had then been up for Salisbury but many had objected to his parentage—his mother was his father's concubine—and a complaint about his lowly birth was sent to the Pope. Herbert finally got his wish in 1194 when the canons of Salisbury unanimously voted for his appointment.

Herbert Poore was a tall man, lank and long-faced, with jowls hanging down like strands of melted candlewax. His eyes were watery blue and his eyebrows matted like sheep's wool. His brother Richard Poore, the cathedral's Dean, looked much the same only shorter and ruddier complected. Richard also looked less lachrymose and had a ready laugh. I did not appreciate the Bishop's presence at this moment, but he was insistent I listen to him.

"Countess, I would speak with you. It is important. Not about the Queen. God grant her peace after such a tumultuous life. About the cathedral itself."

"Speak, if you must," I said, a little rudely.

"Come." He led me through the ambulatory to the niche that held the sarcophagus of black Tournai stone that contained the miracle-working bones of blessed Osmund. Next to it, gleamed a human arm-bone on a silk cushion—the bone of St Anselm that was once Osmund's most treasured possession.

"Lady, look how gloomy it is here and hear how the wind howls. Blessed Osmund deserves a finer place to sleep the long sleep ere the Resurrection. The Earl is not enamoured of the idea of moving the cathedral…"

"Neither am I," I interjected. He ignored me.

"But remember it collapsed once due to high winds, and the lack of water is troubling to all. Also, there have been problems with the clergy accessing the castle at will and falling afoul of your guards. I was hoping you…you might be able to persuade the Earl."

"I am even *less* enamoured of the idea than he," I said tersely—although I had to admit the wind *was* screaming over the rooftop spires. The rare painted glass was rattling in the windows; Mother Mary looked as though she might jiggle the infant Christ off her knee while the Jesse tree resembled a real tree in a gale, buffeted this way and that. "The cathedral has stood here my whole life. What would happen to the people who live around it? It would be like tearing the beating heart from the town."

"The folk of Salisbury would pack up, my Lady, and follow the cathedral down toward the great river to form a new settlement, leaving you and the Earl in solitary splendour in the castle. Fewer villagers would surely remove certain worries should the fortress ever be attacked."

"I pray it will never come to it," I said, unconvinced. "Oh come, Bishop; you may think it rude and overbold for a woman to speak with frankness, but I know your brother Richard is eager to have the new cathedral on his lands at Merryfields. Is there not some profit in this endeavour for him—and you?"

Bishop Herbert turned a rich shade of purple. "It is not as it sounds, I assure you. Merryfields is perfect for a new foundation, Countess Ela. Even the name is an omen, surely—Mary's Fields."

"I have heard the fields are damp, even marshy, from when the river floods. That does not sound safe for building a great church."

"I have already spoken to masons, to craftsmen. The new cathedral, if built, will outshine anything standing on this bleak hilltop. It will be wrought in the new style, with pointed arches; a thing of beauty; a rare gem to glorify God."

"I remain unconvinced. The plan seems a drain of money and resources. The people of Salisbury are happy enough here, despite the wind."

"One more thing, Lady. Let me show you our humble scriptorium before you decide all is well here." He retreated from the ambulatory and opened a small wooden door that led to a cramped spiral staircase. I motioned for Mabella and Felyse, trailing behind, to wait in the aisle, and followed the Bishop up to the cathedral scriptorium and library.

The scriptorium was cramped and dull, lit only by a handful of candles. I spotted an ominous crack snaking up the stonework toward the eroded corbel of a King. Draughts reached through my garments, and the parchment a young scribe was working on flicked and curled, much to his obvious annoyance.

"We have over sixty books here, written by Osmund himself—most importantly, his missal, the liturgical book for the Mass, and his breviary, for the canonical hours," said Bishop Herbert, pulling a hefty tome down from a shelf and blowing dust from the cover. He opened it with a finger and illuminations bloomed before my eyes, exquisite, jewel-like in their rich beauty. "Dusty…not acceptable, but damp too, inside…I fear the illustrations will in time be ruined. Do you not agree these valuable books should be safely kept, Countess Ela? I know the late Dowager Queen—may God smile upon her as she reaches His Throne—was a great admirer of manuscripts…"

But not so often the religious ones, I thought, with a little smile, but then sorrow rose in me again, remembering that Eleanor was dead, lying in Fontevrault beside King Henry, with her beloved son Richard nearby.

Blinking away the evidence of my sadness, I glanced at Bishop Herbert. "Yes, such treasures should be preserved for all time."

He sighed theatrically and gazed at the crack in the wall. "In many parts of the cathedral the roof leaks, Countess. Stones leach apart through the battering of the elements. Repairing it is a never-ending job, and it is dangerous for the carpenters and masons in that constant wind."

"I know all about the rain and wind here, Bishop." Herbert Poore was full of wind himself, at times, but deep inside, I began to understand, just a little, why he might wish to move the cathedral to Merryfields.

As if reading my thoughts, which would be very wicked for a Bishop, he began to expound on the proposed move. "It is not only the weather and the lack of a decent water supply that pains the community, Countess Ela; we also have to put up with unruly knights passing by on the road to the jousting field near Wilton. Sometimes they make a dreadful commotion, drinking and fighting and bringing...bringing common women into the nave. One even tried to ride a horse in; the creature sha...messed upon the tiles and I had to instruct Brother Albert to collect it up before it stunk out God's House. He had nought to contain the dung in, so he had to wrap it in his sleeve and ruin his own cassock!"

I kept a straight face at his final tale, told with much indignation. He was having a slight dig at William because these fractious, drunken knights had not been provided for within the castle. But why should they be? They were only men passing on the road, and the town held far more attractions for them. "I am beginning to see that many of your grievances are real, Bishop, but still, what you wish for is ambitious, to say the least..."

"Lady..." He whirled towards me, his face lighting up like a saint's, enthusiasm glowing through that raddled flesh. "Can you imagine? A great library filled with the most important tomes written in England. A library whose works will be studied for thousands of years in the most beautiful and awe-inspiring of all English cathedrals. And you...you would have a part to play, you and the Earl."

"A part for us? What do you propose?"

"If you back the rebuilding of Salisbury Cathedral at Merryfields, you and Earl William shall go down in history as patrons. You, with others, can lay the first stones. Your names will live forever, clear in God's eyesight..."

If the building does not sink into the marshy ground first, I thought, but the Bishop was beginning to convince me that there was some merit in his plan. It would be most unusual for a town not to have a castle in the centre for defence, but the world was changing, the old battling against the new.

"I will think of all I have seen and heard today," I assured the Bishop, "and I will speak of your concerns to the Earl."

He inclined his head, his dry, yellowish hands clasped as if in prayer. "It is all I ask for, Lady Ela. I do not even mind if the move may not happen in my lifetime; I will die content just knowing it will be done. I *know* it is the right thing to do—God spoke to me in a dream."

I wondered if the Lord had borne the face of Herbert's brother, Richard Poore—but that was a wicked and impious thought! I curbed my own inclination to mock, especially on such a sad day.

But I was sure Queen Eleanor, if still alive, would have thought much the same.

CHAPTER TEN

"Normandy is lost and Philip gloats. What a grave dishonour to the family." William leaned in the window embrasure, staring out over the courtyard. He had returned in the dying months of the year but his mood was not sweet. He was still wrapped in John's business. Plantagenet business.

"Yes," I said, playing the dutiful wife as I worked on my sewing, "it is a terrible shame, but perhaps…perhaps the King will give more of his attention to England. I dare say the country needs it. Richard, God rest his soul, was a great soldier but truth be told, did little for England."

"Woman, watch what you say!" William spluttered, rounding on me in surprise. "He was the greatest warrior ever known—almost. He brought great prestige to England."

"He did, but prestige does not fill the treasury or bring peace amongst those unable to pay taxes raised to fund his wars."

William spluttered again, running his hands through his rough curls in agitation. "Christ on the Cross, you sound like that William Longbeard fellow from London. Do you know what happened to him?"

Primly I put down my sewing. "He died when I was a child, but yes, William Fitz Osbert's name is known to me. He claimed to speak for the poor and oppressed, fomented a rebellion and was hanged on Tyburn Tree. I somehow do not think that will be my fate just for speaking truth. I have no plans to start rebellions, I assure you."

"John hates any hint of disloyalty, Ela. He was counselled by Bertrand de Bethune to throw the hearts of disloyal barons down the privy!"

"Down the privy!" I could not decide whether to be scandalised or amused.

"Yes…it caused much amusement in court, and we all waited to see whose heart would be torn out first. However, John only stripped the faithless of their lands, not that it really helped his cause. Many of the barons went straight to King Philip in France." He rapped his fingers against the wooden table where we had eaten earlier, still covered in bowls, crumbs and empty flagons. "Sometimes it seems no matter what he does, it always goes amiss for John."

I could not argue with that, but put my head down and resumed my sewing, despite the fact the day's distractions had quite ruined my stitchery. "How did you fare at the council? Has the King decided what he will do?"

William's eyes grew steely and he folded his arms, giving himself a pugilistic look. "He passed new laws to curb shirkers Any who will not heed a summons to war will lose his lands…"

"And if a man has no lands?" My sewing dropped back onto my lap, the stitches haphazard. Useless. I would rather hold a book, even an accounting ledger, than a needle.

"They will lose their liberty and be forced into servitude for the rest of their natural lives."

"A harsh punishment."

"Needed in hard times, Ela. John has sent constables everywhere to muster the locals…"

"There is one in the town, I have seen him. He is fat and puffed up with his own self-importance. I won't let him in the castle."

"Let him stay in the town. If he is as unpleasant as you say, the townsfolk will soon teach him humility."

"I trust the King has not given up on Normandy?"

"No, not yet; after he held his great council, we fared north to York. He had business with two of great northern magnates—men he does not trust but whom it is imperative he gets on his side. Ranulf of Chester will have his debts waived, and Robert de Montbegon will have his castle of Hornby repaired—if he swears to remain true to the King. And if he hands over some hostages for his good behaviour."

I grimaced at the thought of Montbegon, or anyone, handing over their loved ones to unpredictable John Lackland. But then I smiled, "I am glad you made it home to Salisbury. The winter is very harsh this year, is it not? I cannot remember the river frozen solid before. I feared you might be confined to the north for a while."

William stroked his beard. "Yes, the weather is always worse in the north country, and the roads are often impassable at this time of year. But God smiled on our company, and so the King is in Marlborough and I am here. The snow blew in behind us, covering our tracks—we were just in time. Another week and we may have had to winter up north. Why do you suddenly look so pleased, my little one? Like a cat that has supped on the cream?"

"Is it not obvious? With so much snow upon the ground, we will have some time together before John summons you again. Let us go to Amesbury, to the manor house where I was born."

"In this weather? It is too dangerous, surely!"

"I've known every inch of the road since childhood," I boasted. "Snow and ice do not make me fear, not here."

"I must have dwelt in the warmer climes of Normandy, Gascony and Aquitaine for too long—the snow outside just makes me want to curl up before the fire like an old dog," he grinned. "Nonetheless, if you wish it, Ela, we shall go. I have not checked on my properties there since we were wed, and I suppose it might behove me to show my face to the Prioress of St Mary's."

"Yes, and I would like to light a candle in the priory church for the Dowager Queen. St Mary's is a daughter house of Fontevrault, of which Eleanor was long a patron."

We left the castle, riding on sure-foot rounceys. The snow had stopped and the little town of Salisbury was wrapped in a white blanket. Behind us, the keep towered, its crenellations touching the low-hanging snow clouds.

Hurrying north with our retainers, we reached Amesbury by late afternoon. The sky had cleared and a hazy sun hung low and red in the sky. We sought out the priory, crossing the old bridge over the frozen river, and William met up with the Prioress while I removed to the church to pray. Lighting candles for Queen Eleanor, I watched the flames surge against the darkness. I envisioned the Queen's age-scored but still beautiful face floating in the shadows. *Lady, if you be in heaven, please lend me your strength. Even if it must be against your own son…Give me some of your courage…*

In the shadows, I scowled with sudden shame. I must not continue to think badly of John. William was bound to him by blood-ties and oaths. I had to accept that in matters of high state, I would always come second…

I clutched my rosary beads, icy against my palm. The church was cold, frozen by the icy winds blowing off the great Plain. I turned my thoughts from Queen Eleanor and prayed to the Blessed Virgin instead, that I should be filled with her grace, that I should fulfil my duties to my husband and bear him an heir. An heir to Salisbury. Such a child would please me too, not just because I desired maternity, but because it would continue on my father's line. He had no son to become an Earl but his grandson would inherit his title and all that it entailed.

William and I spent the night in the house where I was born. It seemed small and quaint now. Servants had rallied round to make it cheerful and bright for our arrival; the flagstones were swept and covered in thick mats of river-reeds, and a crackling fire roared on the hearth. The aromas of fresh-baked bread and roasted beef drifted from the kitchen. Happy memories of my youth flooded back to me, days of playing in the river, days when nurses upbraided me for playing the hoyden and shimmying up trees—days before I received the news of my father's death, heralding childhood's end and a new beginning.

"You smile to yourself, Ela," said William. "What secret happiness does your heart hold?"

The servants and attendants had respectfully vanished after beef and lamb shanks, barley bread and honey wine had been brought. "Secret? My happiness is no secret. I am here, where I was loved, with he whom I love. It is as if, despite all the troubles in the wide world, here I can be content and safe."

It was in the old manor house in Amesbury, that night I am certain, that our first child was conceived in the very chamber where I was born.

The next day, we exited the manor to a clear blue morning with the sun sparkling on snow. The river was a winding ribbon of white ice where village children played, screeching as they slid hither and thither on skates made of cow's shoulder blades. On trees overhanging the river, long icicles tinkled like chimes as the wind blew.

"Let us go up to the Plain," said William. "I would like to see the heathen temple."

The hilly path to the top of the Plain was slippery, but the snow was virgin, which made it a safer jaunt as it had never melted to later freeze into a solid sheet below the surface crust. Reaching the crest of the rise, we turned along the old Harrow Way and viewed in the distance the gaunt outline of the heathen monument, the Hanging Stones, which lay on the priory's farthest flung lands.

Drawing near, the temple appeared to be a roofless building surrounded by a ditch too shallow to use for defence. Lintelled stones were set in a circle, reminding me of stone gallows. Icicles hung under them like huge blue spears, water dripping from their tips to make a sad, constant patter on the ground. I had heard tales that it was a place of execution and shuddered beneath my squirrel-lined cloak.

"I have seen enough," I said, unwilling to walk under those deadly icicles.

William, though, was intrigued and walked in boldly while I stayed outside, whipped by the wind that raked over the Plain. For a few moments, I lost sight of him amidst the grey clutter of rocks, and my stomach lurched as I thought of tales my nurses told—how men stumbled into such liminal places and were whisked away to Faerie for a hundred years…

But then he was back, the snow crunching beneath his leather boots, the crimson of his cloak a splash of blood against the stark snow. "Nothing inside," he said, "no indication what it truly was. At least I can say I have seen it—one of four wonders of England. Did not a chronicler of old say that 'no one can work out how the stones were so skilfully lifted up to such a height or why they were erected'?"

I nodded "Henry of Huntingdon in the *Historia Anglorum*."

William clapped his hands in delight at my answer. "My wife, so clever and well-read—you are a marvel among woman."

"You may thank the late Queen, if my knowledge is truly something you value," I murmured, not entirely sure if he was teasing me.

In my head, though, I was thinking of other words written of these ancient stones, this time by Geoffrey of Monmouth, *As Aurelius looked upon the place where the dead lay buried, he was moved to great pity and burst out in tears.*

"Ela, you look so strange." William was at my side, hand upon my shoulder. His touch was warm but the cold wind went through me like a dagger. I pointed toward the Harrow Way with a shaking hand.

A rider was coming. Seeking us out. He wore the colours of the King.

Philip Augustus was making plans to invade England. He had convinced the Duke of Brabant and the Count of Boulogne to attack first, and he would bring his more substantial forces to join them shortly after. John had summoned William and the other barons to another great council, this time in Winchester. He decreed that one knight in ten was to converge on London by the first of May, ready to fight—and die—for their monarch.

William was his right hand through all the preparations of war. Much of it took place at Dartmouth and Portsmouth, so Salisbury town was frequently full of hard-bitten men marching from the east and north who gave the one house of ill repute great trade, according to the scandalised whispers of the servants. Carts rolled past full of salted pork and venison sufficient for a journey over the Narrow Sea. Other wains brought loads of pikes and spears, crossbow-bolts and fletched arrows.

"Did you hear?" Mother asked, as we sat in the solar, quietly attending needlework. "The King has pardoned all the prisoners in gaols all over England in the memory of dear Queen Eleanor."

I was tetchy, as the midwives had confirmed my gravid condition, and my stomach was in constant sickly knots, ofttimes making me race for the privy. "How thoughtful, how pious of him—*pah*! He only wants those ruffians to swell his ranks!"

"Ela, questioning the King's piety! And you, his sister by marriage. You have not even met him yet."

"I hope the day I do is far into the future."

"Why do you dislike him so? If I were you, I would make the most of being related by marriage to the King."

"Well, I am not you, Mother—you know I favour Father."

"Yes, stubborn and sometimes over-righteous."

I felt furious but did not want to unleash my anger, which I realised came from the changes taking place in my body, none of which were pleasant. "How could you understand? I-I know things about John that you do not."

"Oh, tittle-tattle." Mama waved her hand and gave a loud, dismissive sniff.

"*Not* tittle-tattle. William has told me of his brother's actions."

"Well, whatever he said, I am sure he would beat you for making it into…tittle-tattle."

"He has never beaten me; he is not a vicious man…unlike his brother," I cried, then shut my mouth with a snap, for Mabella had brought a goblet full of mint and balm to ease my roiling stomach.

"Breeding women have such strange fancies," sighed Mother, resuming her sewing as I clutched the goblet. "You must not think unpleasant thoughts, daughter—it might give your child an ugly face."

I glowered and drank the soothing mint.

Strange rumours reached Salisbury, brought by journeymen and wanderers and passing monks and nuns. The fleet was delayed. There was mutiny amongst the crews. Worst of all, there even tales that my kinsman William Marshal, proudest of warriors and renowned for loyalty, had hastened away to France and done homage to Philip. When confronted, he claimed that John had ordered him to do so as part of a secret mission, but the King had flown into a rage and screamed, "*God's Teeth, I did not tell you to bend the knee!*" John had even gone as far as to ask his supporters if they would take on the Marshal in single combat. No one would. Relief filled me, knowing William had declined.

The English fleet was not sailing, that soon became evident. Hubert Walter, Archbishop of Canterbury, had ridden to Portsmouth to confront John and convince him it was folly to sail. He would be outnumbered; he had no heir at home; the throne would be at risk.

John had thrown another tantrum, but Walter had spoken to him harshly, as only one of God's Chosen could, "Your Grace, if you will not listen, then you must be detained, even if force of arms is needed.

England will descend into tumult and strife if you leave with the situation as it is. You are needed here more than in Poitou."

Finally, after much cursing and roaring, John agreed, but the moment Hubert Walter's back was turned, he promptly sailed away under the cover of night with a small band of retainers, including William.

However, he only got as far as the Isle of Wight.

Whether it was weather, despair or persuasion from those closest to him, no one could make up their minds—but I was glad his mad journey went no further.

It meant William would return home, safe, without a single blow struck against the French.

However, when he arrived, salt in his hair and beard and his mouth set grimly, he told me something that did not please me. John was going to distract himself from his latest military disaster with hunting and hawking at his lodge at Ludgershall.

And we were expected to meet him there to keep his Grace company in his misery.

CHAPTER ELEVEN

I thought of excusing myself because of my delicate condition, but William insisted I accompany him to Ludgershall. "The King requested your presence," he said. "He has summoned the Queen to meet him at Ludgershall, but fears she may be bored without female company. It is a great honour for you, Ela."

There was nothing I could answer. I had no idea what I could say to this young girl from Angouleme, whom I heard was both highly-strung and demanding. I had even less idea what I might say to the King but hoped he would be more engrossed with his hawks and hounds than with the wife of his half-brother.

There was no helping it—I would have to go to Ludgershall.

Due to my pregnancy, I was carried in a litter full of soft cushions while William rode alongside. It was June and the sun beating on the roof of the litter made me feel nauseated and giddy. Every now and then, Mabella laved my brow with rosewater to cool me down. I clutched a deep bowl in case I retched up my morning meal of sops.

The journey was about eight leagues but felt more like eighty as the litter swayed back and forth on the rougher parts of the road. It grew hotter and even Mabella began to sweat and look faint. Dark patches blossomed at the armpits of her gown, and I realised mine were the same. Ugh, I might not be able to bathe in the little hunting lodge and would have to make obeisance to the King and Queen doused in the sweet oils Mabella carried instead.

Eventually, I heard the buzz of people and the hubbub of town life—dogs barking, children wailing, pedlars shouting as they hawked their wares. Mabella drew aside a small fold of the litter's draperies so that I could look out. Sure enough, we had entered a compact town of golden-stoned buildings centred around an imposing market cross carved with scenes of Christ's Crucifixion. Excited onlookers gathered on the steps, straining to get a better view of the incoming company.

A few minutes later, our entourage had passed under the gatehouse of the lodge which was, in truth, a small castle built by my distant ancestor, Edward of Salisbury, one-time Sheriff of Wiltshire. Through him I bore the old Saxon blood in my veins; Father used to say that ancient ancestry was one reason why our family got on so well with the common folk of Salisbury, who were mainly of Saxon stock.

Ludgershall had two baileys surrounded by ancient earthworks. One held kitchens, stables and outbuildings, while the other contained a compact stone keep, chapel, hall and apartments. It looked a quiet and pleasant place, yet my belly was in knots as I stepped from my litter and entered the hall block with William.

"Do not be alarmed, wife," said William, observing the pallor of my face. "You have nothing to fear from John."

I looked at him in silence; he had a silly little indulgent smile on his face which made me cross. Had he forgotten what I knew, what he had told me with his own lips about Arthur of Brittany's murder?

The great and terrible meeting came that evening, after Mass in the castle chapel. The King had not attended—William said he often declined, no matter how priests and Bishops tutted—but the young Queen was there, up near the altar ringed by a sea of silk-clad ladies. I managed to get a good look at her as we knelt and rose and murmured prayers. She was not quite the 'Helen of Troy' of whom minstrels warbled. Low in stature, almost doll-like, though shapely, she had a smooth oval face and over-large, luminous grey-blue eyes that dominated her face. Her mouth was bud-like, but small for her face, and her nose, though well-formed, was a little too large. The strands of hair revealed at the top of her headdress were a shade of nut-brown, not the gold beloved of bards and poets.

"You will meet the Queen later, I am sure," William said, as we walked towards John's chamber after the service. "I saw her peering at you throughout Mass when she thought none would notice."

I had grown aware of her surreptitious glances too and did not know what to make of them. Isabella's expression held no emotion; she scarcely seemed a young girl at all.

I had no more time to ponder the Queen's intent as we entered John's audience chamber. Hangings lined the walls, showing scenes of the hunt—a stag was brought down in one, a pack of hounds ran through trees in another, a huntsman blew a golden horn in a particularly large one that hung floor to ceiling behind a dais where the King's chair stood.

John was sitting in the chair. Or rather, lounging, one leg draped over an armrest that had the carved head of a roaring lion. My first glimpse of royalty—and I was not much impressed. I had heard he bore little resemblance to his brother the Lionheart but it was as if I gazed on a changeling, a creature deposited in the royal cradle by malicious fairy-folk. His hair was dark red and curling, hanging dishevelled to below his chin. His face was ruddy and thickly-bearded, the eyes dark and hooded. A ring glittered on every finger; great cabochons polished to a high sheen. He wore a long red robe with golden lions cavorting on the hem; it had slid back to reveal a muscular, furred calf. It was wholly undignified.

"Will!" he shouted out even as William dropped to one knee before him and I dropped a respectful curtsey. Leaping from his high seat, he grasped my husband by the shoulder, almost knocking him off his feet. Bright red, William managed to retain his balance and slowly rise. "Will," the King repeated, "I am so glad you are here. We can do some hunting and drinking, no?"

"Yes, my liege."

"Pah, none of that 'my liege' business in private. You're blood. Family. Ah, I cannot begin to tell you how miserable I've been."

"Chinon…lost." William sorrowfully bowed his head.

John's grin vanished in a trice. "A great loss. How I liked that castle! All my lands in Anjou are now in the hands of that bastard, Philip."

"We will get them back," William asserted. I cringed. I hated the thought of him heading off to battle again, especially since John's cause had little support.

"I have had some delightful news, though, brother. You may not have heard yet—but Hubert Walter, that miserable old wretch, is dead."

William stumbled back in shock. "Dead? I had not heard this!"

John started to laugh; a harsh braying noise. "He had a deadly growth…here…" He pointed toward his crotch, and my cheeks burned with embarrassment. "He was too ashamed to see a physician—and so it killed him. *Sic transit gloria mundi…*" He bellowed with laughter yet again. "God's teeth, Will, I feel like I am finally the true King of England with that old meddler out of the way."

"You will have to go to Canterbury," frowned William.

"I plan to on the morrow. Fights are taking place over the appointment of a new Archbishop already. I am putting forward John de Grey, who alone of the clergy knows my mind…and does not criticise. I have already sent messengers to the Holy Father in Rome."

"You work fast, my liege…John," said William. "It never fails to astound me."

"And you shall come with me, to give added force," said John, clasping William on the shoulder again.

A doubtful expression crossed William's face. John saw and leaned close to him. "You won't let me down when I need you, will you, Will? I would be most…grieved."

I fought to keep from gasping out loud. The smile had vanished from the King's lips; his words were almost a threat or so it seemed.

"It—it is just that I have brought my wife, Countess Ela, and she is with child."

"Ah, yes, the Countess, the one stolen away by her family to spite Richard…" John clapped his hands together in a kind of childish delight. Then he turned his attention to me, stepping over to observe me with those hooded eyes. They glittered as his mouth opened slightly, showing wet, too-red lips amidst the heavy tangle of beard. "Very pretty, William; you are a lucky man. Keep her close always, lest others try and spirit her away—after all, it happened once before!"

"I intend to. She carries my heir beneath her belt."

John, slightly shorter than me, peered up into my face. He was too close; wine and spiced marred his breath. "Ah, she is shy—she will not face me."

"Your Grace, I dare not; I have been told it is a breach of etiquette to gaze directly upon the King's person," I murmured.

"Who taught you that?" asked John.

"Your mother Eleanor, your Grace."

John was silent for a moment and my heart thundered; had I angered him? My tongue was too swift at times.

But then the King laughed and stood back, hands on hips. "I should have guessed. She has placed her mark all over you. Best of luck to you, William, if she turns out like my mother."

"I am very pleased with my wife," said William, a bit stiffly.

"And the earldom of Salisbury no doubt! Now, come, Will, let's have a swift hunt before we depart for Canterbury. Do not worry about your pretty wife; she can spend time with my Queen, who is desperate for conversation with a highborn female her own age. You can imagine how tense things can be between her and Hadwisa."

The King stalked towards the chamber door, gesturing for William to follow. My husband cast me an apologetic look.

I was left alone until a mousy little maid appeared. "My Lady Countess? Queen Isabella awaits you."

The Queen was in her own chamber, and when I entered the room, she was almost shockingly informal. Her hair was down, hanging in coils to her waist, and she wore only a loose green night-robe. Her ladies fussed around the chamber, plumping up the bed covers, tossing rose petals, setting out her gowns for the morrow.

I made to curtsey but she gestured for me to rise before I had even dropped low. "I have heard you are with child," she said. "I will relieve you of unnecessary courtesies."

"Thank you, your Grace."

"Sit, Ela." I sat on a cushion swirling with exotic eastern patterns; it smelt of sunshine and spices…of oranges. I had tasted oranges in France while living with Eleanor, but not a single one since I had returned to England.

"You look wistful," said Isabella, observant for such a young girl.

"I can smell oranges, your Grace. I admit I crave them…in my condition."

She gave a little smile, settling herself on cushions next to me. "You will have them when I can get hold of some, Countess Ela. I will have them sent to Salisbury Castle."

"You are most kind, Highness."

"We are sisters by marriage, are we not? I would like a sister in England. Hadwisa is no sister or friend." A scowl suddenly passed over her face. "She is still bitter. It is not my fault John put her aside."

"No, of course not, your Grace," I said soothingly. *But it was his fault for forcing you together for no reason but spite and avarice…*

"She's an evil old gossip…and ugly," continued Isabella. "She treated me like a child at first, and so did John. I had no say in anything at all…yet I was Queen!"

"You were very young, your Grace."

"Call me my name, I bid you, if we are to be sisters. As for being young, yes, I was, but not so young I could make no decisions. I was past the age of reason. It was outrageous. Even my raiment was chosen by either John or Hadwisa—and the old cast-off chose items to make me look as dowdy and plain as possible."

"Perhaps she was merely a poor judge of taste, Isabella."

"That would not surprise me, as her own dress sense is laughable, but I truly think she took against me from the start. There were vile rumours, Ela…about me and John. Have you heard them?"

I grew alarmed. Was she trying to entrap me in some way? One could never be certain. "No…no, Isabella. I have heard nothing."

She leaned closer, conspiratorially. "Liars and traitors have said that John and I dallied in bed while all his lands in Anjou and Normandy were lost! It…it is not true! He was away much of the time. He looked upon me with lust, it is true, but he refrained from entering the bedchamber till I was fifteen. And now because people believe we…have been in union long, other wicked rumours have sprung up—that I am barren. No one in this cold, unfriendly country seems to like me."

"I am sure that is not true, Isabella." I had heard folk describe her as 'capricious and troublesome' but I would never tell her that. "And I am sure, in due course, a little prince will be born to you and his Grace; perhaps once all the troubles abroad are over. You are still young yet."

"But *you* are with child, and you are close in age to me. And William has served overseas with the King, so has not shared your bed so much."

I was mortified by this discussion of my private life, but managed to stammer, "It is mere luck...and as God wills. I am thankful—after all, my mother gave but one child to my sire."

"As did mine," said Isabella. "Oh, just think—it would be such a disappointment to have only one child, and it ends up a girl."

"My parents were doubtless disappointed, but made the best of it," I said, believing I was offering comfort to the young Queen. "I had tutors, just like a boy. Father said it was so I could assume duties as Countess of Salisbury in my own right until I had a husband, or after I was widowed."

Isabella shot me a ferocious glare, and with a sinking feeling, I realised I had said the wrong thing. "Did they? Mine were not so bothered. They only wanted me to marry horrible old Hugh Lusignan...and then my father Aymer pushed John onto me, almost literally. But, anyway, it hardly matters if *you* do not bear your husband a male child. You are just a Countess, while I am a Queen...and your husband is only a bastard, born in sin. My duty is to have sons; a girl means England would end up at war again as in the time of Empress Maud. The barons swore to her father they'd crown her, but her cousin Stephen usurped the throne."

"There is no need to worry about babies, I will pray for you..." I began lamely, but Isabella's temper was raised. She climbed from her cushions and began to stride around the room, hair swinging. I glanced at her ladies-in-waiting, begging them for help with my eyes, but they stared at the floor, no doubt used to these outbursts.

"You do not understand," said Isabella. "Why would you? No one is after *your* position. If anything...anything happened to John before I bore him a son, I'd be ruined. I'd have to flee back to Angouleme and see who my father could sell me off to this time. There are many, so many, who would see John toppled. That stupid boy, Arthur...Did you hear about Arthur of Brittany, Ela? Do you know what happened to him?"

Again, I had the sensation of a trap closing around me. I schooled my face to blankness. "I know who he is...was."

A sly smile crossed those pert features. "And how do you know he is dead?"

"I do not, your Grace." Gone was the child-like Isabella; now she was *the Queen*, unpredictable and dangerous. "But is it not true that no one has seen him?"

"What does that mean? Nothing! He could lie bound in the deepest of dungeons! But no, he won't be lusting after John's throne again, that my husband has assured me...but he did once, the greedy creature *did*. And forget not his sister, Eleanor. They call her 'the Fair' and the 'Pearl of Brittany.' Even though she's a woman, some support her claim to England's crown."

"See?" A wobbly smile crossed my lips. "There is nothing to fear. Even if you had only daughters, they would still have supporters, even as Eleanor! The world has moved on; it is not as in Empress Maud's day."

She ignored me as if I had not spoken, continuing on her rant about Eleanor of Brittany. Now she began to sound very much a child. She was only one year my junior but with her tiny stature and pouting mouth, she seemed more like a child of ten—an ill-mannered and fractious child at that. She stamped her tiny foot in its jewelled slipper.

"Eleanor is supposed to be so beautiful, yet her hair is red—the red of Judas' hair. She is freckled and insipid and too tall. Men called me the new 'Helen of Troy' when John stole me from Hugh Lusignan, but of late I have heard courtiers laughing that I am neither golden-haired like the real Helen...nor so buxom...that my bosom is as flat as a pricked bladder!"

"Those courtiers were most unkind, Highness. They should have been whipped for insolence"

"Are *you* laughing, Countess Ela?"

I most certainly was not; nervous sweat trailed down my neck, but I heard a muffled snigger from one of Isabella's ladies. It was apparent that the young Queen was indeed not very popular—and for good reason. "No, your Grace."

"I thought we might be as sisters," she said, "and not just because we are wed to brothers, but perhaps I was wrong. You just do not understand—no one in this horrible country understands my plight. I would be alone, Countess Ela. You are dismissed."

Inwardly relieved, I rushed from Isabella's chamber to my lodgings. Passing the privy, I voided the contents of my belly, my nerves tied in knots. I may not have made an enemy of Isabella—I had done nothing wrong—but unless she grew less thorny and overwrought, I doubted we would ever become true friends.

And of that, in the aftermath of our unhappy meeting, I was guiltily glad.

CHAPTER TWELVE

I did not see Queen Isabella at Ludgershall again; she left with her entourage a few hours after John departed for Canterbury. William had been prepared to go with him, but other messages arrived during the night—the situation in Poitou and Gascony was grave indeed, with most of the nobility gone over to King Philip in one region, and King Alfonso of Castile taking over as much of the other as he could grab. The latter was particularly galling for John, since Alfonso was married to John's sister, Eleanor. However, Alfonso had just cause to invade, for Gascony had been promised to Eleanor as part of her dower lands.

After hours of enraged shouting that could be heard from one end of the castle to the other, John sent his bastard son, Geoffrey, to Southampton to take sail with a small armed force. William was ordered to follow him with another contingent of knights.

Worried but trying to keep my composure for the babe's sake, I said my farewells to my husband and returned to the familiarity of Salisbury Castle. Mother was waiting in the hall, but she was dressed for travel. At their home in Herefordshire, Gilbert de Malemains had tried to extricate a cart from the mud, and as it burst free it had run over his leg, snapping the bone. He was expected to live, but she must go to him at once. "My step-son Thomas is coming to run the estate," she told me, "and your half-sister Joan de Tillieres is on her way from France to lend me her support."

"Joan?" I had never met my half-sister; she was a ghost to me, a mysterious shadow. I was surprised she was not married yet and guessed Mama was up to something entirely unrelated to Gilbert's unfortunate accident with the cart.

"I pray you understand," sighed Mother, clasping my hands. "I will return as soon as it is possible to do so."

"You must go," I said quietly, kissing her cheek. "Your first duty is to Gilbert. He is injured; I must do only what millions of women have done all the way back to Mother Eve."

The days passed and the babe grew within me. I became large and round, waddling when I walked. With daily duties now curtailed,

I prepared for my lying-in. A chamber was readied and its shutters fastened and hung with dark cloths to cut out light and draughts. Canopies were hung over the bed and stools set out for the women that would join me. A sard stone sat on a ledge, ready for me to clutch during my travail. I ordered books brought in so that my ladies could read to me and soothe my pains—I particularly chose the *Passio of St Margaret of Antioch*, the patron of women in childbirth. A dragon had once swallowed Margaret who managed, aided by God, to burst unharmed from its belly; therefore, it was known she would help wives bring forth children safely from *their* bellies.

Mother remained in Herefordshire. My assumptions were correct—she had not only gone to aid the injured Gilbert but to see Joan married to Thomas de Malemains. To my joy, Mama's place was taken by an unexpected visitor from the east—Countess Ida of Norfolk.

Warmly, we embraced each other. "I am so glad you have come," I told her. "My own mother Eleonore is indisposed, and it will be less lonely with you here."

"I am eager to see the birth of my first grandchild," said Ida. "You look well. You have bloomed."

"I am stout as a sow," I said, laying a hand on my belly. "And how the little one kicks and turns. If it is a boy, he will surely be a great fighter."

The midwife arrived from the town, a portly woman with a round moon-ish face. "It is not your time yet, but I feel it is drawing nigh," she said with a smile as she examined me. "I would retire to the lying-in chambers, if it please you, my lady Countess."

Summoning the chaplain, I went to the chapel and received a blessing before Mabella, Felyse and Countess Ida, all carrying thin white tapers, escorted me to my special bedchamber. Two midwives in caps and aprons trundled silently at our heels. Once behind closed doors and sealed shutters, further candles were lit and the fire stoked up. Ida hung a crucifix upon the wall, brought all the way from Framlingham, and placed a coverlet she had embroidered with William's coat of arms on the bed. There, in near-darkness, we loosened our gowns and unbound our hair, noble ladies and humble midwives alike. Taking out knots and freeing one's tresses was reputed to aid the babe's passage into the world.

Ida looked years younger with her hair hanging free; she was still very beautiful, her loveliness undimmed by frequent childbirth or the ravages of increasing age. "Would you like me to read to you?" she asked brightly.

"I suppose I would do well to hear of St Margaret."

"Pah, she can come later," said Ida, which brought giggles from Mabella and Felyse—they were not used to seeing a high-ranking older woman behave with such delicious informality. "How about Tristan and Iseult?" She took a leather-bound book from a satchel, brandished it.

"Oh, can I hear about Iseult's love potion?" asked Felyse.

"Why? Do you need one?" teased Mabella, nudging her companion.

We spent the next days as jolly as could be, in our sweltering cocoon of female magic and expectation.

And then, shortly before dawn touched the sky upon a Sabbath morn, I woke with terrible twisting cramps. Niggling pains had plagued me throughout the night, but I had managed to sleep through them, dreaming that I was lost in a marsh with midges nibbling at my skin. I made a soft distressed noise as I woke fully and discovered my linen sheets were wet.

"Hertha!" I hissed to the most senior midwife, who was slumped in front of the brazier, arm over her younger companion.

The big woman roused, giving her fellow a hard finger-jab in the ribs to wake her too. Together, they pressed in around the bed to begin an examination, while my ladies and Ida awoke and climbed to their feet. "It has begun," Hertha informed me solemnly. "Anstice, make her ladyship comfortable."

The other midwife stripped the bed and replaced the linens, while Mabella peeled off my soaked kirtle and dressed me in another. Felyse and Ida helped me back into bed, and then began the rituals of birth—praying out loud, kissing relics, supplicating St Margaret and the lesser-known saints, Bridget, Ursus and Erasmus, the latter of whom was martyred by having his innards removed with hooks, hence his patronage of stomach pains, including those of childbirth. My lump of sard was rubbed over my belly then placed into my hand, where I squeezed it tightly—the cramps were increasing, making my stomach feel as if squeezed in a vice. Felyse draped a string of protective amber around my stomach, while Ida brought out a beautiful prayer-scroll and draped it over my body for protection, incanting the prayers written upon it all the while. The younger midwife, Anstice, a freckled young woman with long yellow hair, patted me comfortingly on the shoulder and even gave me a little gift of her own—a piece of beaten tin inscribed with a prayer to the Virgin.

The pain began to intensify, and I was consumed by a strong fear of death. I had written my will, as all women should do before giving birth, but my situation had become very real, and terrifying. The baby might not survive. *I* might not survive. Death often came creeping for mother and infant both…

Ida's face loomed over me, gentle and comforting. She took my free hand in her own and squeezed. "You will be well looked after, Ela. And you are strong."

The child took almost a day to come into the world but eventually, a small, puling scrap emerged into the flickering firelight. A newborn's thin wails rang out. I wanted to call out and ask if it was a son, but Hertha brought the child, wrapped in a blanket, to the bedside. "You have a daughter, my lady Countess. Hale and healthy. I have sent Anstice to fetch the wet-nurse."

I took the baby in my arms. She was small and red, crying lustily—and she was perfect. A tuft of dark hair stood up like a boar's crest on her head.

"Go find the priest and tell him to prepare for a baptism," I said to Mabella, cuddling my daughter.

"She is beautiful—and I am sure she is only the first of many," said Countess Ida, sitting on the edge of the bed. "What name have you chosen?"

I glanced up to meet the Countess' eyes. "She shall be Ida of Salisbury."

William was back in England later in the year, and if I for one moment imagined he might be disappointed in a daughter, I was soon proven wrong. He was delighted and a proud father. "She must wed an Earl or Count at the very least," he murmured, "if not a prince of the realm."

"If you aim so high, I beg you never tell her," I admonished. "If she grows up expecting a prince, she might well become vain and insufferable."

"What? Should I tell her she must marry the miller's son instead?" he teased.

"Yes, perhaps, if her sire's over-praise turns her into a pompous little prig!"

We were lying together in our bedchamber, glad to be joined once more. Suddenly William rolled away, swinging his legs down from the bed.

"I-I have offended you in some way?" I reached out to stroke his broad back. He had a scar from some old injury; a white stripe followed the length of his spine.

He shook his head. "No, I am sorrowful, that is all. Here I am, home, with my dearest wife and my beautiful infant daughter—but I must return to serve John in Poitou."

I sat up too, naked save for the fall of my long honey-brown hair. "No, not again! When?"

"Not right now." Turning, he cupped my face in one hand. "After Christ's Mass, probably when the winter storms cease and the crossing is safer. We made headway with our foes this past summer but not enough; La Rochelle is still beleaguered, and the land is full of unrest. The King wants a proper campaign with a decisive outcome. He has gathered money to finance a full assault on his foes."

"Yes, I have heard." I kept my voice neutral. Oh, yes, I may have just been a woman but I heard the complaints of knights and nobles, of poor men and merchants in the town. Men were charged huge sums to come into their rightful inheritances; the marriage-rights of wards and widows had assumed new, phenomenal fees. Widows who did not want to remarry could buy their way out of an unwelcome match—but in doing so, they often lost all their lands or emptied their coffers until they were forced to live in penury.

"I also promised John that I would spend the Christmas season with him in Oxford. You may join me if you wish…if you feel well enough."

"Well? I have never felt better. I had a baby, not an ague. I have been churched, our daughter thrives, and so do I. It will be a wrench to dwell apart from little Ida for a time, but her wet-nurse says she feeds well. She will be protected and content."

"So it is settled. You will come to court. The thought cheers me. Perhaps you will learn to love my brother…"

"He is my King; I must love him," I said warily.

William laughed. "I know you better than that, wife—and I know John can be hard to love when his evil tempers are upon him. But at times there is another side to him, I swear. He is more able than may imagine …"

"I promise to try to look for his abilities when next in his presence." Reaching out, I kissed his brow.

In truth, I was not keen to see John but I felt it was time to step forth as the Countess of Salisbury. The barons saw me as young and inconsequential, as well as a weak female, but my father had given me the education of a son, and deep in my heart, I suspected I could match any of John's lords and sheriffs in the governing of castle and town if given a chance. Eve's daughter, I might be, but God had for whatever reason given me swift thought, aptitude, and a way with the common man. Recently, John's fines and taxes had drawn my unease, and I wished to plead for clemency for those afflicted if the subject arose—especially if John did, as William claimed, have a 'good side.'

William stroked my hair back from my bare flesh, touching, admiring. "Now…let us stop talking about *my* brother," he murmured, "and more about…ah…begetting a little brother for our Ida. What do you say?"

"As always, I say yes," I laughed, opening my arms and my lips as we tumbled together amidst the embroidered covers.

Oxford was white beneath a thin veneer of snow when we reached its walls. Mesmerised, I gazed at the spire-laden colleges, the over-arching tower of St Fridewide's, the parties of gowned students bustling through the streets, merry and drunk. In one narrow street, bear-baiting was taking place; wonder-struck, I stared as seven fighting dogs assailed a great hairy creature which swiped at them with huge claws. Men were running about, taking bets; bags of coins jingled so loud I could hear them in my carriage.

"Shall I close the curtain, my Lady?" asked Felyse. "It is not a pretty sight for a noble lady's eyes."

"It is not," I said, "but we will pass it soon enough." I did not want to miss any of my first visit to the town, even the ugly side. I pushed at the curtain again; the bear and its tormentors were lost in the distance. Now before us lay the Guildhalls of the weavers and corvisors, their frontages decorated with stone corbels of crowned Kings. I'd heard that old King Henry had been a regular patron and John too. There were also vintners' shops, busy due to the impending royal Christmas, and dozens of inns, ranging from massive timbered houses with many floors and garish signs to low-slung taverns crammed down unsavoury alleys. All were busy as the King's men and the baron's retainers filled them.

The carriage turned a sharp corner, sending a gaggle of harlots in striped hoods shrieking towards an alleyway, and then before us appeared Oxford castle with its round motte and ten-sided keep, and the battered stump of St George's Tower thrusting into the snow-clouds. The river churned slowly before the curtain walls, sluggish with slabs of broken ice. Once, in the days of the Anarchy, Empress Maud had found herself under siege at Oxford on a snowy eve, and fearing capture, climbed from a window, and crept to safety across the frozen river, dressed all in white and invisible to enemy eyes....

The drifting snow reminded me of the Empress's exploits on a night much like this one, and as the entourage proceeded over the drawbridge, I smiled to myself and hoped I would not feel obligated to make a similar daring escape.

The festivities got off to a start not long after my arrival. John seemed unusually jolly and bragged to William about the increases in his income, "We shall have plenty of money for next year's campaign, Will." He clouted his brother on the shoulder, making him wince. "Never fear, you will have the best ships, horses, armour and supplies. I've collected relief money from inheritances and from the marriages of wards. A profitable little business."

"But not very popular, your Grace." William observed the contents of his goblet rather than his kinsman's wine-reddened face.

John slapped his knee; he was clad in red from neck to foot and wore a belt set with garnets and a golden chain flashing with rubies. I thought all the scarlet made him look rather devilish, like Satan bathed in flame, especially since he had slicked back his unruly hair and had the barber cut his beard to a small point. "It'll be popular when I win back my lands," he said. "Oh, Will, you should have been there…'twas so amusing. There was a knight, Robert Riddell—do you know him?"

William shook his head. "No."

"Never mind. A stout enough fellow—and looking for a wife. He had his eye on Alice, the pretty young widow of a knight called John Belet. Lovesick was our Riddell, but she would have none of him. So he came to me, his King, and told me he'd give me fifty marks and two palfreys if he could marry the wench."

"You gave the money and horses back, I presume?" said William, and there was surprising censure in his voice. Startled, I glanced up from my trencher, to see John's face darken to an unhealthy ruddy hue.

"What do you mean, Will? Of course not. Those were damn fine palfreys he offered."

Will breathed deeply, uneasily, then blurted, "In the time of our great grandsire, a widow was not usually compelled to marry against her will."

John sat back in his seat, staring hard at William, and then he banged his cup on the table, showering wine, and laughed, a laugh that was high, whinnying and forced. "I never knew you were so well-educated on the doings of our forebears, Will. Times change; we do what we must to get what we need! Now…back to unwilling

Dame Alice! Well, I summoned her to come and meet her groom. She came, and oh, she was a fair creature next to old Robert Riddell, and she went on her knees and begged—God's Teeth, I wish she had been on her knees before me in private!"

The courtiers milling around the King's seat like a crowd of gaudy peacocks guffawed with laughter, as did John. "But I am happily married, of course..." he added, peering slyly at Queen Isabella who sat beside him, frosty-faced.

William shifted uncomfortably. "What happened in the end, then? Did she accept the abhorrent match?"

"Her father galloped in to the rescue," sniggered John. "You'll never guess what he did, Will. He offered me twice the sum Robert Riddell did! *Twice!* I had to lose the palfreys, alas, and poor Robert was heartbroken but..." he shrugged. "The wench got her way and I got more coin for the war-chest...."

William the Marshal, who had healed his earlier rift with the King, coughed and leaned in John's direction. "These domestic tales are all very well, Sire," he said bluntly, "but I want to know about Hubert Walter's replacement. Canterbury cannot go long without an Archbishop! Months have passed by..."

"Ah, Marshal, always on about business and never pleasure!" sighed John. "I want John de Gray; he has served me loyally. I have made his nephew Chancellor as well..." He glanced towards a weedy but well-dressed man with a blunt bowl of hair and a ruddy face like a farmer's.

"But will the Pope feel the same—that is the question?" said William Marshall thoughtfully.

"I do not see why not," John snapped. "What business is it of his, in truth? I alone know what my country needs!" He banged his goblet on the table again, this time in true agitation.

A moment's silence descended as all eyes in the hall fell upon him. Then Ranulf of Chester, a lord little liked but mighty in power, rose from his seat, swaying. "A toast for his Grace the King!" he roared. "And after? Let the minstrels play and the dancing begin!"

"Ha! I'd rather have Roland the Farter, who used to entertain my father's court," said John, the sharp edge vanishing from his voice. "But alas, Roland is dead and will fart no more..."

"What killed him, your Grace?" cried the Earl of Surrey.

"Griping of the bowels, I expect!" retorted John, to howls of mirth from Surrey, the Earl of Essex, Ranulf and other barons. William managed a half-smile, as did the Marshal, who then turned his attention to his trencher.

King John gestured to the waiting court musicians and they began to play a stately dance on psaltery, flute, shawm and drum.

John himself rose, dancing with young Isabella before the rest of the nobility joined in, moving around the floor with varying degrees of grace. William was a good dancer and I middling-fair, but the Earl of Essex was half-drunk and his wife Beatrice rather stout and ungainly, her legs puffy with dropsy. They kept bumping into us as we passed, while the Earl, Geoffrey Fitz Pier, laughed uproariously. As we moved around the floor, trying to keep clear of the Essexes, I noticed a woman watching from the sidelines, her expression wistful yet bearing a hint of envy. Tall and spare, she had narrow hips and wide shoulders. Her face was horse-like and lacking in beauty, but she was richly clad in a furred green gown with sleeves slashed through with silver ribbons.

I wondered who she was, and when we returned to our seats, asked Mabel of Chester, wife of William d'Aubigny, Earl of Arundel, who was seated on the same bench. "That is Hadwisa of Gloucester, John's first wife, Countess Ela. The Queen is still in her care due to her youth. What a strange situation it all is! Some say when he visits his Queen, he still beds Hadwisa, but I believe that is a cruel falsehood. It is as preposterous as the tales that he spends all day rolling in the sheets with Isabella. He was never even attracted to Hadwisa, poor creature, and with her ill looks and her lands firmly in the King's hands, finding another husband would prove difficult. At her age, she may even be barren."

"And if any man did want to take Hadwisa on, no doubt he would have to pay through the nose for the privilege," interjected Countess Clemence de Fougeres, wife of Ranulf of Chester. "With all those disadvantages, I would be surprised to see her remarry. Mayhap she will take the veil instead, once John removes Isabella from her care."

"The Queen looks none too happy." I glanced in the direction of Isabella, who had retired to her place at the high table and was sullenly dining on candied violets, sweetmeats and mince pies.

"That one," said Clemence, "is never happy."

The next day John went hunting, taking William, Ranulf, the Marshal and other favourites with him. I was left in the castle with the women and the servants. Accompanied by Queen Isabella, all the noble ladies went to the castle gates and handed out alms to the poor, including scraps from last night's banquet, workaday patten shoes and rough burel to fashion into garments.

It was there I met Hadwisa face to face. All the other women seemed to ignore her presence, but I took pity and worked alongside her.

After the gifts had been distributed, the Queen and her ladies returned to the warmth of the solar for sewing and chatting. I gave Felyse and Mabella leave to accompany them, and they departed with happy little cries, eager for gossip amidst new companions. I did not go; I feared another fiery encounter with the dissatisfied young Queen.

"I would like to walk on the walls, Lady Hadwisa, and wonder if you would care to join me," I said to Hadwisa, who also had not followed the others. "I am not used to sitting so much. Salisbury is a busy place, and as my lord husband is away so often, I have little time or inclination for the feminine arts."

Hadwisa looked surprised but she nodded. "I am sure the Queen will not miss me; she has other diversions."

Passing the guards, we climbed up onto the covered wall-walk. The town looked peaceful and beautiful with its rooves shimmering white and frosted spires hanging in the air. We walked the circuit, side by side, the cold wind stirring our veils and bringing colour to our cheeks. We talked of this and that, trivialities; the price of cloth, the latest fashions.

Suddenly Hadwisa smiled ruefully. "It is good to talk to someone other than the Queen. She never speaks kindly to me but only with disdain. She berates me for what is not my fault. I did not want to be her keeper."

"It must have been hard for you."

She nodded. "John made me his ward again as if I were a child…and yet I was supposed to care for the child for whom he discarded me. I should have been Queen, and instead I have to curtsey and be subservient while she goes about with her nose in the air." As if realising her words were near-treason, Hadwisa pressed her hands to her mouth. "I'm such a fool; I have spoken out of turn…You won't tell will you, Ela?"

"I am no tittle-tattle, and I am no confidant of Queen Isabella. I do not think she likes me either, truth be told. Every word I uttered seemed to cause offense when we met."

Hadwisa let her hands drop. "I am so relieved…"

We had now walked almost the whole circuit of the walls and stood by St George's Tower, overlooking the river. Children were playing on the ice, daring each other to go out to where it was thinnest—a dangerous game. Hadwisa stared down at the river, black beneath its frozen coating.

"Can you not just imagine Empress Maud leaping the walls and escaping?" I asked.

"I wish I had the courage to jump," breathed Hadwisa, "even if I could not flee after."

Horrified at her words, the desperation in her voice, I stared at the homely woman. She spoke of self-murder, a terrible sin. Moving to her side, I clasped her arm. "Am I right in thinking that the King and Queen now spend time together as husband and wife?"

Miserably she nodded. "They both throw it in my face as often as they may. But she is still a child to him, nonetheless, she has no lands in her own name, she plays only the part of a pretty ornament. They are together seldom, which frustrates Isabella for she worries more about producing an heir than John does. I remain her nursemaid for now."

"Have you thought about taking the veil?"

Her eyes, a pale washed-out blue, filled with tears. "He'd never allow it. He is waiting for the time when I am no longer useful, when Isabella takes full possession of her household. Then he will marry me off—I am his ward, remember, so he is in charge of my marriage—and make a great deal of money from the highest bidder. Or so he thinks. I am hardly desirable, and he has made it so that he keeps almost all the lands I came with. But I expect he will convince some baron to pay the price with soft threats."

Anger burned within my heart at her tale of injustice. She had done no wrong and yet she had less freedom than the wives of the merchants in the town below. I thought of John's mocking tale of poor Alice Belet, and my fury grew. One day, such cruelty towards my sex must surely end! "I will get William to speak for you…" I began.

Nervous as a startled hare, she glanced up. "N—*NO!*" she cried. "It is better to leave things as they are. John does not like to be gainsaid in any way; he would make my life worse in some way. It is better to humour him…to obey him. That is the fate of women, to obey…"

I was silent. Yes, we were to obey our fathers and our husbands, but surely not when treatment was cruel and immoral. In my estimation, a woman's lot had grown *worse* since the days of our forebears, with money taking precedence over what was just and fair…

A horn sounded, ringing through the wintry streets of Oxford town. We both turned to look. "The hunt returns," said Hadwisa. She looked ashen and defeated.

Down at the gatehouse, the gates had creaked open. The huntsmen were bringing in the carcass of a stag suspended on a long, sturdy pole. Hounds and lymers yipped and yapped, excited by the smell of blood. Their handlers strove to control them, as the fierce lymers bared their teeth and snarled. John and his party rode behind, their cloaks and furs bright against the starkness of the snow-streaked buildings.

"They've caught a fine stag with many tines." Hadwisa peered between the crenels on the wall. "At least that will make John happy. Nothing he likes better than the hunt…save beautiful women. I could not share his enthusiasm for the first, and I am unlovely to look upon, as he told me often, so I was unsuitable for the second. There was no chance we would ever find harmony—unless I had given him a son, but I failed at that task too."

"You speak too harshly on your own failings," I said…and then fell silent. The King and the hunting party had entered the inner bailey. As grooms took the horses and the dogs were dragged to the kennels, John dismounted and marched purposefully toward the stairs leading onto the wall. "The King is coming!" I breathed.

Footsteps, slow and purposeful, crunched on stone and packed snow. John's head appeared, rising from the stairwell, then the rest of his short, stout form. His mantle was dark ruby, fringed with marten, and he wore an extraordinary cap with dyed feathers and fox trim. A smudge of blood from the kill underscored one eye, making him look exceedingly roguish.

Hadwisa and I sank to our knees. John said nothing for what seemed an eternity. Snow began to fall again, a light shower that dusted the castle wall-walk. It was cold and I wondered if his capricious nature would see us kneel there for hours.

He moved a little closer; I found myself gazing at the slightly-pointed tips of his boots. William had told me he'd purchased them at great cost from the famed cordwainers of Northampton. His scent, sandalwood and myrrh, mingled with horse, sweat and animal blood was heady and not terribly pleasant.

"Rise…" he finally said.

I got up as gracefully as I could. I was close to John, too close. His dark eyes were observing me with amusement—and something else?

Behind me, Hadwisa attempted to rise, but in her heavy woollen skirts, she moved awkwardly and slipped on a patch of ice. She fell back onto her bottom, her headdress coming adrift and her cheeks turning crimson.

"Christ's Teeth," said the King, "Can't you do anything right? Even something you were taught to do when barely out of the cradle?"

"I am sorry, your Grace." Hadwisa's voice was taut with tears.

"What are you doing up here anyway, away from the Queen? I could see you from the bailey with those skirts as bright as a flag, but no sign of my wife."

Hadwisa's mouth hung open as if she had been struck dumb. Eventually, she managed to stammer, "I—I…she didn't…I…."

"Where is she, woman? I wouldn't put it past you to push Isabella off the wall into the river and say she slipped on ice."

"Sire, no, no, I would never do such a wicked thing to the Queen. Or to anyone!" Hadwisa looked terrified, her expression that of a terrified rabbit menaced by a hawk.

"I asked Lady Hadwisa to accompany me, Highness," I cut in boldly. "I felt unwell and needed to take the air, and I did not know the way. If there is any blame to be had, it must be on my shoulders, not Hadwisa's."

John's gaze travelled from Hadwisa back to me. "You are forthright and honest—I like that. You are my brother Longsword's wife, are you not?"

He knew perfectly well who I was, and I had no idea what game he was playing. "I am, Sire."

"He's a lucky man!" he suddenly laughed, the cold air fogging before his thick red lips. "Perhaps, sometime, you and I should become better acquainted. I think I should like that…I should like it very much indeed."

"I would be most honoured, your Grace," I said, with as little enthusiasm as I could muster without sounding rude.

"Hmmm." He gave me a long, appraising look that made me feel colder than the snow-laden wind.

Then, without another word, he whirled about and strode back to the stone staircase. As he vanished from sight in the bailey, relief flooded over me. If I was ever to find John's good qualities, it would clearly not be at *this* meeting.

At my side, Hadwisa of Gloucester, spurned wife, rejected queen, reluctant nursemaid and potential money-maker for the King, burst into wracking sobs.

CHAPTER THIRTEEN

When Twelfth Night was done, William and I set out for Salisbury Castle. John was on the road too, hurrying north despite the inclement weather to meet the King of Scots and visit the royal castles at Richmond, Lancaster, Chester, Carlisle, and Knaresborough. Fortunately, he did not command his brother to join him.

It was a month or so later that I realised I was with child again, the babe conceived sometime around the Twelfth Night revels in Oxford. Pleased, I sought out the cathedral to pray for both a son and a safe delivery. I prayed too that William would be permitted to remain in Salisbury for most of the year, but too soon it became obvious that those prayers were in vain.

In May, John assembled at mighty fleet at Southampton. William was summoned to sail with him to La Rochelle, from whence the King would try to reclaim some of his lost territories.

"I will send messages when I can," William said, as he prepared to ride out of the castle gates. He was dressed in his mail coat, his tabard of six lions on a blue background drawn over it, but his head was still bare, his hair tumbling around his face in the stiff breeze. "God be with you, Ela, my dearest wife."

"I will pray every day and make offerings for your safe return," I answered. Of an impulse, I grasped his mailed hand and brought it to my lips. "Come back to me…to our little Ida and the new child."

I did not truly believe William, a soldier, would find time to dictate to a scribe, but letters came, not many, but enough to dispel the fears that rose in me daily, even as the baby grew in my womb. I imagined William dead on some foreign field; not only would his death tear my heart asunder, but it would mean the King could sell me off to the highest bidder or make me destitute raising a payment to stay free…

"Lady Ela, another messenger has come from the Earl." I glanced to the solar door, where Hobart de Lynom was standing.

"Well, bring him in, sir," I said testily, motioning for Mabella and Felyse to depart.

A dirty, salt-smelling man walked in, his face crinkled and brown from the sun. He had not washed for a long time; I contained a grimace as I saw lice scurry across his receding hairline. I allowed no such filthiness in my household; all had to have their hair combed and any lice crushed before they tended to my needs.

"You have a message from my husband, the Earl of Salisbury?" I asked.

"My Lady." Sinking to one knee, he proffered a grubby, crumpled scroll. I could see the lice more clearly now, nestled in the creases of his neck.

"My thanks." Gingerly I took the scroll from his hands. "Now go. The servants will bring hot water, cloths, and a barber…" I said pointedly, "and then they will bring food. I shall deal with remuneration before you leave."

"My Lady." He scrambled up and bowed, before being escorted toward the kitchen by Hobart.

Drawing near to a candelabra for extra light, I broke the seal on the letter and opened it with shaking hands.

My dearest wife, Ela, Countess of Salisbury,

Greetings and may you be of good health and good cheer. I am cheered because, at last, our fortunes turn. The rebellious Gascons fled to Montauban—do you know of Montauban, my beloved? It is a great castle and walled city steeped in legend; Charlemagne himself laid siege to it for seven whole years yet was unable to breach its walls. But God was with our army, and John took Montauban within days, a great victory and a sign that the Almighty favours us. John brought up siege engines—mangonels and catapults—and at the end sent in troops with scaling ladders from a wooden tower, armoured against the foe's fiery arrows. I was there when the gates fell, fighting alongside my levies in the streets of Montauban. Many high-ranking nobles have been captured and my brother is gleeful, thinking of the ransoms their families will pay! Next, the King will ride toward Brittany, where he hopes to convince the Viscount of Thoars to join his cause. If he is successful in this endeavour, he will head to Angers, the home of our mutual forefathers. What a victory that would be, to hold their castle once more! After that…who can say? It will all depend on the actions of the French. I pray, though, we will be together by year's end. Hopefully, a son will be born to us by the time I return.

May God go with you, and our daughter, Ida.

Your husband, Wm.

I brought the letter up to my face, inhaling the scent of the parchment as if hoping I could draw in some of William's essence where his hands had touched. Inside my belly, the baby kicked. "Do not be afraid, little one," I murmured. "For once, the King is winning…that means your father might soon return."

In October, more news reached Salisbury. Philip of France had brought his forces to Poitou in retaliation. John quailed in the face of Philip's greater army and retreated to Niort. Locked up in the castle, he wrote to the French monarch, declaring that his sole interest was Aquitaine, his birthright through his mother. Philip accepted this declaration, and a truce was made between the two kings for a term of two years.

The fighting was over.

William would definitely be coming home.

However, he would not make the birth of our child. Our second daughter was born in October, during one of the great storms that frequently battered the exposed hilltop. The roofs of houses in the town were torn away; a pinnacle fell off the gatehouse chapel, and the bells went wild, blowing uncontrolled in the wind. Amidst all this clamour, Petronilla was born, after a quick and easy travail that lasted less than half a day. The midwives both agreed that I seemed inclined to healthy, uncomplicated childbirth.

In mid-December, the couriers came galloping up from Portsmouth. The English fleet had docked. "It was a great day, my Lady," breathed the courier, a young lad with an open honest face. "I never saw so many townsfolk turn out for King John…and his lordship the Earl, too. They danced and they sang in the streets; it was like a great fair. Some got drunk and fell off the harbour wall into the sea. His Grace has sent to the Sheriff of Hampshire to buy hundreds of chickens, pigs and sheep for a great banquet at Winchester. It is going to be a marvellous Christmas, my Lady!"

It will be, I thought, *but not because of pigs and sheep.*

A few days later, after kissing little Ida farewell and cuddling Petronilla while her wetnurse hovered, I was riding in a canopied litter on my way from Salisbury to Winchester for King John's Christmas festivities. William awaited me at the royal castle, having travelled to the town with his brother. Winchester was said to have been home to the court of the great King Arthur, which filled me with longing and excitement. I imagined myself as Queen Guinevere—dear Guinevere, buried in Amesbury, according to legend—ready to welcome her beloved Lancelot home…

Winchester was grand. Once the capital of Wessex, it still rivalled London in many respects. The cathedral was one of the finest in England, replacing an older Saxon Minster. King Richard had undergone a ceremonial crown-wearing there after his return from captivity, marking a new beginning for his reign.

I peered out of the litter as my entourage marched through North Gate. Normally, we would have entered from the West, riding on the old Roman Road straight from Salisbury, but the recent storms had blocked the route with fallen trees, causing an annoying detour that cost us half a day's travel.

Inside the town, soldiers and travellers, pilgrims and journeymen milled in the cobbled streets. Camelots hawked dubious relics, potters sold jugs and pots to goodwives in crisp linen coifs. Beggars cried out for alms, extending bony arms, while grimy feral children ran through the gutters, slashing the purse strings of the unwary.

I had never seen so many churches or heard so many bells ringing, the deepest coming from the cathedral of St Swithun. Mabella had family in Winchester and laughingly told me, "You'll get little sleep or rest here with all the bells, I warn you, Countess," and proceeded to name or point out some of the churches and abbeys of the town—St John of the Latin Gate and Nunnaminster, New Minster and St Mary's Calendar, St Peter in Magellis, St Thomas, St Gregory, and St Alphege.

As the litter swayed along into one of the main streets, she pointed out another building, alien in appearance, with stone pillar supports, small windows and extremely thick doors, giving it a fortress-like appearance. "That is the holy place of the money-lenders, the Jews," Mabella informed me.

Turning aside, we then passed through the Fish Shambles, holding our noses against the pungent reek, although it was not so bad at this time of the year as most of the fish was salted rather than a fresh catch.

Next, the party headed up a steep hill, with St Peter Whitbread in a spreading churchyard on the right, and towered Westgate and St Mary in Fossio at the top. Now I could see the castle's rounded towers and massive ten-foot-thick walls. Half the castle had been burnt to the ground during the Anarchy, so most of what we saw was quite new, built by King Henry and undergoing further remodelling by John.

I alighted from my litter and the chamberlain escorted me into the castle apartments. I was anxious to see my husband but it seemed he was closeted with the King on a matter of some urgency, so our reunion would have to wait. After I had been made comfortable and served a small meal of pasties, bread and cheese, I had my maids change my travelling garb for a pale green robe with golden traceries.

"I wonder if there is a garden here," I said. "I need to walk about after lying in the litter for so long."

Leaving the guest quarters, we found a servant to escort us to the garden, attached to the Great Hall by a doorway and paved path. Frost-bitten, it looked a little sorry, the lavender bushes faded and the rosery hung with denuded, thorny boughs, but there was still winter savoury, garlic and chives growing in abundance, resistant to the cold. No doubt the cooks for the Christmas banquet would use them to flavour their dishes, along with the herbs harvested at summer's end—basil, rosemary, sage and tarragon.

As I walked, breathing in the chill air, I heard a woman call my name. To my surprise I saw Hadwisa of Gloucester, the King's former wife, coming swiftly through the herb-beds.

"Countess Ela!" she called. "I am so pleased you have come to Winchester!"

As Hadwisa approached, I noticed she wore a mint-green over-tunic with a pale pink gown below and a linen barbette of the same colours. It was not an attractive combination on a woman her age but I scarcely noticed that. What I noticed first and foremost was that she was smiling in a way she had not at Oxford.

We embraced lightly and I beckoned to Mabella and Felyse to give us some privacy. Sulking, they sauntered over to the garden's well and tossed pebbles into the water, annoyed at not being party to any gossip.

"Are you well, Hadwisa?" I asked. A bright glitter in her eyes and a flush on her wan cheeks reminded me of sickness.

But she was not sick—indeed, she almost danced with merriment. Suddenly she looked ten years younger than her age, which must have been close to forty summers. "I am well, Lady Ela—my fortunes have changed. Soon I leave Winchester…forever."

Winchester was where Isabella and her forced guardian were domiciled, in-between occasional visits to Marlborough, Ludgershall and Devizes.

"What happened?"

"Isabella is what happened. She stamped her pretty little foot and said that as she was no longer a maiden, she refused to live like one anymore. She reminded Johnny that he was nearly forty and needed an heir as soon as possible, and that begetting an heir was just as important as recapturing Aquitaine."

My eyes widened. In my head, I imagined the tiny Isabella, cat-eyed and sharp-clawed, descending like a fury on her husband. "How did he take such an outburst?"

Hadwisa laughed. "Badly at first, as one might expect. Criticising his foreign campaigns, deriding his manliness? An outrage! He roared like an angry lion and his face was a demon's! But Isabella showed no fear, and he ended up rolling around in mirth on the floor while all the court stared. In the end, he sat up, clasped Isabella's hands and said she was right, he had been remiss as a husband. I could not believe it."

"Maybe he *can* change after all." Amazed, I shook my head.

"He has become much more attentive to Isabella, and not only in the bedchamber. He is treating her like a Queen rather than a little child. Just this month he sent her a gilt saddle for her horses, an otter skin to make into a cloak, and three fine hoods of varying colours."

"The King is generous," I said, feeling that I had best find some praise for him in his own royal castle.

"He can be…sometimes," said Hadwisa, and then, her smile crumpling, "although never with me. I was always a failure in his eyes. He did not want to marry me even though my lands were enticing."

"He did, though," I said stalwartly, touching her arm. "In the end."

"For the lands…as you know." She stared at her feet. But abruptly, her rare smile returned. "It is all in the past now. Once Christmas is over, John is sending me to live in Sherborne. Alone. Without my ungrateful little charge. I am sure I have not seen the last of Johnny; I am still of value, or rather my hand is, even as old as I am, but Sherborne is an improvement."

"Whatever befalls, may you find happiness," I said, with true warmth.

"And you. I hear you have borne a second child."

"Who told you?"

"Why, your husband the Earl, of course. He drank a toast to the babe with the King. Maybe that is why Johnny has started thinking of siring legitimate heirs at last…"

"I wish the baby had been a boy," I said, wistful. "What a Christmas gift that would have been. I have not even seen my husband since I got to Winchester."

"Well, we must fix that immediately," said Hadwisa. "In fact, we shall fix that *at once*."

"But is he not busy with the King…"

Guiding me with her hand, she turned me around to face the garden doorway. There stood William, grinning, clad in royal blue and gold. Felyse and Mabella had spotted him and dropped curtseys. I forgot all about my companion, Hadwisa, and raced through the empty flowerbeds like some lovestruck maid, remembering my composure only at the end, when I skidded to a halt.

"My Lady, it seems you are going somewhere in a hurry," William said, taking my hand and raising it to his lips. "Where might it be? A secret assignation with a handsome knight?"

"No, you cannot think…" I started, then realised he merely teased, as he had done when I first met him at Chateau Gaillard. "Oh yes," I said, changing tack, "and I pray that noble handsome knight bears me away to his quarters so that we may become…*reacquainted*."

William flung back his head in mirth, and taking my hand, whisked me from the garden into the torchlit passages of the castle of Winchester.

After Twelfth Night, John journeyed to Canterbury and William and I went to London to await his later arrival for a Great Council. We stayed in the Palace of the Bishops of Winchester in Southwark, sailing along the Thames on a barge to disembark at the palace's private wharf. For several days we enjoyed the Bishop's hospitality and travelled around the city, visiting the Goldsmiths and Silversmiths, purchasing all manner of trade goods that would not be available in a backwater such as Salisbury. Mabella and Felyse travelled with me, shop to shop, screeching in delight as they saw hair-nets and jewels that they admired.

Finally, John reached London. I was left to wander the Bishop's gardens, listening to the street-cries of London beyond its vast wall, while William headed to the Tower to join his brothers and the scores of bishops and abbots who had been invited…or rather ordered, to attend.

At nigh on midnight, William came riding through the smoky streets alongside the Bishop of Winchester, both stony-faced and grave. I watched from the window of our lodgings, wondering what had happened, and apprehensive as I heard William's boots heavy on the stair.

Once in the room, my husband told me how the churchmen had entered the council chamber looking like sheep to the slaughter, uneasy at being summoned in such a blunt and officious manner.

John quickly let slip that he was seeking more funds to renew efforts to recapture his lost territories. With sly and often menacing words, he sought their agreement to take a portion of the income of every beneficed clergyman in England. Needless to say, this idea was met by horror and a stern refusal.

"We had no idea what you wanted, your Grace!" the religious men cried, horrified. "We have no wish to refuse you…" *The liars!* "but we need to gather more of our number so that we might ponder the details of any arrangement."

John had gnashed his teeth in anger at the refusal but with an idea of fund-raising in his head, he was like a terrier with a bone. He called a second council in Oxford for the next month, with even greater numbers of clergy in attendance. And William, his right-hand support, and a horde of voracious barons to intimidate.

"Our half brother Geoffrey the Bishop of York is coming down to speak with the King," William sighed as we left London and began the trek to Oxford. "He is a difficult man, Ela."

"More difficult than the King?"

"Well, as difficult, if less dangerous! He enjoys a good quarrel, brother Geoff. He's perpetually angry because Richard forced him to become a priest to avert any pretensions to the throne. He's quarrelled with everyone—the Archbishop of Canterbury, Richard, John, William Longchamp, the Sheriff of Yorkshire, the abbots of Guisborough and Fountains…and that's just off the top of my head! He likes to excommunicate those he argues with, if he can get away with it; easier for him to wield *that* threat instead of a sword." Sighing, he shook his head. "Poor old Geoff, dreaming of a crown always out of reach. I never have, you know, even though my mother was of good birth. His mother was a common harlot—some camp follower with the outlandish name of Ykenai."

"Never discount a bastard, though, William," I teased, nudging him. "I am talking about the Conqueror, of course."

He glanced over at me. "I am glad you are coming with me to Oxford."

"Truly? I thought you might find me a distraction from your duties."

"I may need a distraction if things go as badly as I deem they might. Dear old Geoff Plantagenet."

Oxford Castle appeared before us, as cold and frosty as the first time, though the snow lay less deep on the ground. I was given a comfortable chamber with the maids, well-warmed and out of the prevailing wind. However, as I watched barons, bishops and abbots arrive, and the courtyard filled with banners bearing the Cross Flory of De Vesci, the silver Water Bougets of de Ros, the DeVere Star, the Fussils combined of Percy, Crosses, Chevrons, and a whole sea of different Lions Passant and Rampant on Azure, Gold and Green, I became curious in a way women were not supposed to be—much like my old mentor, Eleanor of Aquitaine.

I wanted to witness these lords and my husband discussing matters of state. I wanted to deliberate on what was said, even if my voice could not be heard. Father had allowed me to sit secreted in the Great Hall when the townsfolk came to him with grievances, which is why I found it so easy to assume my duties at Salisbury Castle.

"Mabella, Felyse, I am going to take the air. No, stay seated, I do not want your company. I have business of my own."

Felyse looked shocked. "But it…it's not proper, Lady. Evil tongues might wag if you are seen alone. Someone might think you are going on a secret assignation!"

"Felyse!" I rolled my eyes.

"I do not like it, either, my Lady," said Mabella, shaking her head and frowning. "All these arrogant noblemen and crude soldiers all over the place."

"I deal with arrogant men and soldiers all the time when the Earl is away from Salisbury," I snapped, annoyed by their fussing. Stalking to the window ledge, I lit a candle in a cup. "Look, I shall return before this taper burns down. If I am not back…you can start the hue and cry."

Flushed, the maids rose to curtsey as I flung on my cloak, yanked up the hood to obscure my face, and hurried for the door. My heart was pounding as I slipped out into the corridor. Servants flooded past carrying wine ewers and laden trays; no one paid me much mind. As I neared the Great Hall, buzzing with activity and full of raised voices, I veered aside and climbed a little wooden staircase, moving swiftly but not so swiftly as to draw attention. I was in the musician's gallery, and to my relief it was empty. King John was not particularly fond of music, William had informed me, and it was doubtful he would provide entertainment at an occasion as important as this council.

Brushing away dust, I sat on a bench. From the top of the rail of my perch, I could just about peer over into the Hall. The King's dais stood below, and the benches around him were full of jostling, murmuring men, cathedral clergy in vast copes, abbots and priors in sombre hues, barons showing their gems and finery to the world. They seemed upset so John must have suggested something they found abhorrent.

All of a sudden, the King leapt up, agitated, his face empurpled with passion. "It is for the defence of the realm and the recovery of your liege-lord's birthright!"

A baron sprang up, moustache bristling with fury. Robert Fitzwalter of Essex, who was ever at odds with the King. "Your Grace, what you ask of us is too much. King Richard asked for the same and no one would consent. Why would we change our minds now—a tax on income and chattels for every man? Outrageous! It would make many good men paupers!"

"You speak too freely, Fitzwalter!" spat John. "Sit down. What do you say, Salisbury?"

William climbed from his bench on the King's right-hand side. "No one likes to pay more taxes, but for the sake of the realm, and for the honour of England, I must say 'yea' to this plan."

"What about the rest of you?" John glared around at the barons and churchmen, eyes baleful a dragon's. I saw a fat Abbot mopping his tonsured head with a kerchief, clearly ill at ease under the King's scrutiny. "Will you defy me? *Will you*?"

"But, Highness, you've recently begun a truce with Philip Augustus. Surely..." Clearing his throat, Robert de Montbegon stood up.

"*Two years*, man. It will last two years, giving me time to prepare. I have not given up on what is lawfully mine, not by any means. What kind of weakling do you take me for?"

Slowly men began to agree with John, although resentment burned in their eyes, and, in the case of Fitzwalter, and a few others like the northerner de Vesci and prideful de Bohun with his tabard of a crowned Swan, pure unadulterated fury. They knew it was hopeless to argue further and might put their positions and livelihoods at risk. John was too unpredictable and too skilled at confiscation and commandeering the lands and wealth of others.

As the enraged buzzing began to die away, weak unenthusiastic voices began to speak up, "It is a 'Yea' from me, my Lord King." "Yea!" "Yea!"

John's dark beard was split by a wide grin. "I knew you would all come to my way of thinking."

"How is this to be managed?" asked Eustace de Vesci, a jowly man with small darting eyes and an air of ill-temper.

"Local Sheriffs will oversee everything, de Vesci, after the justices have made a record of tax owed."

"What if men do not pay?" asked Roger de Lacy, Lord of Pontefract, nervously drumming his fingers on his bench. Tall and dyspeptic in appearance, he looked as if he wished to rush out and spew. "Or those who lie about the value of their lands and goods?"

"Such a faithless miscreant will suffer as he should for his lack of honesty. Imprisonment for a suitable term and his valuables taken for my use."

A brief silence fell and then muttering began again. John cast his gaze about the chamber, seeking for the dissenters, and this time when the grumbling ended, it did not start up again.

Instead, one of the churchmen leapt from his seat and strode toward the King like an avenging angel, his sleeves billowing like wings. It was the Archbishop of York, Geoffrey—John and William's half-brother. "Your Grace—brother—I beg you reconsider. These taxes will cripple the country rather than make it strong. Only I dare tell you the mistake you are making, for the love I bear you, being of one blood."

John gave a dismissive snort. "Love you bear me, indeed. You've been a thorn in everyone's side, Geoff, since the time you could walk. Pay your goddamned taxes, man—you bloody churchmen are not only damn acquisitive, you are tight-fisted too."

"Me...I...well, you..." Geoffrey began to stammer, biting back rage, aware that overt anger could see him cooling his heels in the Tower rather than aiding the oppressed.

In a last-ditch effort, he flung himself down at John's feet, writhing and heaving on the dry rushes in embarrassing supplication. "Brother, please, I beg you." I heard a theatrical sob. "Have mercy on the poor of England, have respect for Mother Church!"

"Respect for the Church—not while you're in it!" John sneered, and to the shock of the assembly, he flung himself down from his seat of estate to crawl about on the floor beside the Archbishop. Cruelly, he mocked Geoffrey's pleading and fawning, wringing his hands and making mock-mournful faces. "Look, my Lord Archbishop!" he laughed. "Even as you do, so do I! Now, get up, you lowly, conniving worm. Go forth, before I confiscate your lands...No, wait, I take that back, whether you leave or I have you thrown out into the winter night, your lands are mine for this day forth."

"You...you cannot!" Geoffrey staggered up, using his crozier like an old man's cane.

"I just did...*brother.*"

Geoffrey's expression changed from shock to pure loathing. "You...you...God will punish you sorely someday. The Pope will hear of this outrage!"

Slouching back into his chair, John pulled a face. "What do I care, the Pope hates me anyway. Trying to stick Stephen Langton in as Archbishop of Canterbury instead of my choice, John de Gray. Absurd! The Crown has always had a say. Pope Innocent tramples on my rights!"

"God may wait till the afterlife to punish you," admonished Geoffrey, "but I assure you, the Pope can bring much grief to you in *this* life."

"Let him try." The King snatched a candied plum from a tray and shoved it indecorously into his mouth.

Geoffrey whirled on his heel and stormed toward the door. "I will leave England," he said. "You've given me no choice. You are a fool if you offend his Holiness in Rome. God help you, John. God help the people you rule over!"

With that final insult, he pushed aside a page bearing a carafe of drink, sending the flagon flying to the flagstones, and then vanished into a torchlit archway, shouting for members of his entourage.

Upon his departure, the chamber erupted into mayhem. John burst out laughing, slapping his thigh with a hand. Leaping up, he grabbed the fallen carafe from the midst of a blood-hued puddle and hurled it after his half-brother. It bounced off a wall and nearly hit the rotund shape of Baron de Cantilupe, causing him to drop his own goblet into his lap. He rose, furious and dripping, and was pulled back to his bench by Roger Bigod, William's step-father. Red-cheeked and puffing, the irascible Cantilupe began waving his fists at Roger, and William leapt angrily from his seat to keep the two men apart.

I could hear thundering feet everywhere. I must leave before I was discovered. Gathering my cloak around me, I raced down the narrow spiral stairs from the gallery to the lower floor. I flung myself into the press of servants and forced my way through their midst until I reached my quarters.

Bursting through the door, I slammed it shut behind me and shot the bolt.

Mabella and Felyse both jumped up, excited. "We could hear the shouting," said Felyse. "Do tell us all about it...if you can, my Lady," she added.

"I dare not," I replied grimly, "but I am sure you will hear about it all soon enough."

William was in a terrible temper. For the first time since I had known him, he was disparaging about his royal brother, "We must return home, Ela. I will have no more of this foolishness—not at present. I tried to calm John, and he threatened me—*me*, who has given him unquestioning loyalty, even when he did not deserve it!"

I dared not tell him I had heard all, had seen the disgraceful scene with the Archbishop of York grovelling on the floor. Quietly, I stood aside as the servants packed, while William shouted ill-naturedly for them to hurry.

Outside, heavy snow had begun to fall. William cursed and called for lanterns to be lit and carried ahead of the party. The bailey was full of other lords readying to depart; at their backs, the keep rose against the fading late afternoon sky, windows glowing like so many watchful eyes. Guards on the parapets were ominous figures in the gloom, crossbows in hand. I shivered, eager to strike out on the road and get back to my daughters, Ida and Petronilla.

The journey was arduous, and the shorter road still impassable. Every now and then, I glanced out of the litter; William rode sullenly alongside, hood up, the snowflakes frosting his head and warm rabbit-fur gloves. The breath of the horses and the guards made huge white clouds in the night.

Shortly after sunrise we reached Salisbury. The castle earthworks lifted like the frosted layers of an enormous subtlety. William's banner, six golden Lions on Azure, beat against the clear blue of the morning sky.

As we entered the Great Chamber, I laid a hand on William's arm. "You are weary; you have ridden through the night. Go and rest; I will have a bath drawn for you when you wake, and bread, cheese and wine laid out."

He shook his head. "No, I would see my children first."

"Let us go to the nursery then."

I went first and he followed me, lowering his hood. He looked drained, his eyes scored by black rings, the stubble on his upper cheeks blue and rough. The nursery was at the base of one of the lower towers, in a sheltered spot out of the constant wind. I had insisted upon the thickest tapestries to line the walls and plaited reed-mats were laid on the floor three-deep to block draughts. A brazier stood by the far wall; the blaze within was never allowed to go out and always had an attendant to quench stray sparks.

Two nursemaids and the wetnurse were within. As we entered, they jumped up, then sank down. "We didn't expect you so soon, my

Lord, my Lady!" one squeaked. "We would have had their little ladyships up and dressed…"

"No need, Tib," I said. "We will not take long."

I walked to the first little bed, draped in gauze. Ida lay asleep, sucking on her thumb. She was a robust, healthy child, her hair curling like her father's. William's breath touched the back of my neck as he craned to look. "Do not wake her," he whispered as I lifted the gauze and touched her soft cheek with my fingertip. "How peacefully she lies…how beautiful she is. Let her sleep as only an innocent child can, unbowed by troubles."

Nodding, I dropped the gauze and turned to the cradle. Baby Petronilla was awake, gurgling faintly, a milky froth on her rosebud lips. Leaning over, I picked her up, so tiny in her long white gown with its embroideries of leaping antelopes and daisies.

William reached out to cup her small head in his hand. "Her hair…it's dark red!" he said.

"She is a Plantagenet," I smiled. "All I have met of that esteemed line have fire in their hair—even you, my love, when the sun shines heavily upon it."

"Yes, a Plantagenet, with all that might entail," said William wearily. He glanced at me. "If the King is wroth with me, I pray he keeps his distance. I would fain stay at Salisbury Castle with my dear wife and my daughters—and forget I am a King's brother. At least for now."

John had gone hunting. First, he spent time in the New Forest, then in Savernake near Marlborough, and he began building a castellated lodge for future use at Odiham. He did not call William to join him, preferring the company of his Chief Forester, Hugh de Neville, several thuggish imports from Normandy, Faulkes de Breaute, Girard d'Athee, and Engelard de Cigogne, the two de Cantilupes, William and his aged father Fulke, and a mixture of barons and knights such as Geoffrey de Lucy, Robert and Ivo de Vieuxpont, and William Brewer.

Overjoyed that William remained at Salisbury, I quickly fell with child again, which pleased me, for it proved my fertility beyond a doubt. Now, if only I could produce the much-needed male heir.

News reached us that Queen Isabella was also with child and that John visited her regularly at Winchester, bearing gifts of gloves and slippers, gowns and cloaks, imported fruits and delicacies to eat. I thought of Hadwisa of Gloucester, sent forth from her former charge, and hoped she was enjoying her newfound freedom in Sherborne.

"So, my brother will have a legitimate child at last," said William. "He's forty, Ela—he has left it rather late in life but such is God's will."

"He should not have wed a twelve-year-old then," I said impudently. We were alone in my chamber with my maids out of the way.

"No, perhaps not, but he needed to rid himself of that horse-faced one, Hadwisa. She was barren."

"That is unkind. She cannot help her lack of beauty. And who knows if she was truly barren? John neglected her from the start."

"Sometimes it is a pity when a man is forced to marry just for lands."

My brows raised. "You pity the man? He at least can take a mistress of his choosing after his marriage. A woman cannot do the same without dreadful repercussions, even if she were wed to a brute or a man old enough to be her grandsire."

William gazed at me curiously. "You are in a fierce mood, my dearest wife, to speak so."

"The blight of my condition shortens my temper. And my back aches." I rubbed the small of my back.

William laid his hand against my belly. "It will be a boy this time, I am sure of it...and he will be so close in age to his royal cousin, they may well play together which could advance his position in years to come."

"It is all about *that*, isn't it?" I said. "Advancing positions. When I was younger, I studied at my father's elbow about the machinations of the court. He said it was like a game of chess."

"Some would say that comparison is apt."

"Once I wanted to move on that board but now…perhaps the matron in me has come to the fore, I merely wish to live in peace, with my children safe and well, not pawns, not pieces on that board."

"With royal blood in their veins, even from an illegitimate union, such a simple life can never be ours. Our children are born to move with the great and good…and the not so good."

I hung my head. "I know, but I cannot deny what my heart says."

Suddenly a knock sounded on the chamber door; sharp, urgent. "I will deal with it." William rose and left the chamber.

I sought to calm myself as his footsteps vanished down the corridor. Many callers came to Salisbury, asking for an audience with the Earl, but in my heart, I felt a sense of prescience. What could John want? Another war, maybe with the Welsh? Another taxation scheme that William must implement? Already the Bishop and monks at the cathedral complained bitterly about the new, punitive laws…

The clatter of the cathedral bells told me an hour had dragged by before William returned. "Is all well?" I asked, but by the expression on his face I could tell it was not.

"The Pope…He has consecrated Stephen Langton despite John's objections."

"The King will be most displeased."

A bitter laugh struggled from his lips. "One could say so. He has declared anyone who agrees with the appointment as an enemy of the Crown. He also sent the Sheriff of Kent, Reginald de Cornhill, to drive the monks of Canterbury into exile for going against his wishes. Sword-bearing soldiers entered their abbey and told them to depart or they'd fire the building with the monks inside."

I gasped in horror. "That is terrible. Sacrilegious. Did the brothers escape?"

"They sailed for Flanders."

I crossed myself. "Thank God that they are safe."

"Yes, a relief, but there is more. The Bishop of Rochester was summoned to excommunicate de Cornhill, his ally Fulke de Cantilupe and any others who participated in assaulting the monks."

"So it should be. It was a wicked act against the Church, even if the King ordered it."

William walked over to the fire, staring into it glassy-eyed. "His Holiness has asked the Bishops of Ely, Worcester and London to go to John—and impress upon him that he *must* accept Langton as Archbishop."

"And if he still does not?" Here...here it was. I felt I stood on the edge of a precipice, ready to fall. The King at loggerheads with the Pope. If he would not bend his stiff neck, repercussions could descend on all, from the meanest peasant to the highest noble.

William's visage was grey. "Then the Pope may well move against John...and place England under interdict."

Bells rang out from the cathedral, a cheerful paean. Happy tidings had reached us from Winchester—a prince was born to King John and Queen Isabella. He was baptised Henry, after his esteemed grandfather.

"So the succession is assured," said William, contented, and he looked at my own rounded belly. It was not long before my time; I was soon due to take to my lying-in chamber. While I stayed to give birth, William would fare to Winchester to pay his respects to the royal babe, and to stand at John's side as he received the three Bishops designated by the Pope.

"Let us pray little Prince Henry is fit and well."

"They say he is robust and feeds vigorously, but also that he does not scream much and lies quiet in his cradle. In that, he is not much like his father." William grinned.

"Or his mother," I added, remembering Isabella's temper, which took the shine off her poppet-like prettiness.

William wrapped his arms around me, drawing me close. "I wish I could stay at Salisbury during your travail."

I shook my head. "Having gone through it twice already, I know you would not enjoy it. I have a loud scream, I am told. And what help would you be, wringing your hands outside the chamber, barred from entering?"

"I would imbibe wine, lots of it. Is that not what most men do when their wives lie in the birthing chamber?"

"Maybe…but you are not as others." Gently, I pushed him towards the door. "It is time for you to go to John. If you become sotted, it will be on the King's wine. Now I must provision my lying-in chamber—things may well become heady in there, too."

At the end of the month, my child was born, another daughter. She was called Ella, after me and my grandmother, Ela of Burgundy. I hated to admit it but I envied the young Queen, her position now unassailable due to little Henry's birth. Still, I should not complain-God had given me a healthy infant, and my travail had not lasted overlong or caused illness or injury.

Christmas came and went—a quiet affair with the lord of the castle away at John's court in Windsor. Proudfoot entertained us as best he could through Twelfth Night, dancing on the tables and riding around the Great Hall on the back of a man dressed as a bear. Once he juggled silver balls and torches, which made the onlookers gasp for they thought he would set the reed-mats alight, but I stopped him when he suggested farting out a song in the manner of old King Henry's much-missed jester. "If you do, Sir Fool," I whispered in his ear, "I will have you trussed, stuffed and laid out on a platter like a pig, with a plum thrust in your mouth."

"You do not let me show my full range of talents, gracious Lady," he pouted.

"You are right. I do not want to see any 'talents', which includes you dropping your hose and waggling your buttocks at the crowd. Lord William may at times find that amusing; I do not, and he is not here. Sing or juggle or turns cartwheels, but behave yourself."

"Will my Lady smack my posterior if I do not?"

"You should be so fortunate, Proudfoot. No, I will get Eubo, the captain of the guard to do it. He has hands like half hams, no sense of humour and he hates both Fools and dwarfs."

"You mock me so, but I will do as you wish, for I am an obedient Imp." He trotted off down the top of the trestle table, singing

"I'm a foolish dwarf, with a hood and a bell,
a foxtail and a bladder, I'll give ye merry hell..."

'Merry Hell' was what I imagined was occurring in the world beyond Salisbury, and as the days crept on and February arrived with rain-washed skies and wan sun sparkling on the half-frozen Avon, I took to watching the roads from the top of the great Keep, waiting to see William's banners approach. Four months had seemed an eternity.

At last, the blessed day came in a fanfare of trumpets. A terrific rainstorm dulled the sound but it was, for me, as if the sun had returned to light the world. "The new babe...it thrives? And you?" William asked once he had been given meat and bread and changed his travel-worn garb for a red wool tunic with fox trim. His voice slurred, the effects of a flagon of spiced wine and exhaustion from the road.

I nodded. "Another girl, but well and hearty, as am I."

"I will see her and my other daughters later when I've rested," he said, slouching in his chair. "I have much to tell you."

"Christmas was not a happy one, I take it."

"The feast at Windsor was lavish...and merry. The King and Queen spared no expense. They brought in the little prince and paraded him around in cloth of gold, a tiny jewelled circlet on his head. But then, the day after Twelfth Night, the Bishops returned with instructions from the Pope. They were wary, for the first time they sought an audience in October, John threatened that if they continued to defy him, he would send them to their master in Rome with eyes put out and noses slit."

I grimaced. "That was not well done. They are men of God, and emissaries as well. Emissaries are surely sacrosanct."

William nodded. "John was angry at first; he felt they had deliberately come to ruin his Christmas and steal joy from the birth of his heir. However, when he heard the Bishops' words, John grew thoughtful, as I have never seen him. He even said he would accept Langton as Archbishop—as long as he had written assurance that the

Pope would never again presume to challenge his royal authority. However, Langton's brother, a certain Master Simon told him bluntly that His Holiness would make no concessions. I thought John would attack the man, but the Marshal held him back and Langton was hurried out of Windsor for his own safety. Before he departed, however, Master Simon looked over his shoulder and spat, 'You have left the Pope no choice, John of England. He has tried to treat with you, believing you a dear son who merely lost his way. Now he will act.'

"Ela, remember how I once spoke of an Interdict."

Feeling suddenly cold and uneasy, I nodded.

"It is not now a matter of *if* there will be an Interdict. Unless God Himself intervenes and softens the heart of either Pope Innocent or John…it is coming."

At the end of March, on a Sunday, the day most sacred to God, the Interdict was proclaimed upon England. Church bells tolled a brief death-knell, then fell eerily silent. The bellringers then bound them tightly in place and climbed down from their towers, heads bowed as if in mourning. The priests followed, grim-faced, locking the church doors behind them.

From the wall top, William and I watched our chaplain take horse and leave the castle. Below the walls, outside the cathedral, Bishop Poore stood on a podium telling a gathered crowd of townsfolk that there would be no Masses said, no Extreme Unction given to the dying, and no confession, other than to those on their deathbed. No dead could be buried in consecrated soil; anyone who died must lie beyond the periphery of the churchyard. A woman wailed, her voice sharp with grief; the wind carried the sound to my ears, pitiful and horrible.

"What have we come to!" I cried. "This is like the end of the world. William, you must go to John and beg him to reconsider his stance! Surely he will listen!"

A small muscle jumped in William's cheek. "He will not. Not on this matter. Besides, he is right, Ela—the Pope has impinged on the Prerogative of the Crown."

Furious, I turned on him, tears streaming down my cheeks. "Right? Look at what has happened. How can you say that it is 'right'? William, you may smite me as you will for saying it, but you...you are nought but John's pawn...and...and his *enforcer*!"

William's face went crimson; for the first time, I saw not the handsome, gentle knight but the Plantagenet scion verging on the feared Plantagenet rage. His hands clenched into fists and for a moment I feared he might strike me for my sharp tongue.

Then he let his hands fall. "Get you gone from me, madam," he said coldly. "Go where you belong, in the nursery tending to our children. Leave the business of men to men!"

I went without a word, drawing my thick cloak about my shoulders. Overheard, the sky loured, bruise-black, oozing rain. The wind screamed; mocking laughter in my ears.

A dark time was upon us.

The King reacted in wrath to the Interdict, and William sought to give him counsel—which I feared was merely agreeing with his brother's furious demands. Together they oversaw the seizure of the clergy's lands throughout the length and breadth of England. Emboldened by the situation, outlaws and ruffians assailed travelling monks, nuns and priests, even on the King's Road, dragging them from their mounts, beating and robbing them or worse. Under duress, John sent out a writ declaring that anyone caught abusing the clergy would be hanged from the nearest oak tree.

That did not stop him from persecuting them himself. Not all priests were as chaste as they claimed; many had mistresses from the local village, often the woman who would was tasked with cleaning the priest's house. The King captured these women and held them prisoner until their embarrassed lovers paid for their freedom. Many priests, too ashamed or too mean to pay the price let their women rot in town gaols.

Surrounded by castle guards, I walked out amongst the folk of Salisbury, giving comfort where I could. One priest's woman, Avis, had been released from prison but then put out by her lover to fend for herself. This tarnished man of God behaved as if the situation was all her fault and none of his. Knowing Avis' history, certain rogues amongst the townsfolk were throwing fruit and muck at her, taking their own frustrations out on the hapless spurned mistress.

"Harlot!" I heard one of the town goodwives screech, and saw a mouldy cabbage strike Avis upon the head, leaving her dripping green slime. "Corruptin' our priest!"

"Aye, filth!" a man shouted from the doorway of a tavern. "She should have a harlot's punishment; let's strip her and make her walk through town with a lighted candle."

Immediately three hefty men, their faces reddened by drink and lust, rushed from the tavern and laid hold of Avis, ripping at the bodice of her dour, stained dress. She screamed and fought the oafs with tooth and nail, while the riled-up townsfolk shouted lewd encouragement to the attackers.

I had seen enough. Beckoning my guards forward, I rode my palfrey straight up the street toward the tangle of bodies ahead. "Halt!" I cried in my sternest tone. "Stop what you are doing. At once!"

The men released Avis and she fled to my side, gasping and crying and splashing cabbage slime.

"What gives you the right to assault this woman?" I glared down at the three men. "You…you're Bartholomew the Baker, aren't you? Why are you attacking helpless females instead of baking your loaves? And you two, Peter Pieman and John the Fletcher. Have you nought better to do?"

"She's a wicked woman," grumbled Bartholomew. "You must've heard, milady. Cavorting with a priest."

"We are all sinners, Bartholomew. Look to your own misdoings before you accuse others. Be off with you…the others too."

Piggy-eyed and bad-tempered, he glowered at me, his ill-shaven jowls trembling in suppressed rage. I wondered how he dared stare with such malice at a woman of my rank and was glad of the men near me with pikes and swords. But it frightened me too as I realised, for the first time, that he saw me as his enemy, both due to my noble birth and my marriage to the King's brother. William supported John, and now the land lay under Interdict while the King plied heavy taxation on all and sundry. For the first time, I felt a pang of fear in those streets I had known since childhood.

"Be off," I repeated, as I tried to keep my voice from trembling, "or I will have you arrested."

"You heard!" barked one of the soldiers next to me, and he thrust his pike in Bartholomew's direction.

The baker flung up his hands, indicating he would go in peace, and backed off, followed by his two lurching cronies. The crowd that had gathered started to disperse, grumbling that I had ruined their 'rough justice'. Avis was kneeling before me, weeping, as she clutched her torn kirtle.

"Get up, girl," I said. "They won't harm you now."

She staggered to her feet, eyes red, nose oozing snot. "They'll come for me later, milady. I've got nowhere to go. Brian…Father Brian, that is, from St Lawrence's, has put me out."

"Yes, I've heard. You were gaoled already for his sin."

"He had to give up some church plate to get me freed. That made him ever so angry. He called me a stupid cow, and said I should have lied better or run faster when the King's men came sniffing around asking questions."

I noticed she had a blackened and swollen left eye. "Did he do that?"

Dumbly she nodded, and the tears started in earnest. "He was so angry, milady, I can't ever go back. I'd get no mercy. My family won't have me back either, after all the scandal. They're in Durnford anyhow. I can't even walk there to beg 'em…" She pointed to her bare feet, brown with mud and dung.

"Why are you unshod, girl?"

"Brian took my shoes," she said plaintively. "He said he'd paid for them, so he was taking 'em back as I didn't deserve 'em anymore."

"My Lady Countess." The captain of the guards spoke, low and urgent. "The light fails, and I would rather you were back inside the castle bailey before full darkness."

I opened my mouth to tell him that I had no fear of being out beyond dark, but then I noticed that some of the less-savoury townsfolk had returned. They hovered in the alleys and behind buildings like the rats that scuttled from house to gutter to wall. Their movements were furtive, their expressions unfriendly, even hostile. I felt as if I had entered a new, strange, dangerous world.

"Avis, come with me." I gestured for the girl to follow. "You may stay the night in the castle stables and then I will send you to the nuns at Amesbury. Maybe you can find work as a laundress there."

Avis looked happier at this, and I guided my horse around to face the castle, motioning for my men to gather close. Holding my head high, I retreated down the street with Avis stumbling along behind with her bare feet slapping in the mud.

Up ahead, the street veered to the left, running toward the bridge that spanned the dry moat towards the stony security of the gatehouse. Suddenly a cart rolled across the thoroughfare, blocking our passage. An offensive odour emanated from it, making my eyes water and bile rise in my throat. Next to me, Avis started choking and gagging, her grimy hand pressed over her mouth. My guards looked grim.

"Get out of the way!" the captain threatened, striding toward the carter, a grizzled old man in a peaked grey hat with a long beard dangling almost to his waist. I did not recognise him as a local. "Make way for the Countess Ela of Salisbury!"

The old man hawked disrespectfully on the ground. "I've come to take the burdens from the town afore the pestilence comes. I reckon you should all stand back from my cart now, and let me go about my business, for important business it is."

"What are you on about, man?" cried the guard, exasperated.

And then, shifting forward in my saddle, I beheld the load he carried. A dozen dead bodies sewn into rough shrouds lay stacked in the back of the cart. Some were tiny—small children.

Frantically I beckoned to the guards. "Let...let him pass!" I stammered.

The man tipped his hat to me, though in a mocking fashion. "I see you've sussed what I carry, milady. I'm the only one that will care for these poor souls now that the priests can't. I'll even say a little prayer of my own over 'em when I tip 'em into a pit out in the fields, for all the good it'll do." Reaching back, he grabbed one of the tiny shrouded shapes, dandled it on his knee. "This one was fresh this morning, but the others aren't smellin' so sweet."

"Do what you must; just go from the town!" I cried, horrified, and with a spluttering laugh, he cracked a whip over his horse's matted piebald rump and trotted away toward the main gate and the road beyond.

"Should I go after him and make an arrest, Countess?" The captain turned to me, hand on his sword hilt.

"No…no…Just let him go," I said, breathless, the horrible corpse-stench still hanging in the air, a sickly sweetness that turned the gut and clogged the throat. "It needs to be done; he does not lie about that."

I plied my heels to my palfrey's flanks and galloped pell-mell for the bridge, leaving Avis to wander up with the guards. Inside the safety of the fortress, I flung off my clothes and ordered them burnt—the stink of death clung to every fibre. Then, doused in rosewater, I rushed to the nursery, to Ida, Petronilla, and Ella. I wept as I thought of that small child, scarcely bigger than Ida, who had lain in the cart, waiting to be discarded like old rubbish, thrown into a pit in unconsecrated ground.

I wept too because I knew the horrible truth; for all my family connections to Salisbury, for all the care I had given, the locals saw me merely as William's wife, and hence tied to their hated oppressor, the King.

In their eyes, I was part of the evil destroying their lives…

Under Interdict, the people may have come to hate us due to strictures and taxation, but it was not only the common man who suffered in John's blighted England. William returned from his brother's court deeply troubled once again. I kept silent as he unburdened his heart, for I did not want us to fall into arguing again. I merely sat and listened as a good wife was meant to do.

"The King had grown fearful and suspicious of even his own supporters," William murmured. "He has been demanding hostages as a surety. Children, mostly."

My spine prickled with fear. Now I felt obligated to speak, as I thought of my three girls. "Children! William, be straight with me—he has not asked for any of ours, has he?"

William glanced over, expression as horrified as my own. "Ours? No, of course not; they are his nieces. He—he would never…" His voice trailed away as if in doubt. Standing, he began to pace the room. The hounds whined and slunk away into the corner, feeling his unease. Outside, the wind rattled the wooden shutters as if it was a living thing, seeking entry.

"It is Matilda de Braose, Ela. The wife of William de Braose."

I had heard of the de Braose family. They were notorious. William was a harsh man holding many castles in Wales and Ireland, such as Hay, Brecknock, Painscastle and Limerick. The Welsh called him the Ogre of Abergavenny, after he invited the nobleman Seisyll and his followers to a Christmas feast—then slaughtered them all, including a seven-year-old boy. His wife, Matilda de St Valerie, had inspired myths on the Welsh border—she was known as 'Moll of the Night', a wicked giantess who carried stones in her apron to build fortresses along the border of the Debatable Lands. Matilda was an outspoken woman, mother to sixteen children, but like her husband, she was disagreeable and always ready for a fight.

"What has she done? Started a Welsh rebellion with her tongue?"

He cast me a look that said my attempt at levity had failed.

"William de Braose was at Falaise when Arthur of Brittany *disappeared*," said William. "He knows the truth. She knows."

"Surely John already is aware of that."

"Yes, he is all too aware, but recently he has become mistrustful of de Braose, as well he might. He asked for a few children from the de Braose brood as hostages, but it was Matilda who answered the King's messenger. She told him before a packed hall, "I will never surrender any of my children to John. He murdered Arthur, who should have been treated with honour."

My breath hissed through my teeth in astonishment.

"William de Braose tried to soothe John by saying that Matilda was nought but a foolish, hot-headed woman, but to no avail. The royal messenger heard. Others heard. What many had suspected was now out in the open. Rumours raged around the court like fire in furze during a hot summer. The King was…most displeased."

William knelt and took my hands. "Ela, my dearest wife, I ask you one thing—remember, remember, never let your tongue slip on the matter of Arthur. If there is one thing I ask that must be obeyed, this is it."

"I will remember…and never once have I come close to speaking of it to anyone. I am not perfect, only Christ and the Virgin are so—but a fool and a gossip I am not."

"Ela, I was sharp with you not so long ago. When you called me John's enforcer."

"It is forgotten; it was your right to show offence in your own home."

"A home I have only through my marriage to you. I am not a fool, Ela. Deep inside, I'm aware I am but a bastard parading in the shadow of a Prince. A Prince who can be capricious and cruel…but who I still love as a brother, as strange as that might sound. He always had time for me, despite the difference in our ages—look how different it is between John and Geoffrey. Geoffrey still languishes in exile!"

Dropping my hands, he began to pace again. "But I am afraid, this time, Ela. There is talk that the Pope plans to excommunicate John next. The thought has made him crazed, along with all the talk of rebellion among the barons. When Matilda de Braose spoke brazenly of Arthur…he will never forget or forgive her folly. De Braose and Matilda have fled England, but John will hunt that family down…"

In my mind's eye, I saw myself fleeing with my children to an unknown destination. One moment you could ride high on the Wheel of Fate, the next moment Lady Fortune could send you crashing down.

"Is there nothing of the gentle arts that ever pleases John?" I asked plaintively. "Save hunting and hawking, he seems to think of nought but taxation and war."

"He is eaten up with jealousy of Richard, even though our brother is long dead. He cannot bear that he has lost his ancestral lands in France. It is true—music does not please him, jesters do not make him laugh—he likes to play the Fool, but not be laughed at himself—he cannot dance and most games bore him. Occasionally he plays chess with me when he is in the mood, but only me…"

"Why is that?" My eyebrows lifted.

"I always let him win, then tell him how brilliant his strategy was compared to mine." William laughed wryly. "I usually could have beaten him…but it's just a game."

"I thought fatherhood might have mellowed him—he has two little sons now, Henry and Richard." After producing the heir, Queen Isabella swiftly produced a second boy, whose birth would ensure the succession, barring a terrible misfortune.

"It has made him *worse*. He is even more determined to reclaim his supposed birthright to pass onto his eldest son. It eats at him far more than the thought of the Interdict."

"Does he have no care for his immortal soul?"

He sighed. "Not much. I think he enjoys the freedoms he has now, the money that comes rolling in…"

"All stolen or extorted!" I shot back, then put my hand to my mouth. "Forgive me, I should be listening, not assailing you with my loose tongue. You said it before—I should leave the matter of men to…"

William looked rueful. "I was over-harsh. You spoke only truth, and perhaps, sometimes, I need to hear that. Even condemnation, when I do wrong in your eyes. After all, although John is my brother and I am loyal…I do not, in any way, want to *become* my brother."

We rose, with Fortuna the hound trotting at our heels, and went out into the bailey. The light was failing in the west and heavy clouds looming in the north. Standing on the high wall overlooking the town, we gazed down at the darkling streets and the slow, trudging workers on their way home. The cathedral lay enshrouded, its walls painted a pallid unhealthy blue by the dusk. Bats sailed from the tower towards a lonely tree. It seemed no longer a place of God but a place of desolation, its doors barred while the Bishop sat with guards around his palace.

"It is like the words written in Luke," I said, as both the sharp evening wind and sorrow made my eyes damp. "*Every kingdom divided against itself is brought to desolation; and a house divided against a house falleth."*

"Better days will come." William's hand sought mine. I slid into his embrace, wrapped in his warm woollen cloak with its fragrance of dog, horses and frankincense

We retired to our chamber, where the servants had changed the linens, beaten the hangings, set out tall pale candles and decked the rafters with bags of sweet-smelling herbs. The fire blazed and on an oak table sat a flagon of sweet dark wine, alongside marchpane and savoury fancies. But it was not food or drink either of us wanted, but the solace and comfort of each other's arms and lips and bodies…

In September, William was summoned to Marlborough by the King. John feared that with the Pope threatening excommunication as his next step, his subjects might lose their loyalty to the crown and openly revolt. He desired avowals of faithfulness not only from the barons and knights, but also merchants, tradesmen, and poor men. All men aged fifteen and upwards were required to present themselves at Marlborough castle to swear fealty to John and to the little Prince Henry.

"You must come with me too, Ela," said William upon his return. "All the great magnates and their wives will be there…and the Queen."

"She has a dislike of me. Her presence is not much of a commendation."

"She has…matured. A little. But if nothing more, I want you with me because I can spend so little time with you here. Once again I will be required to serve my liege in battle…soon."

"I will go." Gratefully, he took my hand and raised it to his lips.

Marlborough was thronged with thousands of incomers waiting to swear their Oath at the King's bidding. As my chariot navigated its way through the town, I was astonished by the size of the crowds; never had I seen so many folk gathered in one place. They spilt out over the road, a mass of men, women, children, some on horseback, others herding animals; they lurched from a score of inns and taverns; they filled the churchyards of St Mary's near the Green, St Peter's by the castle gate, and the little Hospital of St John. An air of both fear and festival clung to the mob, as mounted soldiers in the King's livery patrolled the streets to keep the crowd in check. Banners streamed and flags flew, and all the tanners, pewtersmiths, burel-weavers and other tradesmen had shut up shop and were instead hanging from the windows of their houses to get a better view of the activity.

Looking from the carriage, I saw William on his bay stallion, forcing a way through the press. He looked displeased, especially when the people pushed in, trying to touch his mount and his fine spurs. Nodding curtly to his men, they used the butts of their spears to break up the crush, making a safe path for my chariot to pass. Boos and catcalls of anger filled the air; a man fell, almost under the wheels of the carriage; his wife screamed and hauled him away over the filthy cobbles. Inflamed by that minor incident, other men began to fight in the road, one slamming an elbow into the face of a man standing too close to him, another lunging at a scruffy, snub-nosed lad while he bellowed, "Pickpocket! Pickpocket!"

Now our guards held their spears in a more threatening position, tips glinting in the sunlight. Gripping my sleeve in fright, Felyse squeaked, "Close the curtain, my Lady, please—if these rogues see that we are women…"

"It is too late," I told her, "they are already well aware who we are. Be brave, the Earl is the King's own blood—they would not dare touch him or his." I hoped my words were true. What if, aggrieved by John's endless taxation, these men who had walked for miles, leaving businesses untended, facing illness and danger on the road, ended up rioting against his demands?

Fortunately, the crowds began to part as the King's soldiers closed in, driving them up to the porches of the nearby houses and shops. The church of St Peter's, used by the castle staff, rose on our right, the four pinnacles of its tower dim against the bright sky. The castle gate gaped open before us, archers on top in formation with bows ready to pick off any trouble-makers.

Felyse and I both breathed a sigh of relief as we passed into the inner bailey. The Castle motte was not as wide as the earthworks that supported Salisbury, and had none of its vast defensive ditches, but it was steeper in height and strangely conical—the locals claimed that Merlin had thrown it up in a single night and that he lay buried inside in a golden coffin. A shell keep built by King Henry stood on the summit, like a jagged crown on the brow of a slumbering king. The royal standard fluttered above the gateway, which was reached by a short wooden bridge. Below, clustered at the mound's foot were the royal apartments, the Great Hall, the chapel, the storehouses, mews, stables and kennels. The latter three buildings were large and busy with falconers, grooms, ostlers and dog-handlers; John loved his hunting and no doubt had been out riding in the nearby Forest of Savernake before our arrival.

The Castellan came to greet William with all the niceties due to an Earl; he had servants take me and Felyse to our quarters, situated alongside those of the highest dignitaries. The din of all the newcomers was exceptional—soldiers shouting, dogs barking, horses neighing, horns blowing.

Tutting, Felyse closed our window-shutter against the row. "I hope we shall get some sleep in here tonight!" she complained. "The noise! My head is pounding already! And it's too hot!"

I doubted I would sleep a wink, but not because of the uproar. Tomorrow I would have to face the King again; a man I had never liked, and now had grown to loathe.

Overnight a vast pavilion had bloomed in the centre of the bailey, its roof red-and-white-striped, its flanks painted with images of the Virgin in cerulean blue. The door flaps bore the Lions of England, ruby-eyed, roaring as they clawed a crimson sea.

Due to his close blood-tie to the King, William was permitted to swear his oath amongst the first of the barons. Although I, as a woman, did not need to swear, I was encouraged to do so due to my own high position.

Inside the tent, we walked stiffly upon a red silk ribbon imported all the way from Syria. This wended its way up and over a wooden dais. John was sitting on a handsome gilded throne wearing crown and ermine. He looked podgier than I remembered and great pouches hung under his eyes. Next to him, on a minute replica of his throne, sat little Prince Henry, aged nearly two, an apple-cheeked boy with golden curls held back by a jewelled coronet, and one eye on which the lid drooped slightly, giving him a perpetual sleepy look. John had a similar flaw, although his defect was far less prominent; it was clear to all whose son this was, even if they differed in other ways.

John's eyes, always hot and glittering, landed on William, then trailed to me, lingering long. "My dear brother…and my best-beloved sister by marriage," he said, with exaggerated sweetness.

"My liege." William bowed before him. I sank in a curtseyed remained there, as John beckoned William forward. "Yes, swear to me, and to the boy…your nephew. Kneel down before me, and declare that you are my man forever."

A small gasp escaped my lips; I had expected an oath of fealty, in which William would declare fidelity to the crown, but what John was insisting upon was homage, a much firmer bond, harder to break.

Head held high, William walked over and knelt, while John took his hands in his own. "I become your man from this day forward, of life and limb, and earthly worship," William recited in ringing tones, "and unto you shall be true and faithful, and bear to you faith for the lands that I claim to hold of you."

John bent and kissed his brow. "Now, swear fealty to my son."

William smiled at the solemn little boy, who was swinging a foot in a bejewelled shoe that did not quite touch the ground. A Bishop shuffled over and handed William a Bible heavily bound in leather and gold. He set his hand upon it and said, "'Know ye this, my lord, that I shall be faithful and true unto you, and faith to you shall bear that I shall lawfully do to you the customs and services which I ought to do, so help me God and his Saints."

Prince Henry inclined his head slightly, and the Bishop carried the Bible away.

"Now you, Lady Ela, my dear," said John. I rose from my curtsey and approached him slowly, sinking onto my knees with thundering heart.

His hands encompassed mine; hairy and strong, easily able to snap my fingers like twigs if he should so choose. Instead, his small finger traced a circle on my palm, making me blush in embarrassment. A bead of sweat ran down the back of my neck, hidden by my wimple.

John grinned down at me, enjoying my discomfiture. "You know the words, I take it? You do not have to say 'I become your woman,' because that would take on a very different meaning, would it not? *Very* different. I might enjoy it, and who knows, you might too, but I dare say Will would be most put out."

"Your Grace, I—I know the words," I stammered. "I do to you homage, and to you shall be faithful and true, and faith to you shall bear for the tenements I hold of you."

"Ah, what sincere eyes you have, Lady Ela." He leaned closer, his hands clamping down on mine, making them completely immobile. "Beautiful eyes." His face was now mere inches from mine. The springy hair of his dark beard, bearing its first grey flecks, brushed my cheek. His lips, slug-like, touched flesh, and I strove to keep from shuddering.

Then I was free and he was gesturing to the Prince, who had begun to fidget on his uncomfortable chair. Quickly I swore fealty to the little boy and then stood aside as John spoke to William. "It's going to be a long day, Will. Bad enough having to receive the wealthy with their half-hearted vows, but all the freemen too. Did you see them all in the street? There must be thousands! Pah, the place is going to stink like a pigsty by the time I get done. And it's going to take days to get through them all. I suppose they'd riot if I changed my mind…"

"Your Grace, I would not advise changing..."

John flapped his hand. "I know, I know. I spoke in jest. I summoned them here, therefore I must meet with them all. It will go down in the annals of history as a great show of the power of the Crown." He took a deep breath, made a face. "Three days…three days. Dally here if you would with dear Ela, and then we shall go hunting in Savernake. I long to get back out there—I spied a huge buck last week, but he eluded me, damn him. You and I, between us we will bring him in for the table!"

When the freemen of England had finally filtered out of Marlborough, the King and a party of his favourite barons and courtiers went out upon the hunt, as planned. Felyse and I walked in the castle gardens. The leaves on the trees were on the change, tipped with gold and red. Large lavender bushes still bore faded purple flowers and a trace of scent. The summer roses were wizened buds, mouldy and unsightly in Autumn's approach. I thought sadly of Hadwisa who had wed John here long ago, a marriage neither of them desired. Perchance, life would turn kinder to her now that she dwelt in Sherborne…

"My Lady…" Felyse's voice buzzed in my ear.

Turning, I saw the Queen drifting through the flowerbeds, her maidens fluttering like butterflies around her. Isabella had matured since we met at Oxford, her face slimmer and less petulant, though her lips held a perennial little pout. She was dressed in a long overgown of pale rose-pink; beneath it rustled cream-hued silk. Both layers were encrusted with pearls. She wore a white barbet and golden fillet, and her hair was contained in a bejewelled *crespine*.

"Your Grace," I dropped a curtsey.

"Countess Ela…it is a long time since we met."

"Yes, your Grace," I murmured.

"And I was rude to you."

I bit my lip against a burst of nervous laughter. "No, your Grace," I managed.

"You do not have to lie; I know what I was. I behaved like a bad-tempered child, because that's what I was at the time. A child seeking to find her place in a distant land—a crowned Queen but one with no lands, no power, kept out of sight, and housed with a woman who loathed her."

"I truly do not think the Lady Hadwisa loathed you,"

"I do…and she had every right to. John treated her appallingly and so did I." She gestured me into an arbour by a little pond. "I have done my duty to John; I have provided him with two sons. I am much younger than the King, as you know—mayhap one day I shall be free to wed again where I will, and it will all be different."

I must have looked shocked by her frankness for she laughed. "Have no fear—I will not poison my husband for all that some might thank me." Mercifully, she changed the subject. "You two have children I fear."

"Three. All girls, alas."

"Do not be sad. There will be more—you are young yet, as you once told me," she said with a tiny hint of malice.

"Yes...and if not, one shall inherit Salisbury even as I did, and her husband shall become Earl in Right of His Wife."

The Queen called a servant over, ordering him to bring spiced wine, wafers and marchpane cakes. "How is Salisbury...with the Interdict in place?"

"The people grieve, your Grace, as you might expect. The dead are being buried in fields like pagans, and some are not buried at all. Can you not speak with the King..." I glanced hopefully at her white, oval face. Queens were expected to intercede with their husbands when harsh punishment had been meted out.

"He'd never listen to a word I say. He thinks I am a ninny. He did not marry me for my intellect, Ela, although I am much cleverer than he thinks." The wine arrived, poured into two golden goblets; we both drank. "I can tell you this, though—John plans to ride from here to Chilham Castle in Kent. He is expecting the arrival of Stephen Langton."

"Langton!" The man the Pope wanted as Archbishop; the man John scorned mainly because he had not chosen him. "Do you think his Grace is ready to come to terms? That he will accept the Pope's chosen?"

"No!" She shook her head. "John may surprise us all, but I doubt it. He will accept Langton only if His Holiness agrees never to meddle in England's affairs again, and that is unlikely to happen. What *may* happen, I fear, is that John might be excommunicated. You may have heard talk of it already."

I nodded; the wine in my mouth tasted sour. "Surely, that threat might move his Grace. To be so cut off from God..."

"My husband is hardly a religious man, Lady Ela. He is unafraid. Like you, I believe he should tremble before the wrath of the Lord and attempt to make amends. But he is what he is."

We talked for a long time until at last we heard the horns of the incoming hunting party. "I must go," said Isabella, "John will demand I attend him after his hunt; he likes me to bathe him alone. Does that shock you? Scrubbing his back like a servant!" She laughed. "It makes him amorous; well, better his lawful wife than a concubine. John's eyes turn too often to pretty women. It is one reason why Robert Fitzwalter's loyalty is always in question—John outraged his daughter Matilda, or so 'tis said. He cares not if a woman is of high status or if she is married…"

She gave me a long look. Was she warning me of the King's intentions? Sick to my stomach, I recalled how he'd held my hands when I paid him homage, how his thick lips had trailed across my cheek…

The Queen was rising, motioning for her ladies-in-waiting. "Farewell for now. I am glad we have spoken. From now on, we can be as two sisters married to two brothers, as it should be, with the past forgotten."

She disappeared back into the castle. Overhead, clouds had gathered; drizzle fell, fine as a lady's veil. "My Lady, the Queen is your friend now," gushed Felyse, overawed at being in such close proximity to royalty.

"I do not know if you can call her that," I said, "but praise God, at least she is not an enemy. And she has given valuable information about what the future may hold."

Felyse looked as though she was fit to burst with curiosity and excitement. But I dared not tell her anything—not only would it be trite gossip, but there was no joy in what I'd learnt.

Unless John had a rapid change of heart and negotiated with Langton and the Pope, soon he would be excommunicated.

A land under Interdict, where the dead lay unburied, rotting; an uncaring King, head of a Christian country, denied the sacraments and the Eucharist.

Shivering, I drew my cloak about my shoulders and hurried for the warmth of the castle.

CHAPTER FOURTEEN

All happened exactly as the Queen had guessed. Firm in resolve, Langton arrived at Dover, telling John no compromises would be made. John arrogantly told him to go to France or to Hell, whichever he preferred. Langton left upon the next tide.

A month later, the King was excommunicated.

It was now near Christmas, and William was ready to leave for John's court at Windsor. I wondered how he might feel about his brother's change of circumstances but he told me, as ever, "I must support him, Ela, although he has done wrong. No man is all evil; John just…does not appreciate the seriousness of his actions. This new folly of his could mean war with the barons; some think the Oath of Fealty is invalid when given to an Excommunicate. He needs me to help placate those who hate him."

"I wish I could journey to Windsor with you," I said. My hands travelled down to my belly. Shortly after Marlborough, I realised I was with child for the fourth time. This may not have stopped my travels but the sickness I had with Ida attacked me again, and much of my time was spent with my head hanging over a foul privy while Mabella and Felyse fussed about, holding back my hair and dabbing my hot face with scented water.

"It is best if you stay here," said William. "Who knows what the actions of the barons will be? I have heard what men whisper that John fears neither God nor man. That might make a few hotheads think it their duty to make him afraid, or even bring him low."

"Depose him?" I said quietly

William toyed with one of his rings; a lion was graven upon the bezel. "It could come to it. The Pope is in a position to declare him deposed. Would the lords of England agree with the Holy Father? Who can tell in these evil times?"

He leaned over and kissed me thrice—once on the brow, once on the cheek and once lightly on the lips, and then he was descending the spiralled stair from the keep, his boots clattering on stone. I watched him from a high window as he strode across the bailey, past the lightless chapel with its barred door, to join with his waiting entourage, their blue surcoats bright against the grey of the wintry world.

I dared not dwell the dangers of John's court for too long. I was the Lady of Salisbury and must put on a brave face in this wretched winter where Christmas would not truly be Christmas and the church bells would not ring.

The next I heard of William, he had crossed the sea to Ireland with John. They were engaged in a hunt—an awful hunt, because it was not beasts of field and forest they hunted, but men and women. John had decided to take his revenge on William de Braose and his sharp-tongued wife, Matilda, who had dared mention the fate of Arthur of Brittany. John had arrived at Carrickfergus, a great Irish stronghold where they had sheltered, but when the garrison capitulated after a short siege, de Braose and Matilda were gone. It was as though they had been spirited away by witchcraft. However, spies soon brought word that they had fled by boat to Man, and so the hunt went on.

It ended for the fleeing family in Galloway. De Braose and one son, Reginald, broke away from the others and hastened for France; Matilda, her daughter Annora, her eldest son William and William's children were captured. Matilda offered money to John and so did her husband, but the ransom was too high—truly a King's ransom, enough to run England for a year. Showing a trace of her old fire, Matilda had supposedly told John, "Then I will pay nothing of this fine. I have only twenty coins of gold, twenty-four silver, and fifteen ounces of gold. If that will not suffice, I must remain your prisoner…"

John agreed that she would indeed remain a prisoner and that the elder de Braose, skulking like a rat in France, was now declared a wolfshead in every shire in England, so that if he dared return, a handsome price would lie upon his head. Matilda and her son William were moved from Bristol to Corfe—famous for its deep oubliette, a lightless dungeon steep-sided and pitch-black. It was where John had starved the captive French knights to death.

In early June, I went into confinement for the fourth time, with Mother attending. I had worried throughout my pregnancy that if my child did not survive birth, it could not be baptised and hence would go to Purgatory or even Hell—a fearful mother's fancy, but one born from the terrible situation throughout England. Although priests could still perform the rite of Baptism, there was much worry that the oil used in the ceremony would run out, since the priest was no longer permitted to consecrate new oil on Maundy Thursday. However, the priests had taken to mixing old oils with the Chrism, so the souls of babes were safe after all...

The birth was harder and longer than my last three, made even more unbearable by the sweltering summer heat. I was given an appalling mixture of vinegar and honey to drink while Felyse rubbed my thighs with rose oil. Mama had brought a silver girdle said to have belonged to a saint and dutifully fastened it around my huge middle, praying for a safe delivery all the while.

Still, the baby seemed reluctant to emerge. I tossed, groaning with pain, biting down on a stick when told to do so. Sweat rolled off my brow and the world became a blur, and fear of my own demise overcame me, making me weep.

"The sard...we have forgotten the sard!" cried Mama, panicking and staring wildly around the birthing chamber.

"Bear down." The midwife ignored her, holding my shoulders in a tight grip. "Breathe...and push..."

"I-I have no more strength to push!" I wailed, writhing in pain.

Mother ran back to my side after rummaging in her jewellery chest. In her hand, she held a polished sard stone, streaked red and white. She rubbed it vigorously on my belly, murmuring an old chant, "*Open you roads and door, in that epiphany by which Christ appeared both human and God, and opened the gates of Hell. Just so, child, may you also come out of this door without dying, and without the death of your mother.*"

"Push!" the midwife ordered. "And again."

Mama was rubbing me with the sard as if it was a slab of Castilian soap. I was still wailing and writhing.

"Push, *push*!" the midwife's command came again, sharp, insistent. "We are nearly there. Nearly..."

I gave one more push and the midwife cried, "The head...I see the head!" Mother leapt back, the sard clutched in her sweaty fist.

A few minutes later the babe, blue and purple from my troubles, slid into the mortal world, and almost immediately set up a robust yelling.

"God be praised!" cried Mama triumphantly. "I knew the sard would do the job."

The midwife, still working vigorously, pursed her lips.

I struggled to sit, my hair hanging haphazardly over my soaked face. "Is it…is it…"

"The babe is well, and strong, as you can hear," said the midwife.

"No, I need to know…"

The woman turned back towards me; she had just hurled the cord that had bound me to the infant into the brazier. Felyse and Mabella ran about the chamber, showering flower petals to disguise the acrid scent. "My Lady, it is good news—you have a son."

"A son!" cried Mama and she burst into heaving, joyous sobs.

"Bring him to me!" I ordered. The midwife carried the baby over and laid him in my arms, red and wriggling. He had a large head and pressed down reddish-brown curls. "Truly his father's son," I murmured. "He will, of course, be named William, both his sire's name and the name of my own sire, God rest his soul."

I stared at the baby's face, screwed up with bawling, unlovely as all babies are, except to their mothers.

William Longespee II, heir to the Earldom of Salisbury.

Never was a man happier than the Earl when he returned home and gazed upon his new son, now carefully swaddled, milky-lipped from nursing and content in my arms. Taking him from me, he held him awkwardly, as if he feared he might break him with his great strength. "At last," he breathed. "God be praised that we have a healthy boy."

"Yes, God be praised," I said. "At one point, I almost despaired of bringing him into the world, but thanks to the Blessed Virgin and St Margaret, he is here and so am I."

"I have brought gifts for you and for the babe, from me and from John and Isabella." He called for his page, who carried in an oaken box. Inside lay a golden chalice with emeralds set amidst carved leaves on the rim; sheaves of white silk, carefully folded; a blue hood with gold trim; a broidered gown for the babe, stitched by the Queen's own hand. All fine, worthy items…yet I almost hated to touch the goblet, John's personal gift. A poisoned chalice? I could not forget Arthur of Brittany, John's nephew even as our little son.

Handing the babe back to his waiting wetnurse, William and I went to the gardens in the lee of the keep. It was September and the sun, although losing warmth as the winter months approached, felt delicious upon our faces and shoulders. That's when he told me the final chapter in the unhappy saga of Matilda de Braose.

"She is dead," he said quietly. "I thought it best to tell you before rumours reached Salisbury. "Dead of starvation at Corfe. Her son too."

Overcome with horror, I could only stare, mouth open.

"Eleven days they were without food…I did not know, Ela, believe me. I had heard they were to have a flitch of bacon or gruel. When they were found, the dead son was propped up against the dungeon wall with Maude crouched between his legs. In her agony, she…she…'" He faltered and turned away, grimacing in revulsion

"What? What had that poor woman done?"

"She…she was overcome; she must have gone mad. In desperation, she…she *ate* the flesh of her son's cheeks."

The world spun, towers and crenels and walls and the yellow eye of the sun. I retched. Such wickedness, such cruelty—and the King who decreed it was uncle to my four small babes?

William knew what lay in my mind, and grasped my shoulders, his face bone-white. "He will never harm them, Ela. Or make them hostages. I swear it—I-I would stop him first, no matter what it took."

I wanted to believe him, but the King had shown his true character. Arthur—some forgave John because the boy had risen against him repeatedly. The French prisoners—it was against convention, but such things happened in war, and they were grown men and hardened warriors. But Matilda de Braose? She was a woman and that line had never before been crossed by an English King; effectively, John had murdered her without trial and without charge.

William's brother, our liege lord, the anointed King of England was now a true tyrant, whose dark face with its too-red lips and mocking grin would haunt my dreams.

Spring. William was gone. This time, in his absence, all changed for me. I refused to dwell overmuch on the world beyond the strong castle walls. I tended my small children, revelled in the garden, prayed to God, who I hoped still listened to those placed under Interdict through no fault of their own. In this time, I found my faith grew, a comfort in the lonely nights when fear clasped my heart—fear for my children's future, for William's safety. Fear of the malice of John.

Trickles of outside news filtered through, though, horrible and disturbing. John confiscated the financial records of the Jews, accusing them of withholding sums of money for the past three years. Demanding payment, he allowed his mercenaries to wreak havoc on their communities. One Jew in Bristol had his teeth torn out with pincers, one by one. Another, in Canterbury, was hanged. Many fled England, unable to pay the punitive fines.

John also harassed the brothers of the Cistercian order, who had once denied him aid. Several monasteries closed, the brothers fleeing into the wilds. Men claimed to have seen them alongside the Jews, begging for food in town and village.

Angry risings began in Wales, instigated by John's son-in-law, Llewellyn. John hastily allied himself with several Welsh princes to bring him down. William rode with the King's forces, marching from Chester followed by great wains packed with weapons and siege engines. However, the host ended up dining on horse-meat when supplies ran low. John retreated over the Welsh border and William returned to Salisbury for a few blissful weeks.

"He has not given up," he told me, as we lay abed the night before he was set to depart again. "He cannot afford to; his hold on the country is precarious. He must be seen as a victor."

"But…he can he afford to replace the men and engines he lost in Wales?"

William shrugged and rolled away, not wanting to discuss it further.

Yes, I thought in the dark, pressed against William's side, his heartbeat loud in my ears…*after all, he can assault monks and Jews to get more money for his wars…*

So William went to Wales for the next phase of the King's incursions, and I continued in my daily tasks, as much as I was able, for I was with child again. My fifth! William and I were certainly obeying the Bible's command '*Be fruitful and multiply!*'

In Wales, John burnt Bangor, dragging the bishop from his own cathedral to be thrown down on the roadside in shame. Joanna, John's daughter intervened, and after fraught negotiations, Prince Llewelyn submitted to John and made terms that spared his life. Faulkes de Breaute, that hard-visaged mercenary, ploughed on into Wales, defeating the native Princes Owain and Rhys in a pitched battle. He built a louring castle at Aberystwyth to cement the English victory.

The Pope, through the subdeacon Pandulf and the Templar Durand, tried to treat with the King again, but flush with his Welsh victory, John was gloating and insufferable. "Why should I accept any peace between the Pope and myself!" he shouted during a council held at Northampton. "My nephew Otto has been excommunicated and also Raymond of Toulouse, my brother by marriage. And yet we all flourish on the field of battle and our enemies tremble—does that sound like God is angry with us? Begone, with your threats to my kingship, before my good temper runs out!"

John's temper ran out in truth when Wales, always ready to erupt into rebellion, refused to remain under his harsh rule. The King's new castles there were sacked, their garrisons put to the sword or hanged.

But there was retaliation. One of John's favourites, Robert de Vieuxpont, angered at being besieged in his new castle, decided to hang a hostage he had taken—a boy of only seven years.

Still fuming at his own ruined castles, John noted de Vieuxpont's response to the Welsh rebels with interest. Then, retreating to the royal fortress of Nottingham, perched like a giant on a hill honey-combed with ancient caves, he promptly brought forth all the hostages Llewellyn had given him as a surety for his good behaviour. They were unaware of why they had been summoned, laughing nervously as the guards encircled them. Among them were beardless youths and young boys of seven and eight.

One by one these Welsh prisoners were taken out onto the walls of Nottingham Castle.

And one by one they were hung.

William's stint in the tinderbox that was Wales ended around the time I gave birth to another hearty daughter, plump and rosy with fair hair. We decided to call her Isobella after the Queen.

My husband was in a nervous mood, pacing the walls and staring out at the road for the signs of incoming messengers. I sought to soothe him with the gentle arts but he was clearly ill at ease. "More than ever the King fears he will be deposed; that a plot is brewing against him," he said at length. "Even his daughter Joanna warned of it and she's wed to an enemy."

I am not surprised if it's true, I thought, but stroked his arm comfortingly. "Nought will come of it. All Kings face such threats. It's all smoke and mist...all silly rumours, I'm sure."

"Rumours!" His face darkened; for a moment I caught a glimpse of John's own visage, the family resemblance coming to the fore. "I am half sick of rumours...However, is best not to live in ignorance—some say John will be exiled and another King chosen. The crusader Simon de Montfort was put forward as a successor."

"De Montfort! But he has no claim!"

William shrugged. "That matters not to rumour-mongers. They also said the French raided the treasury in Bristol. Worse, they claimed that Marlborough castle was sacked, the Queen ravished in her own bed, and little Prince Richard impaled on a sword while his nurses were slaughtered in cold blood. Not one word was true."

"No." I shook my head. "I do not believe the rumour-mongers themselves believe these wild tales. They merely seek to cause more unrest."

The King soon hunted down those who he thought disloyal—lords like Eustace de Vesci, Robert Fitzwalter, and Richard de Umfraville, who lost Prudhoe Castle and was forced to give up four sons as hostages. Even David Earl of Huntingdon, brother to the

Scottish King, was compelled to hand his castle of Fotheringhay over to John, along with his younger son.

And then, almost unbelievably, the King began to soften his stance. Harsh, hated foresters were removed from their positions and replaced by local men. The powers of several oppressive sheriffs were curbed.

"Why would he change so?" I asked William, after he had ridden in from northern England. He had been with John on a whirlwind progress that had ended at the impregnable coastal fortress of Bamburgh. "It will cut his income."

"My brother has learned," said William, "that he cannot always abuse his lords and retain their fidelity. Of course, he *does* seek to campaign in Poitou again in the spring. He will need as many friends as he can get, and at the moment he has few." William's smile was grim.

My heart sank. I had hoped John had abandoned the reconquest of his ancestral lands. It was bad enough to lose William to court duties in England, but to fare across the sea seemed more dangerous. Once over the sundering sea, would he ever return?

"Do those lands mean so much to him still?" I asked. "Surely he needs to set aside old losses and content himself with ruling justly at home."

William's forced, unhappy smile became even tighter. "It is not just the desire for his lost lands, Ela. It is Philip Augustus. I do not wish to voice bad news, but it has become evident that he is eager to invade England. To depose John. Stephen Langton and the Pope support his cause, and already he has a mighty navy assembled."

Fearful, I stared at William. Although I loathed John, deposition by a vengeful foreign power would have terrible consequences for my family. Being John's right-hand man, William would almost certainly lose his lands and wealth, if not end up imprisoned. The castle would revert to the new monarch; we'd soon become destitute, perhaps even forced into exile.

"I pray it does not come to that pass," I whispered, hand to my throat. "We'd be ruined. Oh, if only John would repent and beg the Pope's forgiveness…."

"We shall see." Several candles in the solar had guttered; a black shadow was thrown over half of William's face, an unsettling play of the light. "It is said Philip Augustus has 15,000 men at his disposal. I do not know how many the King can muster…and hold. The common men—the archers and foot soldiers—are wavering. They remember the words of Peter of Wakefield, the hermit who told John to his face that he would lose his crown upon the Feast of the Ascension."

"He said so in the King's presence and lived?"

"The hermit is imprisoned at Corfe."

That great western fortress again, one of John's favourites, with its lavish apartments contrasted to its foul oubliette, from which no man returned. A place where John retired to enjoy local hunting—while below his feet prisoners groaned in the darkness and in the towers above, the Princesses Eleanor of Brittany and Margaret and Isobel of Scotland sat in long captivity, well-treated but unfree. I doubted it would end well for Peter of Wakefield, whatever happened to King John.

William reached up to stroke my hair. "It is in God's hands. I would beat sense into John if I could, but he draws away from even the smallest of my counsels."

"The Feast of the Ascension is not long away," I said nervously.

"No, it is not. And so I must ride to John's side, and face whatever comes next."

The last candle died. Neither of us called for a servant to relight it but sat in the darkness, together and yet apart in silent, troubled thought.

Events had turned. Marvelling, I read the letter William had sent me:

My dearest beloved wife, Great tidings! My brother has submitted to the will of Pope Innocent. At the House of the Knights Templar at Ewell, he resigned his crown to the Legate Pandulf, saying he will receive it back from Innocent as the Pope's vassal. He also promised the Pope one thousand marks per year… But that is not all I wish to impart to you, dearest. John is having a great feast at

Ewell to celebrate. All men are invited. I would have you there, Ela, for shortly after I am to lead the English fleet to Zwin....

I made ready as soon as I might, packing and preparing. Felyse would come with me, while Mabella would stay to oversee minor household tasks; we would ride palfreys under a canopy rather than journey in a slow carriage or litter, and a strong entourage would surround us in the event of any trouble on the roads.

Setting out in the early hours before cock's crow, Mabella and I made good time to Ewell, despite running into the hordes descending on Kent to get the free food offered by the King. Eventually, we spotted John's pavilions, striped blue, white and red, tipped with glorious pennants that flapped in the breeze off the sea at Dover. Beyond the array of tents loomed the tower of Ewell church, built by one of the early Masters of the Temple, and a little further away was the Templar's Preceptory with its massive square frontage and round tower that represented the Holy Sepulchre in Jerusalem.

Quickly I sought out William's pavilion, one of the largest, draped in the banner of golden Lions upon Azure. As my servants flurried to unpack the wains and erect smaller tents, I entered the pavilion and was greeted by my husband, joyous and flushed, his hair in wild disarray.

"Ela!" he cried, flinging his arms about me unashamedly. "Glad am I to have you at my side. What a surprise all this has been. I never thought the King would capitulate—but he has, thank heavens."

"He is very shrewd," I said as William escorted me to a table. His pages raced around, bringing mead and a platter of imported figs and *cryppys*—fried apple slices dipped in honey. "Now that he is but a vassal of the Pope, and England under Innocent's rule, no Christian prince would dare attack the country."

"True, but that does not excuse us from military obligations elsewhere. Philip Augustus has been harrying our ally, Ferrand, Count of Flanders, and so we must sail against Philip." William grinned and sat next to me, sticking his dagger into a plate of meat pasties covered in saffron paste that a squire brought for his delectation. "For the most part, however, you are right. No King would dare attack England for fear of censure by the Pope—excommunication or even Interdict."

I lifted a napkin to my mouth. "So...when will the current Interdict end. Is it known?"

William paused. "Well, no...but it will come. Pandulf must report back to Innocent first. That will take time—the road to Italy is a long one. Then I suspect his Holiness will wait for John's first payment, to make sure he delivers as promised."

"And will he?" I dabbed my lips again; ate another *cryppy*, the tang of apple sweet in my mouth.

"Yes, yes, of course!" William looked shocked that I thought John might renege on his promise. "I truly believe he has repented. He has learnt he cannot rule without God's blessing and the Pope's— and those two blessings are tied inextricably together."

William's face suddenly darkened; the apple soured in my mouth. "Many barons are not pleased by this turn of events, however..."

"Not pleased? When the evil of the Interdict may soon end? Madness!"

"They grumble because England is now controlled by a foreigner who has never set foot on our shores. They see the resignation of the Crown to Rome as dishonourable, even a form of servitude."

"But...but it's the *Pope*, the Holy Father!" I banged down my goblet in agitation.

"Men are men, Ela," shrugged William. "A homegrown lord, no matter how harsh, is seen as better than a foreign master. But come, no more of this talk. The King has bent his stiff neck, Langton shall be the Archbishop of Canterbury, Pandulf shall go to Rome, and before long, church bells will ring out all over England once more!"

"I long to hear them," I whispered, reaching beneath the table for his hand. "And that is not all I long for."

John's celebration at Ewell was lavish, more a festival than a feast, and all the more miraculous because it was arranged at such short notice. The King's grand pavilion was open to the bishops, prelates, barons and their kin; in the fields, trestle tables were arranged for any others who wished to partake. Archers shot at butts to win a purse of silver; tumblers and fire-breathers cavorted through the crowds. A stilt-walker loomed and Fools raced about, cartwheeling and whooping, conspicuous in their motley. Huge carved figures of saints were brought in on a two-storied wagon—St Katherine with her Wheel, St Christopher with the Christ Child on his shoulder, St George piercing a great green dragon with his sword. Adam and Eve came on another cart, Adam hirsute as a woodwose, Eve preserving her modesty with flowing sheaves of braided wheat. A processional giant holding a club lurched through the crowds, while a hobby horse with a real horse's skull for a head galloped about, butting chosen victims and sending them tumbling on the ground.

In the King's pavilion, John was lounging on a makeshift throne, a flagon trailing from his hand. His hosen were splashed with drink, his face bloated and purple. He was very, very intoxicated. Behind his seat stood a statuesque woman in shimmering silks that bore an almost golden hue—when gold was reserved for royalty alone. She was no royal, though, and she certainly was not the diminutive Queen. The woman had an attractive, if slightly foxy face, but she wore a haughty, unbecoming expression. I guessed she might be his mistress Clementia, the mother of his daughter Joanna—men mockingly named her 'Queen' behind her back, for as such did she behave, despite being nought but a concubine.

"Will, Will!" cried the King, seeing his brother. He staggered up, his collar flashing with jewels, and caught William in a bear-hug. "Isn't it wondrous how so many have turned up to my little celebration? So many—it makes me feel so confident, I do not even mind paying for it!" Throwing back his head, he brayed with laughter. "Wait till we get to France and attack those Frenchie fleets! They won't know what's befallen them, will they, eh, brother? They won't bother old Ferrand again, will they?"

"Never in our lifetime, my Liege," William answered, voice muffled by the King's fur-lined robe. "It will be a great victory, God willing."

"And Ela, dear Countess Ela." John released William and suddenly his arm encircled my waist, drawing me close, too close.

Those scattered around the great pavilion gasped in shock at the impropriety. Clementia glared, her cheeks flushed in fury.

"Always so cold, so contained," John hissed in my ear, out of range of anyone else's hearing. "But I would wager you'd burn hot with some...*stimulation*. Dear 'sister'...we need to know each other better. Someday. I've had Countess Hawise of Aumale, you know, and Isabel de Warenne, a *very* dear cousin—she even bore me a child. And then that Matilda Fitzwalter—outraged, indeed! Hah!—outraged only when her father questioned. She squealed like a pig at the trough when I..."

"Your Grace..." A cold sweat of fear burst out on my brow. "Please...I fear you are...you are unwell."

"Unwell? *Unwell!*" He gave another bray of raucous laughter and reeled back into his chair, arms and legs akimbo. "I have never felt better, my dear. Never better. Perhaps we shall continue our most interesting discussion sometime in the future."

Brow dark as a thundercloud, William pulled me aside as Clementia and other toadying courtiers clustered around the King, pouring more wine, spooning sweet dishes into his mouth, dabbing at the sauces dripping through his unkempt beard. On the table before him, a Fool started to caper, the bells ringing madly on his cap as he abruptly dropped his hose to a lewd uproar.

"What did the King say to you?" asked William, his fingers tight on my arm, almost painful. "I saw the look on your face. Tell me..."

I had seldom seen such rage and suspicion in his eyes. I feared what he might do if I told him the truth. "N-nothing, husband. He spoke nonsense, that's all. He has imbibed too much wine. I told him he was unwell..."

"Are you sure?" He still had not released my arm.

"Of course I am sure," I said, "but let us go from this pavilion, if it please you. John is in...high spirits. I do not think either of us fit well with the present company. And I have suddenly lost my appetite."

In late May, William set sail for Flanders, accompanied by Renaud, Count of Boulogne and seven hundred knights, their horses and numerous archers and foot soldiers.

I returned to Salisbury, to my children and the life I loved best, and tried not to dwell on the bloody encounters William might have facing Philip Augustus' fleet. He was doing what he must, and I had my duties to attend to as well.

Much to my surprise, he was back within a few weeks. He rode in from the port at Southampton mounted on his white charger, as people from neighbouring villages and towns flocked to see him pass. Massive wains rolled in his wake, bearing untold amounts of treasure.

I gathered with the household to greet him at Salisbury, a returning hero. My eyes widened as I saw the wagons bursting with booty that inched up the steep incline to the gatehouse.

After he had given a speech to the onlookers, telling them that England's honour was gloriously upheld and Philip's navy trounced, we both retired from public duty for the day. I had a bath drawn for William, with heated water brought from the kitchen in huge copper paniers, and I sat beside the vast wooden tub while his squires scrubbed his back and laved it with rich, foamy soap from Spain.

Once William was content, I dismissed the lads and took over the job of scrubbing him myself. "Well, you look like a cat that has lapped up the cream in the kitchen," I said. "It was more than just a minor skirmish, I take it."

He nodded. "Oh, Ela, you should have seen it all. As my ships approached Zwin, my heart sprang into my mouth, and for a moment I thought we were doomed—there were thousands of enemy vessels! But then…I realised they were all empty of men, save for a handful of guards. Philip had gone to plunder Ghent for supplies. I took the advantage when I saw it, and bore down upon the enemy cogs with speed and fury. I set hundreds alight and cut the others free from their moorings so that they drifted aimlessly out to sea. Now, not only is the threat of French invasion gone, but we are rich beyond words—even with John taking his cut! I have heard men say that so much treasure has not been brought to England since the time of King Arthur!"

"Well, my husband, a brave pirate you certainly are...and you look like one, I trow." I touched my finger to the blue-black stubble above the line of his usually neat, close-cropped beard.

"Ah, that...I have had no time to summon a barber. Ela..." He reached out a dripping, soapy hand to catch my arm and drag me down towards him in the tub. "Would you let this wicked pirate carry you off?"

"I shall think about it," I said primly, "But first...dry yourself, you rogue."

CHAPTER FIFTEEN

"Have mercy on me, O God, and blot out my iniquity!" King John's voice ascended in a melodramatic cry.

The King was standing barefoot, like a penitent, before one of the great gates of Winchester. Nobles and townsfolk stood shoulder to shoulder to watch him, as the Archbishop, Stephen Langton, and a stream of formerly-exiled Bishops entered the walled city.

Snivelling and grovelling, John fell on the ground before their richly-shod feet. "Have mercy!" He raised his hands in supplication. "Absolve me of my sins! Accept me back into the bosom of the Church! If you have no compassion for this unworthy sinner, at least have compassion for the people of England!"

Langton stared down his nose at the prostrated monarch with unfriendly eyes. Nonetheless, he said in a weary voice, "It will be done" while making the sign of the cross above the King's brow.

John raised his head, staring up at the Archbishop. "Is that it? I am forgiven?"

Langton stretched down a gloved hand, assisting the King to his feet. "Come, my son. You must stand before Mother Church in the full view of all."

Ringed by the returning bishops, John marched down the cobbled street toward the cathedral, trying to affect a contrite demeanour. Barons and knights swept after him, with the townsfolk at their heels like eager dogs.

Soon the west front of the Cathedral of the Holy Trinity, St Peter, St Paul and St Swithun, rose up in unparalleled magnificence. Just over a hundred years ago, the cathedral's central tower had collapsed, some said because the bones of the dissolute King, William Rufus, were laid to rest below it; another similar tower now stood in its place. With any luck, this second tower would survive the living presence of the equally dissolute John…

The bishops led the King to the doorway. It yawned like a dark mouth—was it to his personal hell or to salvation? On the steps, the Bishop of Winchester chanted the 50th Psalm as Stephen Langton absolved John of his numerous sins. The King turned to face the assembled nobles and commons in the cathedral close. "I swear upon the Holy Gospels to defend the Church forevermore and uphold the just and true laws of my esteemed ancestors."

Although it was a solemn moment, a joyful ripple passed through the crowd. "A great banquet will be held after Mass," added John.

Even louder noises of assent and pleasure filled the air. Archbishop Langton frowned, and the crowds regained a respectful silence as the King was led into the church. William and I followed, glad that John was curbing his usual behaviour, even if his newfound piety and contrition was a fleeting thing soon to be forgotten.

At the promised banquet that evening, I noted two unexpected faces among the barons. Eustace de Vesci and Robert Fitzwalter, both looking ill at ease as if expecting to suffer an ambush at any moment. Of the rebellious barons, these two were foremost, having been suspected in the unproven but probable plot to kill the King. They had left England in exile, but now they were back, uncomfortable in the John's presence, but very much free and alive.

"Do you see de Vesci's face, husband?" I whispered as William and I danced alongside the King and Isabella and a host of nobles and their wives. "He looks half-mad with fear; he has sweated the whole feast and mopped his brow with his kerchief. I do not think he's taken a bite."

"I suspect he fears an 'accidental' knife between his shoulder blades," murmured William. "John won't harm him, though; not now. Not with the Bishops all around. This is a feast of reconciliation."

"I am just shocked to see both men here."

"They arrived with Stephen Langton. I am told Fitzwalter flung himself at Langton's feet while in France and convinced him that he and de Vesci were being persecuted. Under the terms agreed by Pope Innocent, John had to allow all exiles back into the country. He has even granted them their lands back."

"But not without taking some vengeance…"

William made a face. "No. He has destroyed Fitzwalter's castle of Baynard, and de Vesci's northern stronghold, Alnwick. I do not think you will hear either of them complaining, however."

"At least not yet."

"Not yet."

The musicians ceased to play, as another course was ready to be served, so William and I parted and went to our respective benches. I was seated next to Eustace de Vesci's wife Margaret, an illegitimate half-sister of Alexander, recently crowned King of Scotland after the death of his sire, William the Lion of Justice.

Margaret clutched her wine and stared nervously about her as if expecting assassins to leap from the shadows. "I cannae believe he asked us here, after destroying Eustace's castle," she said to no one in particular. "And with my poor wee sisters Meg and Isobel still locked up in Corfe with the Fair Maid of Brittany."

It was unwise talk, and I tried to calm her and get her to speak of other things—the hunt, the pleasures of falconry, gardens, even the weather. But Margaret continued on, almost in tears, "Alnwick was our favourite castle; it was beautiful, Countess Ela, and mighty...and now it lies in ruins, and beggars from the town creep amongst its stones, seeing what they can scavenge. It is despicable what John has done; Eustace was once a Crusader, too; he went with King Richard to Palestine! When has John ever made such sacrifice and taken the Cross! *Never*! Such outrageous liberties with our castles would not have taken place in the time of Richard or King Henry..."

"You must impress upon Eustace not to *bother* the King," I said, patting her arm. "The grief he will bring you is not worth it. Stay in the north, come to court only when summoned. It may be the safest way."

"You do not know the whole story, do you, Ela?" Her visage growing wan, save for the spray of freckles that crossed the bridge of her nose. "The *true* cause of enmity between the King and Eustace. The real reason Eustace plotted with Robert Fitzwalter."

Mystified, I shook my head.

She leaned closer, gaze travelling up the table toward the King, who was using a large, jewelled dagger to attack a roasted swan, complete with feathers and gilding. "John came north to treat with my father, King William. He stayed with Eustace and I at Alnwick, and there his eye fell upon me while I was dancing the pavane before the dais. He called me to his chamber, but when he attempted to seduce me, I told him straight that I was not a harlot, nor would I be, even for a King, and baseborn though I was, I was brought up as a King's daughter. He appeared to accept that, but later, when Eustace was away, a ring arrived with a messenger, beseeching me to go to my husband in Nottingham. The ring was indeed Eustace's, but I had not seen it on his hand for a very long time and grew suspicious. I sent out my own messenger to Eustace, who rode home at once, guessing what had occurred—the ring sent to me had vanished from his keeping during the King's stay! Eustace was furious and decided to trick John as he tried to trick me. He sent a harlot wrapped in expensive robes down to Nottingham castle, riding in a fine chariot. She arrived late in the evening and was taken straight to a chamber, where she doused all but one candle and waited naked in the bed. In came John, so full of lust he did not even notice he had the wrong woman! A few weeks later, the King attempted to provoke Eustace— 'Your wife is a fine nightly companion,' he sneered. When Eustace asked how he knew, John replied, with boldness, 'She came to me freely at Nottingham and performed all the strumpet's tricks.' To which, Eustace replied, 'That is because, your Grace, your bedmate *was* a harlot and not Lady Margaret. I sent her myself as payment for returning my ring…which you must have mistaken for your own while on your visit.'

"So now you know," Margaret continued, "and you must understand why I am fearful, not just for Eustace's future but the honour of my captive sisters. I realise you are married to John's half-brother, but William is not like him."

"No, he is most definitely not," I agreed.

"And I have heard much good about you, Countess Ela—of your decency and justice to the folk of Salisbury. Of your piety and good works at home. However, I must warn you—do not trust the King, brother through marriage though he may be. You are more than passing fair, and I saw his gaze fall upon you as you danced. The look upon his face—it was one I recognised and hoped never to see again."

I went cold but tried to laugh. "He would not dare. His own brother's wife…"

Margaret looked at me pityingly, as if she thought I was a foolish child.

She was right. John was a danger, a predatory man who cared nothing for blood ties, consumed only with his own base desires. I must make sure he never had the opportunity to get me alone.

Over the following months, the King continued to harass his barons. William came and went at John's will, growing morose, weary and haggard with the amount of travel he endured on a whim. John seemed tireless, travelling north to Durham, Knaresborough and Barnard, then veering back down to Tickhill in Nottinghamshire, where he threatened the castle's new lord, John de Lacy, that he would confiscate all his lands should de Lacy ever rise in rebellion. There were meetings with a new papal legate, a council at Wallingford and yet another council in Oxford.

Christmas rolled around and we were off to Windsor Castle for the Yuletide feast. John glittered, his robe alight with tiny gems; at his side Isabella was striped gold and blue, her headdress a sea of seed pearls on golden thread. French and Gascon wine was served, and food was in abundance—pickled pigs' heads, salted eels, venison pie, squab pastries, stuffed peacock, minced meat tarts, followed by pears and mulberries in red wine, pine nuts in gingered honey, and plums stewed in rosewater.

I abstained from the dancing and kept well out of the King's way. To my relief, he seemed to pay me no attention, although he must have known I was there. A strange restlessness burned in him, and he was often out of his seat of estate, smiting barons and knights on their shoulders in a familiar manner before returning to his Queen's side.

The reason became apparent at the end of the feast. John stood up, clearing his throat. "My lords," he said, "now that his Holiness has smiled upon England and the Interdict is over, England must return to glory."

A weak cheer went up.

"It is time to send an army to France and reclaim the lands that are mine."

The cheering dwindled; John became slightly agitated.

"I have spoken of it before, and I know some of you have *reservations*...but you have my word, such a foray will benefit you all. I promise herewith, that if all the barons agree to join my endeavour, I will not request the usual number of knights from you but reduce your debts to the Crown nonetheless. What do you say, eh? Is that sufficient?"

The cheers came again, still ragged but a little stronger.

"February it is then, my lords!" roared the King, raising his arm. "We will sail from Portsmouth to victory and glory!"

"God save King John!" some lackey shouted from behind John's chair.

The cry was taken up, and repeated, filling the chamber. I glanced to William, who was standing and raising his goblet to the King. "God save King John!"

The blood-ties were strong, too strong; he was as eager as his half-brother to recover the Plantagenet's ancestral lands.

I bowed my head to hide my sudden tears.

The King left Portsmouth for La Rochelle in February, taking with him Queen Isabella, his youngest son, Richard, and, surprisingly, Eleanor of Brittany, who was being taken abroad, not to be released but used in negotiations with her Breton relatives. Her half-sister Alixe and her husband John ruled Brittany, and Eleanor would be on display as a warning that if they did not cede to the King's wishes, they might find themselves hastily replaced by the girl who had a superior claim to the Duchy.

Isabella was clad in floating robes of gold and white, and she had left her hair uncovered for the public occasion, as Queens alone were permitted to do amongst married women. Her locks streamed out in a glossy chestnut cascade, like the bright banners adorning the masts of the waiting ships. Little prince Richard, clad all in white, was carried after her by his nurses, while Eleanor of Brittany walked behind the Prince and his attendants. Like the Queen, Eleanor's hair was unbound, for she was an unmarried maiden and liable to remain so if John had his wish. Fire-red, her tresses blew in wild curls over her deep green gown; I wondered how she felt, returning home but still unfree, the captive of her brother's murderer. She had loved young Arthur dearly, it was said.

From my place amongst the well-wishers on the harbourside, I watched them board their ship, The Trinity, where John was already waiting. In the end, the King had managed to rouse a fair amount of enthusiasm for his venture—but some barons were noticeable by their absence, mostly importantly Eustace de Vesci, who remained in the north, uncommunicative even to when sought by royal messengers.

Beside me, William stood in his travelling garb, ready to depart on his own ship. Unlike John, he was not heading to France; his destination was the Low Countries, where he would liaise with the Counts and Dukes favourable to John's cause.

"Take care of young Will and the girls," he said to me, as the King's great ship slipped out past the harbour wall and his own party began to make its way towards the quay. Overhead, dark skies were hurrying past, threatening to douse us with sleet or snow. I shivered in my lambskin-lined cloak; a chill tainted the air. "Tell them I will bring home lots of booty."

"We have no need of such," I chided. "Just bring yourself home, William, safe and unharmed. Pray to God for an end to all conflicts and a safe journey back to England."

"I am not much a praying man, but for the things you speak of, dearest wife, I will pray with all my heart." He took my hand and brought it quickly to his lips, then he was off striding along the quay, where the wind was making froth out of the grey waves and seagulls screeched as they dived above the swell.

Tallest of all his men, William stood on the deck of his ship, *The Holy Ghost*, looking every inch a King's son with his great longsword belted at his side, the ruby in its hilt flashing sullen fire into the murk. The captain called out orders and the sailors shouted to each other in preparation to depart. The ramp was drawn in and the mooring ropes untied with expert speed. The great cog, with its banner of war flying, slipped out into the harbour and turned its prow towards the open sea.

It was not the action of a highborn lady to wave farewell, unlike the wives and light o' loves of the common soldiers, who clustered along the harbourfront, calling out goodbyes and blowing last kisses...or weeping bitter tears. Instead, head bowed against the wind, I clutched my rosary beads and prayed in silence. Then I took to my carriage, packed high with furs and pillows, and as the sleet fell in sodden grey sheets, furling the dot on the horizon that was William's ship, I departed for home and the long wait.

Tossing in my bed, I dreamed. Fields burning, women and children running screaming through flames. King John and William thundered behind them on powerful war-horses, their faces encased in steel helmets, their swords ready in hand. *Oh, no, you cannot...*I tried to call out, but no sound emerged from my throat. The twin swords rose, shining, streaked with blood, and one of the children turned as the horses drew nigh, hooves pounding, and its face was that of my son...

Shivering, I awoke. That dream again, horrible and persistent. I guessed why I was haunted—rumours abounded about brutal deeds done by the Earl of Salisbury's forces in the Low Countries. A ruse to draw King Philip out so that John might attack his flank, but a brutal bloody one that spared neither woman nor child.

Felyse was sharing the bed since I was so restless of late; I gently nudged her awake with an elbow. Bleary-eyed, she raised her head. "My Lady, what is wrong?"

"I-I do not know," I mumbled, feeling foolish. "I had a dream...a nightmare."

"That is the third one in as many days," Felyse tutted. "I shall seek the apothecary later and get a sleeping draught. For now, I will get you some sops...unless you want to try for more sleep."

I glanced at the window shutters; a thin sliver of light poked through, grey and weak. It hardly seemed like summer, although August had come. "The sun is up; so should I be. I promised Ida I would watch her practice dance, and I am nearly finished stitching a shirt for baby Will. After Sext, I must hear a dispute in the town—old James the Carpenter is accused of riding a cart into the back of Malin the Fishwife's stall, causing it to collapse and ruining her produce. He denies all...says Malin knocked it over in a drunken stupor. Who knows? Both are a problem—he drives his cart as if he owns the town, and she imbibes too much small-beer…."

A commotion outside the castle made me whirl in alarm. Hastily, I unlocked the shutter and stared out into the grey dawn, uncaring that someone might see me with loose hair and in just a kirtle. Far below the window, small figures ran about the bailey; I heard a sentry cry, "Rider incoming!"

I strained my eyes. The gates were open to admit a courier on a steed lathered and muddy to the hocks. The rider himself was windblown and swayed in the saddle. Steward Hobart ran to his side, red robe flapping, a bright beacon in the dullness of the morning.

"Felyse, get me dressed!" I rounded on my maid. "There's a messenger in the bailey! I fear it is important!"

Felyse grabbed a gown and helped me into it, tying the laces too tight in her haste, but I cared nothing for that. She braided my hair with shaking fingers and hid it under a loose veil. "You are presentable now, my Lady."

I was in the corridor when the Chamberlain appeared. "Countess, I was just coming to get you. There is a messenger from the Earl waiting in the solar. The steward brought him inside."

"I heard the noise," I said.

The Chamberlain gave me a pitying, worried look. "He says it is urgent, my Lady."

My heart flip-flopped in my chest and I struggled to keep my composure. *God, please do not let my husband be lost to me.* Whatever news the messenger brought, my tingling senses told me it would not be pleasant.

With as much dignity as I could manage, I entered the solar where the messenger waited, muddy, rumpled, his beard matted. He bowed as best he could, and nearly tumbled over from weariness. I gestured him to a bench along the wall. "Sir, what is your name?" I asked, remembering niceties even as my head spun.

"I am Ralph de Merlion, my Lady," he replied. "I bring news from Bouvines…"

Bouvines? I did not know the name. I shook my head. "Is your message from the Earl?" The words trembled off my tongue.

His face bleached of colour. "No, my Lady...I bear news *of* the Earl..."

A gasp escaped my lips, and the impassive façade I had fought to build shattered. "Speak now!" I rasped. "Is the Earl of Salisbury dead?"

Ralph de Merlion blinked, stunned as if I had smitten him with a fist.

"Well?" I cried, sounding like an enraged crow in my own ears. "Tell me!"

"N...no, my Lady. The Earl still lives..."

"Jesu, thank you," I cried, and my legs went from under me, throwing me to the floor. Ralph jumped up and reached out a hand, then withdrew it in case I would slap it away for impropriety.

"No, you may assist me, Ralph de Merlion. I fear I cannot rise otherwise," I said, and he extended his hand again, helping me up and guiding me to the bench he had vacated.

Once I had settled myself, I took a deep breath. "So...tell me your news."

"My Lady..." He stared down at my huddled form. "A battle was fought at Bouvines. Between King Philip Augustus and the Earl and his allies. Countess, the Earl has been taken prisoner by the French."

"How? You must tell me everything, Ralph! From the beginning. How was my husband taken?"

"It was the King's plan to approach the French forces from both sides and destroy them as a hammer smashes on the anvil—his army the hammer and the soldiers of the Earl and Emperor Otto of Germany the anvil. However, John was defeated at Angers and fled back towards the coast. His baggage train and siege machines were left behind to be plundered by the French. The Earl of Salisbury, Emperor Otto and their other allies were left alone to face Philip's onslaught. It is said Otto was most shocked; he believed he was in hot pursuit of the French, but instead, they were waiting for him..."

"So John did not fight at all."

"Not after Angers fell, my Lady. He was fearful..."

"The coward!" I cried, caring not that I might be heard. "How could he?"

Ralph reddened and cleared his throat. "I—I realise how it seems, but he claims he was thinking of the ladies...the Queen and Lady Eleanor."

My lips drew into mocking grimace. "Oh, I am sure of that, he is such a champion of women...do go on."

"Near the villages of Bouvines, the armies clashed in a marshy field. A melee ensued, and briefly it seemed like victory was ours, for the French King was unhorsed...but his knights surrounded him in a ring of iron and kept him safe until another mount was found. As Philip remounted, my Lord William galloped past the groups of fighters, straight for the nearby bridge, hoping to take it and block a French retreat. However, the bridge was held by King Philip's loyal ally, the Bishop of Beauvais. Have you heard of him, Lady?"

"Yes, Philip of Dreux, a wicked man for all that he is of the Church! He was long a thorn in the side of our late King Richard, even accusing him of murdering the King of Jerusalem! When Richard was imprisoned, this so-called 'man of god' goaded his gaolers to abuse the King. After Richard's release, Beauvais was imprisoned for his actions and was only freed due to a hostage exchange for the Bishop of Cambrai. Richard loathed him...called him a robber and an incendiary."

Ralph nodded. "That is he, a ferocious man. As a Bishop he is not allowed to use a sword in battle; that is forbidden. Instead, he uses a great flanged mace nigh as tall as a man. It was with this weapon he attacked the Earl as they struggled for mastery of the bridge. Alas, the Bishop gave the Lord William a resounding blow to the side of his helm. The Earl managed to stay in the saddle but it was obvious he was disoriented from such a blow."

Coldness ran through me, from head to toe, but I murmured, "Continue..."

"The evil Bishop took full advantage when he saw the Earl falter. He hurled himself at his opponent and struck him a second time with his mace. Now the Earl fell from the saddle...immediately the French surrounded him and took him captive."

"And—and was he sore hurt? To be struck by such a weapon..."

"God be praised, he is not badly hurt. He walked from the field with his captors, although he had a cut on his brow. I think part of his helm buckled in and cut his skin."

"Thank you, Christ and Mary," I breathed, clasping my hands. "He lives... He is a prisoner; they won't hurt him, will they?" I thought of the French knights John had starved to death at Corfe. What if Philip Augustus planned on some vengeance for their deaths?

"I would expect them not to cause harm, my Lady. It is the usual way when a nobleman is captured."

"The King will ransom his loyal brother—have you heard aught of a ransom being offered, Ralph?"

Ralph stared down at the reed-strewn floor, unable to meet my eyes. "I have not, Countess. But it is the usual way a release is secured."

"And the outcome of the battle in the end?"

"Lost," he said bleakly. "William's men broke rank and fled when he was taken. Philip's cavalry charged and broke Emperor Otto's centre. Only Reginald of Boulogne held out with his Brabancon mercenaries—but they soon fell to an onslaught of foot soldiers. Every mercenary was executed on the spot—I fear, my Lady, that King John's dream of reclaiming his ancestral lands is truly over this time."

"I care nothing for John's dreams," I whispered, rocking back and forth on the bench. "I only want William back, alive and unscathed." Tears started to run down my face. "Why has there been no mention of ransom? *Why?*"

My voice rose, verging on hysteria, and a nervous Ralph stepped back in alarm. "My Lady, can I call someone? Your maid? A physician?"

I sprang from my seat. "No...no, I shall be quite all right. I will write to John myself...*I will write!*"

Overcome by emotion, I fled from the hall, leaving the messenger staring after me.

Yes, I would write to John. He had to listen. William was his most faithful brother. Surely, he would see him freed before even leaving France. Surely, he felt some love for him...

I was sure of nothing as I shouted for a scribe to hasten to my quarters bearing quill and ink.

CHAPTER SIXTEEN

Dark and gloomy, December rushed in, the skies brooding, threatening snow. William was still in captivity in France. John had responded to my frequent letters but twice; the first, horribly formal, assured me that '*in good time, all would be made aright*' and the second, more ominous, invited me to his Christmas court at Worcester to '*discuss important aspects of the Earl of Salisbury's release.*' I was disturbed that John had not referred to William by name or called him 'brother' even once…

I had to go to Worcester; I had to stoke up my courage. For the sake of my husband and children, for the sake of Salisbury.

"Must you go away, Mama?" asked Ida, when I came to the nursery to bid farewell. "It is late in the year and if it snows you might get stuck!"

"We cannot change the weather that God brings, Ida. Life must go on despite snow. Don't you want your father back as soon as possible?"

She looked at me with her large blue eyes; she was very like William in aspect. And growing up—soon we would have to seriously think of whom she might wed. Petronilla too, just one year younger; although of all my brood she was the unfortunate one, given to sickliness. She had a contemplative nature not often seen in a child her age.

"I *do* want him back," replied Ida, "but what if…" She bit her lip and her eyes grew teary.

"Do not cry, Ida," said Petronilla, who was leafing through a richly-illustrated prayerbook. "God will look after Mama…and Papa too. You must have faith, Ida."

Ida blinked back her tears but glowered angrily at her sister. "You don't understand, Petronilla. You are always so dreamy…as if you live in another world with the faeries! Outside of your dreams, outside these castle walls, life is hard and frightening and people die all the time, but you are too fey to see it!"

I could sense a forthcoming battle between my two daughters, so close in age but so dissimilar in appearance and temperament. "Be silent, both of you. I cannot have you fighting whilst I am away in Worcester. Ida, you must be the Lady of Salisbury Castle in my absence."

That pleased her; made her cast a smug smirk in Petronilla's direction. Her younger sister ignored her and continued to peruse her prayer book. Meanwhile, Ella played contentedly with a poppet, unconcerned by her sisters' spats, and William crawled around with a painted wooden horse clutched in his pudgy hand. Baby Isobella sat up in her cradle, golden curls a halo; she was getting so large that soon she must have a proper bed.

I did not want to leave any of them; fears clutched at my heart as they did poor Ida's. But I must show strength and do what was right.

"God keep you all," I said, and before emotion overcame me, I called the nursemaids into the chamber and left without a backwards glance. I could not look—I would have run back, weeping, if I had.

Worcester in winter. Cold wind battered the painted roof of the chariot, but at least the sky through the curtain was a rich, unstained blue, devoid of any cloud. Snow had fallen a few days prior, but that had turned to muddy grey slush that hissed under the carriage wheels. The horses in the entourage snorted and huffed, huge clouds of their breath rising into the air. Their riders looked chilled to the bone, their faces raw, water droplets frozen under their noses.

The company crossed the long, arched bridge leading into town, stopping to identify ourselves at the gatehouse built over the central span. Under the bridge, the spirit-haunted waters of the Severn churned, swollen by rain and filled with leaves and bobbing detritus that eddied on the swell. Further along its banks, the half-completed Abbey towers rose in splendour, the most imposing building that the eye could see; even dwarfing the castle that nestled alongside it. St Wulfstan, a Saxon holy man, lay entombed within the abbey church, his shrine a draw for pilgrims from far and wide.

Passing through the winding streets, I marvelled at how new all the houses and merchant's shops appeared. Four times in the last hundred years the town had gone up in flames, the worst damage taking place in the harsh years of the Anarchy. Some of the churches, partly rebuilt, still showed fire-reddened stone, as did the ancient hospitals of St Wulfstan and St Oswald.

I also noticed that the town had many Jews, like Winchester. Salisbury did not have a Jewry, but here I spotted men and women wearing the mandatory square white badges. They hurried along the streets, trying to avoid my horsemen, not daring to glance toward my cavalcade. Peter of Coutances, Bishop of Worcester, had commissioned a damning treatise called *Of The Perfidy of Jews,* and hence they kept their heads down, avoiding any trouble, especially since John's recent behaviour towards money-lenders had stirred up old hatreds.

The abbey drew closer, the sunlight glinting off its pinnacles and great western window. Crossing the Lay-Brothers' cemetery, my party reached the guest-hall, where I would stay while my men lodged in taverns throughout the town. The King had not offered me lodgings at the castle—and I would have found a way to refuse if he had.

The guest-hall was built to the east of the abbey's chapter house and had a gatehouse beside the hosteler's cell. The hall had five bays and was entered by a porch on the western side. Leaving the carriage, I rang the bell for the hosteler; a rotund monk with a liver-spotted head waddled towards me, calling out a welcome. He led me and my ladies through the hall, with its ornate windows and carved wooden corbels of angels, saints and crowned monarchs. The corbel nearest the staircase to the upper bedchambers was a grotesque King, his crown crooked, his eyes big and bulbous, his mouth open with a red tongue protruding. A coin was painted upon the tongue's tip—a warning against avarice and greed.

Immediately I was reminded of John, whom soon I must face to beg for my husband's ransom. I shuddered, and it was not due to the wind blowing through the open guest-house door.

The King could be generous when he chose, especially when it came to food and drink. Townsfolk clustered around the castle gate, waiting in anticipation; they knew that when the feasting was done, the left-overs would be doled out to one and all, and if the King was particularly full of festive cheer, he might even toss a few coins to the poor.

The castle itself was small and compact; it encroached on the abbey's graveyard, which had caused a conflict between its castellan, William Beauchamp, and the monks. For the better part of a century, the castle had been nothing more than a wooden tower upon a motte, but gradually John dug up money to pay for the gate and other major buildings to be fashioned from stone.

The Great Hall was filled with barons and their ladies, excepting the ever-disgruntled northerners who were absent. My table was shared by Johanna, the wife of Philip of Oldcotes, who once held Tickhill Castle; Beatrice, wife of the Justice William Brewer; Christiana, wife of Henry of Braybrooke, High Sheriff of Northamptonshire; and Joan de Cornhill, wife of the chief forester Hugh de Neville, who was also rumoured to warm King John's bed and to have promised him two hundred chickens if he'd let her have just one night alone with her own husband... None of these ladies matched my status as a Countess, and it was a clear snub; we all gazed uneasily at each other, not knowing how to proceed.

The King and Queen were both present in the Great Hall, resplendent in their ceremonial robes. John wore a golden crown, a purple tunic cinched by a belt of *orfrey*, and leather buskin boots reaching the thigh. Over all, he wore a dalmatic of deep blackish-purple, slashed open at the sides, and over it, a mantle with an ornate clasp of gold. Isabella wore a gown of imported blue brocade patterned with birds and gazelles. Tiny gems flashed on bodice and hem when she moved.

John was grinning and jesting with a cluster of courtiers; he hardly looked like a man who had lost his overseas lands for good, although even the lowliest serf in England knew they would forever belong to France from now onwards. He certainly did *not* seem as if he were deeply worried about his loss—or his missing brother, locked in a cell in a hostile foreign land.

A horn blew, brazen and throaty, and the first course of the feast was served. As expected, it was lavish: mustard and brawn, pottage, blancmange and jelly. However, it all tasted like ashes in my mouth.

Second came pheasant, boar, coney, faun and venison dyed blood-red with spices ground from Sandalwood, then *painpuff, doucettes,* bustards flavoured with cloves; I pushed the platters towards the other ladies on my table, favouring my wine goblet instead. Last to arrive were the sage fritters, amber jellies, and gilded gingerbread cut into fancy shapes. I nibbled on the latter only because the strong ginger eased my nervous stomach.

The King had asked me to court, and yet I had no idea of his intentions. Was I to petition him? I would if I had to…but William was his own brother! I had heard the courtiers saying that John would move on to Gloucester within three days. If I had not spoken to him by then…Well, I could not follow his progress like some kind of camp follower. It was irregular enough to be here without my husband, but because I was a Countess in my own right, no one dared speak ill of my presence.

The banquet was winding down. Some lordling had grown offended by the capering antics of the dwarf jester and thrown him across the room. He lay groaning in a circle of concerned servants, one of them weeping. The King paid no attention and the Queen looked as if she smelt something rotten. I could not imagine treating poor Proudfoot with such careless contempt.

Eventually, John rose, teetering slightly, and taking Isabella's arm, paraded out of the Great Hall to a fanfare of trumpets.

The revellers were now permitted to leave. Benches were pushed back, and belching barons headed for the doors followed by their wives. Not knowing what else to do, I let myself be swallowed by the crowd. On the morrow, I would have to rise before sun-up and ask for an audience with the King. I supposed it would be a long wait; he had appeared drunk, and as he did not attend Mass, he would likely lay abed till noon…

"Countess Ela!" A voice called my name and I saw a familiar shape pushing through the crowd. It was Hadwisa, King John's first wife.

"Hadwisa, I had not thought to see you here."

"Or I you!" She clasped my hands. "Court buzzes over the Earl's capture—I will pray for his swift release."

"It is about his release that I am here in Worcester," I said with a bitter sigh. "I would rather celebrate the birth of Christ with my own household and children in Salisbury. But five months have passed, and it seems not one move has been made to free William."

"I do not envy you," she said, as we walked down the torchlit hall. "John does not change. I hope he has not called you here just to taunt you, or extort money from your treasury, or…" She fell silent. Then, licking her thin lips, she said slowly, "Ela, he does not change, not for God, not for family, not for anyone. Have you heard about my latest change in circumstances?"

"You're not still in Sherborne?"

She shook her head. "No, I have married again. *Married.*"

My eyes widened in surprise.

"It was John's decree and John's choice of husband. Geoffrey de Mandeville, Earl of Essex. Geoff did not want to marry me—why would he? I am years older than him; I will never bear him a child, barring some miracle. To add to the shame of it all, John charged him 20,000 marks for my hand and wanted the money within ten months…At least Geoff is not cruel to me as I feared he might be."

"I am grieved to hear of this. At least de Mandeville has not taken out his woes on you."

"He has some small sympathy for my plight, and some lands were tossed in his direction to sweeten him, too. I am his second wife; his first was Matilda Fitzwalter, whom John dishonoured. She died young of suspicious causes; that is why her father, Baron Fitzwalter, hates John with such a passion."

We were now nearing the door into the castle bailey. A tall man with longish hair and a drooping moustache thrust his head around the corner. His impatient gaze alighted on my companion. "Hadwisa, there you are! Let us be off; I've done my duty for this year. Let us depart ere the King decides on some new ply to break me."

Geoffrey de Mandeville.

"I must go, Ela," said Hadwisa. "But I beg you—be careful while you are in Worcester. Beware of John's…*appetite*. To be truthful, I would counsel you to go back home and wait. Before long John will remember William. He will soon realise he needs the support of such a loyal kinsman…"

"I cannot do that, Lady Hadwisa. I cannot let William rot in the dungeons of the Bishop of Beauvais."

Sympathy filled her homely visage. "I suspected you might say that. You are brave, Countess. I wish you the best of Christ's Mass, and hope you are favoured by our Lord in your quest."

She drew her hood up against the night-chill and was gone in a rush, and alone I exited the castle into the hurly-burly of the courtyard. I glanced through the departing crowds, trying to catch sight of the stout-armed attendants that had escorted me from the abbey guest-house.

Peering into the gloom, I took a hesitant step forward, but before I could proceed any further, out of the shadows stepped a cowled figure, striding toward me on swift, silent feet. At first, I thought it was a monk; the cowl was deep, the hands folded in hanging sleeves. However, the stranger sidled up to me and whispered in a harsh voice, "Countess Ela, the King has sent me to fetch you. He has but little time but if you follow me, he will speak to you on the matter of the Earl of Salisbury's freedom."

I did not like this subterfuge at all, but I had little choice. If I refused, I might not see John at all, and my journey would have been in vain. A meeting was all on the King's terms—or else I went home without seeing him.

"How do I know you are truly from the King?" I asked. "You could be any kind of devious rogue!"

The man fumbled in one sleeve and brought out a ring with a purple stone. A star and crescent moon was engraved on the bezel. It was John's; I had seen it on his hand myself. I thought about Margaret, wife of Eustace de Vesci, and her story of the stolen ring, but I doubted anyone would dare steal from John himself. The punishment would be beyond cruel.

"Put it away. I will come," I muttered.

The cowled figure led me around the side of the castle to a door at the base of a tower. It was locked, but the man carried a huge, rusted key which made a clunking noise as he turned it in the lock. Inside was a staircase, dimly lit by a pale lantern hanging on a great iron hook.

Still suspicious, I glanced up the stairs; they opened into another room one flight up. Warm candle-light spilt out onto the landing, and the exotic fragrance of tangy spices wafted to my nose. Only a wealthy man could purchase and use spices to freshen the air of his chamber.

I gestured to the cowled man to lead the way, which would give me a chance to flee back down the stairs if I felt threatened. Thankfully, he made no argument and trudged up the stairs while I followed a few paces behind.

At the top, he stepped into the chamber. "Your Grace, I have brought the Countess Ela."

"You may go then, Hugh," said a familiar, detestable voice.

The servant shuffled away, exiting through a narrow, arched doorway hidden behind a wall-hanging in the little private chamber. I stared around. The King was sitting on a stool, clad in a loose gold-fringed nightgown. Two goblets stood on the table next to him beside a silver carafe of wine. The carafe was patterned with scenes from some Greek myth—a swan mating with a naked woman. Behind him was a canopied bed, its draperies rich and poison green. I began to feel uncomfortable again, especially as John said nought, just stared intently at me, devouring me with his hot, hooded eyes.

I could not speak first since he was royalty, and the silence stretched on. At last, he flicked his hand. "Ela, I am glad you have come. I thought you might not."

"I do not understand why you have brought me to…a private area of your apartments," I said slowly.

"Privacy is needed for any type of negotiation—and, think of it, you would not want to set gossips' tongues wagging by wandering off with me before all and sundry. Therefore, I had you brought in secret to the hidden postern door, so useful if a hasty escape is needed from the apartments. I was merely thinking of you and your honour, dearest sister. Am I not kind?"

I strove not to grimace. He was mocking me.

"I have come to Worcester to ask you about the status of my husband—your brother. He has been imprisoned since July…"

"A sad thing, Ela…very sad," John sighed, "but I am not a wealthy man, you know."

"Your Grace?" I thought of all the taxes he had extorted, the fines he had given out, the fees obtained for marriages like Hadwisa's.

"As you know—I lost the war in France. I had to retreat, leaving my baggage and engines. The soldiers had to be paid lest they mutinied and went on a rampage…"

"It was a sumptuous banquet you held at Worcester tonight, was it not?" My voice sounded bitter, and I was aware that I stood on thin ice. At that moment, realising he was in no hurry to help William, I did not care.

I expected an eruption of anger, but there wasn't one. He spread his hands wide. "The banquet was as it should be. I am a King—a King must be seen as kingly at all times; otherwise, he is no longer viewed as a King…"

You are not a King; you are a tyrant! I thought, but kept my peace.

John shifted, rising from his stool. The light from the fire brazier turned his heavy visage a devilish red. "Now, enough of such unnecessary chatter. Back to William's captivity. Rather than pay a ransom for him, I would prefer a prisoner exchange. I do have a few Frenchmen loitering in the royal dungeons, but so far, my offers have gone unheeded."

"Has King Philip suggested a sum to release my husband?"

"Yes…but it was far too high. A ridiculous amount."

Outraged, I glared at him.

"You're just a woman," he snapped, clearly angered by my expression. "You would not understand such matters. I would look weak if I agreed to the first offer Philip made."

"*William…is…your…brother…*" My words were a harsh whisper that barely contained my anger.

"Half-brother, it might be best to remember. Not a royal prince. Bastard."

A small, strangled sound emerged from my throat. How could he speak of his loyal kinsman in such a manner? At last, I regained my composure. "I deem it best I leave then, your Grace, if there is no more to be said. I will have to see what I can raise to pay William's ransom myself."

Head spinning, I rose, despondent beyond words.

John said nothing…again, moments stretched between us, while his dark glittering eyes roved…and undressed.

"I did not give you leave to go," he then said.

He got up from his stool and approached me, his jewelled slippers making a hissing noise on the rushes strewn across the floor. "You are a brave and dignified woman. I admire that, Ela. I have heard you are quick-witted too, and a practical woman."

"My Lord King?"

"You love your family, do you not? Such fine little daughters…and one son, one solitary son."

Blood began to pound in my ears at his mention of my children.

"You do not want them fatherless for long, do you? A woman alone in a castle, who knows what might happen if William's imprisonment goes on…"

"I said I would try to raise a ransom, my liege."

"Ela…" he sounded like a father chiding a slow child, "you do not have to do that. You would never secure Philip's extortionate amount. Nor, if you are clever, will you have to. There is another way you can pay for William's release…and for that, I would gladly open my coffers."

For a moment, I frowned, confused. Suddenly John was inches from me, his breath hot on my neck, his hairy hand curling around my wrist in a tight grip. "No one need never know. One night, that's all I ask. As I said, you are not a fool…"

"I would be a fool if I betrayed my husband, my beliefs and my honour," I gasped.

"Christ…playing the untouched virgin! For all your pretended coldness, you must enjoy humping; you've spawned five brats almost one after the other…"

"You speak of your nieces and nephew…"

"What of it? Arthur of Brittany was my nephew too!"

The smell of his breath, heavy with spiced wine, reached into my nostrils. He clawed at me, ripping the veil from my head and hurling it into the brazier. It disintegrated in a cloud of sparks and smoke. "That's better; you look less like a nun and more like a whore…"

Struggling, I broke free and ran towards the staircase I had ascended earlier that night. "There's no point in running," John said, grabbing my arm and dragging me back into the chamber. "I had my servant lock it from outside."

"My liege...you must not do this terrible thing." I wanted to strike out, to kick and bite...but then I thought of Matilda de Braose, starved to death in Corfe. Would he have me imprisoned likewise, on some falsified charge if I refused him? What good my honour if I was dead...and with William a captive, what would happen to my poor babes?

"That's a good wench now, none of that drama." John propelled me towards the green-hung bed.

I continued to beg, appealing to any fleck of pity or decency in the man. "Your Grace, *think*, I bid you—I'm your brother's wife, thought of as a sister; what you suggest is against decency. It is forbidden!"

"It is a nonsense law. You are not my blood sister in truth."

"It is written in Leviticus—*The nakedness of thy brother's wife thou dost not uncover; for it is thy brother's nakedness.*"

"Oh, I shall uncover your nakedness, never fear, and never mind William or Goddamned Leviticus. I am the King—you will deny me at your peril. Close your eyes if I offend you so, and think of William returning soon. I'll make sure the money is raised—any sum that is needed—but you must contribute..."

He flung me down on the bed and crashed on top of me, causing the air to leave my lungs. His thick lips were on mine, his tongue hot in my mouth, one hand holding me down while the other roughly groped and fondled. "Christ!" he spat, tearing his mouth away for a moment. "I wish I had my dagger so I could cut this bloody dress off..." His hand slid down to my skirts, trying to yank them upwards.

I struggled even harder; I felt the heat, the strength, the hardness of his rotund body. "I—I cannot breathe..." I lied, hoping to frighten him. "Stop, I beg you..."

"Shut up!"

He wrenched my skirt up around my waist as tears slid from my eyes and ran down the sides of my face into my hair.

And…then, as if by a miracle, the tapestry lying over the room's hidden door was ripped aside. There, still in the rich gown she had worn to the banquet was Isabella of Angouleme. There was anger in her face but no surprise.

"Husband," she said, "These are strange 'matters of state' you deal with tonight. Countess Ela, get up…"

John had rolled off me as his wife entered the room. I leapt from the bed, my knees going wobbly in shock so that I nearly fell.

"Isabella, it is not what you think…" began John.

"It is *exactly* what I think. Christ's teeth, do not try to tell me she attempted to seduce you."

"She did, she always had her whorish eye upon me."

Isabella laughed. "No, I must gainsay you, my dear husband—your eyes have ever followed her. You covet what your brother has. Oh, I know you have mistresses, John—streams of them as Kings often do, and have I ever made complaint? No. But this one…she is not for you. Ela, go now. *Go!*"

Grabbing my fallen cloak, I raced for the door the Queen had entered, nearly ripping down the tapestry in my haste. Beyond was a vast corridor, almost in complete darkness, winding its way into the bowels of Worcester Castle. Stumbling and bumping into the chill walls, I managed to find my way outside.

My servants still waited, thanks be to God; they were dicing with the castle garrison by a watchfire near the gate. When they saw me running towards them like a madwoman, my hair hanging loose, they leapt up to attention, dropping their die in alarm. The Worcester men-at-arms were staring, surprised.

"Quickly, to the Abbey guest-house," I ordered, and as they formed a protective circle around me, I hurried through the gate and toward the Abbey, its tower a black silhouette against the deep velvet sky.

Reaching the guest-house, I rushed to my quarters. Mabella and Felyse were within, waiting for my return. Earlier, they had sighed and moaned because they could not attend the feast, but my position in the hall had been so degraded, my seat placed with women far below my rank, that I was not in the position to bring others to partake.

"Lady Ela!" cried Mabella, dropping her embroidery and leaping to her feet. "Thank Lord God you are back. The hour grows late, most of the revellers are long gone, and we feared that some evil had befallen you…"

Felyse was staring, mouth open, at my uncovered hair. "Countess…what has happened?"

I started to speak, then broke down in floods of tears, and threw myself face-down on the bed, writhing in shame and despair, the foul taste of King John's mouth like bitter poison on my lips.

CHAPTER SEVENTEEN

Wind stabbed like a sword and icicles hung long and spear-fierce from the merlons atop the great keep of Salisbury, sometimes clattering down in ruin on the hard ground below. Glancing out the window of the solar, I saw two young boys, the Cook's sons, playing knights with broken icicles, slashing and thrusting at each other, while the sun transformed their makeshift weapons into glittering magical things: enchanted daggers, hero's swords, faerie lances…

Despite my loneliness, I smiled, enjoying the meagre warmth of the weak February sun and the sight of the lads' innocent tomfoolery. In a few years, little Will would be out there playing too, God willing. I wondered if his father would be here to see him…

Suddenly a resounding *boom* crashed through the relative peacefulness of the morning. The boys stopped their mock-fight and stared at each other. Townsfolk going about their business halted in their tracks and glanced around in alarm.

Another clang, and then a cacophony of bells from the direction of the cathedral. Alarmed, I called for Felyse to bring my cloak. The last time I heard so many bells there had been a death, an important death…

Running towards the gate, I was almost knocked over by a messenger who had come riding under the portcullis. "My Lady Countess!" He flung himself down from his horse. "I come with tidings of great import. I have already told Bishop Poore, hence the ringing of the cathedral bells…"

"Stop!" I held up my hands. "Tell me but one thing, herald. Do these bells ring out in sorrow or do they ring out in joy?"

He was a young man, perhaps eighteen; he looked surprised at my question, then understanding dawned in his face. "My Lady…they ring in joy. I am forward to say this, and I pray you take no offence, but I think, of all, you will be most overjoyed by what the bells betoken. I would advise you have the bells in the castle chapel rung too, in thanksgiving."

"And your message?"

His young face lit up in a broad smile. "Earl William Longespee is free from his captivity at the hands of the Bishop of Beauvais. He sails to Portsmouth on the next tide and will fare to Salisbury as soon as he may."

"Thank Jesu!" I raised the ruby-studded crucifix hanging round my neck and kissed it. "I had not heard of his release. How has this miracle come to pass?"

"The King paid a goodly ransom, and made a prisoner exchange for the French nobleman, Robert, son of the Count of Dreux."

I was stunned. Had John's cold heart melted or had he come to his senses over the fate of his most loyal supporter? Maybe the Queen had pleaded my cause—perhaps she had done even more than that after witnessing the disgrace of Worcester. Neither had informed me that the prisoner exchange had been made, but that did not matter now.

William was sailing on the next tide, and soon my long winter of unhappiness would end.

Spring flowers bloomed on either side of the path as William and I rode towards the Abbey of Wilton, where we would visit the shrine of St Edith to leave offerings in gratitude for William's safe return to England.

I glanced towards my husband from the back of my placid palfrey. He had suffered much in his French prison; his cheeks were gaunt, his complexion waxy. A bitterness clung to him even several months after his return.

I had not told him about the shameful events of Worcester. Although he said nought, I knew from his moods, his stiff actions, how aggrieved he already was over his long imprisonment. I did not want to kindle a flame of rage that might bring him to deeds he might later regret...

The abbey gatehouse rose before us. A portly old nun gazed out from a viewing hatch, then shuffled away with much huffing to unbar the gate and permit our company entry.

The abbey was a House of Benedictine nuns and was both large and rich. Its current Abbess was Margaret, whom I knew from childhood visits with Mama; before Margaret was Asceline, whom I remembered also. The abbey was highly important, one of only four in which the Abbess held a barony, meaning that she must provide knights to fight for the King if summoned. Wilton Abbey was strategically important too, as the usurper Stephen realised when he took control of it during the Anarchy, but today, it was most famous for its two saints, Wilfrid and her daughter Edith, whose shrine was a popular centre for pilgrimage.

Abbess Margaret greeted us with courtesy, a sturdily-built woman of around fifty with a wide, pleasant face. She resembled a winsome grandmother, yet there was almost a manly forcefulness in her stride, appropriate in one who oversaw a barony. "My Lord Earl, God be praised you have returned to us in Wiltshire. Wilton town has missed your presence."

"Has it?" William managed to smile. "Or was it merely the tourneys the townsfolk missed?" One of William's duties was to arrange jousts on the massive tourney field between Wilton and Salisbury. Sadly, these events had been scarce in the last few years.

"It was you, my Lord Earl, I assure you. Many have missed your good governance, though the Countess has done splendidly in keeping town and castle running well and securely."

William's expression showed pleasure at the Abbess's compliments. "I am sure Countess Ela could even make an adequate Sheriff in her own right if she were a man. She is virtuous and just, but takes no nonsense."

Abbess Margaret nodded. "The notion of a female is not so strange. Nicola de la Haye, the widow of Gerard de Camville, has taken on the roles of Castellan and shrievalty of Lincolnshire upon her husband's death this year."

"Extraordinary," murmured William, shaking his head. "She is an old woman."

And why should she not take it on, if she can do the tasks? I thought. *She will bear no more children; why should she do nought but while away the remaining years of her life before the hearth?*

"Everything in this land seems extraordinary at the moment," said the Abbess with a grimace. "I presume you will attend the King in his latest endeavour?"

"I expect I shall have to," grumbled William, "as it is my duty, but I am only recently returned from prison in France, where the King left me long, and my health is not fully recovered. John has assigned me the task of inspecting and repairing the royal castles, but no more than that. I am assuming you know far more than I do, Abbess."

"Oh, dear," murmured Margaret, reading my husband's mood. "Yes…yes, I have heard new tidings. On Ash Wednesday, the King took the Cross. He speaks of a Crusade."

William goggled at the Abbess then burst into impious laughter that rang throughout the cloisters of Wilton Abbey. Half a dozen young novices cast scandalised stares and scurried out of his fearsome male presence.

"Take the Cross?" William cried. "I doubt you will ever see John in Palestine swinging his sword! His finances are low, he lost his battles in France, and he is not the warrior Richard was, nor ever will be. The majority of the barons will never follow him."

"But the Pope plans another Crusade!" remarked the Abbess.

"He may plan as it pleases him! My brother's words are as transient as dust on the wind—forgotten in an instant. He had done this only to protect himself, as it is unlawful to harm a Crusader."

"If you did not know of the King's vow, then you likely have not heard other tales. The barons seek ratification of the Coronation Charter of Henry I. His Grace will not have it and his messenger spoke so harshly to the barons at the Oxford council that they departed in wrath and have fortified their castles for war."

"What day did this occur?" William's expression was one of shock.

"It began days after the King took the Cross and continued in the following weeks."

"I was at sea for some of that time," nodded William. "I mislike that my brother has kept me uninformed about these high matters, but perchance he is unhappy with me—after all, I got myself smitten from the saddle by a fighting Bishop and cost John a fair few marks."

"I am sure his Grace bears you no ill will for that misfortune," said Abbess Margaret, without much conviction. "Is it not true, you saved the life of Otto, the Holy Roman Emperor, at Bouvines? The King's own nephew."

"No, it was his Saxon knights." William's lip curled. "His banner of the Imperial Eagle was carried off by his opponents. Not that John would care much if or how he escaped—he bears little regard for nephews…"

A little gasp emerged from the Abbess' lips. She understood what he referred to, even as I.

"I say too much, Abbess. I have spent over six months in prison, taunted by an unholy Bishop, and have had plenty of time to muse on my sins—and the sins of others."

Abbess Margaret cleared her throat. "I think it is time for your admission to our blessed Saint Edith's shrine."

She beckoned to a younger nun hovering discreetly in the background. In silence, she led us through the abbey church to Edith's shrine near the high altar. She then departed as silently as she had come, her feet making no noise on the tiles, and we were left in the presence of the great Saint. Her shrine was heavily decked in gold; a gold-topped altar, with holes in the lower marble base for supplicants to touch the fabric. The casket that held her saintly bones was covered in golden spires, almost giving it the appearance of a miniature cathedral. Jewels left by wealthy supplicants glittered in the light from three great candelabras.

Edith was Saxon-born, a bastard daughter of King Edgar the Great. She had a claim upon the throne herself after her young half-brother, Saint Edward, was stabbed to death on the slopes below Corfe Castle. But she had no desire to rule. Instead, Edith took vows of chastity and devoted her life to caring for the poor and studying the ways of God's forest beasts. Saint Dunstan had prophesied her death and told men her thumb would remain incorrupt for eternity. After she died, aged but twenty-and-three, miracles were wrought at her tomb. King Canute doubted these tales and insisted the grave be torn open so he might inspect Edith's remains for any signs of sanctity. As he leaned over her stone coffin, witnesses say Edith suddenly sat up and slapped his face. After being hit by that saintly, incorrupt thumb, his doubts were gone, and he began to build the shrine where William and I knelt in reverence.

After we had prayed, we made our own offerings of coin and a golden brooch. Leaving the gloom of the abbey church, we walked for a while in the adjacent apple-garth, fragrant with pink and white blossoms. William seemed troubled and subdued; what he had heard from Abbess Margaret weighed heavily upon his mind.

"Husband, speak to me, please." I reached for his hand.

"I will not go with him if he should go on crusade, Ela. I will not go just because he thinks it will protect his throne, and I'm not even certain it would. From what I gather, he is out of favour with Rome again."

"You said yourself it was unlikely he'd go. He is no true fighter. He would never leave England, for fear another might dash to seize the crown."

William stroked his beard, now cut short; the sun sparkled on a few grey hairs. "There is more than that—my faith in him has been crushed. You might say he was always a faithless man...but he was my brother; we played chess, cards and dice together; he has bestowed a pension upon me and let me borrow money. He has sent tuns of wine for our table. He raised me up, a bastard, and gave me many offices—Lieutenant of Gascony, Warden of the Cinque Ports, Commander of the English fleet..."

"You feel gratitude to him."

"I do! How could I not?"

I bowed my head; tears burnt my eyes. I strove to hide them; failed.

"Ela, what is wrong?"

"William...it grieves me to tell you. At Christmas, I went to Worcester to plead with the King to hasten your release..."

"Yes?" A note of suspicion deepened his voice. "What befell you there? What did John say? Why do you weep?"

"You say he gave you much...but in the end, John wanted what was rightfully yours, what could never be his."

William stood in silence, digesting my words. Understanding. His jaw tensed and a muscle jumped in his lower cheek. His eyes darkened to a stormy hue, and I thought a Plantagenet rage might take hold of him.

"Do not do anything rash." I placed my hand on his shoulder; he trembled with ill-concealed rage. "I am unscathed, my honour intact."

"I will never forgive him for this." William spoke in a harsh, tortured rasp. "I will do my duty to my King, but I will never see him as brother again. May he rot in Hell for what he tried to do."

"It is time for us to go," I said. "Forgive me for giving you this grievous news."

"Forgive you? There is nought to forgive. It was your duty to tell, as it is for me to serve the man to whom I swore fealty—although my eyes have now been truly opened. Let us never talk of this matter again, but also never forget…"

In silence, we returned to Salisbury. Although William still seemed troubled, his brow creased by a perennial frown, it felt as if a great millstone had been lifted from my shoulders.

John had gone too far in his attempt to ravish me, and William had finally seen the truth of his brother's ways. It was time to start disentangling our lives from the dark course taken by the King—the King whose barons were gathering against him even as we reached Salisbury Castle, drawing up a charter of demands to force him to their will…

William began his tour of the royal castles while I remained behind. My courses had stopped, and I was hopeful of pregnancy, of bearing a second son. Having at least two boys was desirable, and a brother would make an excellent playmate for little Will, who was either cossetted or tormented by his older sisters, a situation not ideal.

In the world beyond Salisbury, fighting broke out at Brackley and Northampton, with Robert Fitzwalter leading a company of aggrieved barons who called themselves the Army of God. In May, these rebels reached London, scaling the walls on a Sunday when the townsfolk were at Mass. The gates were flung wide and the Army of God stormed through the streets, capturing the King's men and stealing their goods. The houses of the Jews were raided, then torn down, their masonry used to fashion barricades. The Tower was impregnable and could not be taken, but the treasury within was now no longer accessible to the King; so too the Exchequer. John was left with nought save his own jewellery and plate—and he was soon reduced to selling it.

William was summoned to lead an attack on London, leading John's favoured Flemish mercenaries, but his response had been half-hearted and he retreated from the city's violent streets in the face of greater numbers. Infuriated, John had jeered at him and the Flemings. On his command, they marched onwards to Exeter, where another rebellion had broken out, and this time, William put the rebels to flight and captured the castle. John, however, showed a lack of gratitude to his sellswords—when they came for their pay at Marlborough, he had his servants take up the treasury and bear it before the lustful eyes of the Flemings to the King's own apartments, where he claimed every penny for himself.

William briefly returned to Salisbury in June when the troubles in the West had subsided. "Ela," he told me, "I but come to see you are well and the children, and then I am off towards Windsor with all haste."

"Windsor?"

"To Runnymede, more precisely. The King is meeting with the Barons; they are going to force him to sign a Charter. I should be at his side to advise…but at the moment I am weary, I am heartsick, and in truth, let him swim or flounder as God wills it."

"Do you know what is in this Charter?"

He nodded. "A few things are confirmed. Repeal of forest laws; restoration of lands and castles to those dispossessed unlawfully; freedom for hostages, no fines without fair trial, protection for widows and their children, and most important, I deem, and the part my brother will hate most—the King is not above the law."

The latter made me raise my eyebrows. "I wonder what will happen should he refuse."

"Outright war," said William grimly. "The rebels will seek John's deposition or death."

William rode away and I watched him until his entourage was but a tiny blot in the distance. The world was changing, and perhaps, just perhaps, this time for the better…But it would be born, I deemed, in blood and in anger.

William stood in the solar, opening a scroll sent to him by Elias de Dereham, one of the Archbishop of Canterbury's secretaries. "So here it is…a copy of the new Charter," he murmured, holding it out for my inspection. "Sealed by the King himself."

I stared in wonder. "How did he take it?"

"Better than I believed he would, and the barons have sworn allegiance once more and given John the kiss of peace. After the Charter was sealed, he held a great feast in the fields at Runnymede, and all men enjoy a good feast, even if they loathe the one holding it. I am sure many of the kisses given were no more honest than those given to Christ by Judas." Slightly agitated, he stalked about the chamber. "There have been repercussions for us, Ela. Trowbridge must go back to Henry de Bohun, excepting its castle. This rankles, as the town should have been ours through your ancestor, Edward of Salisbury."

I waved a hand. "We still hold Trowbridge castle; that is enough. When the unrest that grips England is over, we can try to obtain the manor again—through the courts, so no one can say it was unlawfully obtained. Maybe Henry de Bohun might bother to turn up to the hearings this time if he desires Trowbridge so much."

"I can no longer claim scutage from the tenants," William grumbled.

"In these times, we will have to weigh losses against possible gains. Some things are better lost, if peace can be made through losing them."

"Perhaps you are right," he said, dubiously, as he took the Charter from me, rolled it up carefully, and placed it in an iron chest which he locked.

"I do not want my children to grow up in war-torn uncertainty. And now there will be a sixth…" I placed my hand on my still-flat belly.

William grinned. "If there is peace, I can stay on my own lands for much longer, and heaven knows, maybe we will double our brood of children. Think of the alliances we could forge!"

"Double? Husband, you ask much of me!" I laughed. Then, more seriously, "We must work on marriages for the children soon.

As you say, alliances are crucial. We must form strong bonds that will bring us strong support."

"We will," he said, "I have a few ideas in that direction, but it will all depend…" Suddenly William frowned, glowering into nothingness as if assailed by evil spirits.

"What is it?" I was alarmed; his mood had gone from flirtatious to dour in seconds.

Serious, he glanced over. "Dare we talk of happy days ahead, or are we tempting fate, my love? John has sealed the Charter—but when has he ever kept his word when he did not wish to? I know my brother too well—I fear he still may have a few tricks up his sleeve."

The uneasy peace formed at Runnymede was soon broken. Suspicious of John's motives, the rebels continued to refuse to surrender London. Furious, John appealed to the Pope, claiming the Barons had forced him to seal the Charter under duress. Since John was the Pope's vassal, the Holy Father sided with him and annulled the newly-sealed Charter with a Papal Bull. The new laws intended to herald a different, more just England were overturned in a mere ten weeks.

Wrath consumed the barons. The Pope told the Archbishop of Canterbury to excommunicate them all. Langton refused this order and found himself suspended from his office. Afraid for his life, he fled over the Narrow Sea to France. As he departed, men shouted from market crosses and church steps that any rebellion raised against John was just; that the King had broken his word and the truth of his perfidy had been kept hidden from the Pope.

William spent much less time at court with his brother, leaving the great Marshal to be John's prime supporter. He kept abreast of affairs, however, and his cares deepened with every passing day. His growing discomfort was apparent in his expression, the tightness of his shoulders, his clipped walk, the way he gripped the pommel of his dagger. He was fastidious about strengthening the castle's defences, repairing the walls where age had made them sag, replacing the gates with stronger ones wrought from oak-wood taken from Savernake.

"Mama, is there going to be war?" asked Ida, as I instructed Petronilla on their needlework. "That's what the townsfolk are saying. They are frightened. They say mercenaries will burn the town down, and sack the castle…"

"There will be no war," I said, but I was uneasy. Did I lie to my daughter? Perhaps, since she was still of tender years, it was better the truth was hidden, for now. "There will also be no more embroidery for the day—you have done enough. Off to the nursery with you both."

I put my hand to my belly. In another month I would seek confinement again. What kind of world would my latest baby be born into?

"They have offered the crown to Prince Louis." William had called me to his closet, where he sat at his desk. His shaking hand held a scrawled letter. "My spies have told me all."

"And he has accepted."

"He has…and with much enthusiasm. He puts forth a claim in the right of his wife, Blanche of Castile, who is the daughter of John's sister, Eleanor."

"Many might accept such a claim."

"Many do, Ela."

"And you?" I said softly.

Thoughtful, he chewed on his lip, and then said, "I do not know. I truly do not."

"Soon you may have to make a decision."

He buried his head in his hands. "I know, but if I make the wrong move, it may ruin me…us…"

"You must pray, as I do, husband. Pray for guidance…"

Wearily, he passed a hand over tired, bleary eyes. "God seems not to listen to my prayers; after all, I am one of the 'Devil's Brood.'"

"You are no devil." I wrapped my arms around him from behind, leaning my head against his muscled shoulder.

"Maybe you are right. Not devilish enough—torn between loyalty and practicality.

Pulling away from me, he went to stand beside the fire. The flames played on his face; on the surface of his eyes—he looked lost, a man damned. Hearing a noise in the corridor, he glanced up to see one of his squires peering in the door.

"You, boy!" he shouted in a rough manner quite unlike him. "Get me wine, more wine. And lots of it." He grabbed the cup he had imbibed from earlier and dashed it on the flagstones before the lad's feet. The boy, no more than eight, squeaked like a mouse caught by a hungry cat and fled down the hall.

William fell to brooding, staring at the wall. I sighed, touched my heavy belly. I could not help him with his decisions. The choices he made must be his own.

When the first November snows were falling upon Salisbury, I gave birth to my second son, Stephen, named after the holy martyr who was stoned to death for speaking truth to a mob. He was small, dark and very quiet, although healthy and a good feeder. "Maybe he will join the church when he is grown," said William, gazing down at the swaddled shape lying beneath a silk coverlet in his oak cradle.

"I would like that for at least one of our children, if not more—it is a noble profession and a holy one, serving God. I have often thought that Petronilla might make a good nun. She is not worldly like Ida, nor rambunctious like Ella and Isobella. She is already pious."

"It is something to consider if she is willing. Do you think St Mary's at Wilton would take her? It is a convent of great prestige."

"I do not see why not. I will talk to Petronilla, and visit Abbess Margaret after Christmas. Our daughter is still too young, however, to even be a novice. And I would have her with us at Salisbury if there is trouble."

And trouble there was—the French fleet landed in anticipation of the arrival of their prince. A stern summons came from the King; William was to raise levies or face dire consequences. "I must go," William said dully. His eyes looked lifeless, hopeless.

"So that is your choice?"

"At the moment a foreign army lies in wait. I have been summoned or, rather, threatened. I do not see any other course but to support John."

"And where is the King now?"

"On his way north with fire and sword, destroying the castles and lands of any who spoke against him. His temper is such that I swear he would not hesitate to attack Salisbury too, should he feel the need. That is why I join him; to protect you, the children, the cathedral and all the commonfolk of the town."

"God go with you then," I said.

"I do not know if God still listens to me—if he ever did, Ela," he murmured and, without a backward glance, he strode across the courtyard to the stables. His squire brought his helmet, and then he was gone, leaving me standing in the cold north wind, hugging myself for the small comfort it would give me.

News of John's latest depredations reached Salisbury, tales of mercenaries who pillaged houses, fired towns, who even burnt hedgerows in the fields. A subdued mood fell over the town. The residents looked uneasily to the road, fearful of armoured men in the King's colours. I sent the steward into the town to inform the people that if the bell was rung three times in the chapel of St Nicholas, they must leave their tasks and flee to the castle for safety. The monks and priests at the Cathedral were also told to evacuate, although they seemed reluctant to leave for fear of looters making off with the holy bones of Osmund and other treasures.

"It is very bad, my Lady," said Proudfoot the Fool, who had been in the solar entertaining the children with japery, handstands and silly dances. The little ones had all gone back to the nursery now, and I was left with the shaggy-haired little man in his particoloured clothes. "They say the King is on the warpath. He takes prisoners and forces high ransoms; he threatened to starve William d'Albini to death unless he surrendered." Wistfully he rubbed his belly. "Starving to death would be a most dreadful thing, I wager."

"I would like to learn how a Fool has learnt of such events," I eyed him. "Although I dare say they are true. There's more to you than meets the eye, my little Proudfoot."

"Indeed. A small man such as I can squeeze into a dark corner and not be noticed," he said with a roguish grin. "And tiny though my body is, my ears are big!" He cupped his ears with his hands and waggled them. "I've spent time in town, with my lovely lemans and my bouncing bastards, and heard the talk of merchants and traders and rough soldiers in the taverns."

"Would you like to know more, Proudfoot? The Earl has written. John marched all the way to Scotland. He fired towns and sacked Coldingham Abbey. He burnt Berwick and set fire to his lodgings himself, laughing as the building burst into flame. He is mad. He even said he would 'run the sandy fox cub to ground'—meaning King Alexander!"

Proudfoot did a backflip and hooted with mirth. "Sandy fox cub! The King makes mirth even in his wrath. That jape is worthy of Proudfoot."

"I do not think the folk in those towns find John's words or actions very amusing."

Proudfoot hung his head and thumped himself with a little staff he carried covered with bells. "This Fool is being a Fool. That is why I *am* a Fool. I should present my tender buttocks for striking…or a stroke."

"That won't be necessary, you incorrigible little man." I could not help but laugh. Proudfoot was the only male in all of Salisbury—no, in all Wiltshire—who could get away with speaking to me in such a manner. "Now off with you—I need some time alone to think…and pray."

"Ah, my dearest Countess is a good woman, the best of women…while I am but a sinful dwarf. Adieu, great Lady!" He gave a low bow, the tines on his gaudy cap sweeping the floor, and then he scampered off singing merrily.

There were some things I dared not tell him about the deeds of his lord. William had been assigned to the east of England, his own levies joined by Poitevin mercenaries. They had ripped through the heart of Essex, destroying the castle of Pleshey at Christmas. The mercenaries had even taken the horses from the monks of Coggeshall Abbey and used them to ride about the eastern counties like wild Mongols, looting, burning, raping and torturing.

William had written, in a crabbed scrawl, the ink blotted distressingly on the parchment—'*I have protected the womenfolk as best I may, dearest Ela, and I will remember the infamy of Walter Buc, leader of John's heartless mercenaries. If he can be punished, I will see that he is. By God's Throne, I will see to it…*

As I listened to Proudfoot's voice vanishing into the distance, I sat on a bench with a heavy heart. I wondered where God was in all this misery. The Interdict was over, but darkness still lay over the land…

The following months were spent in endless frustration. Rumours flew like twisted arrows. The French Prince was coming, then he was not. Fighting continued in and around London, the rebel barons gaining ground, losing it, gaining it again. John's favourite mercenary, Savaric de Mauleon, was severely wounded and many of his Poitevins slain in a surprise raid; the Londoners, ever eager for the fray, attacked the ships the King had sent up the Thames to ring the city, setting them aflame and throwing their crews into the river to drown.

John retreated to the coast, passing from town to town, his gaze fastened on the waves, watching for any sign of a flotilla coming towards England from France. William was at his side. Every night, alone in my chamber, with the harsh winds sighing over the height of the hill, I thought of him out there, staring out over the sea to the hostile shores beyond.

Spare him, Oh God, I thought, clutching my prayer-beads, *and one day I swear I shall dedicate a great House to you filled with holy virgins, where good works will be done to Your glory and Your praises sung from dawn to dusk…*

CHAPTER EIGHTEEN

The French Prince had invaded. Resistance quickly crumbled, and he marched unopposed from Sandwich to Canterbury, Rochester and finally London. There he was treated as a conquering hero and strode into St Paul's in a regal procession that left no doubts as to his ultimate ambition.

Craven, King John fled west, without even striking a blow at his enemy. It is said he haemorrhaged men like a sorely wounded man haemorrhages blood, with many bending the knee to Prince Louis instead.

I had no idea where William was in all this uproar; whether he lived or was slain, whether he still supported John…or not.

The days dragged long, taking their toll, and the entire household and garrison were miserable and nervous. Even Proudfoot was subdued, sitting on a window ledge in the Great Hall and swinging his stubby little legs.

"I can make no jests today, my Lady," he moaned. "All Proudfoot can think of is the Frenchies slaying him—they have no sense of humour, you see!—and playing ball with his head." He ran his stunted finger across his throat, making a tearing noise.

"It will not come to that," I said firmly. In truth, I was not quite so sure. I watched the garrison sharpening their blades and the fletcher busier at work than I had ever seen him in my life, and deep inside, I was mortally afraid. Not for me, but for my innocent young children, and for my servants and the people of the town. They looked to me, and I felt responsible for their welfare; what could I do to help protect them should invaders come?

Wearily, I trudged about, busy with the never-ending household duties. At least performing these menial but necessary tasks took my mind off the rising threat and gave me a sense of normality when, alas, nothing in the world was normal.

Bones aching like those of a crone of sixty, I retired early to bed after eating a humble bowl of pottage. I dismissed my maids, preferring tonight to sleep alone in my own bed-chamber. Obediently they dragged their paillasses out into the hall.

"You are not sickening I trust, my Lady?" asked Mabella, full of concern.

"No, just tired after a day's work. Tired body and mind. I will surely feel better in the morning."

The maid left the room and I crawled into bed, drawing up the coverlet. My head had barely touched the bolster before I was asleep, the noises of evening castle life fading to nought.

Suddenly I was awake. A scuffling noise had broken my slumber. Blearily, I glanced out the window, left ajar in the warm night. The moon had set and the stars were white watchful eyes. Nothing seemed amiss.

Then it came again—that rustle, swift furtive. It came from the corridor outside my bedchamber.

Throwing my legs over the side of the bed, I pulled on a nightrobe. The door began to creak open, and a shadow stretched over the floor. It was not that of either of my ladies. It was the shape of a man...

Terrified, I reached for the dagger I kept secreted beneath my mattress when William was away—on his advice. *Not all love us, Ela, and a King's brother makes more enemies than most.*

The shape in the doorway slinked forward, a round head, not terribly tall—no taller than I, a tall woman—and no sign of armour or weapon. Still, an attacker who took one unawares could set a fire or use a pillow to smother so that no wounds would show. Hidden by the shadows, I sidled up to the intruder—and laid the long cold blade against his bony neck. "Do you always creep into ladies' bedchambers?" I whispered into a rather hairy ear.

The man went rigid. "My Lady, I am not here to harm you!"

The knife dropped to my side. "Master Hobart! What on earth are you doing entering my chamber unbidden and unannounced?"

"M-my Lady," he stammered, "Do not be wrathful! I...I have orders."

"Orders!" I pushed him out into the passageway where a few low-burning torches cast a wan, wavering light. "What orders? Who gave you these orders?"

"My Lady, they came from the Earl himself!"

"The Earl! Where is he? And where are my maids?"

Master Hobart was shaking. "Not here, my Lady. He sent a messenger...The ladies are downstairs, waiting"

"What? You claim William sent a message to *you*, and not to his wife? I cannot believe that..."

"He sent word that you, my Lady, and the children must remove to Devizes Castle. When he arrives later, he will explain all to you."

"He wants us to fare to Devizes in the middle of the night? I can scarcely believe this is true. Even if I trusted you, Hobart, and I am no longer sure I do, what proof have I that this is not some ruse by an enemy?"

"Here, Lady." He fumbled in a kid-skin belt pouch, drawing out a parchment. On the bottom was William's Seal, a mounted knight with shield and unsheathed sword. My gaze travelled across the writing inside. Short, with no graces...and exactly as Hobart had said.

"Forgive me, Master Hobart," I said. "This has come as a shock. What must I do next?"

"Mistresses Mabella and Felyse are waiting in the hall. I've summoned the nurses to bring the children from their beds. A carriage waits by the gate; plain with no markings, in order to mask your identity. Two dozen men of the garrison will accompany you over the Plain to Devizes. They will wear black like mourners so as to blend into the night. Hopefully, any onlookers will think you merely travel to a funeral."

"What about our clothes and goods? We will not have time to pack."

"The Earl says you are to leave immediately—you saw the proof, Countess. All you need will be sent later when haste is less necessary."

"Let me dress, then. I will join you in a moment." Pushing him from the chamber, I hastily dressed in my simplest clothes. My hair was a bed-tossed mop; my trembling fingers scooped its length into a long braid and I flung a dark veil on top. Then I ran down the passageway as if the Devil himself raced behind me.

Whey-faced and drained, Mabella and Felyse were awaiting me, clad in woollen travelling cloaks.

"Where are my children?" I asked, glancing nervously around.

"Basilia the Nursemaid has already taken them to the carriage," said Mabella. "They are excited and think of it as a wild adventure, save for the babe, who is still asleep."

Together we exited the hall and descended to the bailey. By now most of the household guessed something was afoot; candles glimmered in narrow window-slits and faces peered out. I flung myself into the waiting carriage, my maids scrambling after. It was crowded inside, with the children laughing and fighting each other for cushions to sit upon, while the nurse, Basilia, sat upright in the corner, face white as dough as she rocked the baby. I thought she might cry as she saw me.

"Hush, hush, all of you!" I reprimanded the children, sitting down on a heap of cushions. "Sit down and behave as children of your station! That is the will of your Lord Father!"

Immediate silence fell. The children huddled around me; Isobella's small, sweaty hand clasped my fingers. Outside, men shouted; I heard the clank and clatter as the portcullis straddling the gateway was lifted. A man called out an order; marching feet thudded in the night. The chariot lurched into motion, the horses in front nickering, and we were away, rattling under the gatehouse, over the rain-slick bridge and through the night-locked town to the second gate set within the earth ramparts.

Ida touched my sleeve; alone of my brood, she seemed fearful. She was the eldest and a serious, solemn girl who often imagined the worst. "Mother, are we in danger?"

"No…" I began, but looking at her frightened blue eyes, I could not lie. Not this time. "I do not know, Ida. Your sire sent a message that we must go to Devizes Castle and meet him there."

"Why Devizes?" she asked. She put a hand to her mussed hair, twirling a lock around her finger. Twirling it again and again in nervous agitation. "Father is fighting for our uncle the King in the east, isn't he?"

"Truth be told, daughter. I have no idea where he is. I heard the King has fled…I mean, *gone* to Corfe, along with the Queen and the princes and princesses."

"Fled." She latched on to my ill-advised word. "So it *is* danger we face. Is it the French? All of Salisbury is full of fear of the French.

I heard one of the laundry women saying they would eat our livers, after hours of torturing…"

"Do not be silly, Ida." I wrapped her in my arms, holding her close. "People say such nonsense when they are afraid. Often there is no need, no need at all."

Ida looked dubious. "I wish Father was here with his great sword…"

"We will see him soon," I promised. "He is coming to Devizes too…later."

"Later…" she breathed. She huddled against me, shivering with nerves and the night-chill. I drew my expensive marten-lined mantle over her and soon her breathing deepened with slumber. As usual, Petronilla was engrossed in her favourite missal, her lips moving in silent prayer. Isobella and Ella were wrapped up together in a sheepskin, their long lashes golden-dark on ivory cheeks. William was still awake, determined to show his fortitude.

"I won't sleep, Mother," he said. "I'll protect us all till Father comes. I wish I had a sword, though."

"You may sit on guard across from me," I said, as the carriage bounced and juddered over ruts in the road. "Here, you may hold my dagger." I took my trusty knife from my belt and handed it to him hilt-first. Do not cut yourself; I keep it sharp."

"It must be sharp enough to cut off an enemy's head— especially a Frenchman or a Saracen," Will said matter-of-factly as he laid the dagger across his knees. "You would not understand such things, Mother."

"No, I would not." I tried to hide my smile.

The carriage trundled onwards; I leaned my face into Ida's soft, sweet-smelling hair and drifted into a half-sleep. I woke to a metallic clatter. Will had fallen asleep, and the dagger lay on the floor. Gently I moved Ida and retrieved the blade for safety.

Glancing around, all my children were now asleep. Nurse Basilia was snoring, her head hanging on her chest, baby Stephen locked in her arms. Mabella and Felyse were seated at the far end of the chariot, engrossed in a game of cards.

I glanced through a crack in the heavy drapes. We had reached Salisbury Plain, and the carriage was swaying back and forth across a deep-guttered track shining white in the star-glow. The ground below the wheels was chalk of an almost unearthly whiteness, as if the bones of the earth itself were exposed here in this vast, open space. On either side of the track were midnight-furled humps and bumps, unnatural hillocks with earthen circles surrounding them—were they holding something in or keeping something out? In the gloom, I crossed myself. The mounds were thought to house elves and other unholy spirits—some claimed fallen angels, too wicked for heaven, too good for Hell. The superstitious would even leave bowls of milk upon these hollow hills on All Soul's Night...

Dawn's light was beginning to touch the sky when we reached Devizes, the Castle of the Boundaries. A wan, blue morning mist coiled over the town, broken by the almost surreal grey finger of the castle keep upon its high motte.

Drawing closer, the twin towers of the gatehouse also appeared through the eerie haze, the portcullis rising with a muffled clank. We swept by the sentries, passing through the extensive bailey, and my maids and I woke up the nurse and all the children.

The servants and the little ones were taken to the apartments, while I was escorted into the presence of Thomas de Sandford, the Constable of Devizes Castle. An old man, he had served Richard prior to John. He had a kindly, weatherworn face and striking blue eyes. Although the hair at his temples had receded, it still retained a sandy hue, making him appear younger than his true age. He rose from the desk where he had been dealing with correspondence and made a stiff bow.

"No need for that, Sir Thomas," I said. "Such courtesies are not necessary under such circumstances. All I want is the truth. I was not expecting to have my sleep interrupted and end up on a night-ride over a Plain haunted by cutthroats, outlaws and goodness knows what else, if even half the local tales are true."

"You are aware it was your husband, the Earl of Salisbury, who ordered your removal to Devizes."

"Yes, but his short letter gave me little clue. I am guessing the full story was too sensitive to commit to paper. I had hoped you might be able to enlighten me."

"When the Earl reaches Devises—and he is on his way—he will give you the details, I am certain. All I can say is that there is some danger—Winchester has fallen to the French army."

"Winchester!" I cried, alarmed. "So close…"

"Exactly," nodded Sir Thomas. "Devizes is considered more defensible than Salisbury if worst should come to the worst."

"But the people back home in the town!" I cried. "They are my responsibility. I can understand sending the children away, but William and I should be at Salisbury together, come what may."

The Constable looked troubled and would not meet my eyes. "This is something you must discuss with the Earl, Lady."

"I eagerly await his coming, then," I said, aware that my tone was cold. "Now, may I go to the rooms you have prepared? I have had little sleep through the night."

De Sandford went to the door and shouted for a servant. As I followed the boy out, the Constable leaned close. "Change is coming, one way or another, Countess Ela. Fear not, at least behind these strong walls."

William reached Devizes three days later. I was in the gardens with the children—Ida, Ella, and Isobella were dancing in a faerie-ring, as the wind hurled clouds of dandelion spores over them. Petronilla was lying on her front of the grass in dreamy contemplation, her red hair spread out in long waves, oblivious to the admonishments of Nurse Basilia, who feared she would ruin her dress. William had appropriated a wooden sword from Sir Thomas' small grandson James and the two of them were playing at war, leaping over the flower-beds crying, "Die, you knave!" and "Avaunt, wicked Saracen knight!"

Suddenly I caught sight of a dark shadow against the yellow stone of the garden wall. A familiar shadow. With a gasp, I sprang to my feet and hastened towards it.

Moments later, William's strong arms were about me. He was helmetless but wore mail beneath his dusty tabard; its rings pressed hard against my body, a sweet pain. He smelt of horses, leather and sweat; mud streaked his brow. I made to wipe it; he pushed my hand away.

Before either of us could speak, our brood had come streaming over, shrieking in delight. "Father, Father…you're here! Will you take us into town? Can we ride the ponies in the stable? When can we go back to Salisbury?"

William answered none of the lightning-fast, insistent questions, but he grinned and ruffled little Will's hair. "Enough…*enough*! I have ridden long as you can see, and cannot possibly answer so many of you at once. I must speak with your Mother urgently first…Ponies and days beyond the castle gates will have to wait, I am afraid."

William pulled me into the orchard, amidst the tangle of apple, plum, cherry and pear trees. The wind fluttered the green summer leaves but only the cherry bore fruit, hanging in shining red clusters—the others would not be ready for plucking till later in the year. Where would *I* be at the end of the year? I had no idea. I blinked, and for a moment, in my mind's eye, I saw the orchard black and burnt, smoke rising from skeletal, charred trees and from the castle behind it, split open like the shell of some great beast.

A small moan escaped my lips, and William glanced at me. "What ails you, Ela?"

"What ails me?" A burst of red anger flashed through my body. "Being dragged from my bed in the middle of the night and sent from my home is what ails me. Waiting here for days, praying that you had not come to grief, also caused my temper to grow short!"

"Ela, hear me out. I would not have asked this sacrifice of you if I did not think it necessary. The French…Louis has taken Winchester, and John has gone to Corfe with the Queen."

"That much I know. It seems England reels beneath the Frenchman's armies, and that John has no idea how to deal with the situation, with many barons joining Louis and his mercenaries deserting. What I do not understand is why I had to leave my home. I realise Winchester is not so far away…Was there a direct threat to us?"

William was silent for a moment. Then he said, "Ela…Christ's Teeth, this is hard for me to say…"

"Just say it!"

"I am going to surrender Salisbury to Prince Louis."

A small scream tore from my throat. "Y-you what? Have you gone mad?"

"No, I am not mad. Or maybe I am—mad with despair, mad with rage over a brother who has used me as his tool, then abandoned me to rot while he tried to ravish my wife. I can play his game no longer. He is unfit to rule. I shall offer to swear loyalty to Louis and break my allegiance with John."

"What makes you trust this Frenchman? He will likely behead you as an impostor or spy."

"I have heard he is honourable. The people of London cheered when he rode in with his army. They would have crowned him then and there. If he does not believe in my changed allegiance, then I will have to beg for mercy on behalf of my kinship to his wife, Blanche, who is my niece."

"She grew up in Spain. You do not know the girl or she you! As I said already—you have gone mad!"

William grasped my shoulders, fingers bruising my flesh. "If one surrenders to Louis voluntarily, he has promised to do no harm to castle or town—or so I have heard."

"I heard once that the moon was made of green cheese!"

He gave me a startled look. "And how do you know it's not?"

An urge to hit him gripped me, but it quickly faded, and I began to laugh, a bitter, almost hysterical laugh. Pulling back from William, I leaned against the bole of an apple tree. My unhappy mirth set the fledgeling fruits jiggling in the boughs above. "Ah, the town I've loved, the castle I lived in all my life is imperilled, and here we are talking about what substance God crafted the moon from…"

I sank onto the grass, knees suddenly feeling weak. William knelt beside me. "You always doubted John and warned me. Why do you baulk now when my mind is made up?"

I put my hands to my head. An ache had started behind my eyes. "Because I was foolish and simple then. I saw you walking away from John with no difficulties and your honour intact. Just as if he'd have ever let you be, if you did not support his plans! What I did *not* foresee was subjection to a foreign power. Or the loss of Salisbury."

"I will not hand it to Louis on a platter," William said fiercely. "I will ask for it back in due time."

A sudden new thought came to me, and my hand flew to my mouth as sickness curdled my innards. "William, this plan of yours grows madder by the second. Devizes is a royal fortress; you have brought me and our children here…and yet you plan to hand over another royal fortress to Louis. Once news of your defection reaches John, we will become prisoners here, not guests—we shall be killed for sure. Remember Matilda de Braose!"

"You do not understand, wife. You must be aware that the ranks of the rebel barons have swollen, while John's supporters have dwindled. The Earls of Surrey and Arundel have abandoned the King's cause. The only important men left in his camp are William Marshal and Ranulf of Chester. The rest have all gone. Devizes may be a royal castle but its tenants are no longer loyal to John. Your safety is assured. I made certain that I knew Constable de Sandford's heart in this matter. He remembers Lionheart's day, and it pains him to see what John has become."

William clambered to his feet, leaving me sitting upon the ground, my head still spinning at the thought of what he planned and its possible implications. "I will bathe and eat a quick meal, then set out on the road once more. I must reach Louis ere he moves further west. I need to offer my allegiance before he reaches Salisbury's gates."

Gracelessly I got up, using a tree branch for support. "What will be, will be," I whispered. "I must stand by your decision; it is my duty—but I cannot pretend I am not fearful. But God will succour me in the end."

"I pray He will."

"And I pray, before you go, you hold me one last time and kiss my lips—for I know not when or if we shall ever meet again upon this green earth."

He said no word but caught me in his arms and kissed me roughly, with as much desperation as passion, below the shivering apple trees with their leaves all aflutter—though not so aflutter as my sorrowful, conflicted heart.

And then his hands fell from my waist, and he whirled in his long riding boots and stained cloak, hastening toward the stables and leaving me alone in the orchard. *So alone…*

In the weeks that followed, I listened for any word of William's whereabouts or Prince Louis' plans. It turned out Louis was too cautious to go into the deepest west to besiege impregnable Corfe; instead, he marched to Portchester and Odiham and captured them both. Salisbury was duly ceded to him, but thanks be to Our Saviour, the castle was not sacked or dismantled and the little town remained untouched. I presumed William's submission to Louis had found acceptance. Now the French forces, with, I supposed, William and his soldiers swelling their number, headed towards Windsor and to the great coastal castle of Dover, the very gateway to England. Take that mighty fortress and the French would have the country.

"They say Louis has brought siege engines up to the walls," Thomas de Sandford told me. I was sharing a meal with the Constable, his wife and eldest son. "He's acted as his sire did at Chateau Gaillard, setting up siege-work around the walls, almost making a fort around a fort. On the cliff side, he has his fleet waiting, so no supplies can come from the water."

"I wonder if he shall prevail."

"It may take a long time. Dover is as strong as the Tower. Hubert de Burgh, the Constable there, is well-supplied. So is Louis at the moment, but…" He hesitated. I quirked an eyebrow. "He is now losing men, even as John. The siege is going nowhere, the army's pay has not been forthcoming…many left for home. Many also became affrighted by the King's archer, Willikin of the Weald, who haunts the wildness of the southern woods—he lives only to kill French soldiers in gruesome ways. 'Tis said the French believe Willikin is an unearthly spirit, a woodwose who can turn himself invisible and whose arrows fly by magical means."

De Sandford's wife and son laughed heartily; I did not. So, both royal combatants were losing popularity—and my husband had turned his coat from one and now followed the other. What if King John should prevail in the end? In my head, I envisioned a lightless oubliette and Matilda de Braose lying dead upon the corpse of her son. "Has the King responded?"

"Last heard, he left Corfe and is flying toward the east of England, burning enemy castles as he goes. He will not stay in one place long, though—a division of Louis' army is closing on his tail."

De Sandford's wife, Aliena, a plump woman with over-bright eyes, leaned forward conspiratorially. "The Queen was left at Corfe, and she's not awfully happy about it. I mean, it's so unsafe to have all her children in one place together, including the heir to the throne. Thomas has heard she plans to send Prince Henry here, as Devizes castle is better garrisoned, and so far from the sea that she need not fear an attack from that route."

"Aliena!" Thomas glared across the table. Hectic colour appeared in Aliena's round cheeks and she began to sputter and cough on a piece of dry bread. Her son, Alan, slapped her on the back.

A cold sense of dread ran through me, chilling me to the bone. "The little prince coming here…" My gaze slid across to Thomas de Sandford. "My husband told me certain things about loyalties within this castle. Have you, sir, betrayed him? Is my family, in truth, prisoners within these walls?"

He began to sputter like his wife. Eventually, he got the words out, "No, Countess, you are not. You, the Earl and your children have nothing to fear. However, perhaps, I have not entirely been open and truthful…"

"Then perhaps it is best if you are so now."

He cleared his throat. "My allegiance is no longer to John, that is true. For a while, I decided Louis would make a better ruler. But now his men desert him, and I am not so certain. Prince Henry, although young, may grow into a man more like his esteemed forebears than his father."

"He is how old? Nine summers? What is it they say in Ecclesiastes—*Woe to thee, O land, when thy king is a child?*"

"He would have good counsel, though, and in his young age be malleable. The Marshal is likely to become Regent."

"There is one small problem, however. Henry's sire is very much alive. What are you suggesting?"

Sir Thomas looked uncomfortable. "Lady, with enough Barons in agreement, John could be forced to abdicate in favour of his son and a Regency."

"He'd never agree to such measures."

"Then he might find he suffers consequences, whatever they might be…."

"I am not sure I wish to hear more. I am no lover of the King, but this is dangerous talk."

"It is, and these are dangerous times for all. No one can predict what will happen next. But I assure you, Lady, no harm will come to you here."

"Even if John himself should ride up to the gate and demand I be given to him as a prisoner because of my husband's misdoings? I am sure you are aware of the fate of Matilda de Braose and her family."

He could give me no further assurances and my appetite died. Hastily I went to the chamber where my children played happily, watched over by Basilia. Should I tell de Sandford I wanted to leave at once? That would put it to the test if I was a prisoner or not. But where would I go? William had surrendered Salisbury to the French, and without my husband to vouch for me, who knows what type of reception I might receive?

Mabella entered the room, soft gown swishing against the rushes. "My Lady, you left the table early. Are you well?"

I turned, clasping her hands in my own. "No, I am not, but it is not a sickness of the body that assails me. I am melancholy; I am not a seer, and cannot envisage the end of all these troubles."

"Would you like me to have a posset made so that you may sleep well?"

I shook my head and released her hands. "No, it is not necessary. I shall find the castle chaplain, and seek guidance from God."

I stayed on at Devizes and held my worries close-locked in my heart. The little Prince soon arrived from Corfe; I greeted him alongside the household. He stepped from his chariot looking lost and rather forlorn, a smallish boy with soft waving hair of an indeterminate brown and a slightly drooping eyelid. He was pale, both naturally and through the rigours of his long journey, and the red and gold robe he wore, almost making him seem a miniature King, washed his complexion out even more.

Crowds cheered and clapped as Sir Thomas welcomed Henry before guiding the prince into the royal apartments, closely followed by a dozen finely-dressed attendants. The sight of servants in furs and brocades set tongues wagging; John and Isabella loved luxury, even in regards to their menials, hence even the stableboys and laundrywomen were given rich clothes. John could be generous when he wished—and when it made him look good!

After Mass that evening, a knock sounded upon my chamber door. To my surprise, I saw Thomas de Sandford standing outside. "Sir Thomas, what brings you here? I thought you would be with the young Prince."

"And so I was, Countess, and he has asked to see you. He says he will not settle till he does—and how can I deny our future monarch?"

"I am surprised he asks for me. I only saw him when he was very small. He would not remember."

"I beg to differ, my Lady. He is a conscientious boy, and I believe he takes in all that is happening around him. You are, of course, his aunt too. Will you come?"

"Of course I will come."

I followed the Constable through the castle, which was extremely busy as servants hauled in chests full of the Prince's clothes chests, toys, tapestries and bed hangings. He guided me to a chamber near the top of the castle, not the largest but the most lavish, its floors covered with Spanish rugs, its walls and ceiling painted with gold lions on a scarlet background and trumpeting angels gazing down in a starred firmament.

The Prince was sitting at a small table, with several white-bearded tutors hovering over him as he read Latin from a book. A prim nurse in a starched white wimple sat in the corner, waiting to attend her charge when needed. A lute player stood opposite her, a handsome young fellow in tight green hose and a saffron tunic adorned with silver braid. He strummed absent-mindedly—soothing music to bring calm to the royal bedchamber.

As Sir Thomas announced me, the lutanist let his hand drop and silence fell, save for the crackle of the fire in the metal brazier. I dropped a curtsey to the nine-year-old boy who was, perhaps, a future king—or not, depending on Prince Louis' success.

"Hello, Aunt," he said, and then, with a hand flourish, he dismissed the tutors and Thomas, leaving only the nurse and the lutanist. "You can play again, Humphrey," he told the musician. "Do not make it a sad song."

A merry melody swelled out. "My mother says I have been sent here for my safety," said young Henry. "I wish she had come with me, along with Richard and my little sisters Eleanor, Isabella and Joan. Are you here for your safety too, Aunt Ela?"

"I am, my lord Prince." I managed a weak smile.

"Are my cousins with you?"

"They are. I am sure they will find great delight in meeting their royal cousin. William is a little younger than you, my lord, but he is well-grown and quick to learn—you might well become good friends."

Henry sighed, looking a little sorrowful. "I heard rumours that Uncle William has fallen out with my father. They were always together once. Mother will not talk about it but says she can cast no blame on the Earl."

"Sadly, the rumours are true, my lord," I said. "I hope this does not harden your heart against me and your cousins, some of whom are mere babes."

"Of course not!" said the little Prince, surprised. "I would not do that. I only pray that if Uncle is no longer friends with my Lord Father, he will not turn against me too. He was kind. Father wanted him to teach me the arts of war alongside the Marshal."

"William will not turn against you," I said quickly, with some guilt, for I did not know my husband's true thought. He was, to the best of my knowledge still with Prince Louis, so an enemy to John and all his family. And yet, if what de Sandford said was true, that men were abandoning the French cause as swiftly as they had flocked to it, would William make amends with John, begging to return to the Plantagenet fold? Perhaps, instead of Louis, he would espouse the idea of this boy as King, with my kinsman William Marshal holding the realm in his capable hands during Henry's minority.

Henry smiled at me, all youthful innocence. "I am glad Earl William is still my friend, Aunt. I have worried about it for days. And I long to see my cousins—although not this very minute, for the road was long, and I am tired." He gave a yawn and stretched. "I will see them on the morrow. In the stables. Do they like ponies? I do."

"The oldest ones indeed like ponies," I confirmed, and Henry beamed.

The nervous flutters in my belly began to die away. The future was not mine to see, but this young boy was unlike his sire in every way, and not much like his fiery mother either…

The weather cooled with approaching Autumn. Trees began to turn golden and red. Servants gathered in the ripe apples and pears in the orchard. The air reeked with the sickly scent of spoiled apples lying discarded in the long grass. Henry and William amused themselves catching carp in the fishpond and trotting about the bailey on placid, stodgy ponies. Neither was permitted to venture beyond the castle gates, though, so instead they wandered the wall-walks and poked their tongues out at peasant boys passing below on their way to the market. The peasant lads hurled pebbles up at their tormentors, not knowing their identities but rising to the bait.

It was a strange, cloistered little world, with only distant tales of the battles in the east arriving at intervals. John had continued pillaging and destroying, even burning crops in the fields and plundering monasteries for gold. Now he was hastening for the port of Lynn, where he remained popular for granting the town its charter.

The weather grew more unstable, just like the political climate of England with its vengeful ruler and foreign claimant. Watery blue skies turned iron-grey and torrential rain began to fall, washing down over the great tall keep like the tears of some skyborn giant. Out in the garden, the fallen leaves skirled around me, blood-red, gold, dancing in a frenzy. My skirts and cloak lifted, whirling out behind me. Ida and Petronilla began to scream, as a great gust of wind overturned a basket of apples and sent them tumbling all over the ground. Thankfully the younger children were indoors, including Will, who was having Latin lessons with Henry.

"Girls, take my hands!" I shouted. "Do not fear, it is only a storm, but we must seek shelter."

The girls grabbed my hands and together we raced for the apartments. Rain hammered on our faces; the wind screeched through the crenels high above. Another huge gust ripped through the castle bailey, throwing over a wooden stall and taking a roof off the dog kennels. The hounds began to bark and howl; in the mews, the hawks were screeching and dancing on their perches. A low roll of thunder ascended to a deafening roar, and lightning speared a purple-dark sky. My daughters screamed anew as the world lit up, golden bright, then plunged back into a dark maelstrom of wind, leaves, rain and thunder.

As we reached the door, another bolt of lightning, forked as a devil's trident, shot across the sky, and struck near the top of the keep with a resounding crack and a sulphurous odour. "Look out!" someone bellowed from the gatehouse, a blurred shape amidst the deluge.

From above came a creaking noise, long and drawn out, followed by a sharp snap. The Royal Standard which had flown above the tower came toppling down, together with its broken pole, striking hard into the earth not five strides away. It flapped and whipped as if a living creature in its death throes, then descended into a muddy puddle, the lions contorted and stained brown.

I pushed the girls through the doorway into the relative warmth of the castle and slammed the door against the storm's ferocity. Immediately we were surrounded by agitated servants asking if we were harmed. Now that they were safe, my daughters lost their terror and began to giggle, plucking at their wet dresses and wringing water out of their sodden hair. "Up to your chambers at once and have

Basilia change your clothes," I ordered. "Otherwise you might fall ill."

Petronilla and Ida scampered off and I sought my own chambers, where Felyse and Mabella divested me of my dripping garb and slid my night-kirtle over my head. "I am chilled to the bone after that drenching," I said, hugging myself. "Stoke up the fire, would you, Mabella? I will eat in my chamber tonight and retire early, since dark comes swiftly these October days."

A simple meal consisting of a *mortrews* dumpling and demain bread was brought from the kitchens, which I ate while the thunder continued to roar and the gale buffeted the castle wall like an invisible besieger. Draughts made the candles flicker and long shadows dance on the walls. Afterwards, I climbed into bed and Mabella climbed in with me, while Felyse moved her paillasse closer and topped it with an extra sheepskin. We lay in the dark for some time, listening to the storm growing even wilder. Wind whistled and the very stones of Devizes Castle vibrated. Unseen items clanked and thudded in the bailey. Thunder growled and then rose in a deafening roar, shaking the earth.

"I am frightened," whispered Mabella. "Do you hear the wind? It is as if demons from Hell ride on every gust, dragging the souls of the wicked down into the eternal fires!"

"Oh, hush! Clear your mind of such evil thoughts," I murmured. "It is a storm, nothing more. The first of many winter storms. Go to sleep. It will blow itself out by dawn."

Falling asleep was harder than I thought with the tempest raging outside, but at last, as the thunder trailed away into the distance and the gale dropped from a shriek to a low, mournful keening, my eyelids drooped and I slipped into a deep, untroubled slumber.

In the morning, as I had predicted, the storm had blown itself out. I rose and dressed, feeling strangely light of heart. There was a calmness over the castle, a feeling of freshness and renewal.

I went into the garden. The trees were now thoroughly denuded, the last leaves ripped down the storm to lie like a golden mantle over the wet grass. The sun was out, riding high across the heavens; not a single cloud was visible, even on the horizon. Still that feeling of peace engulfed me, a sense that after every storm a better day would dawn. All one had to do was weather the storm unscathed.

Steps light, I returned to the castle apartments to tend the children. I wanted to tell them I felt certain we would soon return to Salisbury, but perhaps it was too soon to raise any hopes.

Yet my heart of hearts, on this fair, storm-washed morning, told me the day would soon come.

A messenger reached Devizes. Wind buffeted, he flung himself down from his weary horse and stumbled toward Thomas de Sandford. John's star and crescent badge gleamed dull silver against his dour travelling garb. "I bear news from Newark!" he gasped. "News of great import!"

"Well, out with it, man!" said Sir Thomas nervously, hooking his thumbs into his belt.

The rider's arrival had drawn the attention of all the servants and workers in the bailey—and of the elder four of my children, who were playing with Prince Henry in a game of tag amidst the herb beds. They hurried over to where the crowd was gathering, the young royal skipping alongside them as if he were but an ordinary lad.

Recognising the Prince, the crowd parted respectfully, and with sudden foreknowledge, I called my son and daughters to my side. "What is it, mother?" asked Ida, looking worried. "Why have you separated us from Henry, our cousin?"

The messenger had turned to stare at the nine-year-old boy standing alone and confused. "What is it, messenger?" Henry asked in his high, clear voice. "Is your message from my mother, the Queen? Or even my Father, the King?"

The messenger took one stumbling, exhausted step then fell to one knee in the mud. "The King is dead! Long live the King. Long live King Henry, Third of that Name."

A brief silence descended as the household took in the shocking news. Then one by one, the men sank to their knees and the women curtseyed, uncaring of the mud that soaked their skirts. "God save King Henry! *God save King Henry!*" The cry was taken up, growing louder and louder, echoing from tower to tower of Devizes Castle.

"You too," I whispered to my children, and we all did obeisance to the pale-faced, droopy-eyed little boy who was now our sovereign lord.

God save King Henry, Third of that Name!

CHAPTER NINETEEN

St Peter's Abbey in Gloucester stood stark under a gloomy October sky. Earl William and I had ridden to the ancient Roman town to attend the Coronation of the young Henry III. When William had learnt of John's death at Newark, he abandoned the French cause, rapidly crumbling as the English barons flocked to the new King, and galloped to Devizes to pledge his allegiance to his small nephew. "Sire," he had said, kneeling before the boy with tears in his eyes, "forgive me for joining he who had no right to the throne. I see that clearly now. I swear that my loyalty shall be to you for the rest of my life."

Henry had gazed down at him with compassion strange in one of such tender years. "Do not worry, Uncle. You are forgiven. I know my father was not an easy man to love—but you, until almost the end, did so. That counts for much and erases your crime in my eyes. I hope you will teach me the arts of war as my Lord Father hoped—it is well known you are a mighty warrior."

With reconciliation over, we came as guests to the Coronation, although William was to play no great part in the ceremonies due to his recent defection. It was strange to hold the crowning so far from Westminster, but London was still occupied by the French and the danger too great for the boy-king. Haste was also needed to keep any other claimants at bay.

In the Abbey, we walked in procession down the nave, passing effigies of bishops and monks, and the colourful tomb of Robert Curthose, brother to Henry I, who had died as Henry's prisoner, blinded before being locked with Devizes Castle.

Brothers! So often torn between love and hate, blood and destiny. If God and Mother Mary were kind, maybe my own boys would never suffer such anguish and remain in harmony all their lives.

Ahead, the high altar rose in splendour. Cardinal Guala, the Papal Legate, awaited the King on the step. Clad in silver and shining like a moon, his grey hair a cloud around his stern but kindly face, William Marshal motioned the little boy, almost completely muffled by his ermine robes, to step forward in sight of God and the Cardinal. Dutifully, Henry knelt on the tiles, and the Marshal took his sword and knighted him. One touch of the blade to each shoulder. "Be thou a knight, Henry of England."

Now the young King was ready to be coronated. Sylvester, Bishop of Worcester, and Simon, Bishop of Exeter, leaned over Henry, anointing him with the Holy Chrism on breast and back, on shoulders and brow. Then Peter des Roches, Bishop of Winchester, stepped forward, bearing not a crown, but a sparkling golden circlet on a silk cushion.

A murmur rippled through the congregation, dying almost instantly. The Queen, standing with her ladies around her, glared as if daring anyone to comment.

The circlet was her own, a gift from John long ago, and on this solemn occasion, it would serve to crown her son.

The crown of England was lost. It and other royal regalia had perished in the Wash, sucked under by the strong tides as the ailing King John tried to cut across a tidal causeway during his last fevered rush toward Newark. The baggage train had foundered, many of the carts overturning in the storm-swollen water—the crown jewels and all the King's plate and finery had vanished beneath the grey waves, lost forever.

Peter Des Roches took the finely-crafted band and held it aloft with reverence, even though it was truly but a trifle. It glimmered through the smoke rising from the candles as he brought it down and gently set it on the mouse-brown locks of the boy-king kneeling before him. Henry rose and a sceptre was placed into his hand, and he turned to face the congregation as a King.

"So it is done." Beside me, William reached out to surreptitiously squeeze my hand. "A new era begins."

Despite the crowning of Henry at St Peter's Abbey, Prince Louis had not relinquished his idea of becoming King of England. His forces had dwindled so much, however, that he abandoned several castles and sailed back to France to bolster his army. This meant he was unlikely to return for some months; probably in early spring when the crossing was less treacherous.

William and I returned to Salisbury with the children. Situated so far West, the city had turned out to be of little strategic interest to the French, so they had abandoned it and gone to other locations as directed by their captains. I was relieved and even slightly tearful to see the green ramparts appear on the horizon, layer upon layer, and the keep soaring above all. The town was mercifully unburnt, standing in its higgledy-piggledy, daub-and-wattle glory; butcher shops with meat haunches hanging out on hooks, taverns filled with music and mirth, smithies that billowed black smoke, and the workshops of silversmiths, carpenters, bakers, fletchers, bowyers, potters and coopers. It seemed few had suffered during the brief French occupation and of that I was glad.

I wondered if the townsfolk might regard us with suspicion after our absence, but it seemed not—men, women, children, dogs surged towards us as our entourage passed into the first earthwork enclosure with banners flying. A festival atmosphere descended, with the usual hawkers of food and tawdry trinkets pushing through the crowds, shouting in coarse voices as they flogged their wares—"Teeth from Saint Dionysius' skull. Guaranteed to cure your toothache!" "Pretty blue ribbons for your lass' hair." "Love potions to charm the most reluctant maiden!" "Sheep's feet, hot sheep's feet and jellied eels!"

"Can I have a sheep's foot, Mother?" asked Isobella, eyeing the hawker's wares hungrily.

"Certainly not. You will be fed at the castle, at a table; you will not walk about gnawing on a greasy food like a rat," said William, but he was smiling.

The rest of the children giggled, save for Isobella who pouted and folded her arms. "It's not fair…"

"Oh come," I said, scooping her up. It was undignified for a Countess to dandle her children in public, and I heard some gasps and saw fingers pointing, but I cared nought for their censure on that joyous day

King John was dead and William was free of his malignant influence—and we were home at last in the reign of a new young King.

Peace had not yet come to England, despite the change of monarch. Spies brought news to the royal court that Louis was preparing to mount a second invasion with a replenished force.

William had joined the young King's council and, to assure his loyalty to the Crown, he was granted Sherborne Castle and many lands in the west. The custodianship of Salisbury was also officially returned and verified in writing, having been stripped away when he surrendered it to the French.

Louis reached England's shores in May and directed his forces attack Lincoln Castle, which was in the hands of its hereditary Castellan, the indomitable old lady, Nichola de la Haye. The rest of the city had fallen but Nichola held firm against Louis' captain, Gilbert le Gant, who had rolled his engines up outside the castle walls. Now Louis had ordered mangonels brought in to bombard the gates until they shattered. William marched out of Salisbury alongside my distant kinsman, William Marshal the Younger, joining forces with The Marshal and the Papal Legate Guala outside the walls of Lincoln.

A section of the royal army managed to slip into the castle through a postern gate and manned the battered and broken walls, raining crossbow bolts onto the enemy besiegers. Armour was pierced and rebel leaders died as more royalists attacked the French flank; eventually, Louis' army was forced to retreat, leaving their mangonels and their baggage train, which was plundered and burnt.

Louis was defeated and pulled his forces back toward the coast...but still he clung to England with a desperate grip and would not leave. He had been acclaimed King by the rebel barons in St Paul's and the lure of a promised crown was too strong to endure.

William returned to Salisbury a hero, surrounded by high-spirited mobs. "*Longsword, Longsword*!" they chanted, throwing flowers at his horse as he cantered through the town to the castle gates. Bells were rung and the priests in castle and cathedral said Masses of thanksgiving.

Away from the celebrations—the townsfolk were burning a straw effigy meant to represent Prince Louis—William was much more subdued. "I had thought Louis might give up his claim at such a resounding defeat, but no. War will continue."

"He is a proud man, as is his sire."

"Greedy, I'd say," retorted William. "Ah, Ela, but it was a splendid victory. You should have seen it—the Legate in his white robes, shining like a heavenly messenger, publicly excommunicating Louis and all his followers, while pardoning the English from any sin, ensuring that should we die, our souls would ascend straight to heaven! The faces of the French were a sight to behold; anger, mixed with fear and growing doubt."

Leaning back in his seat within our bedchamber, he continued, eyes alight at the memory. "You remember Faulkes de Breaute?"

"A mercenary. A rough man with little scruples."

"Well, he proved himself of some worth at Lincoln. He is brave if nought else. He led a contingent to the castle's postern and found a way to enter without alerting the enemy. He sent his men onto the walls, where they fired on the French with their crossbows."

"Couriers told of that daring deed, but I did not know of Faulkes' involvement." I shook my head. "A bad man, but good to have on one's side. It is often the way."

"The battle was won when the French commander, Thomas, Count of Perche, was slain. He was surrounded in front of Lincoln Cathedral's doors, perhaps attempting to reach sanctuary. Men called for his surrender, but he refused to throw down his weapons. One hot-headed knight galloped at him, wielding a lance; the tip went through the slit in his visor and pierced his brain. I was furious; Thomas was kin, the son of my half-sister Matilda and Henry the Lion, and even blood-ties aside, he would have brought a hefty ransom. But his death *did* halt the fighting and cause the French to flee." He crossed himself. "I will light candles and have prayers said for him in the cathedral."

"God rest Thomas of Perche. And God be praised that you have returned to your wife and children free of any injury!"

He glanced at me and took my hand. "It nearly was not so. At one point, I was surrounded by the foe, striking out strongly and holding my position. But then I saw a knight riding at me, his lance levelled for a killing blow. I was an easy target, as I am taller than most men. I recognised on his shield the colours of Robert of Ropsley."

"Ropsley…Did he not once hold Bristol and Kenilworth?"

"Yes, he was also Sheriff of Warwickshire and Leicestershire. I knew him well; he held many offices under John. But he abandoned my brother, even as I did, and stayed with the rebels even after King Henry's accession. I assume he wanted vengeance for my desertion of the French cause. It was the Marshal who saved my life, Ela— what a lion of a man he is, even in old age. He lunged forward, thrust me behind him, and with one mighty blow, smote the lance from Ropley's hand!"

"God bless the Marshal, England owes him much," I breathed. "I will pray for his continued health…Oh. William, no one mentioned your narrow escape. I feel cold as if a burial shroud has enfolded my limbs."

Forcing a laugh, he poked at the fire with a stick. "No, Ela— there's no shroud. Only the chill winds that always creep over the heights of Salisbury even in summer."

Reaching out, he drew me into his embrace. "It is so good to feel your warm skin and smell the sweetness of your hair, after the reek of burning, of blood, of men who shit themselves in their final death throes. The royal army burnt the town after victory; that was not well done. I could not control them; they wanted blood and plunder. I have sinned gravely by allowing such desecration; they even sacked the cathedral…"

"You said yourself that Legate Guala absolved all English fighters of their sins. You are blameless."

"You have such faith in me, wife; I pray it is justified."

"It is. Now let us retire. I will reward the conqueror of the French in my own way."

"And what way is that?" His hands slipped to my waist, toying with the ties of my girdle.

"Douse the light and you will find out," I laughed as his lips descended on mine.

In August I waved goodbye to William once more as he departed to take on the French. Blanche, the wife of Prince Louis, had sent eighty huge ships bristling with soldiers to give succour to her beleaguered but grimly-determined husband, and this flotilla was accompanied by hundreds of smaller cogs full of sellswords and sellsails. Their leader was a pirate called 'Eustace the Monk' whose daring and bloodthirsty deeds were known throughout Europe.

Richard Poore, now Bishop of Salisbury following the death of his brother, Herbert, gave William blessing as he prepared to march for the Cinque Ports, from whence he would travel by ship to Dover to rendezvous with the castle's Constable, Hubert de Burgh, who was recruiting additional soldiers for the mission.

"You must promise to tell tales of this pirate, Eustace, when you return," I said to him, as I stood at his stirrup. "Little Will demands it. In fact, he says he would like you to bring the pirate's head home on a spike."

"I shall see what I can do," said William, with a laugh, "but no promises, I am afraid. What do *you* want me to bring you, my Lady?"

"Only yourself, as ever, alive and well." I placed my hand on my midriff. "I would not want our latest babe to grow up without a father."

"He—or she—will not. As long as God wills it, of course."

"As God wills." I bowed my head, and with a cheerful wave he rode down toward the gates.

I watched as his figure dwindled into the haze, then, my steps slow, sorrowful, I returned to the solar to watch my daughters' dance and hear a new minstrel sing his repertoire.

Even after all the long years of our marriage, I never got used to my husband's frequent departures, fraught with grave danger as they often were. Behind my forced ladylike composure, I cursed the French and wished for storms to batter their side of the Narrow Sea...

William's fleet was victorious, the wandering monks from Dover told us, breathless with delight. On St Bartholomew's Day, the English navy had engaged the French fleet, bearing down on the rear of the flotilla, after using a diversion tactic to lead them astray.

Arrows blacked out the burning August sun, making the sea darken as if covered by an unnatural night. William's ships rammed the great warships of the French, disabling them, and sank the lesser cogs. By the time the sun set, thirty of the larger French vessels had sunk, leaving the rest under English control, the nobles and knights on board spared death but bound in chains. Eustace the Monk, the cruel and audacious pirate, was dragged from his hiding place in his ship's belly and summarily beheaded.

I smiled wanly when I heard of Eustace's fate and saw little Will's face grow rapt. William had better not bring a gory keepsake home.

Despite his victory, William had still more business to attend to. By September, the disheartened Prince Louis, decided to abandon his pretensions to the English throne. Meeting the King's counsellors, including the Marshal and William, he signed a Treaty known as the Peace of Lambeth. Louis was given a settlement of 10,000 marks—a staggering sum—and all his captive followers were released. He then sailed for France, vowing never to set foot in England again. Many were angered that the Marshal had agreed to such generous terms, but at least it was done and over. Now, at last, England could rebuild with only one King claiming the throne.

William was free to return to Salisbury in early October. The children were brought from the nursery to the Great Hall to greet him. Almost immediately Will began pestering about Eustace the Monk—he had not forgotten. "Tell me about the pirate and how you killed him, Father!" he begged.

"I do not want to hear about smelly old pirates," sniffed Ida primly.

"Then you can go away," blazed William. "Go sniff flowers or do other maiden's stupid things!"

"William!" I warned my son. "You will not speak with disrespect to Ida or any of your sisters."

Will hung his head, muttering a half-hearted apology. Then he glanced up at his father. "You will tell me, though, won't you?"

"Yes, I will. The rest of the children can go back to the nursery."

As the nurses escorted the other children away, Will settled down at his sire's feet like a contented hound. I was minded to chastise him, for an Earl's son should have more decorum, but he looked so contented, I could not bear to do so. Instead, I sat on a bench and tended to my embridery, although I found myself listening intently to William's tale.

"Eustace was the son of a man called Baudoin Busket…"

"That's a silly name!" crowed Will.

"Indeed…but his son wasn't silly, he was sly and evil. They say he fared to Toledo in Spain to learn the Black Arts."

"He was in league with the Devil?" Will's eyes widened.

"So they say…but no, he did not return to France riding a besom and attended by a host of demons. When he returned, he became a Benedictine Monk at St Samer, clad all in sombre black."

"Then he *really* was a monk." William flicked straw strands from the knees of his hose. "Monks are *boring…*"

"Well, this one wasn't, and he was a false monk, with not one ounce of holiness in him. He encouraged his fellow monks to break their holy fast, to curse instead of pray—even to fart loudly while walking in the cloisters!"

Will suppressed a giggle with his sleeve. Like all young lads, he was amused by jests about the ruder functions of the body.

"Fortunately for his fellow monks, he soon left his order, seeking to avenge his sire who had been murdered. Eventually, he joined a noble household and became seneschal. He did not last long there, for his lord soon found out he had stolen coin from his treasury. Eustace fled and his master had him declared outlaw. That's when he decided to become a pirate. He held a castle on the isle of Guernsey and for a while served your Uncle John, but whoever could offer him the most coin was his best friend, and he soon returned to his natural French allegiance and began to fight for King Philip instead. Indeed, it was he who brought Prince Louis to our shores."

"How did you catch him?" asked Will. "Did you fight hand to hand on deck?"

"Yes, there was a melee after we boarded some of the ships under his command. But first we had to get on board—so we threw powdered lime into the faces of the French sailors. Unfortunately,

Eustace the Monk was not on any of the ships we boarded—he saw the way the wind was blowing and sailed off at speed. We had not forgotten Eustace, though; we pursued him and finally caught his ship as he tried to veer into a cove. After his brigands had been dealt with, we searched his vessel to find him. He was cowering in the bilge, under a blanket. We dragged him up on deck, forced him to the ship's rail and…" He made a swift slashing motion across his throat.

"So the evil pirate is dead and gone!"

"He is dead indeed. I wanted to bring his head for you…but your mother would not approve…" He glanced at me and winked. "And the townsfolk on the south coast wanted it anyway; they are taking turns to display it outside their town gates."

"That was a splendid story, Father," said Will, scrambling up from the floor. "I am glad you subdued that pirate…and that you are home." William reached out to tousle his son's hair and then Will, ever-active ran off, no doubt to seek amusement in the kennels or mews, or watch the antics of Proudfoot the Fool.

"Well, you certainly had an adventure," I said to my husband. "What is next, I wonder?"

"Next?" said William. "Sit by the fire in the warm with my feet up by the fire and my handsome sons and beautiful daughters all around me. And my wife too, of course. Finally, for a time at least, there will be peace. Oh—and the Great Charter is valid again, and soon will be reissued with some changes. The Marshal is overseeing it."

CHAPTER TWENTY

Over the next few years, William and I indeed lived a peaceful life in Salisbury. Our son Richard was born and the following year another fine boy, Nicholas. We began to plan out marriages for our children as we had discussed earlier. In 1217, a little girl called Idoine de Camville had been orphaned, her father's death leaving her a wealthy heiress. Knowing the value of a good heiress, William managed to buy her wardship and the rights to her marriage. She came to Salisbury and quickly became as another sister to my four girls.

Soon she was betrothed to our son, Will; I hoped that if they had some closeness in youth, they might form a love-match, although Will would soon be heading to another household for knightly training. For Ida, we found a future husband in Ralph de Somerey, the Baron of Dudley; they were close in age, and he was calm and stolid as she was nervous and flighty. Ella perhaps made the best match of all—her hand was sought by the Beaumont family, the Earls of Warwick. Her husband was called Thomas and he was of a similar age to Ella; they made a very handsome couple even in their early youth. The younger boys we did not make matches for, presuming at least one would enter the church, while Isobella occasionally lamented that she was contemplating a nun's life, so we held off seeking a husband, leaving her to study scriptures, while Petronilla was firmly convinced that her future was in the cloister, serving God.

Ah, my poor little Petronilla with her elfin face and flame-red hair, so dreamy and gentle, caring for every injured bird or hedgehog, seeing angels in clouds, crying when coneys were brought for the pot. It was almost as if she was never quite part of our mortal world.

In the springtime of 1218, we took her to meet with the Abbess of Wilton. She walked around the abbey cloisters in a daze, laughing in delight as a brace of doves suddenly dived through the ornate arches. "The Dove of Peace!" She pointed to one white bird as it soared into the sky. "Christ sent it to tell me of my destiny!"

Abbess Margaret took me aside as Petronilla danced around the cloisters while passing nuns stared in amazement, a few of the elders tutting under their breath. "Lady Petronilla is a kind girl, but she is very young yet…and idealistic. I am not sure if she quite understands the rigours of cloistered life. It is not all singing in the choir and musing on the beauty of God's creations. Wait a few more years—we will have her then."

On the way back to Salisbury, Petronilla went quiet, her usual chatter stilled. I assumed she was merely upset that she was not allowed to join the nuns yet, and ignored her as she huddled amid the cushions in the litter, knees pulled to her chest.

When we reached the castle, she got out and made a moaning noise. "Mother," she said, "there is a horrible pain in my right side. I feel sick."

Going to her, I noticed her face had gone greenish-white and a clammy sweat marred her brow. "Jesu, come inside, I will get the physician!" I said.

Petronella was put to bed and the doctor came, a lean man in black who had a long beard that he liked to stroke while deliberating on his patient. He called himself, very grandly, Magister de la Ronde. He pressed on Petronella's belly, making her cry out in pain, then rubbed his beard, felt her brow, went back to the beard, examined the vomit we had collected in a pewter bowl—and fiddled with that stringy beard until I felt an urge to take a knife and hack it off.

"Magister, you have been here long and have said nought. What ails my daughter? What can you give her to ease her pain?"

Magister de la Ronde hummed and hawed, digging through a large leather bag he had brought. He yanked out a clay jug stopped with wax. Breaking the seal, he leaned over Petronella's sickbed and poured noxious-smelling fluid into her mouth. She choked a little and made a face but with my gentle encouragement, she drank it all.

"I have given her the milk of the poppy," said de la Ronde. "Imported from the Far East. It will numb the pain and bring deep sleep but…" He heaved a great sigh and stared at the floor, twisting his facial hair once more.

Panic washed over me in waves of heat followed by ice. "What are you telling me? What is wrong with my child? You are here to heal her; they say you are the best in Wiltshire!"

"My Lady, can we speak outside the sick room?" He gestured toward the door, his skinny arm in its funereal black looking, to my mind, like the arm of scythe-bearing Death. Fighting the dreadful thought away, I nodded silently and followed him from the room.

In the corridor, the cool air licked at my heated face. The torches shivered, their light dimming and dipping. "Lady Ela," said the physic, "I would have the Earl here as well to hear what I must say."

I was now beside myself with fear but managed to nod. "I will summon him." I gestured to Mabella, who was hovering at the end of the passage, her eyes round and glassy with fear. "Go to the Earl and have him come to me and the good doctor without delay."

William arrived shortly, brows furrowed with concern. "Why have I been summoned? It—it is just some childish complaint, is it not? Eating apples too green? Eating too many sweetmeats?"

Magister de la Ronde cleared his throat, making an awful sound that grated on my shattered nerves. "I wish that were the case, my lord Earl. I have given the child the juice of the poppy…but I fear that is all I can do for her. I have seen her condition a few times; it is thought some facet within the body goes rotten—no one knows why this should be. But when the rottenness ruptures, releasing poisons that are trapped within, the whole body is blighted. Forgive me, for bearing such ill news…." He grasped his beard, fingers moving in agitation as if he might rip the whole thing from its roots.

William gaped at the man as if he could not quite believe what he was hearing. "You are telling me…no…*no*…you lie, *you lie*!" He lunged at de la Ronde, catching his black robes in a clenched fist and dragging him forward, almost causing him to fall.

"William, no!" I clutched at my husband's arms. "You must not! He has done no wrong. It is not his fault. Whatever happens…must be God's Will!"

"*God's Will?*" William shouted and he released the doctor's robes and struck the wall with a balled fist. The rough stone cut his knuckles and jewels of blood glimmered on his skin. "If this is His Will, he can go to Hell, the tyrant…"

"Husband, I beg you, do not blaspheme." Tears were pouring down my face, blinding me. "Railing against God or the doctor will not help Petronella."

"*Nothing* will help her!" William threw out his arms in a helpless gesture. "You heard him. I am her father—and I cannot help her. Oh, Christ…" He was weeping now, his face contorted by the power of his grief. He sank to one knee on the floor and I sank down beside him, clutching his shoulders, my tears mingling with his.

"What can we do, Ela?" he cried. "What light is in this darkness?"

"We must head to Saint Osmund's shrine and pray—pray for a miracle, and if there is no miracle forthcoming, for a swift and painless passage to heaven for our daughter."

Three days Petronella lingered, caught in a half-world, drugged by the milk of the poppy. Near midnight on the third day, she stirred and opened her eyes. "The angel doves are in the room," she whispered. "I see them; their wings are turned to gold. Their wings brush my face…I am so hot…so hot…" Her eyelids drooped again, but this time, they never reopened. The ragged sob of her breath stilled to nothing.

I gave a cry and fell against William, who seemed frozen, his countenance twisted in agony. A warrior who wrought death with the strength of his sword arm was reduced to deep, helpless despondency at his own daughter's loss.

For a week Petronella lay on a hearse in Salisbury Cathedral, surrounded by tall, scented candles. Her small body had been washed with fine white wine, while aromatic spices were sprinkled into her mouth and throat. A rich balsam was rubbed into her limbs and a linen shroud twined around her. A hearse-cloth emblazoned with her father's Arms lay over her. All the folk of Salisbury came to show respect, and her sisters and brothers were brought in to pray. The clerks sang the Offices of the Dead, their voices echoing around the pillars of the cathedral.

On the eighth day, the hearse was raised and the coffin carried outside to a waiting chariot surrounded by black-clad mourners. William climbed onto the back as chief mourner; I was carried behind in a black-draped litter with my eldest surviving children, Ida, Ella, Isobella, and Will.

After consulting with William, the decision had been taken to bury Petronella in St Mary's Priory at Bradenstoke. The priory was strongly connected to the Earls of Salisbury. My great-grandfather, Walter Fitz Edward, founded it as a daughter house to St Mary's of Cirencester, and when his wife died, he entered the priory as a monk of the Augustinian Order. His bones lay within the priory church near the high altar.

Now he would watch over not only Mother Church, but the mortal remains of his great-great-granddaughter, who had also wished for a holy life serving God.

The tomb they made for Petronella was in the choir, small and unassuming. I watched with the quiet dignity of a Countess and Earl's daughter as her lead coffin was encased in stone and a heavy marble lid drawn over it. I was more fortunate than some women, having lost but one child when some lost many, but it felt as if a dagger had sliced my heart in twain, and I wondered if that grief, that pain, would ever cease. My little nun who never wore the wimple—I remembered the white doves flying as she ran after them, and an unexpected sensation of warmth struck through me, and in a flash, I saw with perfect clarity the meaning and reason for my own life. One day, if God willed, I should live so long, I would myself become a nun, and found a handsome house of sisters, and dwell in chastity and poverty, aiding the poor and afflicted. I would fulfil the wish of my poor dead daughter, and do good deeds in the name of Our Lord that she never had a chance to do…

As the funeral cortege departed Bradenstoke after the burial, William came to check on me in my litter. As he observed my demeanour, he frowned. "Ela, you have *changed*. There is a light in your eyes, your face."

"I will shed no more tears," I said. "The Lord has spoken to me. Petronella is at peace and will not be forgotten, and one day we shall meet again, at the End of Days—but now, it is the time of the living, not the beloved dead, and we must do our duty as Earl and Countess of Salisbury. Our duty to the People and to Our Lord."

William continued to back the young King's faction as strongly as he could. Unrest bubbled under the surface but he was proud to hold it in check for King Henry, assisted by the powers of Hubert de Burgh, the Justiciar, a man I had met a few times and never liked. Deep, I called him, holding secret ambitions close to his chest. And his small, dark eyes always followed me searchingly, as if trying to read my mind. Even worse, he had wed the unfortunate Hadwisa of Gloucester, recently widowed, and within a month of the wedding, she was dead. He was granted all her lands. It all seemed a little convenient.

Later in 1218, a Papal Bull was issued regarding a matter that had long lain dormant—moving Salisbury Cathedral down the hill to the fields near the Avon. William was still somewhat peeved at the idea of having to travel two miles to the new town, but I had lost my earlier resistance to the plan. Years ago, I had wavered in the draughty, damp scriptorium, and now the cathedral had grown slightly dilapidated, the constant buffets of wind damaging the fabric of the façade. The town too was expanding and overspilling the ancient earthen ramparts that contained it. With the overcrowding came disease, and even more problems obtaining decent water, the life's blood of the community

William and I travelled down to Bishop Poore's site to oversee the beginnings of New Salisbury. Great trenches had already been dug on the Bishop's instructions. Everywhere was a hive of activity, with men coming and going from the workshops of carpenters, masons, painters and other builders. A heap of stones towered to the sky—good limestone brought from Chickstone Quarry. Timbers from woodlands across Wiltshire, Hampshire and even Herefordshire lay strewn about like a fallen forest. Great stacks of lead to cover the vast roof made a great grey mound.

Whilst there, we met with the Bishop, who was overseeing work on both cathedral and the new town that would surround it. Of old, I had preferred his brother, Bishop Herbert, but now, with a plan in mind, Bishop Poore had strengthened and matured, guided by the wisdom of the Papal Legate Guala. Besides holding the office of

Bishop of Salisbury, Richard Poore had also become a diligent Royal Justice.

"Come, my Lord Earl, my Lady Ela," he said, leading us to a temporary wooden building overlooking the cathedral site. "I have something to show you."

Inside his hut, he unrolled a parchment that, at first, had the appearance of a great map, and pinned it with daggers to a worn old desk. Lighting candles, he beckoned us closer. On the desk was a plan of the town of New Salisbury as Richard Poore envisioned it. "Here…" he said, drawing his finger along a blue line, "is where we shall put canals, and over here in black are the roads. Lodgings for the workers are here…and there is the plot where a church shall rise to serve their spiritual needs."

He swept his hand over one section of the parchment, then another. "We hope tradesmen from all over the west might move here to start new lives. There shall be quarters for various trades—we shall put fruiterers, poulterers, costermongers, wafer-makers, pastrycooks, bakers here, and the fleshers, butchers, egglers and poutrymen just over the way from them. Hopefully, this next section of town will hold the cordwainers, weavers, haberdashers, hatmakers and jewellers…Oh, and not to forget the silversmith and goldsmiths! There are many more possibilities besides once the main town is established. Taverns must not be forgotten, either—important for the ease of hard-working folk! In moderation, of course." He licked his lips as if savouring some newly-brewed Salisbury ale. "I have even marked out sections of the town for those who practice less seemly but necessary trades."

"Less seemly?" My brows lifted. For a moment, I thought the holy Bishop was advocating the building of stews or brothels!

He must have realised my thought, for his cheeks turned a shade of bright pink. "Nothing *too* unseemly, Countess; I meant the fullers who tread in urine to clean the wool, the leather tanners with their odiferous treatments, as well as rat-catchers and gong-fermours."

"Ah," I said, understanding. "Trades connected with filth and foul odours."

"Yes, exactly," said the Bishop. "Nothing to offend the eye or nose in our new town, as much as possible." He beamed, clasping his hands together as if praying that his town would be the finest in all England. "We have a wooden chapel already built, dedicated to Our Lady. It is for the use of the workers. Eventually, I hope it will rise in stone, even as the cathedral. That and many others."

William and I returned to the Castle. Together we gazed down from the ramparts at the old cathedral. It would gradually be dismantled; its massive blocks wedged apart and carried to the new cathedral to provide stone for the encircling wall and for the buildings of the close. Until that time, however, it would remain in use for the clergy and the folk of Salisbury.

"It will grieve me the days the doors close," I said, "but although I was wary in the beginning, I think Bishop Poore's plans for the cathedral at Merryfields are inspired by God. I feel deep within that what is raised shall rank as the most beautiful cathedral in the land."

"I too had doubts, mainly because the cathedral brought trade to the town," said William, "but now I too believe, it is best to start anew. The people of the town must as soon as possible be encouraged move to new Salisbury and begin their trades anew."

"It will be strange and quiet on our hill with only the cry of the birds and the rush of wind," I said.

"It will be peaceful," said William.

"Peace, at last peace...here and in England," I murmured. Together, we watched as the sun set behind the western trees and all the lamps flickered into life around the town.

The great William Marshall died that spring, in his house at Caversham. Before he died, he called King Henry's guardian, Peter des Roches, the justiciar Hubert de Burgh, and many of the barons to a final meeting. The new Papal Legate, Pandulf, in the service of Pope Honorius, who had replaced the deceased Innocent, was given the regency, much to des Roches' dismay and indignation. The Bishop had believed the office was his by right since the boy was in his care.

"The decision was for the best," said William, returning from the council. "No one much likes des Roches, for all he is capable in his own way, and clearly loyal to Henry. I think de Burgh would see him gone from England if he had his way. The Bishop desires more than a churchman should aspire to."

I made a dismissive noise. "Hubert de Burgh is no better. Both men are far too ambitious."

William slumped on a stool and started dragging off his boots. "Yes, it is a great shame the Marshall is gone—although he lived an extremely long life and was strong and wise until his dying days. He had his allotted three score and ten and more."

"He was a good man." I crossed myself. "I am proud to call him kinsman."

"On his deathbed, he was sworn into the Order of the Templars," William said. "His body was taken to the Temple Church in London for burial with others of the Order."

"*Requiescat in pace*, great Marshal," I said. "You will not be forgotten. You were the world's most perfect knight."

Upon the Day of St Vitalis, in the Year of Our Lord 1220, William and I journey to New Salisbury for a great occasion—to lay the foundation stones of the cathedral. Bishop Poore had planned a lavish royal feast, doling out much money from his own purse for food and entertainment to amuse the King. Alas, with only days to spare, Henry had to change his plans, for a Welsh treaty was on the table and he must ride through the night to Shrewsbury.

Bishop Poore was disappointed, but the ceremony would carry on nonetheless, as he had already spread the news of the founding throughout the diocese.

I glanced around as William and I entered the Merryfields. Not many banners flew; most of the barons were with the King in Shropshire as was the Archbishop of Canterbury. However, many folk from Old Salisbury had wandered down to marvel at the New, and at the beginnings of the cathedral of St Mary the Virgin.

The Bishop performed divine service in the temporary chapel, as humble as the stable where Christ was born with its wooden walls and narrow aisles. Then, removing his fine shoes and walking barefoot, he led a procession of clerics and nobles toward the cathedral site.

As he walked, he sang the Litany, his strong voice carrying to the ears of those who clustered amidst the half-timbered first houses of New Salisbury:

"Lord, have mercy on us.
Christ, have mercy on us.
Lord, have mercy on us.
Christ, hear us.
Christ, graciously hear us.
God the Father of Heaven,
Have mercy on us.
God the Son, Redeemer of the world,
Have mercy on us.
God the Holy Ghost,
Have mercy on us.
Holy Trinity, one God,
Have mercy on us.
Holy Mary,
pray for us.
Holy Mother of God,
pray for us.
Holy Virgin of virgins,
pray for us.
Mother of Christ,
pray for us..."

And as he approached the area where the workshops stood, and the great stones, timbers, and leaden sheets were piled high:

"Seat of wisdom,
pray for us.
Cause of our joy,
pray for us.
Spiritual vessel,
pray for us.
Vessel of honour,
pray for us.
Singular vessel of devotion,

pray for us.
Mystical rose,
pray for us.
Tower of David,
pray for us.
Tower of ivory,
pray for us.
House of gold,
pray for us.
Ark of the Covenant,
pray for us.
Gate of Heaven,
pray for us."

Once he had finished the Litany, he climbed upon the earthwork foundations and recited a short sermon with such passion the tears fell from his eyes. Lifting the first foundation stone, he laid it in place in the name of Pope Honorious, who had allowed the cathedral to be moved. Second, he placed a stone for Stephen Langton, the Archbishop of Canterbury, away with King Henry in the Marches; third, he placed a stone for himself, kneeling in the dirt to kiss its pale surface.

As Bishop Poore stepped aside, William strode onto the site, tall and regal in his blue robe girded with a belt of golden wires. With due reverence, he laid the fourth stone. I followed him, kneeling reverently to lay the fifth beside that of my husband. The Dean went next, then chantor, chancellor, treasurer, archdeacons and canons, including Elias de Dereham, designer of the splendid shrine to St Thomas Becket in Canterbury and who was to take on the job of Salisbury's architect. In the fields beyond, the watching townsfolk wept for the joy of this founding, holding their arms up to heaven, to the empty space where a spire would eventually rise—though that would not be for many years, most likely after all of us had gone to our Maker.

The sun shone, and even though the glory of the day was slightly marred by the lack of a royal presence, we felt assured of the success of this great work of beauty and Faith—a cathedral in the Gothic style, lovelier than any seen in England.

Later, at Richard Poore's feast, he leaned over to speak with us, full of joyous enthusiasm, waving a sauce-laden medallion of beef on the end of his knife. "We can now proceed with the greatest speed," he told us, eyes sparkling "I have assurances that when the King has returned from his business more men of rank and honour will come forth to lay stones, and thus bind themselves to contributions for the next seven years. The church is always in need of money..." He peered meaningfully at William.

"You will have your money, Bishop," snapped William, his acerbic tone reminding me of John, but then he smiled and the mood lightened. "This moment, the founding of New Salisbury Cathedral surely shall be one of the great accomplishments of my life and that of my wife, Countess Ela."

The Bishop audibly sighed with relief at his words. "It will be a mighty accomplishment for us all. You will not regret your contributions, my Lord Earl."

The cathedral went up at an almost alarming speed. Consecration blocks set with brass plates were placed around the site and the walls now rose as tall as a man. The east end was the main focus of the building, with great timbers of Irish wood brought in to fashion the roof. The King finally came to visit after his second Coronation in Westminster; now, with a real crown upon his brow instead of his mother's circlet, he felt more confident in his reign.

I visited the cathedral site as often as I could, sometimes staying at the royal palace of Clarendon a few miles outside New Salisbury. Clarendon had been a hunting lodge right back to the time of the Saxon rulers, and it had hosted the King's Court on more than one occasion. Young Henry favoured stays there to enjoy the extensive game-filled forest and ordered its renewal and beautification. The hall from old Henry II's days was remodelled and the plain dark roof replaced with striking red tiles. The kitchens and wine cellars were extended and a treasury put in; Henry also built new apartments with lavish furnishings and grisaille glass.

William and I occasionally hunted there, riding through the green-leaved trees with other nobles. When he was in residence, the young King would join us, delighting in showing young Will his new horses, hounds and hawks. Henry was very generous to all his kin and friends too, giving us gifts every time he saw us—deer or boar for the table, tuns of the finest wine. He even remembered his cousin, Eleanor of Brittany, still locked up behind three stout walls of Corfe. John had stipulated in his will that she never be released, but when he was in the West, Henry made sure she received gifts of dates, figs and raisins.

Trouble was never far away, however. Not surprisingly, it came from the Welsh Prince Llewellyn, along with many of the old rebellious lords of John's time—foreigners such as Faulkes de Breaute, who favoured whatever side would bring him the most plunder. Ranulf of Chester, another man I found loathsome, had gone from the King's confidant to Welsh supporter, having overseen the marriage of his nephew, John the Scot, to Llewellyn's daughter Helen.

William rendezvoused with Hubert de Burgh and William Marshal the Younger and together they marched for Wales with their armies. By October, shortly after the King's sixteenth birthday, Llewellyn submitted to the King at the castle of Montgomery. Shouting and red-faced, Ranulf tried to paint de Burgh as a tyrant who was attempting to corrupt Henry, but Hubert, cool and unruffled, turned to his youthful royal charge and stated, "You must not listen, my liege. Chester has no love of you; he is a turncoat and may even mount an attempt on your life." The Justiciar then retreated from Wales with Henry until they were safe behind the walls of Gloucester.

It was during Henry's stay in Gloucester that Ranulf showed his true colours as rebel and traitor. Knowing the King was still away, he took an armed force to London and seized the Tower. De Burgh soon marched south, and Ranulf was driven out with his treacherous rabble, but that was not the end of his agitating, alas.

With his cronies, Faulkes de Breaute and Peter de Maulay, Ranulf sought audience with Stephen Langton to air their grievances and discuss a peace treaty. Stridently, they blamed all their problems on Hubert de Burgh and demanded that he be removed from his position. Hubert had, in turn, rounded in fury on Peter des Roches, who agreed with Ranulf, calling the Bishop 'traitor' to his face. Long loathing de Burgh, des Roches swore he would bring Hubert to his knees if it cost him everything he owned.

At Christmas, it all came to a head at the King's festive court in Northampton. With William and nine other Earls solidly behind him, King Henry summoned, or rather ordered, Ranulf and his allies to attend him without delay. "I expect to have very fine gifts from you this Yuletide, gentlemen," the young King told them, serious-faced but with a gleam in his eyes. "The greatest gifts you can give me, to show your love and loyalty—your castles."

Grudgingly the rebels agreed, with many shifty sideways looks to each other, while William upbraided Ranulf, de Breaute, Engelard de Cigogne, Brian de Lisle, and other troublemakers, not one of which was born on English soil. "We, the native-born men of England stand against those from without who seek to foment bitter war within this kingdom!"

In Wiltshire, the cathedral continued to flourish, its progress steady. The east end was complete and three chapels dedicated to St Peter, St Stephen and the Holy Trinity were consecrated and in use. Columns of beautiful, polished Purbeck marble reared like frozen trees, ready to take weight of the great roof. A glass window showing the Tree of Jesse was inserted into Trinity Chapel, and its walls were painted with gold, green and red foliate patterns.

At the castle, I oversaw the running of the town while William fared back and forth from Henry's court—and to Lincoln, where he attempted to wrench Lincoln Castle and the Sheriffship from Nicola de La Haye, whose grand-daughter Idoine was now happily married to our Will. He believed that Nicola should cede the castle to our son, who would then hold it in the right of his wife, who was Nicola's heir.

Lincoln Castle and its shrievalty caused one of our few arguments.

"You should not do it, William." Casting my embroidery aside, I faced up to my husband who, for the dozenth time, had moaned about Nicola's 'pig-headed' refusal to cede her positions.

He scowled at me, mouth an angry white line. "What do you mean, wife?"

"You heard me perfectly well. Leave the old woman alone. She held out against the French as strongly as any man, and here you try to rob her of sheriffship and castle."

Now he looked as perplexed as angry. "But you said it yourself, she is old. She should retire gracefully to a manor house and put her feet up before the fire."

"Pah." I made a dismissive motion with my hand. "Do you think after living the life she's led, filled with courage and responsibility, that she wants to sit before the hearth, rocking herself into a stupor of boredom?"

"But...but, she's a *woman*," he complained, "she cannot possibly desire to hold that castle until the day she drops dead. Circumstance forced her to act like a man all her days; surely now she would like..."

I gave an annoyed sigh. "None of you men have any idea what women would *truly* like. Mothers, nuns, or harlots—you see each of us as one of those and nought more, depending on your inclinations."

"I have no idea why you are so angry, Ela. Have I not given you a happy life, with fine children, and treated you with honour?"

"Yes. In no way do I say that you have not!"

"Then what *are* you saying, woman!" he cried, exasperated.

"Merely, that women, for all that they are not men, have talents beyond bedchamber, cloister or brothel. But men do not seem to notice that this is so. Look! Down in Salisbury, many widows carry on their husband's businesses and very successfully too! In your long absences, I received petitions and sorted disputes and other business in the town. I did not faint dead away when required to use the mind God granted me, and on no occasion did I need to ask a man for aid. "

His scowl deepened, although it was mixed with perplexity. "You did those things because they were your duty in my absence, surely."

"Did you never think for one moment, I might have actually *enjoyed* them?"

"No...I did not." He seemed amazed by my revelations.

"Well, now you do know. And I think I would make a fair enough sheriff myself, dispensing justice tempered with mercy. I would certainly be fairer and more honest than some sheriffs in

England, who have caused nought but grief to Crown and commons alike. Leave Nicola de la Haye be, husband—she is so old now, it can only be a matter of time before she goes to her heavenly reward."

William made a frustrated sound and struck his hand against the wall. "You are doing our own son out of a fine castle and Sheriffdom! What mother does that?"

My eyes flashed at my husband's obstinacy. "Will shall have a castle one day, of that I am certain. At present, he is a minor and cannot run a household of his own anyway. It is unseemly for you to filch property off an old woman, who is your daughter-by-law's own grandmother. How to sow disharmony in our son's marriage! And, William, asking Nicola for hostages as a surety—it is like something…something your…"

My voice trailed away as I saw his glacial expression.

"Like my brother, you were about to say, weren't you?" he spat, and he kicked a small stool across the room, almost sending it into the fire.

Then he stormed out of the chamber, the sound of his heavy footfall echoing in the corridors. I realised my hands were trembling, but I was not sorry about what I'd said. I did not wish to argue with William, but there were some behaviours I could not agree with. Not ever.

It had come to my attention that William, working hard in the service of King Henry, had been neglecting the spiritual side of his life. He seldom went to chapel anymore, and when he did, he appeared uncomfortable, eager to be elsewhere. This worried me, for John was known for his impiety, for eschewing Mass, and refusing to celebrate the Eucharist. I wondered if William's lack of charity towards Nicola de la Haye was somehow connected with dwindling faith, a view that the world was solely about 'business' with little thought given to kindness or morality.

I went to New Salisbury to talk with Canon Edmund Rich, a learned man who bore the air of saintliness. One-time vicar of Calne, he had been raised to Treasurer of the Cathedral. A man of high education, he had studied in Paris and at Oxford, where he became a teacher; he excelled in mathematics and theology and introduced the study of Aristotle. When he lectured at Oxford, he was often so weary from spending the night praying on his knees, that he nodded off, to the amusement of his students. But they loved him for his clarity and honesty and overlooked his yawn-filled lessons.

Together, we sat on a stone seat near the Bishop's Palace, which was rising as quickly as the cathedral in its green meadow. Canon Rich was a short, wiry man with an open face full of benevolence. Curling hair touched with grey surrounded his head; his beard was short, striped like a badger's pelt. I had met him several times before at the old cathedral, and we had discussed many issues about both God and the secular world. I considered him a friend.

"You look troubled, Countess Ela," he said. "Is there anything I can help you with? Feel free to unburden yourself. It will go no farther, as you know."

I folded my hands in my lap. "It is William. Our life together has always been most harmonious but now…"

"Ah…" He sat back, hands splayed on thin knees beneath his cassock. "Is it…sin you fear? Wanderings from the sanctity of your marriage?"

"Oh, no, it is not *that* kind of sin!" I cried. "I trust in William's fidelity; no one has ever accused him of adultery and unlike his brother and sire, he has no children born out of wedlock. My fear is that he has become so engrossed in earthly affairs—the machinations of kings and barons—that he has abandoned his spiritual duties. I hate to admit it, but he rarely takes Communion, and he goes to confession even more rarely!"

"Ah, I understand. This, dearest Lady, is more common than you might think amongst hard-working men in all walks of life. If you can convince him to speak with me, I shall try to guide him gently back to the righteous path. I can make no promises but…" he spread his hands and cast his gaze heavenwards, "God moves in mysterious ways, as they say."

William regarded me with suspicion at first, when I told him I wanted him to converse with the good Canon, but he too liked Edmund Rich and eventually agreed to take counsel with him.

It did not take long. William perceived Edmund's holy spirit and was moved by the intellect and gentle humour that had made him a popular teacher at Oxford. Soon he had returned to his religious life as in the early years of our marriage. He renewed his earlier devotion to the Virgin and lit a candle daily before her altar, as he had sworn to do when he first became a knight in Lionheart's service.

Harmony was restored in our household, and William said no more about Nicola de la Haye and Lincoln.

CHAPTER TWENTY-ONE

"Gascony is at risk, one of our last French possessions." William strode agitatedly around the solar. "The King has asked me to go abroad to fight, Ela. He wants me to accompany his younger brother, Richard. Jesu, the boy is only sixteen and has never been blooded."

"Has the King not knighted Richard, and made him Count of Poitou? I have heard he will soon also be named Earl of Cornwall."

"Yes, but what does that change? He's still a green, beardless lad with more eagerness than ability!"

"As it stands, he is Henry's heir. He must learn to defend his brother's realm, even as you did in your youth."

"You lecture me, Ela. I thought you would want me home at your side."

"I do...but I know you too well. If you begged leave of the King and remained at home, you would worry about Hubert de Burgh and others of his ilk usurping your authority and bending the ear of the King in whatever way they desired. You are a soldier, too; soldiering is in your blood. Go to Poitou with the boy. Tell Henry it is to be your last campaign abroad—that you are too old..."

"Too *old*!" he sputtered, almost apoplectic. "I am hardly that, well...I..."

"It is time. After you have seen young Richard blood his sword, you should retire. Remain as adviser and loving uncle, keep the peace at home, if necessary...but stay in England."

William toyed with a small hourglass that sat on the sill of the window. He turned it over, watching grains of sand fall through the narrow middle to the other compartment. So quick our lives pass, like those specks of falling sand! Once a young maid or man, next moment a greybeard and crone...

"You are right, Ela," sighed my husband, still toying with the hourglass. "This campaign in Gascony will be my last."

On Palm Sunday William sailed away with the young Count of Poitou. Philip de Aubigny, the King's tutor and a veteran of the Battle of Lincoln, fared with him on the campaign. As William's ship departed Portsmouth harbour and sailed into the choppy waters beyond, where sea met sky in a mesh of grey, my head began to spin and bile stung my mouth. I stumbled a little, leaning heavily on the arms of my ladies, who had accompanied me to the farewell on the harbourside.

Ill at ease, Mabella fluttered around me, leading me back to our waiting carriage. "You are not ill, my Lady? Or with child?"

"No, to the latter," I said, with a feeble grin. "As to the former, I have no pain, no fever…but I do feel a great sense of doom hanging over me like an ominous cloud. On my way home, instead of heading straight to the castle, I want to speak to Canon Rich in New Salisbury. Perhaps he, in his great wisdom, can reassure me."

I walked along the bank of the rain-swollen River Avon accompanied by Edmund Rich, shuffling in his dark robes, sleep-eyed from another night spent in ceaseless prayer. Sun broke through the clouds, transforming the surface of the water to gold. White and majestic swans drifted by, those birds beloved of both storytellers and royalty. The humbler ducks, green-headed mallards and their sombre brown mates, congregated on the marshy riverbanks, avoiding the larger birds.

I expressed my sense of fear and loss to the Canon, and he sought to console and comfort me with words. "Remember what is written in Psalms, my dearest Lady. *My flesh and my heart may fail, but God is the strength of my heart and my portion forever.*"

"I hope my faith is strong enough, Canon. I encouraged William to go to war, this one last time—but my own spirit quails. I am weak, so weak and foolish…" Shameful tears sprang unbidden to my eyes; I, a Countess, did not want anyone outside my family to see me weep.

Canon Edmund shook his head, the burgeoning sun turning his brown curls into a warm, glowing nimbus, a halo like that which circled the head of a saint. "Be at peace, Ela, my daughter. Think on what is written in Corinthians—"*For our light affliction, which is but for a moment, works for us a far more exceeding and eternal weight of glory. While we look not at the things which are seen, but at the things which are unseen: for the things which are seen are temporal; but the things which are unseen are eternal."*

"I will ponder those words, Canon Rich," I said. "I have long said that if my husband should pass before me—God grant him long life!—that I would seek to become a nun, and with my wealth perhaps found a religious house."

"You would make a splendid nun, even an abbess," said the Canon, "And I would advise you in any way possible if ever you should make that choice. But it is far too soon to dwell on these future possibilities."

"Yes, far too soon. I still have much to do first." I cast him a wavering, unsteady smile. "You have given me great comfort, as ever, Canon."

We continued on our walk, speaking of trivial things, the birds, the glories of nature all around us, the goings-on in the newly-founded town, but a cloud still hung over me, black and malignant, making my steps as slow as those of an old woman.

Beyond the shadow of a doubt, evil times were coming.

William was ill. He had sent a letter from Gascony, his scribe writing down the words, for he could not:

My most beloved wife, Ela. Soon may I be home at your side again. I have been laid low these weeks with heavings of the belly so that no food will stay within. Richard is impossible to deal with, alas. He is full of youthful fervour and unbridled pride and will not follow orders. After we took the castle of La Reole, he became rude and insufferable. Now he is off, without so much a by your leave, chasing after a marriage alliance of some sort. I cannot dissuade him, and I no longer have the strength or inclination to try to bind him to my will. I have written to Henry to state my displeasure, and he has recalled me to England. The sea will be rough at this time of year, but I will not wait any longer. I want only to be home...Look for me around the second week in November...

Overjoyed by this happy news, though worried for my husband's health, I rushed around preparing for William's homecoming. Servants cleaned the castle top to bottom, throwing out old rush-mats and sluicing down the privies. Banners were hung on tower and gate. Minstrels were hired and told to await instruction for a grand procession when their lord returned from war. The townsfolk, from both the old town and the new, made preparations to hold elaborate pageants depicting Noah's Ark and the Assumption.

But, when the second week had passed, there was no sign of William. The weather had waxed stormy; I watched birds struggling in the winds that ripped over the ramparts. *It is just a small delay*, I told myself, the weather will be foul on the other side of the Narrow Sea too. *Tomorrow, his messenger will come, and William will follow swiftly after…*

But no messenger arrived. The roads, blasted by November's chill, were mostly empty save for the odd pilgrim, journeyman or vagabond.

Still, I kept hope, a desperate hope. *He said he was coming; he will come. William has never failed me…*

But…still he did not arrive. The nights waiting were the worst of all. I tossed and turned, weeping in between short bouts of tormented sleep. I did not want Mabella or Felyse to witness my collapse and sent them from my chambers to sleep in the corridor.

Finally, I could stand no more, and sent my own private courier to seek out the harbour master in Southampton. Had he heard any word of Lord William's ship, due to return to England?

No, came the reply. *It is greatly overdue. Men say the night it left France there was a terrific wind storm and the ship was blown off course. None have heard of its fate since then…*

The missive ended with the ominous words, *God Bless you and grant you peace at this time, Countess Ela…*

The harbour master believed the ship had gone down. He had not the courage to say it in so many words, but it was clear to me. He thought William was lost at sea. Drowned, his body lost forever without a proper grave.

"No!" I cried, throwing the harbourmaster's scribbled letter into the fire, watching as it shrivelled away to a coil of black ash. "I would know if anything had happened to William. In my heart, I feel he is alive...*alive*!"

I took to standing near the castle gate at dusk, a lantern in my hand. I stood there in rain, in sleet and snow, and returned by midnight, teeth chattering, soaked, battered by the elements. Those of my children who still dwelt at the castle wept and cried and tried to entice me inside, fearing I would fall ill. Isobella, who had recently discarded the idea of becoming a nun to accept the suit of dashing young William de Vescy of Alnwick, even dared grasp my arm to force me inside.

"You will not!" I shouted at her, shaking her off roughly. "How dare you touch your mother in such a fashion? I am not your child!"

"What has come over you?" she cried back, her voice carried to all and sundry by the chill north wind. Snow was descending; hundreds of white flakes, like falling stars, tumbled into the bailey, whirling, dancing, catching in her uncovered hair. "It will not bring Father back standing outside until you catch a fever and die! Mother, it is weeks now. You must accept the truth—he is likely dead." A great sob wracked her slender frame as she uttered that awful word.

Dead...

"You...you horrid little cow!" I screamed at her like some harridan in a Salisbury tavern. All the sentries and archers on the walls were staring, as they shivered around their meagre watchfires. "How dare you disrespect your father, lie about him in this manner..."

"Lie? I am not lying!" Tears ran in rivulets down her tormented face, mingling with the melting snowflakes that clung to her eyelashes. "The only one who lies is you, Mother—you lie to yourself!" Picking up her skirts, she ran haphazardly towards the castle apartments, her desperate sobs haunting me as she disappeared.

Silence fell as she departed. I glanced around; the guards were all pretending to look elsewhere, to polish a dagger, to test the edge of an arrowhead, to restring a bow. "I know what you all think!" I shouted, shaking with unnatural rage. "And it is not true, it's not. Tend to your duties, and by Christ, show some loyalty to your mistress...and to your sworn lord..."

Waves of familiar, detested dizziness gripped me, and my lantern tumbled from my hand and shattered. I realised my fingers were so cold from hours outside that they had gone numb.

"My Lady Ela." The captain of the guard crunched over through the snow, a bear-like man with a black beard down to his belt, his burly form made even larger by his billowing woollen cloak. "I pray you let me escort you indoors."

I had no more will to fight; weakness washed over me and my head pounded so hard my eyes hurt. I nodded and he took my arm, despite the impropriety, and led me to the solar, where my maids took control, wrapping my shivering form in a warm cowl and rubbing my blue, burning fingers.

"Take me to my bedchamber," I ordered through chapped lips. "Ask me nothing. Just do as I bid you."

In silence, the ladies obeyed, although I noticed frightened, darting glances passing between them. My anger raged at those glances, but I managed to hold it in check. Once the women had escorted me to my bed, I pointed towards the door. "Go, and do not bother me till dawn," I snapped. "Not under any circumstances."

They fled. I thought I could hear Felyse whimpering. It made me almost hate her.

After what seemed like hours of writhing in torment on the sheets, I managed to find the solace of sleep. Only soon, it turned from solace to nightmare.

I began to dream. William's ship was tossed on an angry sea, its mast wreathed by lightning, its sales shredded and flapping like torn shrouds. It rolled and dived, sinking into the swell then rising again, showering spume, triumphant, before descending once more into the watery caverns of the sea. William stood in the prow, by the broken and crumbling figurehead of a woman, shouting desperately for the captain. I could not hear his words and the captain was nowhere in sight. Up ahead, a rocky shoreline loomed, reefs jutting up sharp as fangs, their tips gnashing the waves, seaweed streaming from them like the hair of dead mermaids. The ship was sucked towards the rocks as the wind screeched, and one stone, curved as a dagger, punctured its bow, biting deep, allowing the cold sea to rush into the hold. The timbers shrieked and the whole craft tipped on its side, as men screamed in terror. I saw William flung from the prow into the spray, thrashing and struggling to keep head above water. He struck out swimming as the storm continued to rage, and then, like a miracle, he was crawling on the beach, sand-covered, battered, but alive....

I woke, gasping and weeping. "He's alive," I sobbed, "thank you, Blessed Virgin, for protecting him, for giving me this vision. William lives." I began to laugh, and then to sob, as I scrambled from the bed and fell to my knees on the *prie-dieu* by the window.

William lived. Now all he had to do was make his way back to me.

A knight came to Salisbury Castle. His helmet was polished, his mail new and shining in the weak December sun. A long blue cloak streamed from his shoulders, and the horse he rode was a fine white stallion. He asked to see me, but would not give his name or his mission to Steward Hobart, saying his words were only for the ears of the Countess of Salisbury.

"I would not give him the time of day, milady," said Hobart with a sniff and a scowl. "An arrogant young fool, whoever he is, although he is well-armoured and wears fine cloth, so I assume he comes from a family of means. Just say the word, and I will have the guards remove him and his company."

"No, no, that would be discourteous," I said. "Give his party bread and ale and have the grooms water their horses. Bring this knight to me when he is ready. For all we know, he might bring news of the Earl. But tell him I will only see him if he will allow his name to be announced. I do not play games. This is not a mummer's play where he can assume the role of the *Chevalier de Guise*—the Disguised Knight."

I retreated to the hall, sitting on the dais in lonely splendour. The gilded angels carved on the roofbeams smiled down through a haze of cobwebs. *Please, let this young knight bring the tidings I want most to hear...*

In the doorway, the steward stood clearing his throat. "Reimund de Burgh requests an audience, my Lady."

Reimund de Burgh...So, a relative of the enigmatic Hubert. I was mystified. What on earth could he want with me? "Let him enter," I said.

The knight walked into the hall. He had removed his helmet and carried it under his arm. He was a tall, spare fellow with reddish-blonde hair that coiled around his ears. His face was narrow, the mouth slightly puckered as if he sucked upon a Spanish lemon, and his eyes were almost identical to the watchful, measuring, deep brown eyes of Hubert de Burgh.

As he reached the dais, he gave a low, easy bow. Then he drew himself up to his impressive if gangling height and stood there, almost...*preening*. I suppressed a giggle. He was trying to affect a noble air but he just looked young, haughty and foolish.

"So, Reimund de Burgh, you have come to Salisbury to see its Countess," I said. "I must admit I am *intrigued*. And the secrecy at the gate? How very strange."

His wan cheeks bloomed with two unattractive red smudges. "My message is only for you, my Lady." Reimund's voice was high-pitched and cracked a little. He was young, oh so young. "I wanted to speak to you and no other."

"Oh dear, Reimund, not identifying yourself is a sure way to find yourself apprehended by the guards, especially when the master of this castle is away"

"Away..." muttered Reimund, and his red cheeks became positively florid.

"Yes, *away*." I cast him a dazzling smile.

Reimund took a deep breath; I saw his chest fill with the indrawn air. I thought he might start strutting like one of the fat pigeons that haunted the bailey, looking for scraps from the kitchen. "My Lady, the King has told my uncle, Hubert de Burgh, that Earl William has perished at sea."

"Has he?" I frowned at the young man, making him waver. "His Grace the King is somewhat premature in making such an announcement. The Earl, I am certain, is merely delayed."

Reimund stammered. "N-no one has seen or heard from him for weeks. Parts of ship's wreckage have been thrown up on French shores."

"I do not want to discuss it." My eyes narrowed dangerously, and he took a step backwards as if afraid. "Now, out with the truth. Why are you here?"

He took another gulp of air, mouth moving like a fish out of water. "Uncle Hubert…When he heard that the Earl was missing, presumed dead, he…he asked the King… he asked if I…if I…"

"Have you lost the power of normal speech?" I snapped, shifting agitatedly in my chair. "Come, state your business. I haven't all day."

"My uncle asked King Henry to grant permission to ask for your hand in marriage. He said yes, as long as you agreed."

Shocked beyond belief, I sat in silence for a moment. My husband was missing but a few weeks, and already they were trying to marry me off. Thank God Almighty for John's infamous Charter—widows could no longer be forced to remarry against their will.

I rose from my seat, strode purposefully towards Reimund. The lad looked confused, apprehensive…and hopeful. The latter expression filled me with unbridled fury. Reaching him, I slapped his face with my open palm, making a noise that rose up to the rafters.

He dropped his helmet with a clang and flung up his hand to his stinging cheek. "How dare you, Reimund de Burgh?" I spat. "Even if my Lord the Earl *was* dead, and I have excellent reason to believe he is not, I would not even have had a chance to decently mourn. And yet here you are, gazing upon me as you would a fine cow, a Spanish mare, eager to lay your hands on the Salisbury inheritance."

"No, no, that is not true; you do not understand!" he squeaked, his hands fluttering as if to emphasize his words. It made him look even more pathetic and foolish. "I have long heard of your beauty and piety. My offer to marry you is made in good faith, I assure you."

"This is your uncle's idea, isn't it? I can see de Burgh's hand in this ugly matter. He managed to get his hands on the Gloucester lands after his wife fortuitously died after a mere month, and now he wants an earldom for his kinsman…."

"You do him disservice, Lady. He just wants what is best for me…I mean, you…"

"From the lips of babes," I laughed mockingly. "Oh, Sir Reimund—I assume you are a Sir? How foolish you and Hubert de

Burgh have been. Even if William lay stone-cold in a coffin before my very eyes, I would not marry you. Not only are you far too young, too callow, but you are also not of my rank. I was born a Countess; you were born…with little. It is disgraceful that Hubert De Burgh filled your head with nonsense to make you feel you are more than you are. The King bears some guilt in this unhappy matter too, but he is young—I do not hold it against him but rather his conniving advisors—like your uncle."

"My Lady, how can I make amends for the affront I've given you, and rise in esteem in your eyes?"

"You cannot. Go to your uncle and tell him his plans were all for nought. Go now, before I truly lose my temper and have you beaten and thrown from my gates. I doubt you will want your little company to see you so disgraced, since you clearly enjoy lording it over them, you sad little churl…"

He fled for the door then, forgetting to bow in his haste. Hobart, who had been lurking in the corridor, scowled and chased after him, making sure he departed with no further trouble. Several minutes later, I heard the castle gates open and the sound of galloping hooves growing ever more distant.

Relief flooded me in a tide, but apprehension soon followed. What if he continued to pursue his suit? What if other lords also attempted to win my hand, becoming ever more persuasive, even forceful?

Please, Blessed Lady, send William home to me soon to prove to the world that he is not dead…

Christmas passed without much cheer. Even Proudfoot the Fool was wracked with sorrow. He wandered about the remnants of the meagre and uninspiring feast, mumbling:

"*No lord, no Longsword—
the feast fell flat.
At least the lack of roast pig
kept this Fool from getting fat.*"

December passed to January. Twelfth Night came and went. The holly boughs that had decked the hall withered and servants cleared them away.

I attended my duties, not forgetting my dedication to Christ and the Virgin. However, my resolve, my determined faith in my husband's survival, began, slowly, to fray.

One morn I woke for Matins. The castle was bitterly cold, the braziers making little difference no matter how often the servants stoked them. Ice formed traceries inside the shutters. I had suffered a cough for days and had not moved from my bed. I felt weak and shaky as Felyse dressed me for Mass.

"I can tell the chaplain you are unwell," she offered.

I shook my head. "No, I must go. It is my duty as chatelaine. I must provide an example, even more so without William here."

A lump formed in my throat. Mayhap I had been wrong after all and my dream was nought more than a dream. Perhaps his corpse did lie under the sea, nibbled by the hungry fishes. Everyone in the kingdom seemed to believe him dead, including his nephew the King…and our own children.

Wearily, I sought the chapel with its heady scents of incense and tallowy candles. I knelt, head bowed, as the priest began his sermon. Head pounding, I tried to concentrate on his words rather than the malady that made my eyes water and hurt my throat. It was warmer in the chapel, and soon I felt a pleasant, sleepy sensation embrace me, so much so I wanted to lie down on the floor. I pinched myself to stay wakeful.

During the Mass, the wind rose as it often did, making an incessant dull moaning that almost obliterated the priest's words. He raised his voice a little to compensate—and also to drown out a sudden cacophony of noise in the bailey. Horses neighing and men shouting. I felt irked. What now—another unwanted suitor?

Hunching my shoulders, I attempted to ignore the noise and focus on the message of the priest's sermon. Suddenly the priest halted, mid-flow, mouth gaping. I raised my heavy head, glaring blearily at him. He was standing as still if he had been turned into a pillar of salt by some divine act of the Lord. His face had gone a shade of grey. I realised he was staring over my shoulder toward the chapel door, and as I glanced around, I saw other members of the tiny congregation also facing that way, their faces bearing expressions of wonder and dawning joy.

I craned my head further around as my temples pulsed with pain. Candlelight shimmered in my blurred vision, and I saw a figure standing in the arch, limned by the light of the flambeaux in the corridor beyond.

A familiar figure, though gaunt and windswept, with faded lions upon his rumpled tunic.

"William!" I leapt up from my kneeling position while the room spun about me and the congregation gaped.

My husband reached me in one long stride, clasping me close in his arms. He smelt of the winter, of sleet and mud, and also of the sea, a faint tinge of salt still clinging to his hair. I was so overwhelmed I could not speak, could not weep.

He lifted me up and carried me like a child to my apartments.

With William safely home, I quickly recovered from my own minor troubles, although I kept a kerchief close to contain my sniffles in a dignified way. As we sat before a raging fire, constantly stoked by the servants, and drank warm, mulled wine rich with spices, he told the sorry tale of his adventures at sea.

"We left the port in good spirits, although the winds were rising. Before long, though, we were so battered, we cast our goods overboard to lighten the ship. The waves grew high as mountains and we feared for our lives, but then…" His voice sank and he crossed himself.

I leaned forward, placing my cup aside, my hand upon his knee. "Tell me."

"A light s began to glow on the masthead. It might have only been St Elmo's Fire, but…but I saw—and the men who survived swore too—the face of the Blessed Virgin in that green, fleeting light. Hope renewed in our hearts."

"It was the Virgin; of that am I sure! I dreamt that she saved you; she sent a vision to assuage my fears."

"Whatever we saw, it seemed the storm calmed for a moment and we headed for the Isle of Re, which lies off the coast of France. As we approached the headland, the storm rose in fury again and smashed us against the rocks along its shoreline. I was flung into the sea and swam for safety. Most of my men followed suit, but some were in the hold when the ship foundered and sank beneath the sea."

"God rest their souls," I breathed. "It is exactly as I dreamed."

"When I had regained my strength, I began to search the island and came upon a House of the Cistercians, Notre Dame de Re. The brothers took me in along with the other survivors. I found out where I was and learned that the island was held by Savaric de Mauleon, who once served John but had returned to France to serve the French King. Some of his soldiers knew me from my brother's court, and they sought the abbey under the cover of night to tell me I must flee, for Savaric intended to take me prisoner. A boat was waiting in a hidden cove on the island's far side. The very next night, when the monks had bedded down, I slipped out of the dormitory with my good fellows and climbed over the abbey walls. We found the waiting ship and boarded, despite that the gale was rising again. We set off in the teeth of the storm and were tossed about for many days and nights. No more visions of the Virgin came to hearten us, and often I despaired of seeing England…and you, my dearest, loyal wife. Finally, however, the clouds lifted and the sea calmed and I beheld the priory of the Benedictines rising atop the heights of St Michael's Mount in the sea off Cornwall. I was saved and I was, beyond all hope, home. I kissed the sand as I disembarked at the port in Marazion."

"I kept the faith," I murmured. "Even the King thought you had drowned but I refused to believe it."

"Well, Henry will know the truth by now…"

"I would love to have seen the expression on Hubert de Burgh's face when he heard of your return. And that of his nephew, Reimund."

"De Burgh?" William frowned in perplexity. "What has de Burgh to do with this? Or his nephew?"

"William, once it was known your ship had foundered, Reimund de Burgh asked the King if he could marry me. He rode up to the castle with his helm and armour polished, full of foolish pride. I sent him away the same day, warning him I'd have him beaten if he persisted in his ridiculous mission."

"*What*!" William erupted in sudden fury, flinging the contents of his cup to the floor. The hounds leapt from slumber, lapping excitedly at its contents. "He did *what*?"

"Do not concern yourself, William. I put the presumptuous young fool into his place."

William was breathing heavily, hands clenching and unclenching. "No…no…it *does* concern me. I had hardly been gone before this Reimund was out to grab my wife…and my title. It is even worse than that, Ela. If you had married the knave, he would have taken the title of Earl. Our own boy would be as good as disinherited. Oh, yes, he still would have taken precedence over any child you might have had with this Reimund, but I can imagine de Burgh somehow trying to get around the fact to further his family's interests. Christ! This is not acceptable. I want to speak to the King."

"Oh, William, you are here now and all is well. I wish for no more trouble."

"Hubert de Burgh has brought the trouble on himself," William railed. "I will have my say and demand satisfaction. And I want you to be at my side, to add to his shame."

Uneasiness swelled in my heart but I nodded meekly. I wanted to let the memory of Reimund's unwanted proposal fade from my mind, but I also understood that William was a proud man, a King's son, and to him, honour meant all.

King Henry was at Marlborough Castle, where he was recovering from an illness that came upon him while hunting in Savernake. Doctors declared he had the Little Pox, the kind of pox that affects children and youths in great numbers, causing no harm other than one or two faint marks left on the skin if the afflicted should itch the sores. However, although Little Pox seldom caused death or disability, it made the sufferer very miserable indeed, and so, we heard, was the King, whose physicians had slathered him in unguents and made him wear gloves to curb his urge to rend his own skin. Hubert de Burgh was with him, overseeing his care and trying to keep the young King amused during his convalescence.

"We shall go to Marlborough," William said. "Now. This day. I cannot risk that he suddenly recovers and moves on."

There was no dissuading my husband when such a mood was upon him. Taking our personal guards, we rode for the royal castle, not stopping even once upon the road. Arriving at Marlborough's gates, William demanded in a gruff voice to see the King. The Chamberlain grumbled and prevaricated, but William persisted until the man went to tell Henry that his uncle had arrived from Salisbury.

Within the hour, we had an audience with the King. Henry was sitting on his carved chair, looking groggy, tired and slightly petulant. Several pink blisters marred the skin of his cheek. "Uncle, I am glad to see you," he said, not sounding very sincere. "I thought you were dead, lost at sea."

"So I heard, your Grace," said William. "I heard too that you sought to give my wife, Ela, to Reimund de Burgh, although I was scarcely a month in my supposed watery grave."

Henry gave me an embarrassed glance, then sulkily turned his attention to William. "I did say to de Burgh the choice must be hers alone."

William's face began to take on a thunderous purple hue. "I ask you, your Grace, nephew—was it Hubert de Burgh who suggested this outrage? Or was it solely Reimund's idea with only his uncle's blessing?"

"Hubert's idea, of course! Can you blame him for wanting a decent wife for his kinsman? Hubert is a clever fellow, Uncle William; he always has been. And loyal—that is why I found a Scottish princess for him to marry after his last wife died. One of the girls who were at Corfe with my cousin Eleanor of Brittany."

"He aims too high and asks for too much in my estimation," growled William, adding on a sullen, "your Grace."

"This is no concern of mine," said Henry. "I am still unwell. If you are angry, you must take the matter up with Hubert."

"Well, where *is* he?" William glanced furiously around the hall. "I heard tell he was here in Marlborough."

"Hubert!" Henry shouted. "Come forth. The Earl of Salisbury wishes to speak to you."

The area behind the King's high seat was sectioned off by a large red curtain fringed with gold braid. The fabric was wrenched aside and out sauntered Hubert de Burgh in his long-toed shoes and jewelled collar.

The sight of him made William's eyes flame. "There you are! Did you enjoy listening in, you skulking sneak? Stand forth like a man, if you dare."

Hubert warily approached William. Fortunately for the Justiciar, my husband's sword sheath hung empty; he had left his blade outside with his squires, as was proper when seeking an audience with the King. Nonetheless, his fingers twitched where his sword-hilt should have been.

"My Lord Earl," Hubert began, "you must listen to me…"

"Must I?"

"I made a grave error in judgement; I freely admit it. I want to offer my apologies—both to you and to Countess Ela. I wronged you both by my over-hasty actions. I beg you, do not condemn me; you, of all men, Earl William, know how a man will favour his own nephew and try to make him prosper. Reimund, I must admit, can be gauche and over-eager—I hope you were not too offended, Countess."

"I slapped his face, sir," I said.

"As he no doubt deserved. For the part I played in this unfortunate event, I will make amends as soon as possible. I shall have fine horses sent to your castle at Salisbury, along with furs and silks for the Countess. I will also invite you to a banquet at my humble home. A banquet in honour of your safe homecoming. Do you agree?"

"I-I…" stammered William, his expression still angry but his colour less florid.

"You will give each other the kiss of peace," young King Henry commanded. "Do it now, because your roaring and bellowing, Uncle, is making my poor sick head pound like a drum."

The two men circled each other, almost like wary dogs. Then William clasped Hubert in a hard embrace and de Burgh did likewise, and the two men kissed each other's cheeks to signify that they put aside their enmity.

"A new start," said Hubert de Burgh. "A new peace. I look forward to your attendance at my townhouse in Devizes in a fortnight."

De Burgh's house was a stone manor with a hall and several floors. He had purchased it for his own use when the castle needed rooms for other dignitaries. As befitting his rising station at court, he had it packed with tapestries, imported couches like those of the Byzantines, lanterns filled with expensive painted glass, high-backed chairs with plush cushions that resembled thrones. The de Burgh arms, a red cross on a golden shield, was painted throughout the building.

The house was no castle, so the guests were few due to the constraints of space. I recognised only one or two as William and I were guided by a steward to our place next to Hubert at the high table. As I sat down, I thought of poor Hadwisa of Gloucester, married to de Burgh for but a month back in 1217, buried alone and unmourned. The Justiciar's new wife, Margaret, one-time prisoner and sister to King Alexander of Scotland, was sitting in the place Hadwisa would have occupied, had she lived longer—a small, neat woman with a pretty face, wearing green brocade that contrasted well with the auburn braids under her diaphanous veils.

Soon the wine imported from Bordeaux was flowing, along with Brandywine, burnt wine, and Geneva from the Low Countries, which was made from juniper-berries and burnt the tongue like fire. Food was plentiful, almost ostentatiously so—seethed boar, partridges served with meat dumplings, pike and mullet cooked in ale, chicken and beef in saffron sauce with capers and nuts. As the voiders took the bones and leftovers away to give to Hubert's dogs, pies and tarts were carried into the halls on oversized silver platters, some sprinkled with ginger, others frosted by a paste made of roses and violets.

As the evening progressed, William and Hubert began to converse like old friends, their tongues loosened by the drink and their tolerance of each other much improved—at least until the following morning.

Toward the end of the evening, Hubert stood up, swaying slightly. "I propose a toast to my new friend, William Earl of Salisbury," he slurred. "Page, bring my best wine—the claret mixed with Grains of Paradise and cardamom."

The page boy scurried out of the room and returned with a decanter. He poured out two goblets of the wine, one for de Burgh and one for William. "To a new alliance," said Hubert, raising the goblet to his lips. William did the same, hastily gulping down the fragrant contents.

Suddenly Hubert gave a shout. His goblet flew through the air, spinning, before clanging onto the flagstones. He whirled about and clouted the page on the ear, sending him flying to the ground amidst the spreading pool of red. "You struck my elbow with the lid of the decanter, you foolish, clumsy oaf!" Hubert roared. "Look, the wine is all over my tunic."

"Sir, I did not touch…I mean, I didn't mean…"

"Do you deny what the world has seen with their own eyes!" Hubert blazed, grabbing the lad and hauling him to his feet. I felt sorry; the child was perhaps eight and looked terrified. "Apologise!"

"My-my lord…sir…I apologise," squeaked the boy.

"Go then!" Hubert thundered, giving the child a push that sent him skidding in the wine. "Do not let me see your face for the rest of the night."

The page ran out of the hall and servants gathered to mop up the mess. "I do beg your pardon." Hubert smiled apologetically at William and me. "Children are so inattentive nowadays. If I had been so clumsy as a lad…" He shook his head, giving an exaggerated sigh.

His wife, the Scottish princess, Margaret, said nothing, but stared at her trencher with downcast eyes. It was odd, she had not spoken once all evening. I noted she was toying with her linen napkin as if nervous and wishing to be anywhere but here.

"Ah, do not be over-harsh with the boy, Hubert," said William. "He will learn, and one day he may well laugh about the events of this evening."

"Yes, he may," said de Burgh, and a sly smirk crept across his lips—which quickly vanished when he realised that I was watching him. "And now, it is time for us to rest. Again, this has been a most joyous occasion, with our newfound friendship witnessed by many." He nodded toward the guests at the trestle table further down the hall.

They cheered; a drunken cacophony. Again, I looked at their faces, unknown, a sea of unfamiliar knights. The Justiciar's chosen men, loyal to their master.

William rose and clasped Hubert de Burgh's hand—but there was a strange expression beginning to creep across his face.

As he stepped away from Hubert, he leaned heavily against my shoulder. "Ela, we must not stay the night here. I want to return to Salisbury at once."

Our company rode through the night, hurrying over the mist-enshrouded Plain. After only a short distance, William spurred his steed into a clump of trees, dismounted and was violently sick. "It is just the lingering effects of the ailment I had in France," he muttered when I questioned him, but I suspected there was more to it than that. He refused to answer why he wanted to leave de Burgh's house so quickly and why, rather than staying the night in Devizes as we had planned, he wished to return to Salisbury despite the long, cold night journey.

By the time the company passed through Amesbury, William could barely sit his horse. I demanded a halt at my familial manor house, and with assistance from his squires, I got my husband into bed. He was weak and vomiting; between his heaves, he crawled on hands and knees for the privy, where his water held hints of blood.

"This is not merely the remnants of your French illness," I said, kneeling at his bedside and clasping his hand. His flesh was cool, clammy. "Please, William—tell me why you wanted to leave de Burgh's house."

He beckoned me closer; his breath smelt odd, garlicky and somehow metallic. "I cannot prove it…but the wine, the wine that fell. He did not drink, nor did he offer it to his wife or to you, thank God…"

Horrified, I shook my head, not wanting to contemplate what he had told me. I had no love for Hubert de Burgh but I could not imagine him a blatant murderer. I thought, though, of Hadwisa, plain and unloved, passed from noble to noble—she had only lasted one month into her marriage to Hubert before unexpectedly and conveniently dying...

William's hand clamped on my wrist. "Promise...promise not to tell any of my suspicions if I should die..."

"You will not die!" I cried. "And if there is truth in your fears, why should not that truth be known and punishment given?"

"No one would believe such a tale," gasped William. "And I do not want you or my children placed in any danger. If you publicly denounced de Burgh, God knows what he would do..."

"I am not afraid of Hubert de Burgh!"

"This time...you should be," he murmured and then he fell against the bolster in a daze and spoke no more.

The next morning, I ordered a litter brought and William was carried back to Salisbury Castle. By now he was having difficulty swallowing and pains in the belly; his face and body were awash with foul-smelling sweat. The physician was called and he purged him and bled him into a copper bowl.

"What is wrong with my husband?" I asked. "Can you make him better?"

The physician gazed solemnly in my direction. "I will be frank with you, my Lady. I fear he will not recover. Only time will tell."

Overcome, I sank to my knees. "And...and what do you suppose has brought him to this evil pass?"

The doctor shook his head. "It may well be a recurrence of the grippe that assailed him in France, but yet, something troubles me. The scent of garlic and metals on his breath..."

I clambered up, grasped the man by both arms, which appeared to shock him; his mouth opened in a startled gape. "Tell me, true—spare me nothing. *Do you think the Earl was poisoned?*"

The man started to stammer. "I-I cannot say, Lady. Such things are difficult to deduce in all but the most obvious cases. The garlic scent does tend to indicate…"

"What?" I cried, refusing to let go of his arms. "Tell me what it might indicate!"

Wincing, he writhed in my hold. "Sometimes…arsenic. But it may not be from any sinister source; many medicinal unguents and potions use small amounts of arsenic. If the Earl used too much of such an item, or the apothecary was unskilled mixing it, he may have inadvertently been poisoned. Do you know if he had taken any brews or infusions or rubbed any lotions on his skin?"

I shook my head, released him. "No, he was sick whilst abroad and weaker than normal…but not like this. He took no potions; thought them womanly."

The physician inched towards the chamber door. "I will return after Vespers. We will see how the Earl fares then."

The doctor did not return. During the afternoon, as I knelt at his bedside with Isobella and my youngest two sons, Richard and Nicholas, at my side, William went into a strange, convulsive fever. Once he looked at me, his eyes full of recognition, then he fell back in his sickbed, and his spirit soared free of his ruined body.

The Earl of Salisbury, William Longespee, King's bastard and renowned soldier, was dead.

CHAPTER TWENTY-TWO

William's hearse was carried in a torchlit procession to New Salisbury Cathedral, the first burial within its half-erected walls. Wind shrilled and rain poured down as if the heavens themselves wept for his demise as the funeral cortege began the two-mile journey into the fledgeling town. The candles around the bier flickered and threatened to go out, but they held fast despite the gale; Felyse, dressed in her own mourning gown, leaned over and whispered in my ear—"The candles remain lit, My Lady. A good sign. The Earl's salvation is assured."

Trinity Chapel, already roofed, was chosen for William's final resting place. Bishop Poore spoke the Offices of the Dead, while kindly Edmund Rich gave me succour in my grief. Peter des Roches, Bishop of Winchester, also was there, along with my distant kinsman, William Marshal the Younger, Earl of Pembroke; Earl William de Mandeville; some Irish Bishops whose tongue I could not understand; and a gaggle of nobles who had campaigned with William over the years.

As the last words of the Requiem were sung, I stepped back from the hearse and raised my eyes towards heaven.

"*In paradisum deducant te Angeli:*
in tuo adventu suscipiant te Martyres,
et perducant te in civitatem sanctam Ierusalem.
Chorus Angelorum te suscipiat,
et cum Lazaro quondam paupere æternam habeas requiem."

I laid a sprig of white *Muguet de Bois*, that the English call Lily of the Valley, upon the table-top tomb, as yet without its effigy, and turned my face back toward the daylight and the reality of my life as a widow.

Thirteen days later I was before King Henry to proclaim homage. He was kind and even shed a few tears for his uncle, but then he said words that cut me to the bone, sharp as any knife. "I fear, though, Aunt, I must ask for Salisbury Castle back. It is a royal castle after all. You have other places less windy and bleak where you would prefer to stay, surely?"

"Y-your Grace," I choked. "I have dwelt there for most of my days ever since I was but a little maid."

"I am sorry, Aunt," said Henry, "but I deem my castle needs more attention than you, a widow woman, can give it."

I drew myself up to my full height. "Your Grace, if you do not consider me capable of holding a royal castle in my own name—I implore you to permit me to buy it from you. It is my home."

"B-buy it?" he spluttered, eyes big in amazement.

"Yes, my liege. Longsword your uncle is gone, but I am Longsword's Lady, and I am made of sterner stuff than most other women. I do not wish to leave my home within thirty days as normal under law. After all, I will need a stout castle if I am to be Sheriff of Wiltshire."

"Sheriff!" Henry barked, almost falling from his throne. "You…but you're a…"

"A weak woman, I know." I managed a wan smile. "But do not forget Nicola de la Haye, who served your father so well in his endeavours against the French. She was both Sheriff and castellan. Who can say she did not have a heart and intellect as great as any man? I would fain mould myself in her image; it is, I deem, my right, as the heiress of my sire, the late William Fitzpatrick, Earl of Salisbury."

For a while, Henry sat in silence, staring at me, his drooping lid an almost maddening distraction, for it meant I could not clearly read the expression in his eyes. Finally, he sighed. "Aunt, if you want the castle so much, it is yours—for a price, which we will agree upon when I have spoken to my advisors. As for the Sheriffship, again you only speak truth—it goes with the family inheritance, and I am aware Uncle William only held the post through you. It, too, is yours for as long as you wish it."

"Can I ask you one more boon, your Grace?" I said.

"One more?" he sighed. "Go on, then, Aunt."

"Tell Hubert de Burgh that neither he nor any of his kin is welcome upon any of my lands—and if they should be found upon them, for any reason save tasks set by your Grace, it will be war between us."

Henry looked so stunned, I thought he really might tumble from his throne this time. But he did not object about my request, nor did he make uncomfortable inquiries. Perhaps he guessed the truth. "Yes, Aunt," he said meekly, like the good-hearted youth he was.

I returned to Salisbury Castle, grey and monumental on its layered green hill, feeling as a man must surely feel on the day he triumphs in battle and wins his heart's desire.

I served as Sheriff of Wiltshire for two years, gave it up for two, then held it again for six, and no complaints reached the King's ears that I was too lenient or too harsh, or that men did not abide by my decisions or refuse to pay rents and payments because I was a mere woman.

During my tenure as Sheriff, I had a fine effigy carved for William to lie on his tomb within New Salisbury Cathedral. Depicted in his mail coat, his shield at his side with its painted six lioncels, he lay in quiet repose upon an oaken base with inlays in arcading that resembled a church cloister.

"Sleep well, my beloved husband," I murmured, running my fingers over the cold stone face painted brightly to give it the semblance of life. "You will not be forgotten."

I even managed a smile as I thought of an epitaph written upon his demise by one of the chroniclers, *He was loyal, courageous and skilful in the field; his mother was full of largesse, his banner powerfulness.* In his memory, I also granted lands to St Nicholas' Hospital, newly raised outside the cathedral close, and bestowed upon its residents many heads of cattle.

However, I began to think of promises I had made long ago to myself, and to my daughter, Petronella. I decided to found two religious houses, and, eventually, take the veil myself. With the aid of Canon Rich, I obtained the necessary grants to begin a religious house on a tract of land called Snailsmead, which lay in one of my possessions, the manor of Lacock. I obtained oaks from the royal forest of Chippenham and stone quarried at Hazelbury by a man called Henry Crock to begin the abbey buildings.

At the same time, I granted land at Hinton known as *Locus Dei*, the Place of God, to the Carthusian monks, a rare order which had but one other house in England. Following the rule of St Bruno, the Carthusians ate no flesh, nor did they work their own fields. They lived in individual cottages almost as desert hermits, with slots cut in the fabric of their huts to receive their food. This order was much beloved of William, and so I wrote in the charter that I sealed in the presence of the new prior—

I, wishing for God's sake to complete what my husband had begun well, in my liege power and widowhood after his death have granted by this my charter to the Carthusian order all my manor of Hinton, with the advowson of the church and the park and all its other appurtenances without anything reserved to me or my heirs. I have done this for my husband's soul, and the soul of Earl William my father, and for my salvation and that of my children, and for the souls of all my ancestors and heirs.

The foundation stones for both religious houses were laid in one day, as I travelled on horseback first to Lacock and then on to Hinton, a distance of some four leagues. The end of the day found me weary and saddlesore but content. I was doing both God's work and honouring my husband's memory.

When I finally gave up the shrievalty of Wiltshire, I passed the role of Castellan of Salisbury Castle to my son, young Will. I had already released all of William's lands to him and his wife Idoine several years before. He was a lively, brave and intelligent young man, and it was time he had some responsibility, especially now he had several children of his own

With all the necessary documents signed and sealed, I then gave up my worldly life to join the order of Augustinian canonesses at the Priory of St Mary and St Bernard at Lacock. Several years after taking the veil, the priory was upgraded to an abbey—and the nuns unanimously elected me as its Abbess.

I was content in my new life. The estate was a wealthy one, producing corn, wool and animal hides. The abbey had a huge staff, including stewards, bailiffs, ploughmen, goatherds, wainwrights, and foresters. A head porter met travellers at the gate while the hosteller made any guests welcome. A palfreyman tended the nuns' horses, while millers, bakers, brewers, and poulterers kept the House well furnished with food. St Mary's supplied many jobs to local folk, which put us in good stead with them and made relationships between church and town harmonious.

To bring extra trade to Lacock, I applied to the King to grant a charter so that the town might hold an annual fair, and in time one was duly granted upon the Feast of St Thomas of Canterbury.

My life at the abbey was settled and serene. My children were all now either matched or contemplating church life, with the exception of Isobella, who had sadly died up north in her husband's castle at Alnwick. William and Idoine had four children, the eldest, Ela, named after me, the second William Longespee III. Will himself had taken the Cross and was preparing to do God's work with the King's brother, Richard of Cornwall. Stephen had risen to become Seneschal of Gascony and taken for his bride Emmeline de Ridelsford, with whom he had two girls, Emmeline and another Ela. Ella's husband, Thomas of Warwick died; but she soon wed Sir Philip Bassett, a love match, although they had no children. Ida's husband Ralph succumbed to illness and she wed again, making a far better match to the Baron of Bedford, William Beauchamp. Six children were born to them, the eldest boy named for his sire and grandsire. Richard and Nicholas were set for a future in the church; I hoped at least one of them would make Bishop of Salisbury one day.

Salisbury, fair Salisbury, with its founding stones laid long ago by William and myself...

Oh, how I longed to see that fair cathedral as more of the structure reached its completion; the nave, transepts and choir were all now finished, I was told, and the cloisters nearly done. A bell tower stood alongside the west front, housing a great ring of bells to summon the faithful to Mass. A soaring spire taller than all others was planned for the future—but I knew I would never see such a glorious accomplishment in my lifetime. My children would likely never see it completed, either; the final building phase of the cathedral of St Mary was a promise for the future, for a new generation raised solely within the blossoming town of New Salisbury.

And William lay within those hallowed, newly-consecrated walls, sleeping in death's peace as he waited for the day of Resurrection, the lions on his shield roaring into the incense-heavy shadows, the candles lit daily for his soul eternally burning…

Requiescat in pace, my brave soldier…
I am and will ever be, Longsword's Lady.

****

Epilogue:

In Lacock Abbey, the tomb of the first Abbess, Ela, Countess of Salisbury, stood in a place of high honour in the choir of the Abbey church. Tombs of her children lay around her, attesting to the closeness of her family—Richard, a Canon; Stephen, Seneschal of Gascony and Justiciar of Ireland; the heart burial of Nicholas, who became Bishop of Salisbury, as Ela had wished. Grandchildren and great-grandchildren joined their esteemed ancestress too—Katherine and Lorica Fitzwalter, who became nuns and were buried in the convent where they took the veil; Margaret, Countess of Lincoln, who became a patron of the Abbey in life and a resident in death.

Around Ela's tomb, lit by eternal candles, tended by the good sisters of Lacock until the desecration of the Reformation, were written words of high praise and revered memory—

Below lie buried the bones of the venerable Ela, who gave this sacred house as a home for the nuns. She also lived here as holy Abbess and Countess of Salisbury, full of good works

AUTHOR'S NOTES:

Ela of Salisbury was one of the most important women of the 13th century. Countess in her own right, she became one of only two (maybe three) female medieval sheriffs. She founded two religious houses laid one of the founding stones of the Salisbury Cathedral we know today; before that, Salisbury was a small town set inside and around the ramparts of the great Iron Age hillfort we now call Old Sarum. It had a castle, now in ruins, set upon a motte at the centre of the earlier earthworks, which overlooked the old Salisbury Cathedral, today a mere outline in stone. The whole hilltop was very windy and exposed and lacked decent water supplies, so it was decided to move both cathedral and town to a place called Merryfields, nearer to the river. This new foundation, of course, modern Salisbury, a fine medieval town.

Ela was born in Amesbury, my hometown; sadly, I have no idea where her father may have had his house. She owned many lands nearby and is thought to be the female face carved on a church pillar in the village of Shrewton.

The Childhood Legend—the story of Ela's disappearance after her father's death seems to be true, but she quite quickly turned up again and was married to William Longespee, illegitimate half-brother to Richard I and John, age just 9. She would not have cohabited with her husband at that age so I put her, as King's ward, into the care of Eleanor of Aquitaine. This is my invention but both Ela and Eleanor were in France at the correct time, and Eleanor had similarly looked after Eleanor of Brittany. Later I had Ela live with Ida, Countess of Norfolk, William's mother. (For many years people thought Longespee might be the son of Rosamund Clifford, Henry's favourite mistress, but a document was found where he mentions his mother, Ida.)

The Children—Although he was away for a tremendous amount of time, William and Ela seemed to have had a harmonious marriage, producing at least eight children. Some sources list more, including TWO Idas, but I have gone with eight and only one Ida. (The second one may, in fact, be a granddaughter; in any case, she did actually exist.) I do not know their birth order, although at least one research book gave an order, and the actual years of their births are only approximate. So I randomly chose who was born when. Regarding ages, there is also some doubt as to William Longespee's age, with some accounts making him over twenty years older than Ela, but others say he was 10-12 years older which seems more likely, considering his mother went on to have many more children with Roger Bigod, Earl of Norfolk.

King John's Reign—The middle bit of Ela's life is poorly recorded other than the fact she had many children. I have written about actual events in the reign of John and how the Longespee family might have responded to them—or in the case of William did respond to them.

Magna Carta—William's name is on the Charter and he also owned a copy. He does not seem to have been at Runnymede on the 15th of June but seems to have joined the King on about the 19th.

King John's ex-wife, Hadwisa—There was a King who got rid of a wife before Henry VIII and that was King John. To obtain the Gloucester lands, he married an heiress whose name had been recorded in many ways—Isabella, Isabel, Avisa, Avise, Hadwise, Hadwisa. I went for Hadwisa, as there were far too many Isabellas.

Henry III—Henry came to the throne as a boy of nine and was crowned with his mother's circlet in a hasty ceremony. Some sources say he was at Devizes when he heard the news that his father was dead while some say Corfe. For the purpose of the book, I have made it Devizes, where there is some evidence that Ela fled after William handed over Salisbury Castle.

The Poisoning—It is true that William was shipwrecked and given up for lost, and that Hubert de Burgh sent his nephew to pay court to Ela, who sent him away with a flea in his ear. Upon his return, William did indeed complain to the King, now young Henry III, and Hubert was said to have thrown a feast as an apology, after which William mysteriously died. Rumours of poison spread.

It is interesting to note that when Longespee's tomb in Salisbury Cathedral was opened, a rate in a state of reasonable preservation was found in his skull. Tests have shown the rat had a higher than normal amount of arsenic in its body! So William may have been poisoned—or was taking some kind of medicine containing arsenic.

The Religious Houses. Ela founded both Lacock Abbey and Hinton Priory, becoming Abbess of the former. Lacock was made into a grand house after the Reformation and many of its buildings, including the church torn down, but Ela's tomb was moved to the cloisters, where it is to this day. The Abbey is a popular film location from Robin of Sherwood to Harry Potter and more. Hinton is in private hands and has a wonderful chapter house still standing.

Other items: As usual, the songs are my versions of real medieval songs. They may not all be from the 12-13thc. Occasionally I have compressed events to make the timeline flow more easily. All the main characters are real people; most of the servants mentioned are not, save Amaria, servant of Eleanor of Aquitaine.

For further reading, there are no books solely devoted to either Ela or William Longespee. Biographies on King John will give some idea about William's military service. THE MAN WHO MOVED A CATHEDRAL by Tim Hatton Brown probably gives the most complete information on the Longespee family and the founding of the current Salisbury Cathedral.

OTHER WORKS BY J.P. REEDMAN

STONEHENGE and prehistory:

THE STONEHENGE SAGA. Huge epic of the Bronze Age. Ritual, war, love and death. A prehistoric GAME OF STONES roughly based on the Arthurian legends but set in the British Bronze Age.
THE SWORD OF TULKAR-Collection of prehistoric-based short stories
The Barrow Woman's Bones—short ghost story set around a real archaeological find.
THE GODS OF STONEHENGE-Short booklet about myths and legends associated with Stonehenge and about other possible mythological meanings.

MEDIEVAL BABES SERIES:

MY FAIR LADY: ELEANOR OF PROVENCE, HENRY III'S LOST QUEEN
MISTRESS OF THE MAZE: Rosamund Clifford, Mistress of Henry II
THE CAPTIVE PRINCESS: Eleanor of Brittany, sister of the murdered Arthur, a prisoner of King John.
THE WHITE ROSE RENT: The short life of Katherine, illegitimate daughter of Richard III
THE PRINCESS NUN. Mary of Woodstock, Daughter of Edward I, the nun who liked fun!
MY FATHER, MY ENEMY. Juliane, illegitimate daughter of Henry I, seeks to kill her father with a crossbow.

RICHARD III and THE WARS OF THE ROSES:

I, RICHARD PLANTAGENET I: TANTE LE DESIREE. Richard in his own first-person perspective, as Duke of Gloucester

I, RICHARD PLANTAGENET II: LOYAULTE ME LIE. Second part of Richard's story, told in 1st person. The mystery of the Princes, the tragedy of Bosworth

A MAN WHO WOULD BE KING. First person account of Henry Stafford, Duke of Buckingham suspect in the murder of the Princes

THE ROAD FROM FOTHERINGHAY—Richard III's childhood to his time in Warwick's household.

SACRED KING—Historical fantasy in which Richard III enters a fantastical afterlife and is 'returned to the world' in a Leicester carpark

WHITE ROSES, GOLDEN SUNNES. Collection of short stories about Richard III and his family.

SECRET MARRIAGES. Edward IV's romantic entanglements with Eleanor Talbot and Elizabeth Woodville

BLOOD OF ROSES. Edward IV defeats the Lancastrians at Mortimer's Cross and Towton.

RING OF WHITE ROSES. Two short stories featuring Richard III, including a time-travel tale about a lost traveller in the town of Bridport.

THE MISTLETOE BRIDE OF MINSTER LOVELL. Retelling of the folkloric tale featuring Francis Lovell, his wife and his friend the Duke of Gloucester.

COMING SOON—AVOUS ME LIE. The youth of Richard III part 2 told from his first-person perspective.

Printed in Great Britain
by Amazon